THE WIDER WORLD

BOOK FOUR OF
THE *HOOK* & *JILL* SAGA

ANDREA JONES

REGINETTA
PRESS

Copyright © 2024 by Andrea Jones

The Reginetta Press
www.ReginettaPress.com
www.HookandJill.com

Book jacket designed by Erik Hollander
www.ErikHollanderDesign.com

Interior design by Celia Jones

Library of Congress Cataloging-in-Publication Data:
Names: Jones, Andrea, author.
Title: The wider world / Andrea Jones.
Identifiers: LCCN 2024016229 | ISBN 9780982371442
(hardcover) | ISBN 0982371446 (hardcover)
Subjects: LCGFT: Fantasy fiction. | Novels.
Classification: LCC PS3610.O584 W53 2024 |
DDC 813/.6--dc23/eng/20240411
LC record available at https://lccn.loc.gov/2024016229

Printed in Canada

For men who are heroes,
and women who, everyday, save themselves.

Contents

The *Hook & Jill* Saga
by Andrea Jones:

Book One

Hook & Jill

Book Two

Other Oceans

Book Three

Other Islands

Book Four

The Wider World

Book Five (forthcoming)

The Ever-After End

THE WIDER WORLD

The Unexpected Spouse

When the stranger rang the bell at Number 14, he anticipated the cheery chime it gave out. He expected the appearance of the young servant girl in her starched apron, who soon opened the door to him. What he did not expect was her scream.

Drawing back, he remained on the stoop, annoyed at the commotion the child made as she cried out, skittering away down the hall. Inside, her master's voice chided, "A little less noise, there!" and the man of the house entered the hallway in his slippers and smoking jacket, seeking the source of disturbance. He trundled to the doorway, he looked up at his visitor, and he gasped.

"It's you!" he exclaimed. "You are he! Here, in London?" George Darling stood amazed, his face wary. "You're my Wendy's pirate!"

His guest scowled in disgust, now expecting the name that he so loathed to hear…

"Captain Hook!"

Doctor Johann Hanover Heinrich shook his head. Hooking his walking stick on his arm, he opened his two hands in innocence. The smile he attempted did little to reassure his host. Heinrich had become aware this past year that the scars he bore on his face, while enchanting the ladies, set the gentlemen he met at a distance. Doctor Heinrich appreciated distance. Distance heightened his power.

"Mr. Darling, I presume?" he asked, in his clipped Austrian accent. "My good man, let me assure you that I am no such villain. On the contrary, I am proud to say that I am your son-in-law. You see before you the fortunate gentleman upon whom your Wendy bestowed her hand." In his stiff, formal manner, he bowed. "Doctor Johann Heinrich, at your service, Sir."

"Oh!...I see, I...I am quite unprepared. I did not expect— But please, come in, Doctor, and let us sort ourselves out." Mr. Darling seemed relieved to hear this confirmation of his daughter's dramatic change of heart, but he looked puzzled.

"Indeed," answered the doctor, "I will come in. We have troubling matters to discuss, but I have looked forward to becoming acquainted." In his soft-leather shoes, Heinrich stepped over the threshold of the Darlings' abode. While he did so, he relaxed his posture as far as ever he did. At last, he had wedged his foot in the door of his beloved's first home. From here, he could reach her.

From here, she was his.

Before shutting his host's door, he turned to survey the street with its tidy iron railings and the colors that bloomed in the surrounding flower boxes. What a lovely little neighborhood. Quiet, and kind. This homely square was an ideal spot for a man to house his family.

He expected Mr. Darling would miss it.

An Artist Abroad

Dearest Mother and Father,
    As I live the Bohemian lifestyle, you will be relieved to learn
that I may name only one regret. I refer to the sorrow I suffer because our
correspondence is forced to be so spotty, and so slow. It has taken an age
to secure an opportunity to send this letter off. For all the delay it brings,
it also brings my sincerest love to you, and to the boys. As I write, my
nearer dearest one guards me. The boys, I hope, have described sufficient
facts to color the scene for you.

    I say 'boys,' but no one knows better than I how quickly these little
fellows grow. No doubt John is immersed in his higher studies by now,
and Michael and Curly are become senior students as well. Do you still
call him 'Curly,' or is he grown too much the gentleman? I can hear
him laughing now as he listens to you read this query aloud.

    I wish I could hear, too, your own news. It will be months before
I can collect my letters at the postal bureau to which I directed you
when I first wrote from that quaint, Venetian outpost. I hope that, in
the time between now and then, you cram that empty box full of your
tidings. How eagerly I shall read, once I am permitted to hold them! I
will treasure every word, every syllable, and every serif of your script.

    New things are happening here, too, of course. So many experiences,
of which I am keeping a faithful journal as they occur. My little stories
have multiplied admirably, and one day I shall indeed settle into my
elegant escritoire and pen that novel in three parts, as I threatened
when a girl. Alas, I fear that three parts will not be enough, and
it shall become needful to produce an entire library. As I write here

3

today, I'll give you the best report that my uncommon circumstance allows that I may.

The biggest event first; brace yourselves. Mother, are you nestled at the parlor grate with your mending in your lap? Father, have you finished poking the coals? Are your feet tucked into your slippers, and resting upon the ottoman?

I am married. There. Now you know.

My first husband is not the unnamed gentleman you may presume him to be, and of course it is all quite unorthodox. A marriage became advisable for legal reasons (no, not for a more tender reason in the form of little footsteps. I know you will be relieved and disappointed at the same time, but I am not seeking a return to the nursery to mother more boys). I may not elucidate the details, but know that we three are acting with mature consideration of our interests, and I am officially a wedded woman in the light of the law. Oh— how awkward it is for me to hint to you in this fashion. I wish I might tell the story directly, but my recitation will just have to wait. Until when? Who can say?

I feel compelled to state that I am satisfied, continuing in the life I chose when first I wrote, but with an additional protector, partner, and loved one. Truly, I am granted all a woman could crave, save the company of her loving parents.

I ensured that our marriage— which took place aboard ship with the officiating license of an obliging merchant-naval captain— should be registered in London. You will look it up when you receive this letter, and you'll be able to gather more information through official channels. I may say only that my husband is a foreigner not quite comfortable in his homeland; he is handsome, wealthy, and protective.

As for the less momentous news...

I am older. This condition is true for all of us, I understand, but especially for myself, with one foot anchored in a land where Time advances, not through the usual orderly conduit, but through experience. I am sure you've discerned how John progressed by leaps and bounds while away on our adventure, and how Michael and Curly are wiser than other boys their ages who have lived their whole lives in London. Since leaving home, I've grown quite intriguing. I do not blush to claim that I am a woman in full, and a match for my consorts.

My writing flourishes. I have preserved copies of my manuscripts in a bank box, and shall add to my archive at every mooring there. As I know you worry to realize, life at sea is precarious. Those items that we value must be secured against weather and theft. For those gentlemen who surround me, I am one of those valued articles and, in the same fashion, I, too, am guarded.

I am loved without limit. You might hold fear for my welfare, for which I cannot send a more potent palliative than this sentiment: Those whom I chose to share my world have chosen me to share theirs.

Each of your adoptive grandsons thrives in his elected vocation. In nurturing them all, I told enough stories of the Darlings to ground them in family affection. Whether voyaging with me or 'homing' on the Island, our boys have grown into men, seizing life and love with both hands. In this respect, they and I enjoy the greatest adventure of all.

I enclose small yet significant gifts for each of you. Please do make use of the value, but extract it with discretion.

We disembark soon, and I must seal this letter to post. As I cautioned before, kindly speak of me in general terms. Say only that I travel, an artist abroad. The scandal of confessing the truth may be spared you. I should hate to hear one day that my dear parents have been forced to admit that— horror of horrors— your daughter has become that worst of degenerates...a lady novelist!

I sign this note with the name most familiar, for my woman's name is strange to you and dangerous to me, and although I have outgrown her, I have not forgotten that enterprising girl I used to be.

I believe in you. Believe in your
Wendy

Bewitchery

The Widow Appleton knelt at the side of her bed in the yellow candlelight, resting her elbows on her tatty, hand-stitched quilt. She didn't soften the planks of the floor for her knees with a rug. Penance was her aim, and discomfort might aid her case.

She bowed her head in prayer. "Lord, I thank thee for thy blessings. I never asked for more than you gave us, but my heart is full now, with gratitude for sending my boy back to me, whole and hardy." She sighed her relief, but a twinge of guilt made her backbone shift straighter. "And if I done wrong to hide the truth, I beg your forgiveness. You made me a mother, and ain't a mother's chore the protection of her children? Amen."

She'd gotten this far in her prayers every night since David's resurrection from the dead, but she never got further. She wasn't sure if she'd acted properly, even now, after David shipped out again, rated able seaman with half his pay sent to support his siblings and herself. She kept his secret to keep her family. Bad enough she had lost her husband, and then her brother, the sea captain. She couldn't bear to lose David, too…and most likely to the hangman.

Was it evil at her elbow, or the Lord's own will? The Devil dealt many tricks. Maybe she had been fooled. Since she saw David stride into his humble home, more grown up than his years should make him, Mrs. Appleton knew bewitchery was at work. Deny it he might, but the situation was clear to his mother. David had been touched. Touched by some enchantment.

Looking around the cloistered, shadowy bedchamber first, on guard for any witness, she pulled open the drawer of her nightstand. The wood scraped with the weight of the old family good book that lay nested inside. With skinny fingers gnarled from other women's housework, she lifted it out and set it, with reverence, on the bed. In another moment, she had pried up the false bottom of the drawer, and, without touching the paper, she brought the candle close to read the document all over again. One edge was jagged, where she had torn it from the log book. The weatherworn parchment betrayed David's secret.

> *Joined in matrimony: Giovanni G. Cecco, Captain of the* Jolly Roger, *citizen of the Italian states; Wendy Moira Angela Darling, Spinster, late of London, England. Certified by Edmund Greer, Captain of the* Unity, *Lisbon & London; witnessed by Dr. Thomas Hastings, Ship's Surgeon.*

"…and David Appleton, cabin boy," the widow murmured. "Oh, Davy, how could you think to hand over this evidence to your Uncle Edmund's shipping office?" The name of the brigand ship *Jolly Roger* was notorious. Even a sheltered, god-fearing widow knew of its infamy. In a rush, she seized the paper and hurried it to the fireplace. She fell to her knees again, holding the parchment out toward the coals. The heat hit her face like the furnace of hell.

Yet, as had happened before, Mrs. Appleton could not bring herself to destroy the page. As an official document, it inspired her awe, but the factor that stayed her hand was the sight of her dead brother's signature, the last entry his palsied hand had managed to pen. This painful scribble was, after all, all she had left of her Edmund. What would he want her to do?

Rising from her knees, she returned the paper to its hiding place in the drawer. Along with the scent of old wood and varnish, she locked it away. "I'll keep your secret, Davy, even if you don't have the sense to keep it yourself. No one will know that my honest brother, and my own innocent boy, had any truck at all with the likes of those devils that pillage at sea."

She snuffed the candle and climbed to her bed. She pulled down her nightcap, closing her eyes to the evil. As always, it followed her into the darkness. A mother could tell when her boy was bewitched.

David's soul lay at stake. David's penance was her aim, no matter what discomfort she must call upon to aid him.

"There you have it, Mary, my dear. We must take this doctor fellow at his word. Wendy is wedded to the gentleman."

Mr. and Mrs. Darling's startling caller had departed for his lodgings, and the couple lingered by the parlor fire, their eyes still wide and wondering in the rose-colored room. A grandfather clock stood tall in its authority across the carpets, ticking out the time in brassy clicks.

George Darling inserted a key in a rosewood box upon the mantel, and Mrs. Darling moved to draw the drapes against the gaze of the neighborhood. Mr. Darling revealed the box's contents: Wendy's most recent missive. The parchment no longer crackled. Wendy's parents had fingered it so often that the paper now lay pliant in his hold.

Mrs. Darling gazed upon her husband. Looking like a large, lost boy, he adjusted the quilted lapels of his worn, velveteen smoking jacket, tapping his courage to meet the emergency. She said, "You believe in this Doctor Heinrich. But George, dear, I remember every word of this letter." Mary Darling rested a slender hand on her husband's arm. Her face, with her sweet, mocking mouth, hung close to his, the high collar of her blouse framing her chin. Her voice was lower than her daughter's, yet just as clear. "Wendy plainly indicates that she feels no regret. Surely she would regret contention between her husband and...and that other person she maintains is protecting her."

"Heinrich gave us his opinion of that pirate's form of protection. He insists she is a prisoner! She herself says also...where is that passage?" Mr. Darling's middle-aged face displayed the worry his children had deposited there with their various adventures, in the Neverland and out. At his temples, streaks of gray shot through his hair, and his figure bent a bit. He tipped the parchment toward the firelight.

"Ah, here it is. How grown-up her handwriting has become! She says, 'I feel compelled to state'— *compelled*, mind you, Mary— 'that I am satisfied.' She writes that her husband is 'a foreigner not quite comfortable in his homeland; he is handsome, wealthy, and protective.' If one can look beyond those barbaric scars on his face, Wendy's description exactly matches our caller, this Doctor Heinrich."

Although Mrs. Darling could never doubt Mr. Darling's care for their daughter, her woman's intuition questioned his judgment. "But surely our son-in-law is one of those men who, as she puts it," Mrs. Darling slipped the letter from her husband's hands, " 'who surround me.' " She pointed to the line. "You see, at the time Wendy penned this letter, mere months ago, her husband was close by. And yet Doctor Heinrich claims he was forced abroad by—" she couldn't prevent a little, motherly shudder, "well, by you know whom— nearly a year ago!"

Puzzling, she began pacing the parlor, her long, slim skirts feathering behind. "And I still cannot fathom why Wendy uses the phrase, 'my *first* husband.' What can she mean by it? Has she somehow collected a second? Oh, George, what if this man is an impostor? After all, she has done her best to assure us of her happiness in each letter we've received."

"Yet she sends subtle hints of danger, too. I quote…'I'll give you the best report that my uncommon circumstance allows that I may.' No. Wendy is writing under duress."

"Her circumstances *are* unique, but she asks us to keep believing in her, George. We cannot simply trust Doctor Heinrich on the strength of his word."

"We have more than the gentleman's word, Mary." Mr. Darling's tone was blustery, as he was wont to become when confused. "We saw his marriage lines, signed by this LeCrow, or LeCarbon, that French captain, what's-his-name."

"And how can we verify his paper? Why should we trust it above Wendy's own script?"

"Your instincts are correct, my dear. We have done all that we can on our own. I've applied to the City repeatedly, and to the Navy, and to the various merchant shipping bureaus, inquiring as delicately as I might about the registry of her marriage. She spoke so confidently on that point. Yet I feel a fool every time I walk into another office— a father desperate to prove that his errant daughter is properly wed! It's no use inquiring again. And the doctor claims that the French vessel on which they were married never returned to port. Heinrich's paper is all the confirmation we may ever find. Perhaps…perhaps it is time we called in the authorities, just to be certain?"

Mrs. Darling stopped dead, and her cheeks pinkened. "No, George. The last thing we must do is involve any kind of official. John has always been adamant in this matter. Ever since he came back from that Island, he has impressed upon us the fact that Wendy's welfare depends upon secrecy!"

"How I wish Heinrich's ship wasn't due to sail so soon. I should dearly love to learn John's opinion. Dash it, if only his school term had started next week, instead of last. Heinrich's timing could not be worse."

"Or, his timing could be very, very good, George." Mrs. Darling's brows drew together in a rare sign for her, of suspicion. "I'd thought of consulting John, of course, but, inconveniently for us, to do so discreetly is impractical."

"A detective, then?"

His wife stood in thought, biting her lip, then she answered, "No. We simply cannot risk it, nor do we have the time. We must proceed according to our own lights."

"In that case, I will humor the man. After all, it is not *me* about whom we must feel concern, but our Wendy."

"George, darling…please don't rush off—"

"I am sorry, my own one, but I know my duty to my daughter. I will accept this man Heinrich's invitation and accompany him on his voyage. I shall get to know him."

"If you go, you will have no *choice* but to get to know him."

"I understand your fears, my dear. He is not quite what we'd hoped for in a son-in-law." Mr. Darling's bluster had come over him again, and he rocked on his slippered toes with his hands locked behind him. "Still, he may be better than the man whose company she *first* chose."

"The pirate captain for whom you mistook him? Despite the doctor's efforts to hide his feeling, I believe he was offended at your assumption, and deeply so. Well, he managed to explain those unbecoming scars, but why, if all Wendy tells us is true, would one man she trusts turn a sword on another?" Clutching the brooch at her throat, she blanched to think of such violence. "Dueling! And both armed with blades!"

"If the Fates are willing, I will soon learn everything, from our daughter's own lips."

"You will pay a price for that knowledge, George. In venturing abroad, you must become dependent upon Heinrich's goodwill."

"Ah, I am glad you reminded me. I have ample means from selling Wendy's diamonds! What a happy coincidence. Or do you think, perhaps, that our Wendy hoped we would use those diamonds for this purpose? No matter. I am provided against emergency in good British pounds, and I shall hide my private funds in a money belt."

"It does appear that Wendy prepared us for just such a situation. And for the boys' futures, too, safely banked for them. We mustn't touch her gifts to her brothers, though."

"Mary, I swear to you. I will satisfy myself of Wendy's welfare, or I will aid in her escape. By gad," George Darling flushed with long-reserved emotion, "Wendy's misadventure has weighed upon my shoulders! I have been powerless to help her, but today I am granted my one chance to rescue our daughter from that pirate, that scoundrel— Captain Hook."

"Oh, George! Never think of challenging that man!" Mrs. Darling gazed at him, anxiety written in the delicate lines upon her face. The hidden kiss at the corner of her mouth begged Mr. Darling to stay.

Mr. Darling couldn't see it. He placed his hands on his lady's shoulders, soothing. "Never fear, Mary. I know what I'm about. It is clear to me that Heinrich has a plan. He may be our single hope of redeeming Wendy." Mr. Darling stood straighter, then, and adjusted his cuffs, unwittingly following the lead of his visitor's strict bearing. "And whatever his character, he cannot hurt me. We are both gentlemen, after all."

Dispirited, Mrs. Darling bowed her head to gaze upon Wendy's letter. She sighed, and then she warned her husband— her loving, foolish husband.

"You say he is a 'gentleman,' George. It is the very word Wendy uses to describe her pirate."

The crossing was only slightly disconcerting for the woman. Dover to Calais, by paddle steamer. The atmosphere was chill, but the breeze failed to keep the lady inside. She understood that through the next weeks she must stay hidden away, unseen and unheard. For these few hours, she desired to breathe fresh air through her lungs, and feel the mist and the thin, clouded sun on her face. She welcomed even the lonesome cries of the seagulls that pierced her hearing. Soon enough, her veil would enshroud her, and cabin walls close her in. No, the travel was not disconcerting, but her destination augured a different emotion.

The portrait was packed in her trunk. She no longer needed to view it. In simply closing her eyes, she saw his image. She had been curious, all this time. She, too, had attempted to render his likeness. Now she was curious to learn how close both painters came to reality.

'Reality' was not a word that she associated with him. 'Fantasy' was more like. Even all those years ago, he'd seemed like something untrue. When he disappeared from her life, her suspicions seemed borne out. Had he not left physical evidence of his attentions, she might have gone mad with wondering. He had stepped into her world, uninvited, and stepped out again.

Soon, she was meant to step into his.

She must enter his world, which, by all accounts, was disconcerting. She took a breath of sharp sea air; she adjusted her old-fashioned traveling cloak, and set her face toward France.

Rendezvous

Twice in his lifetime, James Hook steeled himself against the unknowns of paternity. Now, a world away from that first experience, his tension reached its height, apace with his suspense. With a will of iron, he had put off the moment of knowing. Hook had chosen today to re-enter the Neverland, and appointed this hour to reckon the truth.

Sweeping his coattails aside, he sat down upon a stump in the herb garden behind the house he had established in the Clearing. Here he hoped for a modicum of privacy. For the coming revelation, he shunned even the company of his consort, the woman who had created him Hook, and whom he created Red-Handed Jill. Much as he loathed the curse of solitude that had plagued most of his existence, this ordeal was one he resolved to face all alone.

It was Jill who had formed his story in the first place, and lengthy months of waiting for this day raised the old specter of his early manhood in London. He had been reminded of the unfortunate end that the beginning of a child's life had wrought.

On that occasion, long, long years ago, the beauty of an infant's golden hair proved an ugly portent. Back then, his new brother displayed all the wrong traits for the son of a dark father. That birth blighted a scion of aristocracy. It slashed a noble family's ties, and drove young Master James away to sea. Thus he'd embarked upon a life devoid of his hereditary company, never to see his birthright restored. This tragedy, dictated by his Storyteller, proved to be the underpinning of Hook's existence.

The deadly barb at the end of his arm twitched, pricking his knee as Lelaneh approached. The native woman made her way down the garden pathway with soft, slow footsteps that swayed the fringe of her deerskin skirt. Hook did not observe his custom of removing his hat for the lady. Instead, he allowed the broad velvet brim to obscure his features. A pair of purple butterflies flirted with one another, brushing Lelaneh's arm, and the drone of bees in the blossoms buzzed in Hook's ears. The woman smiled down at a child. She crooned to him, and cradled him in the fullness of her bosom. When she neared, though, Lelaneh looked up at her benefactor, and he read the concern in her Indian eyes. She, too, envisioned some disaster.

"Here he is, Commodore," she said. "Mrs. Hanover's babe, born four moons ago. He came early, and I am sorry to say that his path into this world was a difficult one." As she held the infant nearer for the pirate's inspection, the buzzing in Hook's head increased. With a twist of his lip, he dragged his gaze from Lelaneh's, and let it rest upon the wee face before him.

Within moments, to Hook's ear, the song of birds in the Clearing became audible, and the pleasant scent of flora floated up, roused by the warmth of the Neverland sun.

This time, the babe's coloring delivered relief. Hook felt a sense of liberation as he viewed the pale tufts of hair. The boy's gray eyes blinked at him. *This* time, proof of non-paternity was the desired condition, and this child displayed it, in spades.

Mrs. Hanover's son belonged to her father.

Yet Hook's eyes narrowed as his scrutiny increased. Thank the Powers, his own trouble with the child was ended; the unfortunate Mrs. Hanover's had only begun.

Abruptly, Hook stood, causing Lelaneh to pull the babe to her breast and step backward.

"I have learned what I came here to know."

"Yes…one can see it," Lelaneh's voice lowered with sorrow. "The child does not easily suck sustenance from his mother, nor from any of us."

"I thank you for your care of them, my dear. I expect that Mrs. Hanover's tribulation shall not be long-lived."

"Mother Moon will decide it."

"Yet the girl herself is recovered?"

"Yes. She is able to go back to sea, if she wills it."

"And, this one…?" With his claw, Hook indicated the infant.

"On shore or aboard, it will make little difference to Mother Moon."

"I understand."

Supporting Lelaneh's arm, Hook escorted her and the child up the path and around the dwelling, to the open, oaken doorway of the House in the Clearing. He tipped his hat to her, and, now allowed access to sunshine, his filigreed earring sparkled in its rays. He turned his back on the children at play in the shade, striding away to apprise his Jill of good tidings— and raise the specter of less happy ones.

These experiences, agreeable and otherwise, wove the intricate tapestry of his history. He had endured a brief chapter this time, but what might emerge next, from his Storyteller's lore?

He stepped up his pace, and his sapphire eyes anticipated the sight of her. His half-smile slid to his lips.

He expected she'd always surprise him.

The *Jolly Roger* and her sister ship, the *Red Lady*, had a rendezvous to keep, and a lucrative one. Shore leave would be short, this anchoring. The commodore and the captain allowed only a week for this rest, and their sailors were determined to make the best of their stay in this most welcoming of ports.

Chores must take precedence, though, and on this first morning the ships' boats ferried back and forth, rolling in the surf of Neverbay, from their moorings to the beach. Sporting the bright-colored shirts customary to the *Roger*'s crew, and the French blue jackets of the *Red Lady*'s, the pirates assembled on the sand. Those assigned to hunting parties milled about, priming their weapons for game. The ship's carpenters and their mates rambled into the forest for timber, with axes on their shoulders, while Chef and Cook erected spits in preparation for the hunters' bounty. By nightfall, the sailors expected to have earned a rendezvous of a more personal nature, with the ladies of the Clearing.

As bo'sun's mates, Nibs the Knife and Tom Tootles were perspiring, hustling with their men to offload barrels for fresh water. As fast as the cooper sent the casks up in nets from the hold, the crew on deck swung the yardarm and lowered the barrels over the side. Empty now, they bobbed in the bay water, to be towed to a stream and filled.

Nibs and Tom hoped that when the bo'sun, Mr. Smee, emerged from the commodore's quarters, he'd find the job mostly done, and send Nibs and Tom to bob their merry way to the Island too.

The lookout high in the crow's nest watched for Lost Boys and indigenous warriors. One or two of the former could be seen peeping from the treetops; the latter were seldom perceived unless they intended to be. As always, the pirate crew kept a weather eye on the commodore when he returned from his early errand. Nibs and Tom were no exception, and they eyed their foster father as he scaled the companionway toward his quarters— and Red-Handed Jill. Tom spoke under his breath to his brother. "From the spring in his step, I'm guessing Hook's in good humor again."

"Who wouldn't be, who got first crack at the Clearing?" Nibs rejoined. Like the other men, the bo'sun's mates smirked and went on with their work. Whatever cloud had been causing Commodore Hook's temper to darken in these last weeks seemed to have dissipated today, and life on the Island was good. Soon, the sound of chopping rose from the timber, and a rainbow of birds fluttered up above the trees. The fresh scent of vegetation piqued the men's senses, tempting swabs and officers alike to indulge in the isle's wonders.

As the last boat dragged its casks away, Nibs pulled the orange cloth from his brow to mop his neck. The breeze from shore blew balmy air through his dark hair. His prized kerchief showed bloodstains, but Nibs felt that these marks only enhanced its character— and his own— since the blood came from wounds inflicted upon him by a warrior here on the Island. Jill had won the kerchief back and restored it to her son. Only Jill's inner circle knew how she'd taken revenge on the man who murdered one of Hook's sailors, and who had attacked her and Nibs. Knowledge of the topic was hidden from anyone beyond family and first officers, and, as of the time of the ships' single visit to the Island since the brave's disappearance, the tribe was ignorant of what Fate had served up to Lean Wolf Silent Hunter. As contrived by Jill, the knave seemed to have disappeared— with nary a bloodstain behind him.

Nibs looked over the rail at the *Red Lady* while he stretched his long limbs. "We'd better pick up Guillaume before we head for Marooners' Rock. By now, he's like kin to the mergirls. They come rushing up from the waves whenever he dangles his little toe in the Lagoon. He's never once had to use the conch Zaleh gave him, to call them up."

"Brother, befriending LeCorbeau's second mate was the best idea I ever had. You should be grateful for my intelligence."

"Too bad your intelligence doesn't extend to learning Italian." Jeeringly, Nibs bowed and chanted with musical tones, *"Ciao, bella ragazza!"*

"Leave off the jargon, Nibs. You know I'm mortified that I couldn't keep up with Jill's language lessons." Tom scowled, an unusual expression for him. A barrel-chested, good-natured sailor, it took a missed opportunity to knock him out of sorts. He rubbed the scar at his temple. "It's bad enough that I can't stay with you on the Continent after we deliver Jill to Captain Cecco's clan."

"Sorry, mate," Nibs relented, and the crease between his eyebrows deepened. "I know you're disappointed. Jill and I'll miss you while we're in Italy, but we'll bring home some fine stories to entertain you."

"Stories are well and good, but if you can bring home some *'bella'* Italian women, even better." Restored to geniality, Tom slapped Nibs' back. "Now let's get Mr. Smee's blessing and give Guillaume a lift ashore. I'm ready for a dive— among other things." He thought for a moment, then cocked his head. "How do you say 'mermaid' in Italian?"

Stymied, Nibs shrugged his lanky shoulders.

"Oh, never mind, mate." Tom got a wicked gleam in his eye. "I expect the gypsy girls would never believe you, anyway."

As he scooped Mrs. Hanover into his arms, Mr. Yulunga spoke in the rich, deep tones she loved to hear. "I missed you, little woman." She was so small and he so large, she nearly disappeared in his embrace.

Nodding into her master's shoulder, Mrs. Hanover squeezed him back, demonstrating her pleasure in their reunion. She loved to touch his body, but she wasn't comfortable with words. On Captain Cecco's advice, he humored her. When he pulled away, he brushed the brown hair from her face, and saw a tear glitter at her eye.

"You missed me, too."

The oddly-matched couple had withdrawn to the children's room upstairs in the House in the Clearing. The big nursery window stood open, according to tradition, draped in the long green curtains that Mr. Smee had sewn. The drapes framed a view of the garden trellis, and the delights of the outdoors seeped in. Striped rugs woven by the native ladies softened the wooden floor beneath their feet. The room was padded and cozy, with no echoes to frighten a child. Though the little fireplace hosted no flame this temperate day, the smell of ash and applewood lent their aromas. On the mantel, cornhusk dolls stood side by side with ships whittled by sailors' hands, in an interesting blend of cultures. The home of the Women of the Clearing was an appropriate place for a daughter of Europe and an African prince to reunite.

Mrs. Hanover asked in a husky, neglected voice, "Why so many months?"

Yulunga was one of the few who knew why Hook had steered the fleet away from the Island for such a long time. Even Mrs. Hanover had no inkling that she might have mothered Hook's son; she had been unconscious during their carnal exchange. Thanks to her father's drugs, the girl had given Hook no choice in their coupling. The commodore used his power to choose, now, to keep his distance until the infant she delivered showed indications of its sire. Yulunga didn't care one way or another who fathered her child but, like all Hook's officers, he relished the lighter atmosphere since Hook learned the truth. He answered his woman's question with another truth.

"We had other islands to visit."

Mrs. Hanover pursed her lips in a pout.

"Lelaneh tells me you made a lot of work for the ladies, birthing that babe." Yulunga grinned his wide grin. "Typical." He chortled, making the orange, red, and yellow beads bounce on his ebony gullet.

"He made *me* work," she said, but her aspect wasn't sullen. Mrs. Hanover's spirit seemed to have grown a new dimension: she was a mother now.

A mewling sound came from the cradle that hung from the ceiling, and Yulunga glanced at the child who lay swaddled there.

"Is he a cat, then?"

Mrs. Hanover answered, sadly, "A child, but not yours." She swung the cradle. Her hearing was her primary source of perception. Listening to the plaintive cry of her baby brought pain to her. His keening did not echo in this comfortable room, but it resonated in her young mother's heart, and it frightened her. "Your child would be stronger."

"I have a strong son, already. By now he is chief of my people." To Mrs. Hanover's sensibilities, Yulunga's pride seemed to vibrate in the air. Her shoulders sagged as he stirred her worries, saying to her, "But in all the village, I never heard a baby cry like a kitten."

She shook her head. "Not in my medical books."

"He is unwell, then?"

"No diagnosis."

"So, you have kept up with your studies. I see you are taking my advice, making your own way. You may be ship's surgeon, one day. You will not need a man once you can be your own woman. But what does Lelaneh say about the boy?"

"Not knowing." Mrs. Hanover squeezed her hands together.

"Little woman…what are you thinking?"

Her gaze strayed to the cradle, then she bowed her head to hide her face. She whispered, "Consultation."

Yulunga's dark face turned stern. "He will not help you." He gestured to the cot, where the baby's frail wailing grew louder. "This boy came from his shame."

"I can try."

"I expect that we will see him at our rendezvous. I would have to get the captain's and the commodore's permission. Even if Hook agrees, you won't go near Doctor Hanover without me there to watch you."

Hook had bestowed Mrs. Hanover's name as retribution for her transgressions against him. A clever and conscienceless girl, she generated the conditions for her father to abduct Hook, and the two of them nearly starved him to death. While a captive, Hook had witnessed the pair's unseemly liaison, and she shuddered to hear her father mentioned by the same appellation with which— daily, hourly, and expertly— Hook punished her.

"He is 'Doctor Heinrich,' now," she ventured.

"You cannot slough off your punishment. Whatever he calls himself in Europe, Mrs. *Hanover*, you are burdened with his pirate name. Do not forget what the doctor did to you, and what you did to Hook."

"Heartless!"

"Call me what you will, but tell me now. Do you truly want to show this child to his father?"

Mrs. Hanover was small, but she was stubborn. She fixed her gray eyes on Yulunga. "Afraid to go with me?"

Yulunga jutted his jaw, glaring, and then he broke into a laugh. He was a lover of trouble. "Oh, little woman." He snatched her to his chest. "I missed you."

He kissed her heartily, arousing *all* her senses this time. Mr. Yulunga nudged the cradle with his knee. As it rocked, the baby's cat-like mewling petered out in exhaustion. The daughter of Europe and the son of the same had made an oddly-matched couple— and an unhealthy offspring.

The water drumming on the ledge made a steady sound, soothing to the soul. Daylight filtered through the mouth of the cavern, softened by the waterfall's flow, so that the stone enclosure glowed like the Fairy Glade when its denizens lit up the evening dews. As happened in that magical circle, the damp here was not unpleasant, but gentle, smelling of rock and of rain, and cradling its guests in its closeness. The two who bathed in its sun-warmed waters held together, wet but affectionate, sharing a final hour before separation.

Taking her buccaneer's face in her hands, Red-Handed Jill pressed her lips to those of a man with whom, although she was young in years, she had shared many trials. As the water fell in a perpetual stream outside the grotto, the beat of it lulled the lovers, dulling their senses. With their eyes closed and their kiss so engulfing, neither took note as the waterfall parted. Against the light of late afternoon, a silhouette loomed.

The figure stood dripping in the doorway, his dark hair bound beneath a red silken scarf at his brow. Water from the falls collected in a rush, to swirl about his ankles. His clothing hugged his chest, which swelled as he watched the two lovers' embrace. The atmosphere grew charged, and, startled, the couple turned to see him. They held together still, but their gazes sharpened, and the magic of their moment dissolved, like a sprinkling of sugar.

Whatever the intruder's emotion, he didn't miss a beat. "I expected I would find you here, together."

"As I anticipated you," Jill returned, her voice bold and clear.

Captain Cecco drew back from his wife, but did not free her hips from his hold. "No secrets can survive between the two of you." Pointedly, he eyed the lethal hook that armed his rival's wrist, "For which circumstance, at this particular moment, I am grateful."

Swiping the moisture from his face, Hook located the captain's weapons on a bench at the side of the cave. The dagger and pistols reposed atop a jumble of clothing. Hook tossed a satchel to the bench, then turned to stare back at Cecco.

The captain stood proud next to Jill, unclothed and unarmed. Gold gleamed at his neck, arms, and ears. His hair fell free of its usual binding, hanging loose about his powerful shoulders. Hook yanked the sopping shirt from his own body and threw it aside, exposing the barbarous harness that anchored his hook to his arm. He stepped down into the pool, where he towered over the twosome. Pulling his woman from Cecco's arms, he drew her to his side.

"Your job is accomplished, Captain." Hook's gaze roamed over Jill. Her long, light hair curled with moisture. She wore a gypsy blouse that slipped off one shoulder and hung down to her thighs. The garment was made of a jewel-blue linen that emphasized the color of her eyes. The fabric clung to her every curve. Hook felt a twitch at his lip.

"Che bella!" he declared, kissing his mistress, indulging in the wet scent of her skin, provoking her ardent response, and only then, with her fingers raking his hair, did Jill realize they had all been speaking Italian.

Hook read her thoughts. He tilted his chin toward Cecco. "You see? Your lingo is now second nature to our lady. Or, shall I say, your Italian tongue? After all, I *did* witness that last, happy embrace." Slyly, he smiled, and then his throaty laugh erupted to coat the cavern walls, while Jill's mirth and Cecco's chased after it.

"Sì, Signore," Cecco countered, then reverted to English and his Mediterranean accent, "and I see that my Italian tongue brings success to you, too."

"Amori miei— my two loves." Seizing both of her men, Jill laughed again, and the sound of their unity created an amicable cocoon— one that, not for the first time— brought the three allies solace as they anticipated an ordeal. They all expected trouble, and, together, they had striven these past months to make ready for it.

Preparing Jill for her sojourn with his tribe, Cecco had tutored her. He found that speaking with his wife in his own language lessened his tension, so that along with her learning, their time together brought a new ease to their marriage. This ease, in turn, brought contentment to the threesome. At Hook's suggestion, Jill had taught Hook what Cecco taught her— or most of it. Because of their bond, storyteller to story, what Jill did not voice, Hook intuited. As Cecco claimed, no secrets could last long between them. "And," Jill answered Hook's unspoken thought, "I am most painfully honest."

"A fact the good doctor learned to his cost, while aboard the *Roger*." Casting off the rest of his clothing, Hook sank into the pool, which was shallow and pleasantly tepid, the surface constantly agitated by the flow from the falls. He leaned back and relaxed his body, but set his mind back to work. "My apologies for dampening our spirits," he said, flicking a spray of water at Jill as she and Cecco eased down beside him, "but time is short." His humor evaporated. "Now tell me what I don't already know."

"Giovanni approves the gypsy garb Mr. Smee made for me." She raised her bare shoulder to show off her blouse. "I can see you approve also. Giovanni gave me a pouch of trinkets to go with it, and a lovely little blade," Jill indicated the items on the bench her twin sons had crafted for this cave, where Hook had spied the weapons.

Cecco explained, "It is a sturdy brass knife, in place of the jeweled piece she carries now. No need to tempt my people with such a prize, and fewer questions will be asked."

Jill teased, "I hope my new jewelry isn't made of brass, too?"

Cecco laughed, refuting this suggestion. "No, no. Only true treasure for you. The gypsy boy has grown up, and no longer trades trinkets of brass for golden ones. But, as I warned you, my people will tell tales of this trick. I earned their admiration for deceiving rich girls with rings— until the day I was thrown in a cell."

Hook added, "Thus setting in train the events that brought our trio together." He angled a look at Jill. "Yet, even in her youth, I doubt that our Jill could be fooled by base metals. And, my love, how else have you made ready?"

"On Giovanni's advice, I'll bring my whip as well. I've been honing my skills this afternoon," Jill rubbed her muscles, "but I seem to have overdone."

"Smee will have a remedy. In the meantime," Hook drew Jill nearer, and with his one good hand massaged her upper arm. He had left off his own golden rings; his long, fine fingers were free, and he touched her tenderly. "You have lived a full life since coming of age. We are none of us as young as we used to be."

"Indeed, *Bellezza*," Cecco gripped her hand in his— her crimson hand, stained on the inside from palm to fingertips with the bloody mark of her experience. Jill's right hand had earned her her pirate name. On it she wore a circle of emeralds from Hook, and at her wrist lay a bracelet of sapphires, matching the stones of her anklet. On her other hand, she wore her husband's wedding band, enhanced recently by a ring set with topazes. Both her men reveled in her lust for pirate treasure, and they all felt the benefits of indulging her. "Whatever your age, in our eyes you are perfect."

" 'The perfect woman,' *sì*, Giovanni? Your words will go to my head."

"As you go to ours." Her husband kissed her scarlet palm; then, intertwining the fingers of his left hand with hers— wedding band to wedding band— he addressed Hook. "And you, Commodore, are to be congratulated. You are finally free of the bondage Mrs. Hanover so wickedly imposed upon you."

"I am unencumbered, and so also is a family in London." To Cecco's questioning look he answered, "Jill desired that, should the child be confirmed as my progeny, it should be offered to her parents to raise as their own."

"An excellent solution, if such an event had come to pass. Because you were pressed into that liaison, naturally you resented the possible fatherhood forced upon you. But, Sir, I dare to ask, have you changed your mind about siring a family…with Jill?"

"I have not."

"In my opinion, this is a terrible waste." Cecco shrugged. "Why should a man refuse children by the lady he loves?"

"I turn the question back to you. Why should a man crave an heir?"

"Many a male would say, to prove his manhood."

"I have proven myself."

"Then, perhaps, to grant your woman's wish?" Cecco slid his eyes sideways to study Jill's reaction.

"Should Jill wish to bear a child of my body, my concern for her safety forbids it. Her role as my consort is dangerous enough; I will countenance no further cause for my enemies to threaten."

As was his custom, Cecco had created his opportunity. Now he seized it. "Not long ago, you applauded our marriage, claiming our union discourages your foes from taking Jill hostage— or worse. I should be delighted to advance your scheme for her protection. I should like to tie her to myself, for all the world to see, with the tender bond of motherhood."

As Jill's cheeks took on a rosy hue, she said, with appreciation, "I champion your gallantry, Giovanni, without committing to your proposal." With her hand still joined ring to ring with her husband's, she turned again to her lover. "For a woman, Hook, to nurture the seed of her man— engaging her flesh so completely— is a demonstration of her devotion."

"A sentiment I do not require you to prove."

"Ah," Cecco raised his finger, and the golden bangles on his arm chimed. Commandeering the moment once more, he declared his own hope. "Sons and daughters are a comfort to lean upon in age." Cajoling Jill, he confessed, "I long for this boon for myself!"

Hook replied, "My dear Captain, I have already reached an age in which life is complete. When I lean at last, the sea will catch me."

Jill had smiled at Cecco's audacity, but she shuddered now to think of her lover's demise. Hook ceased stroking her shoulder to wrap his arm about her as Cecco presented one last argument.

"To guarantee a legacy?"

"My legend will outlive me." Hook cupped Jill's chin, lifting her face to his. "As I suppose, my love, you shall also do."

"No...oh, no," she protested, alarmed. "We are linked in such a way that we'd each be half alive without the other."

"True, indeed, and only untrustworthy Time can reveal our destiny." Beneath his scarlet scarf, Hook's aspect turned steely. "But now I shall ask and answer another question: why should a man like Johann Hanover sire a child? Vanity; pride; to secure his hold upon the woman who brings him the admiration of lesser men. In short, the doctor craves to prove his power. The infant I encountered this morning will bring none of these triumphs to his father. The boy is sickly. To one who believes so ardently in virtue, that child is the sinful product of seduction."

"And incest," Jill spat out. "It is fortunate for Mrs. Hanover's boy that she chose to remain among our company."

Leaning forward, Cecco confided, "I had meant to wait to discuss it, Commodore, but since you introduce the subject...Mr. Yulunga requests permission to arrange for mother and child to meet with Doctor Hanover, at our rendezvous."

Hook raised a single eyebrow. "Is the girl so addicted to discomfort?"

"So I wondered, too. But she wishes the surgeon to examine her son, in hope of a cure."

Jill was astonished by her husband's news. "It seems Mrs. Hanover has truly transformed into a mother. Facing this danger in the interest of her child…who would have predicted such selflessness? Commodore, will you allow Mrs. Hanover to take this risk?"

"Mr. Yulunga's woman means nothing to me. Captain Cecco may decide."

"Aye, Commodore. I shall think on the possible consequences."

Considering Mrs. Hanover's dilemma, Jill frowned. "When the doctor proposed to me, I scoffed as he pledged to make me an 'honest woman.' He swore he would defend my honor with his sword. I wonder; if he regains influence over his daughter, will he wish to redeem *her* honor? Or will he strive to hide her, for his own honor's sake?"

Hook's lip curled in a sneer. "Honor is beyond his power to bestow. We do well to send you far, far away from this monster, to the bosom of your husband's family."

"And as we all agree," Cecco asserted, "to doubt the mettle of Jill's honesty is absurd. She is as true as the steel of my knife."

"Jill's candor is another of the weapons she will carry as she travels to Italy. But, Jill, as your commander, I warn you." Hook set his jaw. "Do not allow your frank nature to be turned against you." He exchanged a significant look with Cecco.

"Aye, Sir, I will be wary."

Cecco nodded, "Red-Handed Jill will be as prepared as the three of us can make her, with her weapons, her wit, and her sons at her side."

"And with Jewel as our guide along the way," Jill added. "What report did the fairy bring you, Sir?"

"Jewel has found the caravan's new encampment."

"Ah, yes?" Cecco beamed with joy, but then he sighed. "This wonderful news means that Jill must leave us, no?"

"She, Nibs, and Tom will depart tonight."

"So little time!" Jill exclaimed.

"Yet this scheme is a year in the making, initiated by our captain's covenant with LeCorbeau. We shall collect our tribute, and— if he gives me no cause to kill him— I will ship Doctor Johann Hanover Heinrich back to Europe," Hook smiled, half-way, "empty-handed."

Jill, too, could not resist smiling. "To Vienna, I suppose, where he'll concoct more of his love philter…"

"…and amass another fortune to share with us," Cecco chuckled. "Jill, I look forward to thwarting the surgeon in his pursuit of you, yet I wish I too could fly along home. But my presence can only bring trouble to my family. The bounty on my head is a rich one, and many people of the villages wish us gypsies ill."

"From what my Jewel observes," Hook said, "the offered bounty is a point of pride with your mother."

" *'La matriarca'* I used to call her! I left her little but pride to repay her for my absence." Cecco's even teeth flashed as he grinned at Jill. "Yet soon she will know her enchanting daughter-in-law, and hear all the tales you can tell of her most handsome son."

With a gleam in her eye, Jill returned, "Surely one or two of your many brothers are as striking as you." She laid her scarlet fingertips upon his cheek. "But I thank you, my dear, for your kind education these last months. I shall be pleased to bring your mamma your love."

"You were quick to learn the language of the land, and your phrases of Romani may be of some use to you." To the commodore, Cecco explained, "I have cautioned Jill to conceal what she understands of our own gypsy tongue. With her fluency in Italian, the tribe will not expect she would seek to know also the old Romani. She will hold this advantage. One can never be too careful, among my Cecco clan."

"Giovanni says I am very like his mother." Jill cocked her head. "I suppose I shall discover what he means."

"*Sì*, lovely one. As a pirate queen, you will feel simpatico with our gypsy women. Raising me to win over girls for their gold, my mother taught me some secrets. Gypsy females are subtle, and sly. They need to be clever, to rule the menfolk without seeming to." Once again, he and Hook shared a glance, then, with a casual gesture, Hook saluted him.

At this signal, Cecco rose and dried himself, then reached for his breeches. He wore only one of the two golden armbands that usually bound his biceps, and Jill watched with reluctance as his most intimate piece of jewelry, a golden ring at his loins, became hidden. A wave of warmth surged through her being.

Tucking his pistols in his belt, Cecco prepared to slip around the waterfall and descend from the ledge by a rope. He enjoyed this pool behind the falls equally with Hook and Jill, but he alone among the three was unable to enter or exit this grotto by the power of flight. Nodding his respect to the commodore, Cecco turned to bunch his fingertips at his lips, and he tossed a kiss to Jill.

"*Addio, Bellezza.* I go now, to seal up my letter to my family. I know that, read aloud in my storyteller's voice, it will be cherished by her audience. As soon, my storyteller herself will be cherished there."

"*Arrivederci*, my husband. I will kiss you goodbye with your letter at my heart."

"No, Jill," Hook countermanded.

She and Cecco turned to him.

"You are *Signora* Cecco. You require the favor of *la matriarca*."

"Aye, I am…and I do."

"Kiss your Giovanni *now*, Jill."

Jill and Cecco gazed at one another.

"Make it a lasting impression."

After some seconds of wondering, Jill obeyed him. "Aye, Commodore," and she rose from the pool, and her husband held her hand to help her out. She looked up into the brown, gypsy blaze of his eyes. They stood face to face, and toe to toe, fully and freshly aware of one another's presence.

Hook asked, in his velvety voice, "Do you hold the magic in this moment, Jill?"

"Aye….I feel it."

"Then commit this time with your husband to memory."

Hook stopped speaking then, and Cecco folded his wife in his arms, to garner her loving kiss and give it back to her. Their hearts thumped in tandem, their pulses vibrated with the beat of the falls. The water drummed on the ledge outside the door, collecting in a rush to swirl about their ankles, and the cavern cradled its guests, in closeness.

Commodore Hook turned away. While he waited for passion to peak and the couple to part, he leaned back to bask in the pool.

The very next ordeal was his, alone, to anticipate. It might prove a shock to the *Signora* but, in its execution, he did not expect her to cause him much trouble.

As Cecco climbed from the ledge, Jill waved to him. She reentered the hollow behind the falls to find Hook divested of his harness;

his chest was free, broad, and bare. His hook was hidden from sight, and the pouch he had carried lay within reach. As she rejoined him in the warmth of the water, she settled on his knee, and he spoke to her, most sincerely.

"Amore mio." Once again, some seconds passed before Jill realized Hook was speaking in Italian. She started to say so, but he forestalled her with a finger to her lips. Puzzling, she now took notice that his five fingers were unadorned— as was his earlobe, at which an ornate circlet usually dangled. But he brooked no questions, and, in her husband's language, Hook conducted the rest of their rendezvous.

"When two lovers have created one another, as we have done, their story is simpler, yet more complex. We two did not need to learn to know one another. Rather, once we met, we reminded ourselves who we are. Our memories are ever present but, sometimes, they require to be nudged, or teased out."

"I sense that the memory of *this* encounter will stand out quite clearly."

"I undertake to ensure it will not."

"Hook?" Jill's brow furrowed. "I don't follow you."

"Excellent. As of this minute, you must drive thoughts of me from your mind."

"What..." As his meaning seeped into her thinking, Jill's jaw dropped. "You believe we must suppress our connection."

"Sì, Signora, although you are my very soul. For your protection, we will place our spirits at a remove."

Jill set her crimson hand on the ragged scars of Hook's stump, where his flesh was taut and tender. Since these lovers became one, her red hand served, both symbolically and in practice, in place of the right hand she caused him to lose. "I wonder what I may not know still, Hook, about you? As closely aligned as we are, you hold depths I dare not sound."

"All the better, my love." Hook withdrew his wrist from her touch, to leave her hand feeling empty. She sensed that his thoughts, too, were receding from her grasp. He went on, "You have known me, in truth, and I you, and yet I cannot be sure of you, either. How many stories did the Wendy begin? And how might her past tales transect our future?" Lowering his chin, he insisted, "Now is the time to surrender to these mysteries. We can *know* nothing." He incanted, like a spell, "So mote it be. Our souls are blind to one another, until I see you safely aboard once again."

"May that day come swiftly."

"I refuse to contemplate your homecoming, and I forbid you to dwell upon it. As of now," he conjured, "your home is a bright gypsy caravan."

"But I wish to carry your strength with me."

"My strength is *your* strength. But Captain Cecco warned you, Jill. Gypsies live by intuition. Romani women must be subtle, and sly. The only man for you is your husband; otherwise, your family will sense a deception."

"*La matriarca* is a fortune-teller…"

"When she studies your palm, the trinkets on your hand will be those her son bestowed."

"But your blood colors my palm. Our mark is indelible!"

"You play the game of Time. Like all mysterious ladies, you have a past. And Cecco's love, also, left a mark."

Jill lifted her arms to study her wrists, where, once upon a time, Cecco's own leather laces had scored her. She remembered their grip— binding tight, and yet lending security. Cecco's care had sustained her all through the nightmare of Hook's disappearance. She murmured, "His mark encircles my heart."

From the pouch, Hook pulled another string of leather. "Let us now delve into this more recent story. The story of Giovanni and Jill." He offered the leather lace to her. Its musky scent brought back dual memories: Hook, and Giovanni. Hook knew it. He nodded. "*Per favore*, lovely one, you will do us this service." He dragged his crimson scarf from his head and turned his back, so that she could gather his hair and bind it with the leather lace, wrapping it in the manner of Cecco's.

In a daze, Jill did as Hook asked. Having served her husband this way, she felt the texture of the leather to be familiar in her fingers, and, like its smell, akin to the straps that fastened Hook's claw. Hook's waves of hair were finer than Cecco's, and more difficult to tame. At length this job was accomplished, and a long black tail hung down his back.

He handed her the scarf. She guessed his intention, yet, in order to accustom her to a new habit of mind, he waited to hear her speak the question out loud.

"This cloth is to be a blindfold?"

"*Sì*. And although your Giovanni has two hands, he asks you to tie it yourself."

"He knows what you're about, then!"

"Gypsy magic, Jill. And there is nothing your loving husband would not do for you." So saying, Hook collected a set of bracelets, beckoning to Jill to slip them on his arm. Once she complied, the bangles rang with his every movement, and with a spike of emotion that tugged at her gut, she listened to their chimes. The sensation swelled as she watched him pull one wide, shining armband from the pouch, to fit it round his biceps. This band was the missing mate of the one Cecco wore this afternoon. The memory was potent; with these ornaments, her husband had played upon her yearning for treasure, just as Hook played on his behalf now.

While comprehension sank in, Jill's heart cinched tight, and tighter. She cried out, "No! I won't allow Hook to vanish."

"You will please humor him, with the proper form of address."

Jill sucked in her breath at these words— borrowed from Cecco, as even his language was commandeered for his purpose.

"Your captain asked, *Signora*. Please to follow his order."

Jill hesitated to indulge in this pretense. Still, as a member of the company, she was sworn to obey both her captain and her commodore. Her own welfare, too, demanded that she act. She must leave her lover behind. Reluctant, she began to fold the silk in her hands. She shaped it into a length.

Hook stared into her sapphire eyes. One final time, their color mirrored his own. As Jill returned his gaze, he saw the beads of her tears. But, with his hand, he commanded, and she raised the cloth to her face. The swath of scarlet broke their connection. She pulled it back, she knotted it tight behind her head. She perceived only a rose-colored aura. Hook saw her shoulders sag down, and her blue gypsy blouse crumpling.

His voice came to her, stern. "You will not see me again."

"Hook…"

He leaned close to her ear, careful not to let his beard brush her skin. His whisper tickled as, slowly, he declared, as in a prophecy, "*Lui è solo una fantasia*….Hook…is but a fantasy." She felt his grip on her wrist, felt him pulling her, until her fingers pressed the muscles of his chest. "Here is your reality…*Bellezza*."

Listening in darkness, her ear distinguished his voice not as a sound, but a touch. It vibrated down through her body, and her nether parts throbbed like the drum of the waterfall.

He eased Jill backward, to rest her head upon the ledge of the pool. As he caressed the fingers she held to his breast, her tension diminished a little. Then, sightless, she felt him pull at the emerald ring, wiggling it off. The bangles tinkled. His hand settled again, warm, on her forearm. His few fingers fumbled with the clasp of her jeweled bracelet, and, perhaps to mask this clumsiness, he thrust his hips between her thighs. Her breath escaped in a rush at the sensation of his flesh there, and she heard the echo of her sigh as it flew through the cavern.

When the bracelet had seemingly abandoned her wrist, the hand that purloined it moved higher up her arm. As Giovanni's had done, moons before, this hand circled her neck; as at that time, his thumb stroked her throat. Traveling up her jawline, he outlined her ear, and next, unhooked the golden crescent Hook's one hand once hung there.

His whisper stirred her again, insinuating words in the hollow of her ear, "I have not too much dignity to wait upon you." His fingers brushed over her cheek, to disengage the other earring, "And you have done the same for me." The sound of gold jingled. His words, his terms, his chimes…so familiar…

Captivated by his game, Jill anticipated the task he would undertake next, and she bent one knee to meet him. He kept her waiting a while, and then he stroked her thigh. Wending his way to arrive at her calf, he raised gooseflesh that prickled, and his touch fixed at last near her foot. Her anklet of sapphires slid along her skin, and soon it swirled away in the pulse of the water. The tail of her blouse eddied, too, fluttering round her more private places. Before long, with her treasures all gone, she would wear nothing else. Anticipation washed over her again, more tantalizing with every moment. She reached out with her naked arm to seek the gold at his biceps.

She didn't need vision to see it. This circlet was the symbol of Cecco's power. Molded to his muscle, it had been the object of her eye, times without number. She had caressed this armband, as she caressed it now, in times of turmoil, and in hours of joy. Her fingertips knew this sleek feel of metal. She herself had borne it on her arm, when she and Cecco were one. As she and he were one, now.

With a jolt, Jill remembered who truly wore the twin bracelets: *two* men. She was distracted from her accounting, though, by the feel of one of her men kissing her instep. Holding each foot in turn, he nibbled every toe, rubbing her arches, massaging her heels. Again, her rings were his playthings. One by one, he toyed with the two silver rings on her toes until each one slid off at his tug— and, behold, three more slipped on in their places. Beneath the blindfold, Jill blinked, then she wiggled her toes to enjoy the new trinkets. She'd not been offered a chance to unwrap them earlier; these pieces were embellishments to her costume. Her husband had provided them— as she now understood, destined to adorn her this minute.

As always when jewelry skimmed her skin, Jill trembled with pleasure. She was eager, now, to advance the playacting, for were they not players, staging a scene for their own private purpose? Smiling, she uttered his cue, "I want our first kiss to be one I will remember… always." With one hand, she seized the lustrous metal at his biceps; with the other she cupped her breast, as an offering. In twilight, she waited, expectant, impatient.

He answered only with his actions. Sliding his hold under hers, he formed her breast to a crown. The linen of her frock was rough enough to chafe as he fondled her. Just as his whiskers might do, the scrape of the fabric incited her nipple to tighten, and, soon, as she requested, he covered it in a kiss— a long, searching kiss. It drove her mad to feel the barrier of cloth between her skin and his tongue, and, yet, the texture against her taut flesh intrigued her. She reveled in the contrast, glossy gold at her fingertips, the coarseness of cloth at this pinnacle. Just like Cecco's very first kiss, this touch lingered— never, ever, to be forgotten. The sensations made Jill shiver with rapture, and the peak of her breast on his tongue spurred the peak of her fervor. Waves of pleasure surged through her center, until she huffed out her breath to collapse in his arms.

Yet this gift was not the last that he held for her. As she relaxed in the water with the current swirling round, his bangles rang again. He slipped a ring on her finger, in place of Hook's emeralds, and then he coaxed another on her thumb. Languorous in her afterglow, she touched them; one held a setting of gems, the other was a band, with decorative indentations. Before she finished her visionless tour of them, a light, cheery pealing broke out, soon to be drowned by the pool. He scooped up her ankle and wrapped it in a new bracelet. Chuckling, he murmured in his admirable Italian, *"Tu tintinni."*

Her laugh rang out like the bells of her anklet. "*Sì…sì*, I shall sound just like Jewel!" Shaking her ankle above the surface, she listened to the chaos of a chain full of tiny, tinkling spheres. It was a silvery sound. Clearly, this merry music was meant for dancing. Before she fully took stock of this present, he clipped two crescents of metal on her forearms. She explored them— they were tight to her wrists, and silent, and next she inquired, "What has my husband brought to bedeck my ears?" She opened her hand.

Into her palm he pressed a disc of metal. It was heavy, not a solid disc, but cut with some design. With her fingertips, she felt ridges on its surface, and a hoop to secure it. Was it gold, or was it silver? She smelled it…"Copper!" Happily, she hung it from her earlobe, and reached for its partner. Once both baubles dangled in their places, she smiled, holding her hair out of the way and waggling her head. The earrings bounced nicely against her jaw. "*Signora* Cecco offers her thanks. *Grazie mille!*"

Jill couldn't see him, but she didn't need to view her men to see how she was loved. The blindfold remained, a rosy radiance, while, in her mind's eye, she followed the directive to focus on her husband. He it was who pledged protection on behalf of his family. It was he in whose arms she reclined. Her mystic gypsy prevailed. No other entity impressed her consciousness; the former face receded, to hide behind Cecco's.

Gypsy magic.

So mote it be.

The spell was cast.

"Giovanni…" she whispered. She turned to lay hold of his shoulders. She felt the might of the muscles under his flesh, and, compelled, she pulled herself toward his loving embrace. Her blouse dragged in the water behind her, the sleeves clung, damp, to her arms. The grip of his bracelets emboldened her wrists. Feeling for the rugged coil of leather wound round his hair, she visualized his ponytail— hazelnut brown, matching his eyes. As he fondled her backside, his jewelry sang to her, and her heart responded in kind. No matter who he was, he sacrificed his own needs, to shield her.

She did not attempt to press his kiss to her lips. The memory of their last kiss loitered there. She sought the next best thing. Stradling his lap, she found him eager to fill her. He came to her gradually, though, measure for measure, making her ringed toes curl with the delight of impatience. But when finally she met him in full, she inhaled in a gasp. The shock of pleasure left her quivering. Again, she groped to clutch at his armband as, moving with the current, he stoked her craving for treasure with yet one more ring. As before, as always…it circled the shaft of his manhood.

As he loved her, inside and out, the strokes of his gold, slow and assertive, gave way at last to a rush of elation. She shook with it. He surged within her and, with their ardor, the pool sloshed and splattered the cavern. Droplets touched their tongues with a flavor of mineral. At the entrance, the waterfall splashed. Like the lovers, the storm of waves crested, and ebbed. Soon the pair floated, in a following calm.

He clasped her left hand in his. Sharing this moment before separation, Jill and her man held together, wet but affectionate. They intertwined their fingers, holding fast, until, beneath her blind, Jill's eyes opened in certainty. She felt something she should have expected.

Her wedding band tapped against metal. Gold to gold, her ring met its match on his finger.

"…Giovanni!" She held her breath. She turned her sightless gaze his direction. Her thoughts were fixed on her husband.

He murmured, *sotto voce*, "There is nothing I would not do for you."

He spoke these words, most sincerely, not in his Italian…but in the older, Romani tongue.

Relativity

With Jewel above and Nibs and Tom on either side, Jill touched down, and her ringed feet settled on her husband's native soil. Her skirts ceased billowing to drape about her hips, resolving into multi-colored layers of ruffles, with one side hitched up to her knee. She felt windblown and wild. No longer buoyant with flight, she eased to a standstill as her body reassumed her weight.

Sunset lit these woods, and the four travelers were surrounded by a kind of tree they'd never seen before. The gray, smooth trunks reminded Jill of dancers, lithe and leaning. They held up their boughs like arms, their leafy fingers clutching clumps of flora like ladies' bouquets. Jill sniffed the pleasant scents of ground and greenery. After so long in flight, high above seas and continents, the earthbound smells centered her spirit. A hint of smoke from a campfire told her Jewel's guidance was true; they had alighted near Cecco's troupe. The Italian earth underfoot felt fresh and springy, making the visitors welcome. She hoped that her in-laws would make them welcome, too.

Nibs linked his arm in Jill's, ushering her to a recumbent log. "Here at last. Let's take a minute to collect ourselves. There's no hurry. We're not expected." They sat down, and he tightened the knot of his kerchief. Its orange coloring matched dainty flowers on the bushes behind him. Likewise, as Jill unwound her shawl, she revealed the gypsy blouse that complimented deep blue forget-me-nots blooming in the grasses at her feet.

Now that Jewel had guided the party to their destination, she toned down her light. She alone wore muted colors. The film of her gown was meant to blend in, not with the Romani, but with their surroundings. Not a sound did she make, and, placing a tiny finger to her lips, the fairy flitted from Nibs to Jill to Tom, reminding her companions to stay quiet. She roosted on a branch, then, to tuck up stray flaxen curls, and to watch and to wait.

Jill spoke softly. "Thank you, Jewel. We count on you to observe our reception. I am grateful, too, for the little vial of dust you allowed us. It's a relief to know that you may find us again as the troupe travels the countryside. But the flight home is so lengthy, I want you and Tom to rest before you carry news of our safe arrival to Captain Cecco."

Jewel's wings dropped as she remembered her master's preparations. Captain Cecco was not the man to whom she'd report, but Hook had forewarned her. Jewel was steeped in magic herself, and she recognized at the start of the journey that, as the commodore implied, some particular power veiled Jill's thinking. After a glance at Nibs' frown and a shrug from Tom's beefy shoulders, Jewel was confirmed in her opinion that Jill's linkage to Hook was successfully obscured. She responded to Jill's instructions, merely nodding her acquiescence.

Jill went on, attempting to calm both herself and her sons, "I've awaited this visit so long. The captain assured me that, once the folks know who we are, all will be well."

"He also said no coward walks into a gypsy camp uninvited." Nibs felt for his knife, then remembered he had positioned it discreetly inside his boot. No need to antagonize the gypsies.

The four intruders could hear sounds of the camp a short way away. Low voices of men floated through the trees, and here and there came piping calls of children, a harness jangling, and a wagon's wooden creak.

"Brace up, mates," Tom advised. "We'll soon be among family." He rubbed the scar at his temple. "I admit I'm a bit nervous. Maybe more than you two, because I don't ken the lingo. I'll take my cues from you. Just tell me when to go home to— uh…to the *Red Lady*." He glanced to Nibs, who signaled with a thumbs-up. Tom reddened, realizing how close he had come to the blunder of reminding Jill of her home on the *Roger*, and of Hook. Her safety lay in the gypsies' hands, now, and she could not afford to offend Cecco's clan with any whiff of any other man.

When they'd all caught their breaths and watered their throats, the young men hefted their packs, while Jill opened the pouch that she wore slung from her shoulder to her hip. She pulled out six silken handkerchiefs from the interior, one wine colored, one yellow, one green, sapphire, purple, and turquoise. Each of the handkerchiefs sparkled with threads of silver woven through them. Jill draped them to hang from her waist. She felt their festive effect, but because her destination was so close at hand, their secondary effect was to key up her nerves.

Next she retrieved her anklet from the bag, glancing at her sons to ascertain that they were ready. Satisfied, she fastened the chain of bells round her ankle. In the hush of the woods, their merry peals were startling. Jill shook her foot to make certain they were heard.

A sudden silence confirmed it. The people at the camp came alert.

Jewel ducked into foliage. The other three travelers arose, and strode forth to meet their unknowing hosts.

With his mates Nibs the Knife and Tom Tootles away on the Continent, Guillaume was left to pursue his own risks and pleasures in the Neverland. This being the *Red Lady*'s third sojourn to the exotic shore, he was still exploring its possibilities. His favorite haunt was the Mermaids' Lagoon, where his foster father ruled his clan of seafolk. For the *Lady*'s second mate, any excursion to the Island must include a visit to the resident sea king. As much as these meetings filled Guillaume with joy, he approached this mystery of a merman with awe, and with some apprehension. Merfolk were known, after all, for their whims, which more often than not led humankind to disaster.

Having obtained his captain's leave and alerted Mr. Yulunga, the young Frenchman felt courageous enough to row a skiff to the Lagoon on his own. The sky this afternoon loomed low, overcast with bulbous clouds, and the breeze turned into a low, whistling wind. The other sailors ashore preferred to wait upon the Women of the Clearing, where they were sure to find warmth, if not roofing. Guillaume, however, when an urchin in the gutters of a port town, had stowed away to follow a cousin. He'd been snatched up and used by Captain DéDé LeCorbeau; he longed not for female attention, but for the guidance of a true father figure. His dream had materialized on this Island, most unexpectedly, in the strange and alluring figure of Zaleh.

Indulging his daring today, the young man tied his boat at the northern entrance of the Lagoon, where the Lost Boys had marked sunken treasure with an X etched in the cliffside. Listening, he heard no mer-song, only the slosh and suck of gentle breakers. He peeled off his dapper blue and red uniform and slid into the water, cooler this day because of the cloud cast. With goosebumps rising along chilly limbs, he submerged to search for his kin. They might not expect him on this inclement afternoon. Was it possible, he wondered, to sneak up on a mermaid? Thanks to LeCorbeau, Guillaume was no longer naïve, but, with a sense of humor netted from his good friend Tom, he put his question to the test.

In his first act as mentor, Zaleh taught Guillaume to swim in the sweet, salt waters of this bay, redolent of kelp and protected by high mossy cliffs on three sides. Now the slender Frenchman put his learning to work, gliding beneath the waves to inspect the crevices and hollows where his sisters liked to lurk. The Lagoon was generous with such crannies, its waters deep and wide enough to hide many a maiden. Guillaume wound his way smoothly among the rocks, surfacing for air without a ripple, then diving down again in the murk of sunless currents. He determined that without sunrays it was useless to seek the multiple colors of the merladies' tails. But even the clouds couldn't dim the silvery glow of Zaleh's scales, and, smiling through the bubbles of a laugh, Guillaume found him. Lounging in a downy bed of seaweed, the merman wore the enameled bracelet Guillaume had given him, and his many long silver plaits swirled round his majestic head. Zaleh held his muscular arms crossed, tapping his tail in impatience as he awaited his foster son. All Guillaume's stealth was for naught.

The mergirls whom he'd sought in vain levered up all around him, teasing. They urged him to the surface, where he treaded water with them as they giggled in musical measures— and then spit in fountains, tossing their sodden locks. Looking around with eyes of vivid and various colors, they searched for his brethren.

"*Non, non, mes demoiselles,* today I come alone. My brothers flew off on another adventure."

Enthralling in spite of their pouts, these sirens of the sea made even Guillaume find it difficult to breathe. The mermaids lured him closer, then pelted him with shells until Zaleh emerged from the depths to disperse them. "Go your way, my dears," Zaleh flicked his

silver-backed arms. "You will find no bait today." Hauling his son
through the sea, he hoisted Guillaume to the expanse of Marooners'
Rock. He flipped his own dripping body up beside him, and the two
creatures stretched out. The air was chill, but to Guillaume's relief,
Zaleh's welcome was as warm as before. The mer-king directed his
daughters to tow the boat hither, so that Guillaume could towel off
and don his clothing, for comfort. Yet, wise as ever, Zaleh intuited
that his foster son felt unsettled.

"Speak, my son, and I will advise you." Zaleh's timbre was like a
cello made flesh.

"*Merci*, Papa. In our short acquaintance, you have learned
much of me." Guillaume scooted closer to the place where his true
comfort lay. "Soon our fleet will rendezvous with my former captain.
As you understand me, I understand him. When I chose to join the
commodore's company, Captain LeCorbeau did not wish to part with
me, nor did my cousin Renaud, who sails with him. *Monsieur* will
demand to ransom me back."

Zaleh's silver eyes burned brighter. "And shall your officers give
way?"

"Not unless *Monsieur* effects some clever scheme."

"Then your own scheme must be cleverer."

"Oh, I believe that he is!"

" 'He'?" With no loss of dignity, Zaleh flashed a smile.

"You, Papa. You have bestowed upon me your seashell, with
which to alert you. Would it be seemly, if I find myself taken aboard
Monsieur's ship, to use the conch to call for your help?"

"I can think of no better occasion to summon me. You seek my
counsel, yet you already know what to do. My only caution is to
remind you that, if you must be taken, be taken as if willingly, so
that you may assemble your belongings to bring with you. If you are
in danger of abduction, though, instruct your friend Tom where to
find the conch and how to blow it for you."

"Indeed, I had not thought to ask Mr. Tom, or Nibs. They are
true friends. They will act as my second protection." In continental
style, Guillaume embraced the mighty mer-king, right cheek and
left. "Thank you, Papa! I am truly content, now. A man who has a
father, and friends, need not suffer alone among adversaries."

"I am proud to foster such a brave son."

"*Moi?* Brave, Papa?"

"Daily, you dwell among humankind, who are known, after all, for their whims. For many an age, I have watched this race. More often than not, men lead their own kind to disaster."

With a thoughtful countenance, Guillaume considered. At length he conceded, "An unexpected lesson, Papa. Always, you open my eyes."

Jill braced herself to step within Cecco's world, an unexpected spouse.

As she, Nibs, and Tom emerged from the woods and into a clearing, a cadre of men formed in front of them. Over their shoulders, Jill caught only a glimpse of wooden-roofed wagons with steps leading down from doorways, and paintwork of intricate design. Horses grazed, tethered; families milled about, and the smoke Jill had sniffed earlier rose from a common fire in the center. She smelled a trace of sweet pipe tobacco, but, swiftly, her observations were barred as the Romani men she'd surprised pressed forward in protection.

They wore flaring shirts and short, loose riding breeches, muddy boots, sashes, and long hair. Like Cecco, they wore jewelry, but none boasted quite as much as he. In other circumstances, Jill would have smiled at the comparison. To a man, their expressions were hostile. Their hands touched their weapons. Jill sensed the women and children gathering closer, beyond them, but she didn't dare lift her gaze from the menfolk.

To the accompaniment of the bells on her ankle, she moved in front of her sons and dropped a quick curtsey. In Italian, she spoke before the gypsies could question her. She used the words Cecco suggested.

"Please excuse our intrusion. We are family, and we bring you news."

An elderly man pushed between the others. His white hair was tied back in a braid, topped with a gold-colored scarf, and over it he bore the kind of headdress Cecco wore since his elevation to captain, a ringing mesh of coins and medallions. Unmistakably, this sage was the headman. Although aged, the gypsy king formed a formidable figure. His face was lined, but his arms were still muscular, his back straight, and, clearly, he commanded his wits.

He scoffed, and in a vigorous voice he exclaimed, "Hair like winter wheat, and you think to gull us that you are family?" He flung up one hand, dismissive. His rings flashed in the late, slanting sun. "Go back whence you came."

"*Padre*, my husband commands me otherwise."

"Your husband....He tells you to thus address me?"

Jill waited as the old man's shrewd, sharp eyes appraised the two young men behind her. His long white mustaches dangled below his chin. Assessing this man in return, Jill was grateful she and her sons had tucked away their weapons. Her whip and her dagger were concealed in her bag. The elder's gaze returned to her.

"Your husband is a fool."

"A fool he may have been, once. When he was young, and a boy in your tribe."

"If he was stolen away, we do not want his English wife." Turning on his heel, he pushed back through the line of men to return to his pipe and his chair by the fire. His action signaled to the others that he disdained any threat. Now the cadre relaxed their stances, and, with curious looks, the middle-aged women walked around them to draw nearer to Jill. Younger mothers hung back, protecting their broods. As the old man had indicated, the stealing of children was not unknown to them.

Jill surveyed the women's faces, alert for familiarities. Some of them wore bright, patterned skirts, swollen with petticoats. Others wore rusty black, with embroidered girdles similar to her own, and shawls of many shades tied round their shoulders. In the silence of curiosity, their jewelry, like Cecco's, hung notes in the air.

"Good evening, mothers." Jill offered another curtsey. "I am the pirate Red-Handed Jill, a storyteller. These buccaneers are my sons." Her claim to piracy made little impression but, as she gestured toward her boys, she heard the intake of the ladies' breaths. Their scrutiny now included her blood-red hand. Purposely, she'd left her fair hair uncovered, nor had she hidden her marking. No secrets must interfere with this parley. Uppermost in her mind was her husband— their tribesman.

And, sure enough, one of the women resembled him, strongly. Jill hadn't expected the impact that hit her sensibilities. Seeing a variation of Cecco's likeness before her, devoid of his love, reminded her of the precariousness of her position. She was an outsider, one whose mere presence stimulated suspicion. She stepped back to draw on her strength, then set her blue gaze to catch that woman's eye.

"I seek the one a lost son named…*la matriarca*."

The ladies exclaimed in amazement. Chattering all at once, in Romani, they turned toward Cecco's mother. She herself did not speak, but her posture grew prouder. She was petite in stature, and comfortably plump. A red folded fan swung from her girdle. Her dark hair was coiled, collected in netting. As her brown eyes took in the trespasser, they seemed to kindle, like charcoal. Jill recognized that look.

Pulling the lady from their cluster, the women ushered her before Jill, then formed a supportive gaggle behind her. *La matriarca* did not smile, but stood staring, demanding, through the eyes of her son.

Her tone was biting. "Besides reading your palm," *la matriarca* looked askance at Jill's hand, "what use should I be to a *straniera*? A stranger?"

"I thank you, but my fortune has already been read. My marriage was foretold to me, by the bridegroom himself." Softening her tone, Jill pronounced, "Your own Giovanni."

"Indeed, you *are* a storyteller." At the mention of his name, Cecco's mother betrayed no vulnerability. "But all of Italy knows the tale of my Giovanni, and the bounty on his head." Her pride in him rang in her words, underscored by mistrust. "You will get no coins here to tell lies of him."

"I've no need of coins." From her pouch, Jill pulled the letter Cecco sent. "And I needn't make up the story. Your son has written it, himself."

La matriarca only eyed the parchment.

"He did not write it in letters of blood, though. Not this time."

Again, the crowding women gasped at this intrigue, although *la matriarca* stood stoic.

"It is natural that you should doubt, and Giovanni warned me you would. Allow me to prove my claim." Jill pocketed the letter, and indicated the menfolk. "Let me guess which are his brothers."

La matriarca smiled sideways at this notion. Her teeth were strong and even, like her son's, and as she tossed her head, the loops of her earrings danced. "Agreed!"

A young woman approached the elder one, a girl of Jill's height, with thick, auburn curls and green eyes. Loose ringlets fell over her forehead. "*Nonna*, you must not ask the impossible." To Jill she explained, "Lady, Papa Cecco and most of his sons are not here. Some have married elsewhere, and the others led a string of horses to fair."

"And how many remain?"

"Two only."

"Only two of Giovanni's six brothers?"

"Yes...two of six." The girl's face curved in dimples, as if she was pleased to bear out Jill's knowledge. She dared to arch her eyebrows at *la matriarca*.

"I will find them." Passing her bag to Tom, Jill indicated that he and Nibs should hang back. She strolled to the center of the camp. The line of men edged away, as if her proximity might bring bad luck. Most of the troupe, some eighty-odd Romani— men, women, and children— had congregated round her by now. Some grinned, some scowled, but all were riveted by the intruder, and her audacity. Clearly, like Cecco himself, his clan were impressed by her courage. Jill felt the keen stare of their king upon her, from his rug-covered throne by the fire.

Had she not held an intimate acquaintance with Cecco, recognizing his kin would be challenging. But Jill knew the man. She knew his shape and his structure, she knew how he moved, how he held himself. As she felt her way with her feet through the dry, bedraggled grass, now quickly, now carefully, she gazed into each face she encountered. She held silence, trying not to be distracted by the youngsters' questioning voices, or the cluck of women's gossip.

Cecco had advised her not to hurry. The gypsies enjoyed a good show. She was a novelty, this Englishwoman with waves of pale hair and a bloodstained hand. As instructed, she took care not to smile at the men, nor to test the pride of the women. Having paced the full circle twice over, she stopped. She drew the wine-colored silk from her waist.

Holding it up, she moved to stand face to face with a man slightly taller than her husband, perhaps slightly older. He bore a visage of the same mold as Cecco's, his chin cleanshaven and firm, the cheekbones angled just so, and his eyes the same, too, but set deeper beneath his brows. Where Cecco sported noisome bracelets, this brother wore bands of leather that silently wrapped his forearms. The shape of his shoulders was so familiar that she felt tempted to touch him...and this feeling pierced her with a sudden pang of homesickness. Drawing a breath, Jill fended the feeling off and plucked up her spirits. She dropped the handkerchief. It floated down, past the scuffed cuffs of his boots, to puddle at his feet.

"You are one of Giovanni's brothers."

"*Sì, Signora,*" was his curt reply.

"An older brother. Too young to be Giorgio. Is it Jacqui, or the closest to his age, Nico?"

He jerked back, opening his lips in surprise. Then, begrudgingly, he named himself, but did not deign to bend in a bow. "Nico."

"Nico. I am Jill, your sister-in-law, and most pleased to greet you." Turning, she located her second target. "And you." Sweeping toward the man, she drew forth the silk square of turquoise. This brother was also broad shouldered, but slimmer than Giovanni, and younger. He wore flamboyant trousers, a red bolero, and bangles. Jill proclaimed, "I know you; you are the youngest son. Trinio!"

Not as concerned with dignity as his mother and brother, Trinio bent to accept the turquoise kerchief from her fingers. His laugh echoed Cecco's. "*Certamente!*" He flourished the fabric. "You are sent by my brother, indeed. Welcome, Sister!" He raised his fingers to his mouth, and blew three shrieks of a whistle. The other men followed suit to burst into cacophony; the people clapped and laughed in delight.

From the tail of her eye, Jill watched Nico exchange a look with his mother. Before accepting the congratulations of her tribes-women, *la matriarca* flicked open her fan, concealing the lower half of her face. The fan was made of wooden laths carved in elegant lines, stained in varying tones of crimson. Jill recalled that this style was called *brisé*, because where a common fan would be all of a piece, its slats were separate as if 'broken,' and stitched together with ribbons. It was inlaid in an Oriental design— a little white bird, balanced on the interlacing twigs of some strange, foreign tree.

Moving with grace, the auburn-haired girl hastened to Jill. Her voice was musical. "You *do* know our famous outlaw. Giovanni Cecco is a legend among his people. I want to hear all about him, please."

Struck by this young woman's self-possession, Jill accepted the hand that she offered. "He has commissioned me to tell his stories, and I have many to relate for him. What is your name, my dear?"

"Stella. And this lady is my mother, Bezzi." A tall woman had taken Stella's arm. Under her flowery headscarf, her hair was a shade of auburn somewhat lighter than Stella's. She kept her eyes on her daughter, unsmiling.

"Mamma," Stella trilled, elated, "Now we can know—"

"We can know Giovanni's wife." Bezzi turned to Jill. *"Ciao, Signora."* Her words welcomed, but her manner was reserved. "And… these boys are your sons….May be…Giovanni's boys?"

Nibs materialized at Jill's side, interrupting her answer.

"Giovanni Cecco is my foster father," he explained. *"Buona serata, Signora e Signorina,"* the foreign words rolled off his tongue. "I'm called Nibs. I am most honored to make your acquaintance. May I present my brother, Tom?"

Jill smiled, pleased at his linguistic proficiency, and, at first, attributing the joy in his voice to his skill. She looked again, though, and saw that the crease his troubles had etched between his brows had smoothed, and in his eye shone a new kind of light. With a single look at lovely Stella, Nibs the Knife was disarmed. After nearly a year of preparation, this adventure might change her son with a dizzying speed.

Off balance for a moment, Jill was grateful to feel Tom's arm go round her waist. At his questioning look, Jill allayed his doubts, "It's all right. I've been accepted as Captain Cecco's wife, and his mamma and papa are well. You may fly away home soon, to tell him how we've fared."

Tom sighed, "That's a relief! Looks like Nibs has been accepted, too." He winked at Jill. "You keep an eye on him for me. He's fierce, but he's no match for *amore*."

Nico Cecco joined them. Jill spied the wine-colored kerchief spilling from a pocket of his vest. He called, "Stella, Bezzi, let our guests settle, and then we will ask all our questions. Mamma," he waved *la matriarca* closer, "you must present our company to the elder."

With a wooden clack, Cecco's mamma folded her fan. "Come… you fair one…you lovely one," she cooed to Jill, almost slyly, and although softly delivered, her words struck through Jill with a sting. How often had she heard Cecco speak this very endearment? And how often was it used, years ago, and falsely, upon the girls of various villages, whom the gypsy mother and her boy conspired to rob? Jill could almost hear Cecco utter these words— *lovely one*— as he must have employed them in the final seduction that led to his exile.

His mamma steered Jill with a firm grip toward the fire. "We will get you the blessing, and then find you your places."

Aiming a harsh look at Nibs, Nico urged him forth from fair Stella's side, then shepherded him and Tom after Jill. The escorts lined up the three strangers in front of the patriarch, retreating to stand behind them. The gypsy king glowered under shaggy white eyebrows. Jill watched him consider the scar at her throat.

"And so, you are no impostors," he judged, at last. *"Bene, bene."* Leisurely, he puffed on his long-stemmed pipe. "The Ceccos will care for you. Feed you. And then, Storyteller, you will recompense us for our hospitality. Come back to the fire, we will smoke, we will drink to you, and you will make us glad of your company."

"Signore, grazie. We will find it a pleasure.*"*

Nibs and Tom repeated Jill's thanks, and bowed their respects.

Jill ventured, "This young man is Nibs the Knife, and this, Tom Tootles. You should know, though, that although they are my sons, they are not Giovanni's. He is like a father to my boys, but he knows no children."

"No children, eh?" The old man clamped his pipe between his teeth, cradling it in his palm. He leaned back, but his gaze upon Jill remained intense.

"Let me see your wedding ring."

"You may see it, Sir." Jill held out her fingers to him. Night was now drawing down. The trees overhead shed a fragrance of dew-dampened leaves. Her wedding band and its companion ring of topazes glowed in the fire's light. The gypsy king would not touch it, she knew, nor would he ever touch Jill. No man of this troupe might lay a finger upon her. Only cloth must pass between unmated and unrelated men and women— hence the handkerchiefs Cecco sent, six innocent filaments between his wife and his brothers. She continued, "You can see that my rings are golden, *Signore.* Not the brass you might be expecting."

He unclenched his teeth from the pipe. For the first time, he smiled at Jill. It was a wide, wise smile, with a gap of two teeth missing from his lower gums. To Jill, his grin was beautiful. She had won the blessing of the patriarch.

"Yes, yes," he cheered, loud enough for the whole troupe to hear, "these rings *are* made of gold. As for brass... *Signora* Cecco," he poked his pipe toward her, "the only brass here— it is your very own boldness!" He took up an earthenware jug, and toasted her. "Look, Mamma. See, Nico! Our Giovanni has changed his ways! No more brass counterfeits. He traded *true* gold for this golden girl."

"*Sì, Padre,*" Nico conceded to the man in authority but, to Jill's ear, his voice betrayed skepticism. "Against all expectation."

As the patriarch flung up his arm, Jill and her sons were dismissed. Jill rejoined Cecco's family. Relieved and fatigued, she felt more than ready to be led to their caravans. Stella pirouetted to follow, but her mother, Bezzi, stood tall and handsome at the rim of the fire. She seemed lost in thought.

Jill watched Bezzi stare at her hands, then clasp them together. Her fingers were bare, Jill noted. She wore plentiful bracelets and other trinkets. She was a parent, the mother of a young woman. But, as Jill witnessed, Bezzi bore no rings at all. No gold, and no brass.

Jill turned to study the girl, Stella, more closely. A flush of heat suffused Jill's cheeks, as, all at once, comprehension dawned. She had recognized Cecco's mother, and each one of two brothers. Now, rosy from her realization, she had discovered a daughter.

Did an unexpected spouse dwell here already, besides herself?

No, Jill decided. As the patriarch had judged, only Jill wore the ring of Cecco's wife. Bezzi had once been his lover.

Brassily, Jill had stepped into Cecco's world. Yet, now, as the blood pumped through her heart, every instinct informed her that her tread must fall far, far more delicately than either she or Cecco expected.

Fortunes Fair and False

Many questions must be answered. Rested and fed, the travelers separated as Jill and Nibs bid Tom farewell. He traipsed to the woods to meet Jewel, while his mother and brother joined the company round the fire. The old man smoked his pipe in the comfort of his rugs, and the families crowded in, chattering with anticipation in both Italian and Romani, eager to hear what the newcomers might reveal.

Nibs found a way to wedge his tall, lanky self into a spot on a blanket, in the vicinity of Stella. Under the ringlets on her forehead, the girl slid a glance his way. She cradled something in her arms and, looking closer, Jill saw that it was an ornate, painted mandolin. Jill was pulled to a bench by Cecco's mamma, who arranged herself next to her, there to wave her fan in languid strokes, shooing campfire smoke from her proud Roman nose— another feature she shared with her sons. A brooding Nico loomed at Jill's other side, his profile much akin to his brother's.

Over the bonfire, wavering eddies of heat rose up toward the moon, the night creatures chirred, and, up high in the stardust, Jill glimpsed the silhouette of Tom trailing a small, star-like light. "Safe passage," Jill whispered to her son, wishing she, too, held a fan, to shield the words meant for his ears alone.

Soon the patriarch pointed the stem of his long pipe at Jill, and the gypsies hushed to hear. "And so." He sank back into his throne, disposed for a full night's diversion. "Your Giovanni was a clever boy, until he was caught. He is a clever man, now?"

"One of the cleverest men I know." Jill uttered these words easily, but found herself wincing. She'd come too close to a memory she'd had to force from her mind. Something rattled down in her thoughts, like a shutter, and, for one moment, she blinked in confusion. At her side, she sensed Nico reading her every emotion. He, too, she suspected, was a clever man.

As the patriarch continued, his white mustaches waggled beneath his chin. "He avenged the wrongs perpetrated against him."

"Yes, *Padre*," Jill answered, "with the aid of his brothers." As she accepted the mug of wine he offered, both parties took care to avoid brushing fingers. "But you've all heard that story," she said. "He himself does not know its full ending. When Tom arrives home, Giovanni will be relieved to learn from him that Nico, Giorgio, and Jacqui returned to you safely."

"I was against their going." The medallions of the old man's headdress chimed as he tossed a nod toward *la matriarca*. "Their mamma, here, induced me to allow it."

Mamma angled her face from him, and, again, took shelter behind her fan, where no one could read her expression. Jill would have wagered she wore an artful smile. But, speaking for her husband, Jill defended her. "One must never doubt a mother's instinct. I assure you, *Signore*, that Giovanni is aware of the dangers his three elders risked. Their loyalty freed him from prison, and even death. He is grateful." Raising her wine to Nico, she toasted him. "As am I."

Nico replied, "We Romani believe that in this world, no one should wander *solo*...alone."

His choice of words caused the breath to catch in Jill's throat, but she had no time to consider why the thought of living alone grieved her heart so, as if the concept of solitude deepened a rut already worn there. "I agree. Love and company make our troubles lighter, and our joys more complete."

The *Padre* asked, "And so, lacking his brethren, Giovanni found a place in the company of pirates?"

"Indeed. He now captains a ship of his own."

The listeners gasped with appreciation.

"Regale us, Storyteller."

"Willingly." Jill obliged, at long last beginning the narration that would surely continue throughout her stay. "As a girl, I dwelt on an island where this band of pirates take shore leave. I adopted seven boys who were lost there, and raised them. But the boy with whom I fell in love was unkind to us, so we all chose to leave him behind." Involuntarily, Jill touched the old wound at her throat. "I joined up with those buccaneers."

Nico snorted, "So, then, foolish boys— they appeal to you?"

"Spoken like a brother." Jill turned her smile upon him. His resemblance to her husband was uncanny, and her gaze lingered over him; she couldn't help it. "And, yes, unlike my husband, this boy *was* foolish, to my way of thinking. But I've learned. We must each be who we are. We change only through Time and experience." Cecco had advised Jill of the pace at which this audience would best embrace her storytelling. Allowing Time to work for her again, she indulged her listeners with it, gazing into the fire, and into her past with the Island boy, Peter. "And, sometimes, we learn through a well-worded story."

"Which seems to be your talent." Nico challenged his new sister-in-law, crossing his arms so that his leather bands met in a formidable union. "But how do we know your stories are true? Shall we hear only what you need us to believe?"

Mamma snapped her crimson fan shut, and shook it at him. "Let our golden girl speak, my son. We are not so heedless as to be led into lies." She beamed upon Jill, with her sideways smile. "And even if it were so, to behold such a beauty as she speaks is pure pleasure."

"Ah, Mamma," Jill sweet-talked back to her, "I see where Giovanni got his golden tongue."

Mamma agreed, "Giovanni is a great one for the gold, indeed. He loves the coins, he loves the trinkets. He loves also the girl with the golden locks." Here her flattery turned to concern. "But..." she addressed the elder, redeploying her fan to flutter at her chin.

Jill knew from Cecco's teaching that his mother was both wise and manipulative, and this little, feminine gesture made Mamma's question seem an appeal for the patriarch's guidance. No wonder she had gotten her way when her favorite son required rescue.

"But *Padre*," Mamma continued, "shall not such a brilliance invite questions? After all, the people of the villages seek always after Giovanni, and they lust for the prize his capture promises."

Pushing his pipe in and out through the gap in his teeth, the old man considered. "A stranger among us will spark gossip. In this case, there may be stories about our storyteller herself." Sagely, he nodded.

"Because we must remain in this place until Papa Cecco's return, we cannot risk raising attention."

To Jill's wondering look, Mamma said, as if it hadn't been her intention all along, "It is decided, then. Tomorrow, we will make you to blend like a gypsy." She'd used a Romani word with which Jill was unfamiliar, but before Jill could ask for clarification, Mamma insisted, "Now, tell us how my son won command of a ship?"

Stealing a second to sip from her cup, Jill savored the cool, fruity taste of Italian wine. She used the moment to smooth her composure. A few yards away, Stella watched her steadily with her sea-green eyes, and, although no one had, as yet, divulged Stella's bloodlines, Jill intuited her need to learn more of her father. She smiled at the girl. "Becoming a captain was his way of wooing me."

Stella's dimples reappeared, and Nibs grinned in tandem. A chorus of "Ah!" rose up all around Jill, as men and women alike indulged in the romance. *La matriarca* clutched her fan, to all appearances enraptured. As she leaned forward to hearken, the loops of her earrings swung with her.

Jill related the tale. "When I stole aboard ship, Giovanni was the first of the sailors to bid me welcome. He was a valued member of the company, and, by then, quite wealthy. On his biceps he wears golden armbands. I remember how his bracelets reflected the flame of the lantern he held up to guide me— just like your earrings, Mamma, in this fire's glow. As you may well believe, he was a most handsome seaman. But he was not yet an officer."

Trinio joked, "That is just like Giovanni. Why do the work, if he can still win the treasure?"

Nibs joined the merriment, "I can vouch for what you say! Tom and I signed on before our mother did. Until he laid eyes on Jill, Captain Cecco had not much ambition. Now he drives us like slaves, more's the pity!"

Trinio's bangles rang as he laughed, applauding Nibs' wit. "I know what it is, to be a slave for one's mamma." He bunched his fingers to toss a kiss to *la matriarca*, just as Cecco might do, belying his words with his fondness.

Jill laughed, too, then continued, "Soon after we met, he set his sights on the captaincy. He wished to win not simply my heart, but my regard." She turned to Mamma and laid her hand on the woman's skirt. "The truth is, he is lonely for you. He owns the soul of a wanderer, but he has lost the family he loves—" Jill spread her arms to include the Romani band, "and his tribe. All these years, you have been his anchor."

"And now, his anchor is you." Mamma tapped Jill with her fan. "So, my Giovanni has found his way in the world, and a love to walk with him. How does it happen, then, that he sends her so far away, here, to us?"

"*Sì*. This is my question!" the *Padre* agreed, and the people all around echoed, "*Sì!*"

"In all he does, Giovanni thinks to protect his beloved. He sent me here to hide me—" Jill threw her blue gaze around the sea of expectant faces, "from an evil adversary."

The response of Jill's audience was gratifying as, employing the motions she'd seen Cecco use, they banished bad luck. With murmurs and gestures, they signified their interest. These people loved a good tale. They were eager to learn of Cecco's exploits. Jill was primed to please them, and pleased for her own sake, too. She need use only truth. With such a store of adventures, no lies were invited.

"Trinio, tell me. What stories are recounted of Giovanni?"

"Everyone here knows how he inflicted his vengeance on the governor of the prison. Nico and the others bore witness. With the knife they gave him, he cut his name in that vicious man's back."

"He and his knife are famed for this deed on the high seas as well. Yet, even so, his crew were surprised when, one fine day, he required revenge once again. This time, he acted for my sake. The evil man of whom I spoke behaved despicably."

"And?"

"And now, that man bears his shame in indelible letters. *My* name is etched in his skin." Jill bent forward, and, with one blood-red fingertip, sketched the letters in the air. "J-I-L-L…writ in pretty red ink."

Applause, shrieks, and whistles filled the air. Trinio stoked the fire, his handsome face bright in the night as the flames leapt up to join the celebrants. The ladies flounced their skirts; a tambourine clashed.

"The rogue is not dead?" Mamma asked, indignant. "What is my son thinking, to leave such a scoundrel alive?"

Grave now, Jill replied, "We both felt the urge to kill him. But a cunning counterpart calls for more cunning, and Giovanni's shrewdness prevails. He holds leverage over this villain. The man is a physician, famous in Europe for a love philter he formulated. He makes much of his reputation, and makes much money by it. Very soon, the two rivals will rendezvous, and Giovanni will seize his percentage."

"But my brother guards you," Nico retorted, his eyes narrowing. "A ship's crew answers to his command. I think there is more to this story. Some other menace puts you in danger."

"I confess it. To discover the source of this physician's wealth, I led him on. The man is convinced he has the law on his side." Jill squared her shoulders. "He believes he is my husband."

"Why should he believe such a—" Nico's face darkened. "No. No— Not even Giovanni would allow such a ploy. Not from a woman…" his dusky eyes looked Jill up and down, "not his wife!"

"*Sì*, brother Nico. I used my husband's signature trick." The young *Signora* Cecco smiled. "An exchange of rings."

In sly, rising tones, Jill's hearers moaned. Understanding spread, and their approbation grew louder. Trinio whistled through his fingers, and soon Jill was surrounded by drinks hoisted high in her honor. She felt as welcome here, now, as ever she'd felt aboard Cecco's ship. As Giovanni's people bestowed their acceptance, Jill's heart, too, filled with affection.

Even Mamma smiled broadly, her fan neglected on her lap. "*Straniera*, I called you. My splendid one, I should have trusted my son and his judgment."

Jill was willing to believe her— but she didn't. Still, sitting shoulder to shoulder, the two women understood; an alliance was possible.

"When you are ready, *Signora*, I will read his letter to you."

The woman nodded. "Tomorrow. Tomorrow, lovely Jill."

"And I want you to know, Mamma, I did not wish to leave my husband's side. I desired to face the danger with him. I now understand that, just as Giovanni makes me safer here, I make him safer there. He is free from the burden of protecting me."

The old man pulled his pipe from his teeth. "I see you love him, truly, to part from him thus. I understand why he prizes you. You are loyal. And, like your man, you do not shy from lies and larceny."

"From larceny, never. But as for lies, *Padre*, I speak only truth."

Nico grunted. Mamma shot him a look.

"Giovanni taught me his own gypsy principles." Jill raised her mug and saluted the company. "To courage, and loyalty, and a healthy disrespect for the law." She drained her cup, and, hoisting their elbows, the people joined her with bottles, mugs, and wineskins. When all had partaken, Jill stood to gather her skirts and sashayed in a circle, setting her ankle bells chiming. "I also learned that you love the music. I see Stella waiting with her mandolin. Please, my dear, may we hear you play?"

Many questions had been answered. Many more lay ahead. Jill drew a deep, relieved breath. From the comfort of his rugs, the old man smoked his pipe. Gleaming, his intelligent eyes studied her. Stella rose and handled her mandolin, other musicians crowded in, and Jill took Stella's place on the blanket next to Nibs, to listen to strains raised in gypsy tradition. She felt weary in both mind and body, but she was eager to hear what the old Romani songs might reveal.

At the break of day, Jill awoke to the unfamiliar. She was alone; her bunk did not rock upon the waters, but lay motionless. In place of seabirds, sparrows squabbled. The breeze wafting in carried scents of earth and dung, while horses snuffled on the other side of the wagon wall, munching meal from a trough. She opened her eyes to see sunshine, and Mamma's hair, the same rich brown color as Cecco's, coiled in netting. *La matriarca* sat on the caravan's steps with her back turned, allowing Jill privacy in which to dress in her new, foreign garb.

Jill rose to slip her blue blouse over her shift. She layered her trio of skirts and hitched them out of her way, then she cinched the embroidered girdle round her ribs. She slid the brass knife from under her pillow, tucking it into her belt. As she hung the copper discs from her ears, she paid homage to the goddess some artist cut into them, a kneeling Isis, with her feathered arms spread. Jill imagined this deity might have watched over the long flight that ended last night, here in the heart of Cecco's family.

The noise of children romping outside reminded her to rummage her pack for her tin of tea. Finding an urn of water steaming on the little iron stove, she steeped a cup of her daily brew. Mamma heard her movements, and climbed the wooden steps to join her.

"Good morning, my daughter," she smiled. "Tea, is it?" Mamma lifted the tin to sniff the herbs. As she recognized the scents, her brows twitched. "Ah. And not only tea."

"No, not just tea." Jill had asked Cecco if the women of his clan might object to this medicine, but he was uncertain. She asserted, "I find that seven sons are enough. Perhaps, Mamma, you feel the same?"

"Seven sons. We have this in common!" Jutting her chin, she declared, "I cherish my *bambini*, each and every one. But seven is a lucky number to keep. I, too, have my remedies, as do some of my sisters." Mamma's expression set in shrewd lines. "We do not tell the menfolk, and they do not dare to ask."

"We women must remain mysterious. It is part of our charm."

"Mystery is our power." *La matriarca*'s voice resonated with it. "I taught my Giovanni more than the others. In him, I instilled an understanding of females. He will have told you these secrets." Mamma fingered one of Jill's earrings. "He understands this goddess, too. He found these earbobs for you, no? The 'Gyptian Isis. Another proud mother."

"These ornaments were his parting gift to me. And what is the story of this *brisé* fan from Japan that you carry? It is beautiful, a rare find. I have seen only one like it before, in faraway days spent in London."

"A treasure to pass from mother to daughter."

Turning away, Mamma sliced bread from a loaf, and laid wedges of white cheese atop it. Vegetable cuttings lay scattered on the bread board. A bowl of some concoction simmered on the stove, redolent of vinegar, and pots and utensils hung from the wall just above it. The wagon was tidy inside and, although compact, it held three cushioned bunks— two at the sides, and a crossways one curtained at the back, for Mamma and Papa— a table and stools, garments on clothes pegs; the wagon's every inch was filled with shelves, cabinets, and drawers. An aged but good Persian runner lined the narrow patch of floor. Everything Mamma needed lay within reach, ensconced in soft, lively fabrics. Jill felt at ease here, in this traveling home so like to a tiny ship's cabin.

"You must break your fast, my dear one." Mamma gave the bread to Jill, and a small bowl of olives, indicating that she should sit down. Dusting her hands first, she opened the fan to display its little white bird on a branch, inlaid on the mellow red stain of its ribs. "My own mother received this fan from hers. It lay across my *nonna*'s table-scarf one night, as she read a fine lady's cards."

"And, like her great-grandson, she seized her opportunity?"

"I see how well you know my boy! My grandmamma understood the potential of women's weapons. She had seen the lady wield this fan, acting prim, or shy, or seductive, or secretive— implications conveyed by how her hand moved the piece. *Nonna* felt in this fan a magic, a hidden means of power, and of protection." Mamma's head slanted like the bird on the fan's. "She felt she must acquire it, and, so…" in a gesture reminiscent of Cecco's, Mamma shrugged, "she made sure the lady's fortune was favorable."

"Giovanni's great-granddame left a legacy of intelligence," Jill observed, and then she sobered. "I hope, Mamma, that you find *his* fortunes favorable." She swallowed the final bite of breakfast, the bread crumbly and sweet, the cheese a bit sour, all complemented by her last sips of tea.

"You will read for me his letter, then I will read for you the cards."

"I don't know how long I may stay here, but, when I go, I'd like to bring Giovanni your blessing. I'd like to bring Papa Cecco's, too."

"I can bestow both. But Papa will be unhappy if he misses you, and so will the others. He spoils his grandchildren." Mamma said, indulgently, "He cannot be parted from them; he made Giorgio and Jacqui bring their families along."

"Do Nico and Trinio have families?"

"Trinio, ha! He is flashy and laughing. He cannot be serious long enough to go courting. This is not to say that he remains lonely."

"Should I be shocked, Mamma? Does not Trinio respect the law of the cloth?"

Mamma collapsed her fan and shook it like a finger, but the twinkle in her eye gave her amusement away. "No more than Giovanni did, when he was young. Or his papa!" she laughed.

"And exceptions are made for your clientele? For those *non tribale* girls Giovanni played so profitably?"

"Oh, yes," Mamma waved compunction away, then let the fan drop to hang from her waist. "And within the troupe, the people respect the rule, for the most part. But just try to keep young lovebirds from loving."

"I don't attempt the impossible."

Mamma smiled her sideways smile, "*Sì*, lovely Jill. I already know this." Squinting, she surveyed her daughter-in-law. "You surrendered, I think. You found it impossible to resist our Giovanni."

Jill admitted, with only mild surprise, "You read me like Giovanni does. He bewitched me, with his gypsy magic."

"No need for magic to read *you*, my lovely one. Your right hand, the hand of power, signifies both lifeblood and death. You carry intrigue. Is it not so?"

"It is so. Giovanni knows it. We don't deny one another's stories." Jill hinted, again, "Do not fear to speak of him— of his past— if something hides that it would help the two of us to know."

"His past I leave to him."

Changing tack, Jill asked, "Well then, no woman has settled Trinio, as yet. And...Nico?" Jill considered the possibility that she had guessed wrong about Stella's parentage. Nico and Giovanni were so physically similar. "Pretty Stella resembles him, and I've seen him watching over her. Is she his daughter?"

"Stella is a daughter to Nico; Bezzi is not a wife to him." Mamma turned her back, clearing away the breakfast. "I wish now I had not scolded Papa so, insisting he get a good price for every one of those animals. He is a fine horseman, and he will sell only to men his intuitions say will care for them. But where his beasts are concerned, he holds no measure of time."

"He must be a kind man." Sorry that she might not make Papa's acquaintance, Jill felt disappointment for Cecco's sake, too. She had hoped also to thank Giorgio and Jacqui for breaking him free from the prison at Gao. As for his younger brothers, next in age— "Stella says two others of your sons married outside this tribe. These would be Pietro and Mischa."

"They married sisters. We see them every half-year, at the gathering. Their little ones are still tiny."

"Giovanni longs for little ones of his own." Jill watched Mamma, offering her the opportunity to return to the subject of Stella. Mamma only tended her chores, stirring the pot on the stove, then sweeping up the cuttings that gave off a crisp smell of greens. She tossed them out the wagon door, to the horses.

"Yet," Jill continued, gently, "I don't expect that I will be giving you grandsons."

"Of grandsons I have plenty, and of granddaughters also." The older woman sat down, and patted her daughter-in-law's hand. "No, my Jill. You cannot help that Giovanni's luck twisted. You did not tear him from his home. It broke my heart to see my crafty, handsome boy dragged away, thrown to a cold, hard cell." Gazing into memory, she heaved a sigh. After a moment, her brown eyes rekindled, and she fixed them on Jill's. She said, fiercely, "You may not give me grandsons. But, lovely one, you *will* give me something."

"Yes?"

"You will give something that no one else can."

"I am gratified to learn this." Jill felt the hypnotism of Mamma's gaze. "But, besides loving your crafty, handsome boy, what else might I do for you?"

"You will alter their fortunes."

" 'Their' fortunes? Whose?" Hearing the conviction in Mamma's prophecy, Jill felt herself start to tremble. "Mamma…I do not know what you mean."

"No," *la matriarca* answered, her expression steeped in mystery. As she had claimed, mystery was her power. "I do not suppose that you know."

Her words held the storyteller spellbound.

"You will alter the fortunes of not one son…but two."

Until this moment, Jill had warmed to this woman. She was the mother of her beloved. She had taken Jill in, to protect her, wrapping her in this cozy home. In their brief acquaintance, roads to understanding were laid down between them, a path to common ground. On edge now, Jill pulled back to study her.

With her eyes, her face, and her words so familiar, *la matriarca* was everything Cecco had indicated. She was acute and intuitive. Yet, Jill now knew, Mamma was more— much more potent than, even warned, Jill anticipated. And, once again, at the break of this day, Jill awoke to the unexpected, the unfamiliar.

The wagon steps creaked then, and, as the hairs rose up on her arms, Jill felt some gypsy intuition of her own. When Nico darkened the doorway, she found herself unsurprised.

After her exertions in guiding the travelers, Jewel's master allowed her luxurious days to rest upon her green velvet cushion. Pampered and refreshed, the fairy addressed her next task with zest.

She raced through the air above bushes and boulders, hurtling over rambling terrain. Except for nesting birds, not a creature stirred on this empty islet. The ground below her fell away in a cliff, and a craggy coast leapt into view, stinking of the dead fish and seaweed stagnating by the sandbanks. Seabirds wheeled squealing around her, and she slowed, dimming her glow to hide herself. Her master had warned her when he sent her on this errand. The utmost of caution was called for.

As the commodore predicted, a ship nestled here in the swells. From her mast flew the colors of France: blue, white, and red. The vessel lay anchored beyond towers of rough, reddish rock jutting up from the shallows— all as foretold, yet the fairy pulled up in surprise. Her eyes were dazzled by the flash and gleam of swords. She had expected to locate the ship and its company. She had not thought to find that company fighting.

Cautiously, Jewel dropped to a perching place on a rough, furled swag of sailcloth, where none of the sailors would spy her. Fascinated by this foreign ship full of strangers, she set herself to watch. A cluster of sailors in waist-length, brass-buttoned jackets, like those worn by Captain Cecco's Frenchmen, grinned and cheered at the edge of the action, which the fairy now perceived as a duel. She had never before witnessed this kind of combat without the gut-wrench of caring which swordsman prevailed. The combatants' voices rose up to her roost, vigorous but breathless, as metal clashed in stroke after stroke. Jewel gripped the sailcloth and leaned in to listen.

"Have at thee, again, *Monsieur!*"

"As you please, Sir. I am at your command."

These men spoke in English, with foreign accents. The first seemed a soldierly fellow, with a short cape thrown over one shoulder. He slashed away with a military saber. Red and gold cords dangled from his hilt. As he lunged, his legs surged forward and back, the long crimson stripe down the side of his French blue leggings bending and straightening with his knees. Stirrup bands beneath the arch of his boots held his trousers tight to his ankles. He was just as athletic but taller than his opponent, and his proud posture matched the other man's. His expression, also, mirrored his adversary, with a look of intensity.

As Jewel now studied that adversary, she found that his face did not quite mirror the younger man's after all. Handsome in early middle age, yet the opponent's visage was marred by marks. She knew him at once, from her master's description— this swordsman was the dishonorable doctor. A villain.

Still, he put up a fight worthy of his company's attention, and the watching crew urged on his efforts. His sandy hair was tied back in a ribbon. He wore a loose cream-colored blouse and an elegant vest, both of which, Jewel was disappointed to note, hid his disfigured back. She smirked to think of Jill's name carved there, now written in scars.

The engraving in his flesh did not seem to afflict him. His footwork, in his soft-leather shoes, was light; he trod deftly as he countered the Frenchman's blows. He appeared to be succumbing to his foe, every thrust driving him backward, yet his manner remained calm, and— thanks to Jewel's close attendance upon both a boy and a man who each excelled at deception, she was expert at identifying this trait: he was calculating.

This doctor's effort was pretend! He was losing this duel, on purpose.

Jewel re-examined the young Frenchman. Seeming larger than life, his energy dominated the deck. A fire burned in his eyes, and she wondered what inspired it. In recent experience, Jewel had seen that kind of flame fueled by a female— Red-Handed Jill, to be exact. No woman decorated the deck of this ship, so Jewel searched for some other cause.

Ah! The man wore a badge on his sleeve. Stealthily, Jewel worked her way lower, clinging to the scratchy cable of a backstay, gaining a closer look. The badge was sewn of smooth, golden threads, in the shape of a shield. Upon its field, three stylized lilies were embroidered in a royal shade of blue. This emblem, she thought, was a tattoo for his clothing. His cropped hair curled longer over the peak of his forehead; the man was clean-shaven. He seemed confident and clever. Jewel found him altogether dashing, just like Peter when playing at soldier. The Lost Boys had shammed many a battle for King and for country. Thus, the fairy surmised that the hot blood that blazed in this man's breast burned for his nation— for France.

This reminder of duty jogged the fairy back to her chore. Quickly, she completed the tasks she'd been assigned. The vessel boasted three masts, like the *Roger*. Jewel inspected the ship's weaponry, touching a finger for each cannon she saw, twice on each finger of each hand, counting the chaser at the bow and the swivel gun at the stern. As the commodore ordered, she compared the ship's size to *Red Lady*'s, but found its dimensions more petite. The prow was sharp and the deck narrow, a design, Jewel guessed, that made it swim like a fish. It would be quick in pursuit, and agile in battle.

Slipping down to hover round the hull, the fairy found no sweeps and no gunports. The rows of cannon lined only the main deck. A set of windows along the stern allowed her a glimpse into the captain's cabin, bedecked in paisley trimmings. No one was visible within, and all port and starboard portholes were shut. Jewel couldn't read the name painted on the bow, but she peered at a design rendered there in gold paint, a rare species of flower floating in a puddle of water. A curiously pacific symbol, for a preying privateer.

Yet, most important, according to the commodore, was to mark the setting in which this ship moored. Was it a solitary vessel, or did companions lurk in the vicinity? Jewel had flown a wide circle on her approach. Save for the commodore's fleet a few leagues away, the open water lay vacant. Nor did she spot any boats round the islet, which her officers had chosen for this assignation because of its inaccessibility. Jewel ascertained for her master that this ship's captain— the small, cocky man in a coat of iridescent green with a wattle of ruffles at his throat, and who stood clutching a spyglass— had obeyed his instructions. He'd sailed to this rendezvous without the protection of a partner...or the law.

With one last glance at the duelists, Jewel turned back toward the islet. The ringing of swords stopped abruptly, and in his exacting accent the doctor declared, "Hold, de Beaumonde! I yield." Some intuition caused Jewel to pause before flying. Setting her nose at the level of a scupper, she peeped through the opening, inhaling scents of oakum and sawdust. She didn't know what to expect, but her master would demand full intelligence.

The doctor smiled, and his long, symmetrical scars flexed on his cheekbones. He held out a hand to his adversary. "Olivier, you are too accomplished for my inferior skill to defeat. In any case, I meant no offense to you, nor to your birthplace. My remark, no doubt, suffered in translation." The doctor bowed, and the two men tucked their sabers away to shake hands. "Come, let me pour you a glass." Turning to the captain, the doctor called, "LeCorbeau, shall you join us, or will you remain on your watch?"

The French *commandant* observed the duelists with a cynical eye. His accent was heavy, a challenge for Jewel to follow. "*Mais non*, I thank you." He seized the lull in hostilities to raise his spyglass, propping it close to his beak of a nose. As he searched the sea, he exclaimed, "And how you are able to swill wine, let alone play at dueling, is a mystery to me! These, eh, pirates..." LeCorbeau fluttered his free hand, laden with lace at his cuff, "I expect them to bloom on my horizon at any instant."

"Bloom, like *La Fleur de Lotus?* You have named your ship aptly, my friend. A good omen for our endeavor. To the lotus flower we owe our futures, and our good fortune. I shall drink to her!"

"Good fortune you call it? With Hook at our heels?" The wind kicked up, the French flag clapped the mizzen with a crack, and LeCorbeau jumped in surprise, flailing like a capon. The spyglass tumbled from his grasp to clank on the deck. His men managed to keep their faces blank, but Jewel had to stuff her fist in her mouth to silence a jingle of laughter. Not as diplomatic, the man called de Beaumonde chortled.

LeCorbeau seethed, malevolent, "*Mon Dieu*, Doctor Han— that is, eh, Doctor Heinrich! Leave me to my vigil, and take that other idiot with you."

The other idiot, de Beaumonde, stiffened to a pose of attention, but, this time, took no offense. His tone was heroic. "*Vraiment, mon Commandant, Monsieur le Docteur* and I will protect you." He flung his cape over his shoulder. "No passel of brigands shall prevail, while we live to wield weapons!"

Jewel recognized two shrewd men, and a fool. She also understood that, as such, each man comprised a danger. As always, Commodore Hook was correct. The utmost of caution was called for. With this information, she zipped away toward the *Roger*. Confident that these 'brigands' would soon meet their match, she unstoppered her shiny-bell laugh. No wonder her master so anticipated this adventure. It should prove as daring as any game Peter played on the Neverland!

Other Lovers

My dear husband,

I sit alone tonight. I am musing at the little tabletop in the caravan, with an alluring glow of empty parchment before me, shining amber in the light of the oil. I promised myself to keep a journal of all I see and hear on my travels. I think of you so constantly, though, that I decided instead to write not to myself, but to you. In doing so, I feel that I am sharing this time here in Italy with my loved one. You feel as near to me as my shoulder. I know that I am in your thoughts, too. Yet you must wait and wonder what I see, and what I feel, until next we meet. And here is the answer: what do I see? Your face. What do I hear? The scratch of a pen whose ink conjures you.

In order to keep this journal private, I am writing in my native tongue. It's odd to think in English again. You taught me and Nibs expertly and, for the most part, I am keeping up with the language. Every now and then, and maybe deliberately, Mamma keeps me guessing as to her meaning.

Your mother judged it wise for me to blend into the troupe. You will be amused when you see me. You might call me 'Red-Headed Jill' now, and I'm a more apt namesake for your ship, for with an aromatic concoction of vegetable dye, Mamma made my hair match my hand. Not blood-red, of course, but a shining shade of copper. A day or two passed before I stopped smelling of beets and vinegar, but I'm quite content with the change, and when I tell Curly one day, he will be pleased that his mother takes after him. Maybe I'll have a portrait painted— perhaps just a miniature— to send to him.

Tom will have told you that both your Papa and Mamma are well. Your brothers are married, save for Trinio (too flashy and laughing for marriage, according to la matriarca*) and Nico. I've yet to penetrate the enigma of Nico, but, my dear, give me time. He is as dark and ruminating as you've been known to be. After adapting to you, I can manage to handle this brother's moods. As for which of you seven I judge to be handsomest, I shall allow you to wonder until I fly home.*

Mamma revels in your letter. Upon the first reading, she couldn't hide her tears from me, and I felt the moisture burning in my eyes as well. The two of us are simpatico in our yearning for you— she for a long lost son, I for my faraway lover. Mamma insisted that I read your eloquence aloud five times, and at least twice every day after. She'll have your letter memorized soon, so that when I must leave her to return to your arms, she'll still be mining pleasure in the message from your heart. May that time arrive soon. Even writing of that day makes me feel the burning now, and not, amore mio, *whence the tears spring.*

But I must bring myself back to earth....

Mamma returned the favor of my reading to her by reading her cards for me. I am not quite sure what to make of my fortune. She concurs with your prediction that I will raise no more boys. It is no surprise that I'll travel; my heart knows much love; I am doubly protected— perhaps she means by both you and my sons? Halfway through the spread of cards, though, she went quiet, and ceased to look in my eyes. Nico hunkered next to me, listening too, but where Mamma seemed troubled, Nico seemed heated. They spoke over my head, in Romani, so rapidly that, knowing just the basics of the old language, I couldn't keep up. One word only stood out for me. 'Weapon.'

I don't know Mamma or Nico well enough yet to read their expressions, and I must say I am hampered on dry land. Everyone who set foot aboard the ship is, in some degree, my own creation. I've played a hand in establishing their stories. But, here, I cannot intuit the people's histories. For once, the clan around me sense more of me than I of them. I suppose it is only fair, but I find it...unsettling. I've remained somewhat off balance since my toes touched the ground here.

Nibs, on the other hand, is off balance for an entirely different reason. Love has discovered him. The young lady is pretty, poised, and practical. In every way, she suits him, and I approve of the romance. He is keeping to Romani code, behaving properly (although I am now aware of accepted exceptions). With a cloth at the ready, he escorts her to the village, carries her market basket, and takes her walking in the evenings, under the silver Italian stars that pulse through feathery tree boughs, high up above. Yes, even the heavens appear exotic here, and both Nibs and I have fallen under the spell of your homeland. No wonder you are such a romantic, amore, having entered your manhood in this place, where the air is perfumed with passion; the earth, so soft, begs to cushion us lovers; and music floats into one's ear from some twilight glade far beyond eventide. How I miss you. How I crave your strong, loving hold.

Yet I am not just a redheaded lady yearning for love. I am a mother. Shall I trust in Nibs' affection, or is he a victim of atmosphere? Once he learns who the girl's papa is, I believe he'll ask him to part with her. The subject seems to be a delicate one. I've an inkling as to why, but my queries about her are parried. Whatever my suspicions, as you know, your people can hold a secret. Because I can keep my confidence, too, I will not write my guess down. No. Not even here.

I've been regaling your troupe with my stories, and I'm delighted by the attention of my listeners. They are curious and, naturally, ask about the legend of my hand. I've attempted on several occasions to relate that tale, but somehow my tongue becomes tied. I cannot quite find the words. Whenever I speak of my history thus, however fluent I believe that I am, my Italian fails me. Perhaps I've been struck with modesty. I live the story of Red-Handed Jill— it defines who I am— but I cannot stammer it out. I began to tell it again last night. I described myself as a girl long ago on the Island— whip and dagger in hand— and the next thing I knew, I'd told the tale of David's rescue by my tiger kill, scant months before, my right hand imbued in the blood of my very first kill, fresh spilt from the beast that had stalked us.

Why should I shy from this triumph? Surely, in all my repertoire, no more potent story exists than that of Jill. When I arrived at its conclusion, with the people's eyes as big as walnuts, an image hovered at the edge of my mind. Something sharp and shining. Mamma seemed to sense my distress. She leaned toward Nico, her fan at her lips, and she whispered into his ear. With newfound intuition, I deduced what she said. It was that image she saw in my fortune, come back to mystify: some kind of weapon.

I must close this note soon, and I turn to a grimmer topic. I will not dwell on my anxiety for your meeting with our adversary. Your prediction came true; your people thrilled to hear of your heroism in avenging me with your famous knife. They appreciate my deception of the doctor for the sake of his riches, and they applaud the expected outcome of your rendezvous. I trust you will prevail. My heartfelt hope is that you will turn that odious man back toward Europe, relieved of his fortune— or relieved of his life.

I leave us both with the sentiment Nico murmured, soon after I made myself known to him. "In this world, no one should wander alone."

What a lonesome word that one is, most especially to hear in Italian. 'Solo.' More ominous, really, than Mamma's mysterious 'weapon.' Much as I miss you, I sense to the depths of my soul that I am not…that we are not…alone.

Ship's discipline demanded discretion, and Pierre-Jean respected the rules. He knew Mrs. Hanover's habits, and where she could be found this night, and every night, since the fleet broke free of the arms of Neverbay, under way for its next adventure.

In the lowering aura of twilight, he saw her. She leaned back against *Red Lady's* foremast, one arm holding tight to the column behind her, her eyes gazing forward. After her confinement on the Island, she seemed to welcome the force and the foam of the sea. He could see that Mrs. Hanover had changed, as women do, with motherhood. A trifle uplifted, a trifle more grounded. Just a shade older. Across her chest she wore a soft sling made of skins, in which a little lump reposed, whimpering. Her free arm lay poised, protective, around it. Wasting no time, the young French sailor approached on the pretext of securing a brace to the mast that supported her pretty figure.

He daren't talk to her here in view of the company, but his china blue eyes could speak for him. A glance, and she knew he would wait for her down on the lower deck. A nod from the lady, and he knew she would meet him there, in their secret corner.

As his gaze encompassed the baby, the cheer of his Gallic smile dimmed. As little as she liked to talk, he understood that she would want to tell him about her child. He would listen to her few, measured words, and then he would comfort her with his touch, protect her, maybe, from the blow of her sorrow. He was a Frenchman. His English was spotty, but *les mains*, his hands, well, with his hands, he conversed with fluency— and with discretion.

La Fleur de Lotus was a fighting ship, compact and efficient like her *commandant*. Her dimensions were petite, but, handled carefully, the ship was tight enough to accommodate a captain's secrets.

Sleepless, DéDé LeCorbeau tiptoed from his quarters, his paisley dressing gown sweeping behind his slippers, his first mate, Renaud, creeping ahead. Once on the quarterdeck, LeCorbeau waved Renaud away to awaken the surgeon. The time had come for the two partners to finalize their schemes. With scant prospects for privacy, the dead of night in the open air seemed the best option.

The captain retreated to the taffrail, as far from the watch as possible. Days had passed since *Le Lotus* moored at this rendezvous point. Strategizing to avoid surprises, LeCorbeau arrived early to this site. Hook had vowed that he would see LeCorbeau before LeCorbeau saw him. The result of this threat was a crew steeped in superstition, nervous, always scanning the sea, the islet, and, absurd as it seemed, even the sky, to catch a first sighting. Tonight, the *commandant* ordered just a skeleton watch topside, allowing his men respite as the ship rocked at anchor, in the darkness and silence of this dead island's air. LeCorbeau pressed a scented handkerchief to his overlarge nose. Along with the unpleasant odor of the shore, the ship's atmosphere filled with anxiety, seeping into every soul aboard as the hour ticked closer to reunion with the *Jolly Roger*'s buccaneers.

The last time these two crews engaged, LeCorbeau lost, and lost badly. The pirates commandeered LeCorbeau's ship, three quarters of his company and, perhaps the most galling of losses, his Chef and Guillaume. The moon this eve hung low and subdued. Free of lunar influence, LeCorbeau's face caught a blue tint from the dark-lantern at the stern. Still, in this meagre light, his eyes of beady black shone with resentment.

A confident captain even in extraordinary circumstances, the Frenchman chafed under the foul effects of his deal with that devil, his *bête noire*, Captain James Hook. He'd required every day of the past year to recover his footing. First, the grueling row in search of a friendly shore— one dozen drenched, fatigued men in a longboat, and Doctor Hanover sprawling senseless over the boat's ribs at the beginning, betrayed, robbed, and drugged. Then, their obligation to serve that very demon of a pirate king again!

At last, dragging ashore like a damp, bedraggled peacock, LeCorbeau had felt close to broken. Sheerly by will, he rallied to return to the sea, reconstructing his lucrative but lurid trade. His partner, the surgeon, had lost treasure, too— a trove of diamonds, and his new-wedded wife. The nature of the physician's character, a mix of righteousness and obstinacy, drove him to recapture his lost work and his woman. LeCorbeau found these traits in his partner both a requisite and an irritant. Privateering was LeCorbeau's camouflage. His more profitable interest lay in the physician's love philter. Otherwise, he'd have shed the man Hanover, and his obsessions, as a molting fowl flings off its feathers.

The cohorts held hopes, but no guarantee, in regard to this rendez-vous' outcome. They were forced to meet here with a percentage of the year's profits in hand, extorted by Hook in exchange for the ingredient most vital to the potion. Along with LeCorbeau's ship, the wily pirate had sailed away with two crates of Egyptian lotus blossoms, leaving a supply just sufficient to last out the interval. LeCorbeau finessed a financier and outfitted a new vessel while Hanover concocted more product and, surprisingly, contrived a plot to hold Hook at bay and yank Red-Handed Jill from Hook's clutches.

The appearance of Jill's father in Hanover's wake, the quaintly-named Mr. Darling, was a shock to LeCorbeau. Sputtering with passion, he fumed, declaring that Hanover presumed too much on his hospital-ity. Yet the revelation of the other leverage the doctor produced, to ensure Hook's comeuppance, was nothing less than— even LeCorbeau had to admit— genius. LeCorbeau rearranged his cabins and his plans, and, tonight, his slippered feet toed the edge of success...or of failure.

However stubborn the surgeon might be, his skills worked for LeCorbeau, and LeCorbeau had one more scheme for him to act out, if the upright physician's principles could be nudged a trivial bit further. As he heard graceful footfalls on the steps to the quarterdeck, LeCorbeau forced his features into a pleasant, persuasive guise. He greeted Hanover with a smile. *Zut alor, non, non!* Not 'Hanover.' *Herr Doktor* Heinrich. When among strangers, LeCorbeau must discipline his tongue.

With a salute of lavish proportion for two men in their nightclothes, he hailed, "*Bonsoir, mon ami!* Tomorrow may produce our prey. Hook's greed will not allow that we wait forever."

"My own greed is a sentimental one. I anticipate the joy of beholding my beloved, and the happy glow upon her face as I reveal her father's presence."

With the small, jerking movements of a curious bird, LeCorbeau inquired, "Now that we are free of other company, and I am, eh, somewhat the more tranquil, you might confide in me…however were you able to find this gentleman?"

"Our marriage lines, LeCorbeau, which you were so good as to salvage as we cast off from poor, doomed *L'Ormonde*."

Not for nothing had LeCorbeau avoided private conversation with the physician. Having yet to confess that the marriage he had conducted was counterfeit, he now feigned self-effacement, averting his eyes. He shrugged. "Yes, well, eh, a fortunate stroke."

"The night I met Jill, she told me of her girlhood in London. With her maiden name revealed in her signature, I hired an agent to inquire, discreetly, about town. He found her family home."

"And the beloved parents, of course, welcomed with open arms the husband who might resurrect their daughter's, eh…" LeCorbeau's fingers wiggled as he groped for the circumspect term, "propriety." Red-Handed Jill herself left the decision of enlightening Hanover— no, no, *Heinrich*— about his marital status to the French captain, whom she knew would be guided by their mutual gains. Keeping the surgeon in the dark on this question allowed her *faux* husband to focus on business. "But, I think, you overestimate the lady's ardor for you. Another man, as you know, set his so-abominable hook in her heart."

"You heard her yourself, DéDé. She acted in the only way she knew how to protect me. And still, with the last words she uttered, she swore she would come away with me. I return to collect on that promise."

Having argued with this logic during last year's long row toward shore, LeCorbeau changed the subject. "I myself will be elated to see the face of *mon petit* Guillaume. Hook cannot have use for him! I shall present an offer of ransom." The loss of his second mate, whom he'd schooled with his own hands and heart's blood, was a wound that had not healed. He had shaped Renaud, also, into an admirable helpmeet, but Renaud's cousin Guillaume, first discovered as a stowaway, rounded out a neat trio to which LeCorbeau became partial. As the fervency of the Frenchman's gaze met the doctor's, Heinrich's frown of disapprobation appeared, even under the dark-lantern's light. Over the past months, LeCorbeau had— mercifully, he reflected— forgotten how easily the man's sense of decency became bruised.

Heinrich railed in disgust, "I tire of the sea and its infamies! Upon returning to Vienna, I shall wash my hands of it. A gentle punt on the Danube is all the voyaging I will wish to pursue."

"And your medical practice, it, eh, thrives there?"

"Certainly. I reestablished a connection with a prominent colleague, who referred the Grand Duke to my care. My associate put the word about and, thereafter, Doctor Johann Heinrich, physician and scientist, received society's brightest at his surgery door. Then, too, the miracle of my philter has brought many others to my practice. I have become known as an innovator, and my *avant-garde* experiments are financed by interested parties." In the darkness, Heinrich neglected to don a look of humility. "My reputation is revived, and enhanced. I have accepted invitations to the best salons, where I promised to introduce my entrancing wife."

LeCorbeau's eyebrows elevated to hide beneath the fringe of dark hair at his forehead. "And where, exactly, do these noble persons believe the lady to be?"

"I remain strictly honest. Jill's predicament proves useful to me. All parties are intrigued by my mission to save the lovely *Frau* Heinrich from these rogues of the sea."

"Just how will your daughter fit in, to this, eh, how shall I put it," the *commandant* tipped his head to one side, "household of nobility? And, also…your grandchild? Always supposing, that is, that you manage to pry them from pirates."

In his habitual manner, Heinrich reached for his pocket watch before remembering his attire of only nightshirt and robe. If he was discomfited by LeCorbeau's questions, the deck was too dim to betray a ruddy glow beneath his scars. "You need not fret about Liza. I have always found means to manage my daughter. She will come to Vienna, and I will deal with her progeny."

"Oh…*bien sûr*…I, myself, have no doubt of it. I ask merely as a matter of practicality. There seems to be no end to your family! As far as cabins are concerned, this ship, fond of it as I am, has its limits."

"I am aware of your superstitions about women aboard. As a man of science—"

"Ah, yes, well, as you are a man of the science, I trust you are able to count. Which brings me to a certain favor I should wish to receive." LeCorbeau lowered his head, and his voice. "It is, *hélas*, a most delicate affair. But, I think, we may make an occasion to relieve ourselves of one of our number. One who, we might say, requires more cabin space than his worth."

Heinrich's backbone grew rigid. He knew LeCorbeau well enough to divine some blatant immorality. He braced himself for the next, not unexpected, outrage.

"You yourself gave me this so-opportune idea! We both know that you, eh, 'threw' your duel. Your swordsmanship is superior to de Beaumonde's. You tested him, *non?* And found his skill wanting?"

"Without immodesty, yes. I discovered his weaknesses, not only in swordsmanship, but in character. I am pleased to find that the man is in love with France, and France only. I see no reason to expect he will attempt a seduction of Jill." With a twist of his generous lips, he added, "In company with yourself, a brace of Frenchman *sans* sentiment for the fairer sex."

"*Eh, bien!* I agree with him! What female could rival *la France?* In spite of our fraternity in this opinion, however, I require a small favor. I wish for *Herr Doktor* Heinrich to provoke one more duel… and dispatch him."

This time no doubt remained; Heinrich was severely offended. "I am no murderer, LeCorbeau!"

"Are you not." With a penetrating look, LeCorbeau did not ask. He implied.

"You go too far!"

"You go not far enough. His father, my financier, *Le Baron* de Beaumonde, paid me a bonus to sweep young Olivier away. Believe me, his family is grateful to be rid of him, and to be freed of his troublesome tangles. Even the army of France has expelled him! Like everyone else, I wish to be quit of him, but, eh…I also wish to keep his papa's gold."

"The boy is rash, I grant you. Why not simply abandon him at the next port?"

"And let him make his way home, to set *le baron* regretting his investment? *Non!* I am enamored of my new ship, and do not wish to kiss it goodbye."

"I decline to soil my sword with your petty grudge. No doubt Olivier will tire of life aboard, and you can encourage him to enlist in some faraway regiment. Perhaps, when you return to Egypt, he will join the Foreign Legion? After all, in another year's time, I shall be in need of more lotus."

"Your needs are no more pressing than my own, *mon ami.* I suggest, if you expect to retain my assistance in peddling your product, that you reconsider." As Heinrich had witnessed too many times, LeCorbeau's hand dipped to his pocket, where, always, he kept a stiletto on guard. "As I say, this ship holds room enough only for those whom her master requires."

"You threaten me? When I am the instrument with which you orchestrate your fortune?"

"Threaten you, *Herr Doktor,* while you act as my indispensable partner? *Jamais.* But, as you remarked, I am a Frenchman with no sentiment for the fairer sex."

"By heaven, LeCorbeau! Jill's husband, her father, our daughter— we will all be watching you— not to mention your sailors. You cannot slit your passengers' throats without consequence!"

Pulling the stiletto from hiding, LeCorbeau swiveled it, allowing the blue light to play, up and down, on the silk of its surface. "*Quoi?* Slit a lovely lady's throat? I need not sully my lily-white hands." He dropped the blade in his pocket. "Who knows? At sea, much perversity of fortune occurs. It is possible, is it not, that your lady wife, or *peut-être,* your daughter, may simply trip with a slip of the so-delicate foot, and plunge, too tragically, into the brine?"

As alarm spread over Heinrich's countenance, LeCorbeau leaned closer. He said, softly, "*La Fleur de Lotus* is modest in dimension, but, I assure you, Doctor, this ship can accommodate all of our secrets."

Nico Cecco bumped his powerful fist on the table. The lamp oil sloshed in its glass, and yellow rays swayed on the woven flowers of Mamma's table-scarf.

"A cunning counterpart calls for more cunning. The woman says so herself."

"Our lovely Jill is a storyteller," *la matriarca* reasoned. "She speaks to entertain." Stella's mandolin thrummed outside by the fire, where Jill and Nibs mingled with the troupe, to unruly music. This other mother and son had withdrawn from the gathering tonight, to sit in the caravan, conferring.

Giovanni's bride had been their guest for some weeks, now, getting to know his relatives and friends. She acted as his emissary, recounting story after story to color his life for those who loved him. A hot-blooded woman, Jill could not disguise a wife's desire for a husband. With knowing smiles, the tribe sensed what she did not describe: the depth of her physical need for Giovanni. Despite her efforts to satisfy the family in any question of her dedication to him, Nico, who among his brothers had known Giovanni best, could not shake the feeling that, behind her yarns and fairy tales, some secret veiled this woman Giovanni called wife.

"Sailors, Indians…parks and palaces in London! She does not answer our questions. Where is this island? What power did she employ to find us? The words she does *not* say are where she deceives us."

" 'Where?'…'how?' These questions hold no significance." The loops of Mamma's earrings wobbled as she shook her head. "I have the power of sight. The visions entered my eyes the first day of her stay, even before I read the cards for her. I know *why* she is here. Her very presence alters the future…" *la matriarca* stared at her son, her gaze full of meaning, "and not just Giovanni's."

"Such a prophecy makes me more apprehensive! You laid out the cards, Mamma, and I heard what you said. I feel it in my being." Nico touched the scarf Jill had given him, where it cascaded over his heart from the pocket of his vest. "Everywhere Red-Handed Jill walks, her ankle bells resonate, but the woman herself rings untrue."

"She is honest as far as she takes us, Nico. No one can deny that she is in thrall to the pleasures she finds in Giovanni's embraces. I see her torment, sometimes, when she is craving her man's arms around her. But I need to know more, so I asked today to read her fortune again. The outlook remains as I claimed at the first, Where she, perhaps, perceives emptiness, I sense a presence. Looming over her shoulder—" Mamma's fingers fanned out in the air, "— I see a figure."

"Is it not this villainous physician?"

"The doctor is depicted in the cards, too. He is a fair man, light of hair and light of eye. He deals in poisons. The influence I feel is a dark one. It wields some sort of…barb."

"No doubt you saw Giovanni. Him and his dagger."

Emphatically, she said, "Yes, I saw Giovanni. I felt this other power as well. He stands opposite your brother." Mamma closed her eyes and laid her hands flat on the tablecloth, where her cards had lain spread before Jill. Her fingers circled, brushing the weave of the fabric as she evoked recollection, searching for answers. "No. I was wrong. A blade of some manner threatens, yes. But it is also…a name."

In silence, Nico listened. Over the years, he learned to heed *la matriarca*'s presentiments.

"The name of a man who lurks in black shadow. I believe Jill herself is unaware of him."

"Then, you will warn her?"

Mamma's eyes opened wide. "I would not dare! My role this time is not to light darkness. Some vital reason makes Jill thrust this influence from her thoughts."

Nico's face, olive toned by days in the Mediterranean sun, turned darker still. "What better reason for deception, than the influence of another man? Her pleasure-seeking nature might have caught her in some trouble. She says she needs protection. Perhaps she hides from this fellow— a paramour, maybe— and to hoodwink Giovanni, she blames the physician!"

"Giovanni is a strong man. He holds a position of authority. If he knew of this man whose name is a weapon, how could he fail to protect her?"

"He cannot be aware of this threat. If he were, he would have warned us in his letter."

"He tells me only to place my trust in his Jill, and watch over her."

Nico confided, "I must act to safeguard someone else too, Mamma." His features tensed with concern. "If Giovanni must send his wife away for safekeeping, can he protect little Stella?"

"Hold, my son. The first question is this: can you trust Stella to Jill's son?"

Thoughtful, Nico answered, "It is well that he has been my guest in my caravan. It gives me the opportunity to watch him. He looks after his mother, as a good man should. He is tough, but not cruel. Everyone in the troupe likes him, and in all his conduct, he shows our Stella respect."

"Stella finds Nibs appealing," Mamma observed. "I see how her aura glows in his company. But she is sensible. She reserves judgment. Nor will she make him a promise without your approval."

"You found nothing dubious in his cards, but— but, Mamma..." Nico's fist hit the tabletop again. "Nibs the Knife! A dark man, whose name is a weapon?"

"I, too, wondered if Nibs the Knife is the man in Jill's readings. Yet, in spite of his piracy, Nibs' spirit is benevolent. He poses no threat to our family."

"I am relieved to hear that your intuition approves him. And I consider, Mamma, that if this young man takes Stella from *us*, he also takes her toward Giovanni." Nico's robust figure sagged. "I do not like to contemplate our family without her."

"Nico, think. What would our family be like, now, if Giovanni had never been sentenced to Gao?"

"He would be here with us. He would be a son, and a brother."

"And?"

"He would be Stella's papa."

"*And*— he would be husband to Bezzi."

Nico's brows drew together, and he ceased to speak.

"You see?" Mamma coaxed, "Just as Jill does, when an uncomfortable thought enters your head, you push it away."

"I do not push it away. I think of it constantly."

"You have thought of it all Stella's life. She knows no other father."

"Bezzi loves another man."

"Tcha! You must overlook this. She was young, and no girl could resist our Giovanni. It does not mean she does not love you, too."

"She remains true to my brother, and for this fidelity I revere her. Far beyond her beauty, the auburn locks and the delicate skin that I love, Bezzi's loyalty is the trait that I treasure. As for resisting him, Bezzi cannot. Nor, in spite of whoever else she might hide, can Red-Handed Jill."

"I foresee change, Nico. I'll wager that if you pursue her, she'll not long resist, now." To encourage him, Mamma pulled the wine-colored handkerchief from his pocket, and strung it out before him on the table. Its silver strands glittered in the lamplight. "Go, Nico. Hold the cloth out to her. The music sings to the moon. See if she will not dance with you."

Nico's brooding air lifted. "Ah." He sat straighter. He drew the kerchief nearer, and gazed upon it. Its rosy color reflected on the strong, clean cut of his jaw. "Yes, that is the answer....Mamma, you will help me to gain her trust."

"My son," Mamma smiled, "no one trusts you better than Bezzi."

"I do not speak of Bezzi. I speak of my brother's wife."

Mamma's smile faded. She studied Nico's determined face, so similar to her long lost Giovanni's. Her gaze drifted outside the comfy caravan, seeking guidance in visions beyond the door. She saw, illumined by the fire, a flash of turquoise, and flowing hair the color of copper.

Still staring, she uttered, as if in trance, "Trinio is dancing with her. Why should not you?"

"*Sì*. And Jill is a passionate one. In every way, she indicates her longing for the loving touch of Giovanni. If my brother cannot be resisted, so much the better." He tapped his chest. "I resemble him. Jill reveals her feeling, every time her eye lingers on me."

"In you, she sees her lover." Mamma sat quiet then, calculating. Outside, the wine poured, the music whirled, the dancers laughed. She took up her fan, and tapped it to her chin. As she considered, her deep brown eyes began to glow, and then they blazed. "Red-Handed Jill is a warm-blooded woman. She longs for him. But, is she constant? If tempted, is her heart true?"

Nico murmured, affirming, "I will put our storyteller to trial."

Slowly, *la matriarca* nodded. "As Jill herself tells us…a cunning counterpart calls for more cunning."

Nico stood to go, plucking up the handkerchief. His mamma broke her reverie, and, turning to him, she stopped his hand. She clutched it in her own. "My son. For Giovanni's sake, do whatever you must. If his Jill proves to be *non tribale*, it is best that we know. It is best that *he* know." Mamma let go of Nico then, to take the kerchief and caress it, fondling the silky thing in her fingers. "Even if you must drop the cloth."

The wine-colored square, a symbol of separation, floated past the scuffed cuffs of his boots, to lie limp on the carpet.

My husband,

The pages of my journal fill quickly. I do look forward to sharing these entries with you, and to describing all the details I don't have ink enough to include. Your family— our family— make me more welcome each day, and I now understand how difficult it must be for you to live apart from your tribe.

I've already written of the Padre, *and how he came to lose those two teeth. I've described as much of your absent brothers as I've been able to glean. Trinio, as you've learned from past night's depictions, is sheer joy to know. Tonight, I will concentrate on the one* fratello *who, up until recent days, remained aloof. The mysterious Nico…*

I do not blame Nico for holding back from me. He resisted longer than Mamma, and I would do the same in their places. Such a tight-knit community remains strong— even safe— by distrusting newcomers. Whatever test the two of them set for me, I must have passed, for now our interactions are easy, and, with Nico's acceptance, the last bastion has fallen. I am a Cecco.

Nico takes after your father. He is a horseman. He took me to see the mares, and he introduced me to the new colts and fillies. I know little of rural husbandry but, from what Nico teaches me, I infer that next year's offerings for the fair will be choice. I've discovered what fuzzy, warm muzzles these animals have, and how much they relish a crisp bite of apple! Now, when they hear the bells on my ankle, their heads bob up with their big, velvet eyes, and they come nuzzling my pockets for treats. I don't dare arrive empty-handed. Nico laughs and slaps the darlings away when they're too boisterous, but I can't refuse, and more than once I've been butted, to end on my backside in the straw, dazed and waiting for Nico to pick me up (as easily as a foal), and dust me off. It's funny to think— you're a man of the sea now, but once upon a time, you must have felt one with the grasslands, and a friend to these creatures of earth, just like Nico.

He is teaching me to ride the gentlest mare, a satiny dun, and one of his favorites. Soon we'll mount up and take a tour of the countryside. Mamma promises a picnic and a flask of good wine. I've agreed to bring my whip, to compare my technique to Nico's. Nibs will come too— although a sailing man through and through, he is tall enough not to feel cowed by the horses— and he'll invite his sweetheart, Stella. The two of them can enjoy a bit of time to themselves, still chaperoned but away from the camp and the village. Nico appears to accept Nibs. Stella's mother relies on his counsel, and if he did not approve of Nibs, this freedom for the lovers would never be granted.

And the lovers here come in all ages. Mamma smiles when I ask about Papa. She employs a special flutter of her fan when she speaks of him. Her eyes soften with that tender look I love to see in yours. I've caught a glow in Nico's eye, too, and heard his breath catch, when a certain lady is near. I believe he's in love with a handsome redhead. Nico seems very much the family man— again, like you. I never see him without your token, the wine-colored handkerchief, in his breast pocket. He hid his heart, at first, but I am peering past the kerchief at last, to see it. He says he stayed behind when Papa left for the fair, in order to look after not only the horses, but Mamma and the Padre, *too. I'm surprised he's remained unmarried so long. After all, it was he who advised me that no one should wander alone.*

Perhaps he only needs a nudge to declare to his loved one. Trinio is handsome and dashing, but Nico's seriousness is, to my mind, more attractive. He has begun to tie his hair back the way I told him you do, which, naturally, I find flattering. I am convinced that he wants to take me away on this excursion in order to court my advice. And, frankly, amore mio, *who better to advise him? I need only remember our courtship, which seems a dear dream to me now.*

I hear Mamma yawning in her bunk, so, speaking of dreams, I will say buona notte. *Good night, my dear one. I turn down the lamp, close my eyes, and illumine imagination.*

Reunion

L ike a rooster guarding his coop, LeCorbeau stood alert at the rail, juddering his gaze across the horizon. Puzzled, he looked to his crew. His sailors remained silent, with the same attitude of unease they had worn the whole voyage.

Too long, the French captain anticipated this rendezvous. *Sans doute*, the year of worries had eroded his senses. The sky continued clear of smoke, his best men stood on watch in the rigging, reporting no sightings. Sinking his chin back into his wattle of ruffles, LeCorbeau relaxed, concluding that the far-off roar of cannon he'd heard was merely imagination.

With a flourish, he gestured to his slender mate Renaud to hand him his coffee. Served in a bone china cup on a serviette, its robust scent wafted up to his nostrils in a graceful curl of steam. He sniffed, he sipped, he smiled, then java shot through his nose as a second boom erupted in the distance, in the opposite direction from the first. *Le Lotus'* men yelled, Renaud lurched to rescue the cup in midair, hot coffee splattering his fingers.

This time, the *commandant* bridled with understanding. James Hook was playing with him! The pirate king sought to gain an edge by unnerving both captain and crew! But how? Two ships hailed *La Fleur de Lotus*, and neither vessel, as yet, lay within view. For all his precautions, LeCorbeau was taken by surprise. Leave it to Hook, to use devil's tricks to win his way!

LeCorbeau dabbed the drink from his chin with the serviette, recovering his wits. He, too, was armed with devil's weapons.

"Renaud! Alert the doctor! Make sure that Darling man is prepared." At Renaud's bewildered gawk, LeCorbeau spat, "The Darling...*Monsieur* Darling, *hein*, that harridan's papa— I do not trust him to remember his place. Ensure that he keeps below until called for...hatches closed! Also," the lace at the captain's cuffs swirled with his wrists, "send a swab to mop up this mess." He dropped his voice to mutter to himself, "And I will mop up this other."

Quickly, the two ships became visible. They sailed from behind the islet, approaching *Le Lotus* on either side, enlarging as they came, dominating her horizon. LeCorbeau sneered as he recognized the *Jolly Roger*; Hook's flagship, to starboard, her banner of black fluttering like an ensign of honor. His sneer deepened to a scowl as he beheld the delightful lines of his beloved *L'Ormonde* to port. He saw that she was refitted, her masts raked, and renamed as— LeCorbeau steadied his spyglass to squint at it— *zut*, how revolting! The *Red Lady*. Named no doubt for the red-handed female who so distracted the doctor and disrupted a golden flow of commerce. Soon that woman's dainty feet would walk the decks of *La Fleur de Lotus*. Gritting his teeth, LeCorbeau swore to himself that, this time, bad luck would not walk with her. He glanced down at his peacock green coat, inspecting it for droplets of coffee.

Stamping over the boards in his military boots, Olivier de Beaumode came bounding to join him. The captain ignored him; due to the height of the man, conversation with him made LeCorbeau's neck stiff.

"*Commandant*, are these, then, the ruffians who so insulted you as you strove to serve France?" He huffed, "Had I been aboard then, to succor you with my sword, Fate may have taken a more favorable turn."

Regretting that he'd sent Renaud below and out of call, LeCorbeau replied, "Yes, such a shame...but you may be useful to our country now."

"Command me, *Monsieur!*"

Along with his other arrangements, the captain devised a tactic to keep young de Beaumonde out of the way in such moments of crisis. "You are a soldier, sir, what we call, eh, a landsman. At sea, we follow a custom. It is the province of our marines to guard our noble flag. *Alors*, I would be much gratified if you would station yourself at the base of the mizzenmast. Your honorable obligation is to ensure that no insult to our colors occurs."

The former soldier snapped to attention, fingers at his forelock and his short cape swinging behind him. "*Oui, mon Commandant!* I accept this sacred duty." Executing a military turn, he marched off toward the foremast.

LeCorbeau called him back, and, dryly, directed him with a nudge of the spyglass. "*Non, non*, my boy, the *mizzen*mast, at the stern. The, eh…backside?"

Corrected, de Beaumonde subsided to the rear, and LeCorbeau, hoping this pest was stowed for the moment, returned his attention to the fleet.

The sister ships coasted closer. Their officers hollered and men rushed along yardarms to haul up and furl sails. Bow facing bow, the two vessels slowed, their crews hustling to splash down the anchors and settle at last, penning the first, smaller ship at her berth by the shore. His ship's caging did not faze the bantam captain of *Le Lotus*; he had expected it. He smiled, secure in the knowledge that, in spite of his size and his mooring, he held the winning position. Astutely, he inspected the vessels' decks to determine what changes occurred since that last, disastrous battle one year ago.

Hook's first mate, that brute-like, bespectacled Irishman, still held authority. Smee bespoke him first.

"*Lotus*, ahoy!" With an offhand wave, the redheaded bo'sun hailed from amidships. "Commodore Hook has ordered your crates readied for you, and I'll be sending a boat for your tribute." Turning away, he signaled to his crew to drop a dinghy, then set a second party to make ready the block and tackle.

"*Bonjour*, the *Roger*," LeCorbeau returned, with a limp wag of his napkin, indicative of the degree of his enthusiasm. He searched for the two spies, Nibs the Knife and Tom Tootles, who had sailed with him during Hook's abduction by the doctor. He missed Mr. Nibs as he missed his Guillaume, but, as for the Tootles, *ce bâtard*, he hoped with a vengeance that the devil had drowned him! LeCorbeau's thoughts turned more cheerful as he identified the two precious crates of lotus petals, labeled in a flowing, foreign script and bound in nets, all set to lift and swing over to his hold.

Relieved to see his precious resource so close to the nest, the *commandant* felt free to consider Smee's words. 'Commodore' Hook. *Oui*, yes, of course. With the theft of *L'Ormonde*, the arrogant captain had risen in rank. Hook's original ship remained, however, the same, her paint pristine, filled with glinting fittings, and, in contrast, an abundance of rough, ugly men. Tapping his fingers on the chill brass of his spyglass, LeCorbeau observed with distaste, "As always, *mes amis,* you present a spectacle for the eyes."

More hesitantly, the former captain of *L'Ormonde* rolled his gaze to *Red Lady*. Ah, a lost love! Taking in the changes, he wiped at a tear. Pierre-Jean was there, his long pale pigtail swinging as he toiled in the rigging. Chef, the dear soul, must be secreted below decks, concocting some supreme meal in his galley. As for the others...LeCorbeau's moment of nostalgia turned to amazement as he recognized the man on the quarterdeck, clearly, her captain. With a refined sense for these subjects, LeCorbeau remembered the muscular mass of his body, and this body was very much alive. *"Sacré bleu!"* he whispered. "This cannot be! This gypsy, he escapes the wrath of James Hook?"

Feeling the Frenchman's stare, Giovanni Cecco raised his arm in salutation. The bands on his biceps gleamed in the morning light. *"Ciao, Commandant!"* He smiled widely enough to show his white teeth. "I congratulate you on finding yet another fine ship."

LeCorbeau rose to the bait. "Do not look so hungry! I intend to keep her— unlike the case of you with your so-fickle female! Although you somehow survive your crimes of mutiny, eh...I see her not at your side."

"Perhaps not, but as you do see, I prize my able second mate." Cecco, looking far more happy and healthy than he had any right to expect, indicated another of LeCorbeau's losses; not far from him on the quarterdeck stood *petit* Guillaume. LeCorbeau's heart throbbed to see the boy's slim figure still sheathed in his blue and red uniform, his posture respectful, his visage, so grave. Solemnly, the young man saluted, but he did not reply to LeCorbeau's greeting. No wonder, for, overcome with longing, his former *commandant* could barely articulate it.

As if he'd waited for this moment of weakness, Commodore Hook himself swung wide his cabin door on the *Roger* to stride down the steps of his companionway. Dressed to the teeth, as expected, his jewels at ear, hand, and hatband glowed in the glaze of the sun— along with his hook. His luxurious coat of tawny velvet brought to mind his reputation as the Lion of the Sea. Abaft the mainmast, he halted his gait and called in his silken voice, "Welcome, LeCorbeau! I trust we find you well? And wealthy?"

"You need not feel concern. I hold your portion, and will, eh, most willingly, give it over. Upon receipt of my baggage." Hearing the soft step of Heinrich behind him, the *commandant* added, smirking with a resurgence of confidence, "And, of course, *after* the spouse of my partner, our good doctor, is restored to his arms."

Hook's smile enlarged. "Doctor Hanover, how very daring of you to confront us once more. I suspected you'd not disappoint us." He touched his magnificent hat, broad of brim and bedecked with feathers. "But, alas, *I* must disappoint *you*. The lady declines your company."

Strutting up to the railing, the surgeon stood stiff, glaring at his enemy. He wore a high collar and cravat above a tan satin vest, but left off his coat in favor of his saber. After twelve months of healing, the scar Hook awarded him had paled to match its counterpart on the other side, extending downward from cheekbone to jaw. The mark Jill had administered, a short, horizontal score across the bone, appeared less dramatic, though its sting of betrayal must have cut much more deeply. "If you delude yourself that I trust your word, Hook, think again. Produce Mrs. Heinrich, immediately, and I shall hear my wife speak for herself."

With an instinct for business, LeCorbeau intervened. "*Messieurs*, let us first deal with practicalities. Hook, I beg, send over my crates, and I shall descend to weigh down your boat with your tribute. I ask, also, eh, that Captain Cecco should allow *Monsieur* Guillaume to parley. I have missed him, and, *bien sûr*, I feel the responsibility to attend the boy's welfare."

Agreeably, Hook answered, "But of course, DéDé. As it happens, one of our officers desires parley with *your* guest, as well. Mr. Yulunga?" He swept his hook to indicate the *Red Lady*, where Cecco's first mate dwarfed the gangway. Tall, black, and broad, he had arms so thick they hung at angles from his hulking shoulders.

The two pirate crews had awaited this moment. As one, the men abandoned their chores, turning toward their African officer. All parties stared, while Mrs. Hanover stepped from hiding behind him. Her father inhaled a sharp breath.

She wore a yellow blouse and a plain but elegant skirt of pale green, cinched in a sash at her waist, where Heinrich last recalled a gentle swell of pregnancy. Her hair fell loose to her shoulders, a lustrous brown. Still petite, still reserved, yet something about her had altered.

"Liza!" The doctor's face drained of hue, and the dual scars now stood out in red. Repressing the severity to which she was accustomed, he offered in his brusque accent, "I did not know what to suppose. How greatly you have changed." He extended his arm. "Look at you…a mother now, I expect? And…the little one?" His gaze raked the deck, his tenor half anticipating, half dreading, "*Have* you brought forth a child, after all?"

Yulunga spoke for his woman, in one slow, rich sentence.

"Congratulations, Doctor; you have a son."

As the words rolled over the waves, the only sound to follow was the swill of the sea. Pierre-Jean bit his lip. LeCorbeau coughed into his serviette. Mrs. Hanover studied her father, who, as if to dodge the awkwardness of his position, did not allow his gray gaze to leave hers. She lifted her face. Her lips, generous like her father's, parted. Her low, steady voice emerged, audible to all.

"I must speak, protecting my child. Ask that you help him…as physician."

With an air of considering, Heinrich inclined his head. "I see." He soon followed up, sounding somewhat relieved, "Of course, Liza. I shall let the *commandant* arrange for our meeting." His expression turned almost smug now, as if he'd been granted a gift. "I shall fetch my medicine bag from my quarters." Pausing first, he addressed the commodore, now applying his old severity. "And, afterward, I shall wait upon my wife."

"Indeed, *Herr Doktor Heinrich*." Hook sketched a mock bow. "You will wait."

Hook observed the surgeon's departure. With a nod to Smee, he ordered the lotus to be hoisted aloft. He raised a single finger. "One crate only, Mr. Smee. And you may row for the gold. One half, I presume, LeCorbeau?"

"*Et voilà!*" sang LeCorbeau, "We begin! I and Renaud will row toward the *Red Lady* for parley with Guillaume, the good Mr. Smee will collect from my boat one half of the pirates' percentage, and the doctor's daughter and eh— " carelessly, he fluttered a cuff, "whomever— will play the hosts to our physician." He rubbed his hands together. "All my chickens now fly home to roost!"

With a sigh of satisfaction, the *commandant* turned to look to his sailors. His happy grin perished. They bore the same look of unease they had worn the entirety of this voyage.

In the cabin that housed his wayward daughter, Heinrich rolled down his shirtsleeves to refasten his cuffs. His examination was over, and the child lay limp on the coverlet— a padded fabric sprawling with paisley, which the surgeon recognized as LeCorbeau's. He recalled the hedonism that used to hang within the perfume of the French captain's quarters, one deck above. Innocent of such debauchery, the babe before him suffered from sin, nonetheless. His fair hair clung in patches to his head, his pale gray eyes were closed now, in the sleep of fatigue. He was so tiny, he might fit into the medicine bag that sat open on the bedding beside him. Heinrich's lip curled as a vision came stealing to his mind, of Liza and her lover moving under those secondhand covers. He blinked to banish it.

The physician's daughter stood twisting her fingers, waiting. Yulunga loomed at her back, their two bodies touching. He had to bend his head to fit beneath the beams of his quarters, but, as a man who loved trouble, no discomfort could keep him from witnessing this meeting.

Postponing an unpleasant moment, the surgeon pulled his watch from its pocket and rubbed the smooth metal with his thumb, remarking, "I see you have enlarged this cabin since I attended Mr. Guillaume here. A bulkhead has been removed, the *commandant's* furniture brought down." He stepped a few paces, taking in the surroundings lit by windows at stern and at starboard. "A beveled mirror, a chest of drawers of fine quality and, beneath our feet, a carpet from the Orient." He took the opportunity to play upon his daughter's memory, linking her present to their past. "This room is far more comfortable than the quarters we found ourselves sharing on the *Roger*, do you not think, Liza?"

"I do not think about our sharing."

Unused to hearing her voice, her father listened closely enough only to catch her meaning. Without doubt, she had caught the implication of his own. From their past, he moved to their future. "Well, I see no sense in glossing over the situation." He pocketed his watch to resume a professional pose, preparing to divulge the damage. "Your infant is ill, and seriously so."

Mrs. Hanover flinched. Yulunga's hold on her shoulders grew heavier. Once again, he spoke for his woman. "*Your* infant, Doctor.

'No sense in glossing over the situation.' " Over Mrs. Hanover's head, he leered with his wide, threatening grin, enjoying the surgeon's disquiet.

"Regardless, the child must be treated."

Mrs. Hanover looked at her baby. For all his similarity to her father, she much preferred to rest her gaze there. "Can you cure?"

Heinrich's brow wrinkled. "This disease is a rare one, and not well understood. As yet, it has not been named. There is, however, a chance…"

The little mother held her breath.

"If, for instance, we were able to consult with specialists, with my colleagues, the very finest minds in Europe…" Heinrich slowed his words, coaxing, "In Vienna, I may be able to bring about some improvement."

With a sob, Mrs. Hanover released the breath, along with some of her anxiety. Then, again, she fell silent. Behind her, she felt the tension of Yulunga's body as a dilemma he had not foreseen was revealed to him. His grip slid down to her arms, tautening.

He sneered, "And you expect your daughter to trust you? To pick up and follow?"

The sternness returned to Heinrich's tone. "I expect a mother to do what is best for her child."

"And what is best for you? We all know why this boy is sick. With their 'very fine minds,' your colleagues will understand, too." Yulunga snorted. "Shall you ruin your reputation, Doctor, expose your stinking secret, to save that secret's fruit?"

"I warned you to keep away from my Liza. Instead, you have pulled her down, degraded her— in spite of these lush, purloined pamperings—" he indicated the furnishings, ending with the bedstead, "you have pulled her lower even than I ever dreamed. Now, sir, you will stand back and release my daughter from bondage." He gentled his voice. "Liza. I will leave it to you to consider. LeCorbeau has agreed to your passage. All that stands in your way is a test of your courage. In this virtue, you never failed your father. Do not fail your son, now."

"If I go, I will not be silent." Stubbornly, she shook her head. "I speak, for my son."

Heinrich deliberated. "Very well. You are a grown woman now, after all."

Making the bright beads bounce at his throat, Yulunga rumbled, "And she will *not* go alone." He turned Mrs. Hanover around to look into her face. "I cannot leave my station on the *Red Lady*, but I can command one of our men to protect you."

Eagerly, Mrs. Hanover grasped at his arms, grasping also at this promise of security. With relief illuminating her face, she nodded agreement.

Her father's expression soured, but he did not object. Of the battles he'd have to wage to regain her, he would fight only one at a time. His primary priority was to lure Liza under his wing. With this new circumstance that turned a transgression to his favor, he could abandon his intention to pass the child off as Jill's. Awkward as this babe's birth might be, the boy brought an advantage to his father, all unexpected, in the form of ill health. Heinrich felt his trap tightening around the girl, and he hid his satisfaction.

From this cabin that housed his daughter, they would journey to a much finer place. And once at home in his house in Vienna, she would never find means to stray.

Crumbles of Justice

The horses paced single file through a grove, the four riders careful to duck under outreaching branches. Sunlight flecked their path, crosshatched with pine needles. Preparing for this jaunt, Jill left off her ankle bells and dressed in her forest-green tunic and fawn-colored trousers. She toted a supply of apples in her pouch, along with her whip. Her hands, extending from embroidered cuffs, held the reins lightly, for she was enjoying the ride rather than imposing her will, and trusting her mild little mare to know best.

Once clear of the woods, Nico led the procession at a competent trot, and Jill gripped the mare more tightly. She felt the thrill of warm, living horseflesh beneath her, a more personal mode of travel than sailing, yet not unlike maneuvering a small, responsive craft. Watching Nico's broad back before her, his thick brown hair bound with leather in a ponytail like Cecco's, she smiled to think that, except for the silence of his armbands, she might have been following her husband. A twinge of missing him constricted her stomach, but, determined to enjoy the day's outing, she comforted herself by gathering her fingertips to her lips, and sending a kiss to fly Cecco's way.

As the grasslands began, Nibs the Knife clicked his tongue to urge his mount abreast of Stella's. She looked contented, borne jauntily on her favorite black pony, her disorderly skirts tucked up and her auburn curls bouncing. Nibs rode a gray colt, and brooked no nonsense from him. He was a man with purpose, this day. He and Stella had been granted time together, with more privacy than they'd ever known. Like his mentor, Captain Cecco, Nibs was about to seize his opportunity, whatever form it might take.

Nico Cecco felt the same way. He'd created this opportunity to bring pleasure to Jill, and, in doing so, to draw her closer in confidence. Giovanni's wife was not a fool; Nico knew he must lull the woman into trust before he could test her. Now that he'd begun to court her goodwill, he found it easy, thanks, no doubt, to the loyalty Giovanni taught her to expect from his family, and from Nico in particular. Conducting this trial on behalf of his brother, Nico felt that his job was tricky, but not onerous. Jill was intelligent and strong. She was daring, good humored...and she was beautiful.

Since Mamma turned Jill's blonde hair to ginger, she was, in Nico's eye, more dangerously lovely than before. Unlike Giovanni, however, he was not a captive to beauty. Integrity was the trait to tempt Nico. Above all other qualities, the woman who would hold Nico's heart must possess loyalty. She must be constant not only to her man, but to her family, and to her tribe. Jill alluded to Giovanni's belief in her virtues, but talk was easy. Nico and Mamma both felt the need for proof. Giovanni as a young man gained a vast experience of women. He admired them; he manipulated them; with the prosperity of his family in mind he preyed upon them for their gold. Cast away from his people, had Giovanni allowed his prey, in the person of Jill, to turn his own weapons upon him? Had she, in the artful arms of his seduction, become his seducer? Who knew but that his loneliness had diminished his perception? Giovanni's judgment, so sound when he belonged to his Romani troupe, might now be corrupted by his wife's many charms.

In the course of keeping company with Jill, whether working with the horses or listening to the *Padre* as he smoked his pipe and held forth to the troupe around the fire, Nico's suspicions eased— until Jill moved her hands to gesture. Then, the blatancy of her bloodstain arrested him. At the sight of her mark, he was seized again with premonition. Mistrust yanked him back to a dusky cave of doubt. That blot of blood returned Nico's thoughts to Mamma's vision. He recalled Mamma's warning of a shadow that lurked behind Jill, and the question of a weapon that defined some dark master.

Lightly, for luck, he touched Giovanni's wine-colored silk in his vest pocket. Out of the woods now, he felt the sun shining warm on his shoulders, in contrast to the shadows in his mind. He'd have to keep his misgivings at bay so that, when Jill searched his eyes with her jewel-blue gaze, she would see her affection returned there, as Giovanni's eyes would do. Always, now, Nico strove to remind her of Giovanni. Turning, he fabricated a smile to flash upon her, then broke into a canter.

The other riders applied their heels, and the horses jumped to catch up, their hoofbeats thudding the turf. As Nico watched the horizon ahead, he held a vision of Jill with the pine woods behind her, the sheen of her hair in the sunlight, and her earrings of just the same color. To all appearances, she was a bright, copper goddess. If she carried some underworld taint, it was Nico's chore, for his brother's sake, to discover it. This thought spurred him on toward his purpose, like his heels to his horse. He was determined to discover the truth, whether his findings justified Giovanni's trust, or exposed Jill in perfidy.

Before long, his destination came into view. A majestic cedar tree reigned from a hilltop. Its huge, ancient boughs stretched out at intervals that spiraled up the trunk. Its greenery was sparse underneath, the lower branches a reddish color, as thick as Nico's waist and bare toward the center, so that a man could stand on the tree, or lounge at his leisure beneath it. Above, the boughs were as lush and clumpy as the tails peacocks drag, deep green, full, and feathery. The cedar king provided a generous circle of cool, dense shade for the riders.

The moment Jill saw this tree, she thought of her sons' play in the Neverland, and the old oak there that endured their capering. She exclaimed, "What a glorious cedar! I can picture you brothers shinning up into it, when you were young. It offers enough branches for all of you, and looks hardy enough to support seven men, let alone seven boys."

"So it is!" Nico grasped a bough, swinging from his saddle up into the tree. He stood balanced on his bare feet, looking for all the world like Cecco aloft on a yardarm, smiling down at his 'ideal woman.' Jill's heart ached as the memory took hold. She saw Cecco as just a sailor, before his election to captain. The gypsy magic with which he enticed her still held her in thrall. She pressed her red hand to her lips, remembering the seductive strokes of his thumb as he read her future in her palm.

Nibs, too, swung up and into the tree, perfectly at home in the heights. Laughing, he and Nico both reached out for Jill. She trotted up on her mare, pulled her whip from her saddle, and, next moment, she cast her lash up. Whistling, it caught a higher branch, and she pulled herself up by this strap to alight between the two men. Nico was amazed; Nibs, knowing that Jill had employed her secret power of flight, merely grinned and tightened the knot of his kerchief. Stella clapped her hands in delight, almost singing, *"Brava, brava, Signora!"*

Jill gathered her lash and bowed to the girl. The bark was ridged beneath her feet, easy to navigate, and the scent of the cedar was heavenly— sweet and spicy. She breathed it in.

Stella, more practical than her companions, remained on the earth with the horses. She dismounted to arrange the picnic. She shook out a quilt, then set out a basket of Mamma's providing. Nibs hopped down to tend to the animals before joining her. Jill took two steps along her branch, then looked out, over the hill crowned by this cedar. She gasped at the sight, and nearly missed her footing. She barely felt the strong hand that grasped her own, steadying her.

The scenery was so magnificent that, once she recovered her balance, she stood entranced. The hill sloped away and away in a series of mounds and hollows, all covered like a patchwork quilt with squares of vineyards. The squares consisted of line after line of grape vines, in parallel rows of green, leafy plantings. Even from a distance, the air was permeated with a heady smell— grapes, basking in the love of the sun. The only sounds were the sighing of the breeze as it sauntered through the cedar, Nibs and Stella's murmurs on the blanket below, and, far away, the bleat of a goat. A dun, dusty lane climbed up and down, winding as far as Jill could see. On either side, the road was studded with the peculiar kind of pine that grew in this latitude, tall and thin, like dark green sentinels with pointed caps and their elbows tucked in. Upon the rise of the farthest hill perched a pink villa with terra cotta tiles on the roof, and outbuildings to match. Jill had never viewed such a vista. She was about to remark upon the sensations it inspired when, disconcertingly, she discerned another sensation at her fingertips. She looked down.

Nico Cecco was holding her hand. She remembered, then, how he had seized it to keep her from falling. She was not falling now, and, yet...Jill looked up at his face. Nico, too, seemed enraptured with the scenery. His lips curved in a smile as he gazed at the countryside. He appeared quite unconscious of the fact that he possessed her hand, and that the wine-colored kerchief meant to connect them remained in his pocket. As pleasant as it felt to stand side by side with a shared sense of wonder, Jill loosed her fingers and, diplomatically, drew away. In doing so, she drew his gaze, too.

He did not apologize. He cast a glance at Nibs and Stella, who watched their elders with amusement, and he said, enigmatically, "What is not hidden, cannot cause shame."

"That outlook is one of the first things I noticed in Giovanni. He never hides much of anything." She curled her whip into loops.

"We Cecco men can be brazen."

"Trinio being simply the least subtle one."

"Subtlety requires the extravagance of time. As I have grown older, I find I've lost patience."

Clearly, the younger couple were impatient, too, to draw away by themselves. Knowing they must not stray from Nico's sight, Nibs guided Stella from the picnic blanket to take in the view from the hill. He bent down toward Stella, so that they walked preoccupied, heads together, but not quite touching. They looked to be exchanging confidences. Nico chuckled to see them thus, then he dropped from the branch to the ground, holding up his arms to help Jill descend.

She ignored his offer, and slipped from the tree to fall so gently that she seemed to glide. Nico blinked, wondering at her agility. Again, he sensed she was shielding some secret part of herself. Something raw, he felt. Something she'd assimilated from her primal island. He allowed his doubts to show on his face, and twisted the subject to his advantage.

"It seems, though, that Giovanni has hidden at least one secret from you." He spoke low, and his smoky eyes turned to indicate Stella.

"No," Jill rejoined, "Giovanni could not know about Stella."

"He knew about Bezzi. I see that he has not confessed his love for her."

"And so, at last, I have my answer. Stella is his daughter; my daughter, now; your niece." Toying with the tip of her whip, Jill studied him. "And you, Nico? What do you hide?"

He startled. Her easy acceptance of Giovanni's fatherhood astonished him, but, so too, did the speed of her riposte, and her question.

"I feel the subject of Giovanni and Bezzi's love to be a sensitive one. And I believed all redheads to be jealous."

"I know Giovanni's story. At the moment, I am thinking of yours. Why, Nico— if, as you say, no one should travel alone— why do you?"

"I am hardly alone from one moment to the next. I enjoy this sense of family, this belonging that you say Giovanni misses so badly, since he was arrested and forced to leave us."

"You dance around my question. I can see you are a loving man, and a man who longs for companionship."

Carefully, he stepped closer. He watched her face tilt up, to challenge his gaze as he neared her. Her copper tresses lilted with the breath of the wind. "I *have* longed for a companion. Since learning of Giovanni's marriage, I have desired her, even more."

Her voice remained clear, as when she indulged in her tales. "Nico, you have some reason for bringing me here."

He recovered from his surprise to smile, roguishly, "You have caught me…red-handed." Jill's laugh relieved his tension, but made him wonder again— asking these intimate questions, how could she behave so cavalierly?

"Perhaps I can guess," she said. "You wish to discuss the young lovers…" With a toss of the hand he had referenced, she indicated Nibs and Stella, dallying at the crest of the hill. "And, I think, you wish to discuss more mature lovers, too."

"What power gives you your intuition?" he asked, half in earnest, half in guile. "You were not born a Romana, yet you hold arcane wisdom." As she edged toward his trap, his heart skipped a beat beneath Giovanni's kerchief. Surely, she'd not fall so easily.

And he was right. "Like draws its like," she replied. "I am no stranger to magic." Abruptly, Jill strode to his horse and unhooked his whip from the saddle. "We'll soon learn how Nibs and Stella feel." She handed him his lash, but, as he grasped it, she did not let it go. "Let us talk of other lovers later. Won't you honor your promise to share your technique?" The next moment, she had freed him and turned back to the horses. Unseen, Nico scowled.

Jill treated each animal to an apple, leading them away so that they might not be frightened by the snaps of the lashes. The couple retreated to a meadow, where they each exercised their skills. Side by side, the two enjoyed the open space, the beauty of the land, and the freedom a new friendship offered. Nico reflected that this pirate woman had turned him into a rule breaker. Now that the subject he wished to pursue had been broached, he was emboldened by this ease of familiarity, and he felt the pricking of a particular expectation. Had she tempted him with an apple, like the horses, he'd have supped from her bloody hand, too— but not for the sweet taste of fruit. For the deception.

As they practiced their methods, Jill acknowledged that she'd never yet used her whip for destruction, but, as in the legend of Red-Handed Jill, she had sworn to bring down any male, or anyone, who tried to tame her. For his part, Nico assured her, he disdained to apply the lash to his horses. He employed it, he said, as a command to be heard but not felt. Only rarely would he use the tip to tickle a horse to obedience. Jill watched him, pleased to see that, when speaking of his animals, Nico radiated kindness. Nico's sensibilities were much as she imagined Papa's must be, and like Cecco's in his tender, shared moments. And yet, Nico possessed a severity.

Jill felt it most when he spoke of Giovanni. When Nico first met her, he opposed her, protective, no doubt, of his brother's heart. Now he'd accepted her, but he could still be prickly at times, and she wondered if he was protecting his own heart as well. Like the tickle of his whip, he was guiding Jill to some destination, and it was a place, maybe, more perilous than the cedar king's hill.

But Jill could be prickly, too. When Stella laid out the lunch, the aroma of Mamma's repast made their mouths water. Under the pretense of hurry for his meal, Nico brushed past Jill, so that his bare, muscular shoulder rubbed her cheek. As he returned his whip to the saddle and patted his steed, Jill waited for the moment he would turn toward the blanket. Gripping her own whip, she aimed and shot out her lash, deftly wrapping its end round his leather arm brace. He exclaimed, their eyes met, and Jill yanked, sending him tripping toward Stella, who laughed and caught her uncle in her arms.

"Giovanni advised me to keep the handkerchief between us," Jill asserted, "but the whip can work just as well."

As he unwound the lash from his wrist, Nico stared at her. He smoldered with a mix of surprise and injured pride. Stella let go of him with a squeeze, her green eyes alight with her teasing. "Uncle," she trilled, "I do not know my papa at all, but I think my papa knows *you* very well."

Having snared him, Jill tossed the whip aside. In the shady shelter of the cedar giant, the four sat down to partake of the feast. Undaunted, Nico reconstituted his composure to pay Jill every attention. The group grew merry. The wafts of wind on their backs were warm and fragrant, the food fresh and wholesome. Nibs had stolen some clusters of grapes from their canopies, perfectly round with a frosty sheen, and, between juicy bites, the ladies wove the tendrils into garlands. With his two hands, Nico crowned Jill with a wreath, leaning as close to her as he dared, so that she smelled the kiss of the sun on his skin. Then he helped her weave another garland to adorn her mare's tail. As Stella shared out the last of the wine, Nibs abandoned his relaxed recline, and sat up straight. Jill saw the crease between his dark brows deepen as he drew breath to speak. Nibs, too, had been captured, but with a pressure more gentle than his mother's whip.

"*Signore,*" he began, "Stella and I have been talking today, and we're in accord. I want to take her back with us, to meet Captain Cecco aboard the *Red Lady*." He turned to the girl, who nodded solemnly.

"*Sì*, Uncle, I would so like to go. It is my one chance to meet my papa."

Nico sighed, then admitted, "I will not pretend that I have not considered this opportunity." His firm jaw set against the loss. "But the troupe will be moving on, and Giovanni resides a long way away. We must ensure that, should you wish to come home, you can do so."

"I'll see to it myself, *Signore*, if that's what Stella wants, in the end." Nibs the Knife frowned in his earnestness, looking as fierce as his name. "But what I want is for Stella to marry me."

Stella's dimples curled with a resolute smile. "I have told Nibs that I will make one decision at a time. Before I consider marriage, I must learn to know my sire. And I cannot commit to a life at sea before I find how it suits me. But I will need your help to persuade my mother to let me go."

"My son has chosen well," Jill said, with pride. "One day, Stella, you will be a wisewoman like your *nonna*. I am delighted, and I know Giovanni will welcome you. For long, he has dreamt of a daughter." She nodded to Nibs, "And *my* dream is for my son to win such a wife."

"My little Stella," her uncle said, reluctantly, "Bezzi will not be pleased. Yet I will speak to her on your behalf, and then I will consult the *Padre*." The young lovers exchanged happy glances.

Jill hesitated, considering, then she reached for Nico's handkerchief. Slipping it from his vest, she draped it over his forearm, just above his leather bracer. And there, to the wonder of the company, she placed her crimson hand.

"Nico, I am here to speak for Giovanni. I have just done so in the matter of his daughter. If you want his advice in securing your own contentment, I am willing to give it." But a rush of hot blood coursed through her arm and into her heart, and she leaned back. "Oh!" she said, and, with her hand still clasping Nico, she focused on the hills, and the vineyards, as they glowed green in the sunlight, down and down, stretching into infinity.

"Jill! What do you see?" Nico asked, at a loss as to where to place his own hands. With Stella watching, dare he return the woman's touch? Again, the bloodstain on her palm made him doubt her. He spoke angrily. "Is it the magic you claim to know? Some power, some dark force, that pulls you from us?"

"I do sense a power, and it pulls me *toward* you." She sat still on the quilt, her gaze engaged with the vista, and she let the breeze speak to her. "Nico, I know Giovanni's story, and I know your tale, too. It has just come to me, mingled with your brother's. I know what withholds happiness from you. It is faithfulness. It is betrayal."

"Will you tell us this story?"

"Will you tell me Stella's?"

Nico's countenance darkened, as Giovanni's would do when he felt reluctant to speak.

"You yourself told me today, Nico. What is not hidden, cannot cause shame."

Stella, too, looked grave, but urged, "It is all right, Uncle. I must soon meet my father, and it is best that I know whence I came."

"Very well, then." Nico turned his face to Jill. His every nerve stung with the heat of her scarlet mark, penetrating the cloth on his skin. Resentful of her power to affect him, he wanted to shove her hand away. Yet the scarf was trapped beneath her bloody palm, and he could not bring himself to feel her flesh again. This woman's touch, even sheathed, made his stomach churn.

"You already know the gambit Mamma and Giovanni ran years ago, taking advantage of rich girls to steal their rings." With begrudged veneration, he said, "They were artists, those two. Bezzi fell in love with him, just like those other girls, he was so sharp and handsome— if I say so myself." Nico's lips twisted in a bitter grin, while his modesty fought with his pride. "But Bezzi is *tribale*, she is one of us— she is not like those village girls who paid for their fortunes— and Giovanni should have sensed that she is no light of love, but an *innamorata* to be cherished in sincerity. No one is truer than Bezzi. Once she loves, she will not take it back."

"My uncle is right," the girl chimed in. "Where Mamma loves, she is steadfast."

"I have tried to make up to Bezzi for her lover's carelessness, and for his absence. Had my brother not been arrested, I do not doubt that he and Bezzi would, even now, be married. And blissful." Nico's gaze pierced Jill's. He hoped she felt its darts.

Jill did not look away. If the subject brought her pain, she compounded her discomfort. "And Stella would, by now, enjoy the company of numerous brothers and sisters."

Nibs ventured, "I see how you care for Stella, *Signore*, like she's your own daughter. I think you love Bezzi, too."

Nico turned away, but his connection to Jill did not weaken. Her touch still seared. She asked him, "Has Bezzi refused you?"

"Bezzi? She does not allow me near enough to ask."

"Yet you helped her raise Stella."

"Bezzi is sensible. She knows when to accept assistance."

Jill returned, "Giovanni hurt her. He is her past. I believe that what Bezzi feels now…" Quickly, Nico faced her as she concluded, "…is a wish for you." Her connection to Nico complete, Jill withdrew her hand from his body. She no longer needed to read his memory; she'd intuited the tale. She dropped the scarf in his lap. "A story for a story. This was our bargain."

Her three companions eased down again on the quilt, composing themselves to listen as Jill leaned back, finding a rough means of support from the king cedar's trunk. Each of her listeners had reason to feel unsettled: Nibs with his hope, Stella with her history. Nico, with his schemes. He twisted the scarf in his fingers.

In entering into this intimacy with Nico, Jill was alert to the danger. As with her mare, she held the reins lightly. She trusted her heart to know best.

After all, what is not hidden, cannot cause shame. She began her recounting….

"Expecting more trouble from the *conestabili*, half the Romani men hang back at the camp. They are protecting the women and children. The gypsies have settled this time in the hollow of a farmer's field, under the azure of a Mediterranean sky. The caravans are packed now, the horses in harness and flicking their tails. In the safety of mothers' arms, the young ones peep from the wagons' windows. In the center of the meadow, where the grasses lay trampled from work and from play, the great ring of fire sits steaming. The morning's wash water drowns its heat, slowly, while the drenched embers hiss in complaint.

"With equal outrage, the other half of the men ride to town, where they crowd the courtroom. Their boots hit the floorboards. The outdoor smells they bring invade the stale, paper air of bureaucracy. The ancient town hall is turning to dust, and these flesh and blood men are a threat to its integrity. Like Giovanni's clansmen, the crimson brick, the plaster patches, the shreds of red velvet, stand witness. They all watch the crumble of justice that constitutes his trial.

"The magistrate is a pinched little man, with pinched little spectacles on his little, pinched nose. Squinting at the gypsies, he taps his gavel for quiet, which is grudgingly given. With a flare of his gown and an imperious wave, he summons the prisoner, then he straightens his stringy gray wig.

"The watchers murmur when they hear the approach of their lost boy, Giovanni. In place of the ringing of his bracelets, the youth is preceded by the jangle of chains. He emerges from under the arch of a doorway, dragged between officials in uniform. He is barefoot and beaten, his handsome face swollen with discolored flesh. Wherever his skin shows, dried blood patches his cuts. Raising their voices, his clansmen protest, but the magistrate pounds his gavel again— a flat, wooden order for silence.

"Giovanni, his head hanging, his eyes half blind from brutality, does not witness much of his trial. The magistrate asks; the officers jab; Giovanni jerks, but says nothing. His head throbs, his wounds sting, his wrists and his ankles blister in irons. His ears hear friends' whispers, hear the gavel, he hears the garbling and gabbling of the mayor whose daughter is disgraced, but, when he's accused, he refuses to let his lips form the answers.

"One of the onlookers sits gingerly on a bench at the back, sniffling. A fringe of hair slips from his cap, but he doesn't notice. He's an awkward lad, too small for his jerkin, and uncomfortable in his breeches. His breakfast sits as uneasily in his gut as his garb sits on his frame. The chamber is full of kinsmen and countrymen, but all he can see is Giovanni. His Gianni....His heart tears in two.

"In a pinched little voice, the magistrate names the verdict. The mayor nods in triumph, his chain of office glimmering from shoulder to shoulder. He turns to the prisoner, shakes his fist, then, deliberately, he spits at him. Beruffled and primped, his sycophants rise to follow him out, babbling congratulations. They eye the gypsies, sneering. Pointedly, they draw scented pomanders from their sleeves, and hold them up to their noses.

"In shock, the Romani men sit quiet now, without the magistrate's bidding. The strain shows on their weatherworn faces; they expected the cell and the beatings, the scorning, the spite. They did not foresee transportation, to faraway Gao. Young Nico's silver was meant to prevent that possibility. Now that the courtroom has cleared of its villagers, more men in uniform enter, to line the surrounding walls.

"Bolstered in his arrogance, the magistrate pulls a pouch from the pocket of his robe. He smirks from his high table as he tugs the bag open. Giovanni, propped up by his guards, hears the merry chink of coins. Finally, he raises his head.

"The magistrate stacks the money, pinching each piece of his bribe. The sheen of the coins is softer than the glint in his eye. The Romani men shuffle, exchanging belligerent looks. Nico jumps to his feet, but his papa grips his elbow to forbid him from speaking, for the *conestabili* bring their batons to attention. The boy at the back sits alone, stupefied.

"Everyone listens as the magistrate mocks. With twisted little lips, he berates the Romani, threatens further arrests. He sits back then, weighs the coins in one hand, and, with a sudden sweep of his sleeve, flings Nico's bribe back at the gypsies.

"The men throw their arms up to avoid metal rain. The coins ping on the floor, rolling in all directions. Links of chain ring, too, as the officers haul Giovanni by his shoulders, through the archway and down to the gaol. The magistrate rises, and, aiming at Nico, hurls one last silver piece to his hands. Nico is too surprised to throw it back. The young man stands, horrified, as the sounds of his brother's links fade.

"The boy at the back holds his hand to his mouth. He stares at Nico. He waits, but Nico stands stubborn, still gripping the cold silver piece in his fist. At last, Nico gestures to his elders, urging them to scoop up the lucre.

"The boy rushes out, and into the daylight. At the edge of town, he flings off his cap. Bezzi's auburn hair tumbles down. It blazes in the Mediterranean sun as she runs all the way back to camp. Dry dust from the road coats her feet. Her disappointment tastes bitter. Just before she turns home, she sheds her boys' clothing. She shivers into the skirt she has hidden in the bushes, and she collapses. She gasps, she shrieks, and she weeps. She will never see Gianni again. He will never know he is a papa. He will never lay eyes on their child.

"She will never forgive this betrayal. Where is Nico's loyalty? He grips the silver! He hoards the cursed, bloody money, pinched by the magistrate's fingertips.

"The men take too long in returning. By the time they ride back and whip up the caravans, the wash of morning's tears has drenched the heat of her anger. The embers remain, though, to glow through her years, and, sometimes, to hiss in complaint."

Nico sat remembering, his eyes wide with awe. Eventually, he said to Jill, with a touch of suspicion, "You speak as if you had been there."

"Now I understand," said Stella, her melodious tones hushed. "Now I have heard my mother's voice, in a way I could not hear before. No wonder she is hurting. No wonder..." She studied her uncle's face, shaded by the cedar boughs, but she said no more.

"Not even Giovanni knows the full story," Nico declared. "All through that farce of a trial, he was only half aware."

Jill answered, "Nor has he spoken of it. Yet, through my own kind of magic, I know his story by heart."

"Bezzi...I never knew she was there, that she witnessed Giovanni's degradation. All these years...and she believes I betrayed him?"

Jill lifted her shoulders. "You know her far better than I. But, I think, you must tell her what you did with the silver."

"Too many years have passed. To her, I cannot speak of it."

"You never kept that money, Uncle?" Stella's green eyes pleaded. "Mamma was wrong. You could not have kept such a curse!"

"No. I could not." Reluctant to ask Jill this favor, Nico forced himself. He opened his hands. "Jill, if you please, enlighten Stella, and Nibs."

Sitting back, braced by the strength of the cedar, Jill paused to pick up the threads again, then related the rest of the tragedy.

"In the courtroom, the magistrate withdraws with all the pomp of his office. Nico speaks to the Romani men in an undertone, then they exit, quietly. They mill about the town hall's square, watering their horses, examining hooves. Some lean back to doze in the shade of the trees, one mends a bridle, one stokes a pipe. Each man of the tribe takes his turn to wander, pacing round the hall's lawn. Each man, in his turn, hunkers down, an elbow on a knee.

"One by one, the silver pieces are planted, discreetly, shoved deep by the thumbs of the gypsies. Each coin carries a curse, whispered to the earth by its sower. In the end, a circle of silver seed lies, hidden, each piece at an interval, ringing the courthouse. Nico gives a short whistle, and the Romani men swing jingling into their saddles, and ride.

"Days later, Giovanni is hauled aboard his first ship, to sail his first voyage, in irons, trapped in the hold. Beyond the pain of his injuries, he is homesick with aching as deep as the sea.

"Days after that, seated at his high desk, the pinched little magistrate straightens his wig. Something taps its top. Something else plunks on his gavel. He looks up at the ceiling, to discover a cleft in the plaster. As he watches, the rift widens. His twisted lips frown. The rain in the courtroom, this time, isn't silver. It is gray. He can't catch the drifting powder like Nico caught the coin. A ponderous old structure, the town hall trembles. The ancient edifice of justice crackles, then shudders, then groans. Imploding, it thunders its verdict.

" 'Death,' it pronounces. And executes the sentence.

"From the crumble of justice that constitutes this trial, a cloud of dust rises to heaven. The cost is dear— a son, and some money— but flesh and blood men restored the court to integrity."

◢

Stella's pony led the way back to camp. Nibs followed on his colt, Jill's mount prancing at its heels with a garland of grapevine twined through its tail. The last of the riders, Nico Cecco hung back, and brooded.

All these years, Bezzi blamed him, as a betrayer. The man whom that loyal woman loved betrayed her, too, in a way, by sending this storyteller to expose her mistake. Giovanni's wife, the woman who won him, had returned in his place to cut Bezzi again, with the truth.

Nico, who took his brother's place in her life, but not in her heart nor in her hold, now knew what kept her so far from him. One honest question from Bezzi, and they could have been happy.

Whatever Jill's intentions, whatever change Mamma foresaw in his fortunes, the story Jill told did not raise his fate; it sank him lower in misery. Bezzi loved Giovanni. Nico had accepted that fact. He revered it. But he now knew that Bezzi resented Nico— resented him too much, even, to simply ask for an explanation about the tainted silver of the bribe. All these years.

Derisive, Nico huffed. Red-Handed Jill, with her truth-telling! Giovanni had not intended to leave Bezzi. So many years later, he could not guess the cost of Jill's visit. It would be too cruel, now, to set Bezzi straight. She had lost Giovanni. She endured sorrow enough. To learn at this point, too late, that she was wrong about Nico would surely drive her mad. Why double her heartache? Better that she never realize the joy she had missed, the life she might have shared with the man who adored her. Giovanni was blameless. Nico was blameless. It was the women who caused all this grief.

Bezzi made a foolish, petty blunder, and Nico would not humiliate her by correcting it. But, where Jill was concerned, Nico felt no compunction. He'd make her pay in shame for what she did to his loved ones. He could never win Bezzi now, never offer her happiness. Stella could misunderstand his reluctance, might interpret his discretion as yet another desertion; because of Jill, the girl would soon abandon her home and her uncle to go to sea with her father. Jill and her beauty blinded Giovanni, so that he did not see the danger of her soothsaying, nor could he perceive the man in her shadowlands.

Bitterly, Nico grasped what little Jill left to him: a new freedom. No rules bound him now. For whom did he need to be virtuous? Mamma had encouraged him to break with tradition, to test Jill's fidelity. Bezzi set her face from him. Stella was determined to depart for the sea. Thanks to Jill, her son, and her story, he now had nothing, and no one, to lose.

And, perhaps, Mamma's vision proved more acute than she knew. Her prophecies had a way of coming true. Nico felt his heart harden. His disillusionment whittled it sharp, to a knife point, to skewer through Jill's. All he required was opportunity. A single moment of intimacy. One touch. He would prove that, as Mamma predicted, a dark and dubious man loitered at the source of Jill's soul, waiting to snare her.

That man's face lay revealed. He was *tribale*. The dark man was Nico. Himself.

He watched his brother's wife riding ahead, her head held high, her copper hair blowing back in the wind like the mane of her mare. He knew two things he loved. Two things to be sacrificed.

Already, he had given up Bezzi. And once Jill was driven off by the gypsies at last, exposed as the disloyal spouse he despised, Nico would sell that mare to the first man who offered— with the wine-colored kerchief twined through its tail.

Departures

*M*onsieur Guillaume sat at a safe distance on the *Red Lady*'s mainchains, his feet hanging down toward the water. In the boat below him perched his onetime captain and his cousin Renaud. Renaud handled a boat hook, to keep their craft close, but not too close, to avoid a clash with the ship. As he had told Zaleh, Guillaume knew this duo well— sufficiently so to suspect that, if he allowed them near enough, these former lovers and shipmates would not scruple to abduct him.

"So, my boy," concluded LeCorbeau, his ebullience subdued, "we are to be comrades no more?"

The two Frenchmen bobbed on the surf, gazing up as hope dwindled in their eyes. How to dash that hope, and yet remain friendly? Guillaume tried to be gentle, but he had rarely seen LeCorbeau so morose. Even the lace at his throat seemed deflated somehow, and the buttons of his green coat less shining. Volatile as the man was, Guillaume hadn't seen his captain so depressed since his prized bottle of cognac went missing.

Guillaume smiled in secret. Tom Tootles had caused that trouble, swiping the prize from under LeCorbeau's big nose. Tom used the cognac to manipulate both Guillaume and LeCorbeau— before restoring the bottle and allowing Guillaume to take all the credit. That memory warmed him, just like the taste of aged oak that had hung on his tongue from the cognac they shared. The recollection gave him heart to hold fast. This kind of friendship was the fixative that bonded him to the commodore's service— as was the fact that, divorced from this fleet, he might never again swim with a merman in a magical, mystical lagoon.

"I sorrow with you, *Monsieur*, but my new life pleases me. I thank you though, for your generous offer of ransom."

"*Zut alors!* I would toss at these thieving pirates twice as much, to bring you home!…Although, eh," with a furtive air, LeCorbeau glanced about, and toned down his vehemence, "you need not mention this fact to your captain."

"Come, Cousin!" Renaud broke in, his narrow face growing livid with impatience, "Do not tear the *commandant*'s heart. You are cruel to our benefactor, not to mention forgetful of family! Who on this ship loves you as we do?"

"Captain Cecco respects me well, and he is wealthy enough not to sell me against my will." This claim was one that, in all honesty, Guillaume could not make on behalf of LeCorbeau.

The captain complained, "But these are not honorable sailors, these are buccaneers! They steal, they plunder!"

"With respect, *Monsieur*, you taught me how to ply these skills."

LeCorbeau clutched at the sides of his boat, as if in danger of swooning. He gasped out, "Our work is performed in the name of France, for *la patrie!*"

"And I work for my friends."

Collapsing at last, the *commandant* subsided into the arms of his faithful first mate, wheezing.

"Ungrateful Guillaume," Renaud hissed, patting his captain, "see how he suffers. But if you refuse to champion France, have pity on me. I perform the work of two officers! With so many new crewmen, our *commandant* trusts no one as he trusts you and me."

LeCorbeau plopped a hand on Renaud's sleeve. "Never mind, Renaud. We shall give the boy some time to consider, eh, the consequences of remaining with these pirates. After all, Hook's good luck cannot last forever. *Sans doute*, the authorities will sniff him out," he turned his jaundiced eye upon Guillaume, "and then, my child, where will you find yourself? Dangling in the loop of a noose!"

"I accept the word of all the company that, if taken, my comrades will swear I was forced into piracy. I should then be pardoned, and sent home to France. Our good Chef, as well, is protected so."

LeCorbeau's eyebrows soared. What was he to say to this miracle, or rather, to this trickery? His grip on Renaud became pinching. Renaud understood. He scoffed.

"Cousin, you dupe yourself! These men are felons, not philanthropists. If you carry on in this delusion, you will learn your mistake— in a reeking brig, as you await execution!"

His kinsman, Guillaume, stood up to climb back to the deck. "To my ears, no insult to my shipmates is welcome." Clapping his heels together, he saluted. "Again, I give you my thanks, *Monsieur le Commandant*, and I bid you good day. No doubt I will greet you one year from now, when we meet for our next exchange."

Quite like his old self, LeCorbeau countered with a chill in his voice, "Do not rely on that meeting, young Guillaume. I have in mind to make the, eh...alterations...in our terms with the commodore." LeCorbeau dismissed his former mate with a gesture, and Renaud unhooked the boat to cast off. "Seize the tiny bit of time to reconsider. You may not be so fortunate as to find a second opportunity." He flapped his handkerchief. *"Adieu, Monsieur Guillaume! Et,* eh, *bon chance!"*

Saddened yet relieved, Guillaume clasped his hands behind his back, watching Renaud row the boat home to *Le Lotus*. He recalled Zaleh's warning, and he grew firmer in his decision. Best to keep these two creatures in the past, or, at least, at the length of a boat hook. These were men whom he knew, much too well.

"Pierre-Jean did not need my command. He volunteered." The oaken slats of the bedstead groaned as Yulunga lowered his weight onto it, reclining against the bolster where his woman sat propped. "He will travel to Europe, as your protector."

Mrs. Hanover's baby lay tucked at her breast but unable to suckle. In his struggle, he made little mewings, his sour breath barely brushing her flesh. Yulunga wrapped his hands around the tiny body and set the boy down in the cot beside the bunk. "I brought the goat's milk, you can try that again, like the Ladies of the Clearing taught you."

At the mention of Pierre-Jean, Mrs. Hanover had blushed. This habit was unnecessary in her life with Yulunga, a mannerism left over from her days in more genteel surroundings. Yulunga plumbed many of her secrets. He seemed immune to them. She nodded, and kept her gaze on his face. She did not bother to draw closed her blouse.

"I warned Pierre-Jean not to trust the doctor, ever. Nor should you. If Heinrich finds a cure for this baby, I am the one who will be dumbstruck. Even so, little mother, you believe that you must take this chance."

Lifting the heavy weight of his hand to her lips, she held it tightly, and kissed it.

He had learned how to hear her, with words or without. His eyes lowered to take in her nakedness. The babe didn't pull much of her milk, and her breasts swelled with it, her tips taut and hard, all open to his view and inviting arousal. His nether parts pricked as he said, "In name, you are a captive, but you will miss this free life of ours, won't you?"

"I will miss you." Moving his hand from her lips to her ribs, she made her lover caress her. She felt his body ripen along with hers. He was her captor; he was her liberator. He did not want her to go, but he would send her away, with protection, and that protection provided by a rival. As always, his care and his carelessness stirred her. His proximity was, however, not her sole stimulant today.

"I lied," she said. "With Father. I think about our sharing…all the time." The blush on her face spread over her bosom.

True to form, Yulunga laughed at her confession. "I am no jealous man. I know your appetites."

"What if I falter…fall back under his spell?"

"With good reason, I chose Pierre-Jean to tend to you. You two already enjoy dallying, and it will serve to your benefit. If any man can keep your hands occupied and off of the doctor, he is our blond, blue-eyed Frenchman."

He had won her again. A product of her father's upbringing, Mrs. Hanover could not resist that mix of protectiveness and indifference. To the depths of her being, she craved the contradictions Yulunga served to her.

She wrapped her arms about the column of her lover's neck, thick, and bedecked with beads, pressing the gold of his earring to her cheek, the match to the hoop on her own lobe, and thinking as she held him that this time might be the last. This too-likely possibility made her push closer, to climb on his thighs, desperate to cling to her man, to experience him palpably, to memorize the rich feel of his skin, the scent of him, and the colors of his presence.

He indulged her. He opened his breeches. With his hands sliding under her skirt, he raised her hips, to settle her, slowly, along the length of his cock. She arched into him, abandoning the few words she might use, to pant instead at the entrance of his mouth.

Nursing a babe made her nipples tender, and the touch of his chest against hers provoked a tingle of both pleasure and pain— exactly how she longed to be loved. Guiding his fingers, she made him squeeze her teat, then pushed her breast between his lips to feel his kisses there, and the rub of his tongue, till her discomfort stung and inflamed and exploded, and his lips drew, not blood, but milk, and she hurt, and she loved, and she perished there, in his arms, in his bed, in the negligence of his passion.

The babe woke and fussed. As the brutal blend of sensations eased and ebbed, Mrs. Hanover rolled to the edge of the bed, to gaze at the child. Weakly, he beat the air with his elbows. She sat up and cradled him, thinking each time she did so, that this time might be the last. As Yulunga rose up behind her, he supported her back with his hot, heaving chest, while the little mother stared at her child, committing to memory the thin feel of his skin, the scent of him, and the colorless ghost of his presence.

Yulunga asked, "Will you return to me?" His teeth bit into her shoulder, sharp and piercing, leaving their indentations. "Whether with, or without him?"

"How to know? But..." her head drooped over her baby, her nipples dripping, and her brown hair shrouding his face, "if you command me, I volunteer."

In the balmy air of late afternoon, white swirls of seagulls screeched and dove, fetching up fish that flashed in the shallows. Commodore Hook's station on the bow of the *Roger* set him slightly above Captain Cecco's, at the fore of *Red Lady*. The fleet's crews manned their posts, inhaling their last smells of land. The men were primed to sail as soon as the second crate of lotus was transferred. Their two officers concluded their conference.

Hook turned toward the more distant figure of the French captain, who waited amidships of *Le Lotus*, drumming on the gloss of the rail. At the *commandant*'s right, Doctor Heinrich stood with his customary air of dignity, his dress formal, a tailored brown coat over his splendid tan satin vest. His decorum could not mask his anticipation. Hook, too, anticipated, harboring the knowledge that Red-Handed Jill remained safe from this danger, a continent away. Restraining a smirk at the advent of the surgeon's imminent defeat, he opened the parley.

"Well, LeCorbeau, shall we make our final exchanges before the sun sinks?"

"Certainement." LeCorbeau flicked his fingers at the boat in the brine below him, containing two oarsmen and Renaud, and a weighty leather bag. "As soon as we see your boat lowered, transporting toward my vessel the so-charming *Madame* Mrs. *Frau* Heinrich."

"Captain Cecco has a word or two to offer on that subject. Captain, if you please?"

Cecco's gypsy regalia caught the slanting sun's light. The medallions resonated as, in seeming sympathy, he inclined his head. "Gentlemen, I must disillusion you in this matter. Mrs. Heinrich lives only in your hopes."

The would-be husband insisted, "Do not play with my patience. I will wait no longer for our reunion."

"As I say, no Mrs. Heinrich exists." The Italian captain crossed his arms and leaned against the braces. "But there *is* a Mrs. Cecco."

As Heinrich clutched at his watch, he burst out, "Desist these absurdities! I demand to see my wife."

"*My* wife, you mean. Red-Handed Jill married me, the day we boarded the *Unity*. The good Captain Greer performed the honors. You were not invited to the ceremony, Doctor. You were injured during punishment, as I recall, and lay flat on your belly, unable to rise from your bunk."

Speechless, the surgeon blinked in confusion. His thoughts whirled as he reconstructed the events of that terrible day. He darted a look to LeCorbeau, who, with pursed lips, acted on an urgent impulse to inspect the embroidery on his lapels. Remaining mum, the *commandant* picked at lint.

Hook took up the story. "I missed the wedding myself! By a strange coincidence, I too lay confined to a bunk." With the tip of his hook, he peeled back the lace at his wrist, exhibiting the traces of shackles.

As if he felt the incisions of Cecco's knife again, Heinrich drew back his shoulders, declaring, "You are deceivers, both of you. Jill plighted her troth to me, in a sacrament sworn and certified by Captain LeCorbeau. You will allow the lady to attest for herself. I demand to speak with her!"

Hook replied, soothingly, "I understand your disappointment. We are all three enamored of our lady. Few men can resist her. Yet the fact remains— you, Doctor, have no claim to Red-Handed Jill, lawful, or otherwise."

Cecco added, "Even were we inclined to grant your very civil request to speak with her, we are unable to do so. Our Jill is not aboard the *Roger*, nor does she sail on this vessel that I, her loving husband, named in her honor."

"What? Impossible! I know you both well enough. Neither of you malefactors would let her out of your grasp. Have you locked her up in the brig?"

At the thought of their pirate queen imprisoned, and, further, imprisoned against temptation from the even worse restraints of polite society, the sailors grinned and chuckled in derision.

Hook scoffed, too. "As you are aware, Doctor Hanover, Jill refuses to be bound by so much as a corset." The company burst out anew in guffaws, slapping one another's backs.

With a look of distaste, LeCorbeau broke through the merriment. "I warn you, Sir, to guard your tongue. You do not guess who may be present, to witness such, eh...indelicacy."

Hook's earring swung as, with narrowed eyes, he swiveled to study the Frenchman. "Coming from you, *Commandant*, this remark is a strange one." Catching his suspicion, the men on deck observed the French captain too, and fell silent.

LeCorbeau looked down his nose. "*Hélas, mon Commodore*, he who laughs last..." With a lazy gesture, he raised his right hand. He twitched two of his fingers.

A bustling arose on *Le Lotus'* deck as her sailors pushed a man forward to struggle through the crowd. He tottered his way toward the rail with the unsteady steps of a landsman. Wedging himself between LeCorbeau and Heinrich, this fellow removed his hat, and peered across the waters that separated the three dormant gunships.

"I beg your pardon," he said, in the modest manner of a man at his tobacconist's. "I don't mean to intrude, but," he cleared his throat, "to which of you gentlemen must I appeal for the release of my daughter?"

The two dashing pirates, Commodore Hook and Giovanni Cecco, resplendent in costume and at the height of their powers, observed this mild, middle-aged Englishman. His bowler hat and city suit with striped trousers inspired their twin looks of astonishment. Their gazes absorbed him; then, slowly, each man turned his head to stare at the other. Beyond the shock, their widened eyes, sapphire blue and smoldering brown, communicated. Their final exchange was a crystal clear cypher that signaled a mutual conclusion:

Defeat.

Tonight, I address my journal to myself. No other eyes will read this entry. While my husband is always in my thoughts— too much, indeed; I see him where he isn't— my feelings this evening are secret.

Yesterday was lovely in all respects. Our outing to the cedar king brought visions of breathtaking beauty. This country is full of color, the people warm, generous, and true. I feel fresh empathy for my husband, having learned of all he was forced to leave behind. How can he bear such a sadness?

Our picnic party offered our members companionship, a pleasing memory, and cause for celebration— Nibs and Stella may drop the cloth. They are accepted as a couple. Stella's uncle, mother, and the Padre *have consented to her travels. Instead of boarding with only a story to relate to Giovanni, I may present to him the living, breathing daughter for whom he has wished. To compensate the family here for her absence, the history I related clears the way to a new couple's bliss. Stella confided in me her belief that her mother, while stubborn in her longtime rejection of Nico, would certainly accept him— if she knew the full story of how Nico put that cursed silver to work. Nico and Bezzi should join hands, and make up for their losses, with love.*

These lovers should join hands, but will not.

Nico refuses to tell Bezzi the truth. The time is too late, he says. He claims she is no longer the woman he loves. When he tells me these things, he looks at me through the eyes of his brother. He utters no more. He does not need to speak. His gaze, as deep and as heated as my husband's, tells me his story. Truly, the law of the cloth, if applied properly, would hide those eyes behind a wine-colored blindfold.

This image has disturbed me. A blindfold...a rose-colored aura. My mind shuts it away, my head hurts. I don't want to think. I can't think—

I must sleep....

Dancing with Destiny

Mamma handed the lantern to Jill, then hitched up the hem of her skirts to lead the way into the wood. She had released her hair from her netting, and her long dark locks hung down to her knees. Lit by the loving light of the moon, her face revealed the young girl who had captured Papa Cecco's heart, years ago. She had a little silver sickle tucked in her belt and, alongside her red fan, a basket hung at her elbow. "Best to harvest the roots I am after on a bright, moonlit night like tonight," she said. "One learns when each plant's properties wax the most potent."

Jill's ankle bells jingled as she stepped through the mossy undergrowth, following Mamma. This close to the camp, stealth wasn't required. Indeed, the song of Stella's mandolin reached their ears as Nibs and the other young folk sat on the wagon steps, gaming and gabbing, and making music. Mamma hummed along with their tune as she beckoned to Jill, indicating where to shine the lantern's light.

Every clump of vegetation underwent Mamma's scrutiny. When she found the right flora, the woman knelt to dig or slice with care what she needed, showing Jill how to harvest without damaging the plant or its cuttings. Each herb and root gave off its own fragrance to spice the night air. Under this moon, Jill felt, the evening promised something. She could sense it, but she wasn't gypsy enough to guess what that promise might portend. She must study her surroundings, expecting the unexpected.

The two women moved along in harmony, and at length Jill observed, "One of my friends on the Island is an herbalist, and she is respected by her tribe. I venerate this skill of yours."

"Lovely one, if you stay with us long enough, you will learn many useful skills."

"You've been most generous, Mamma." Jill hesitated, remembering Nico's refusal to enlighten Bezzi about his revenge after Cecco's trial, and his silent declaration— with no nuance for doubt left to linger— of affection for his new sister-in-law. "I feel at home here, but I've no wish to overstay my welcome."

"Nonsense. You are a Cecco now. You may remain with us as long as you like. And Papa will come riding home soon. He will want time to get to know his daughter-in-law." She pointed to the side. "No, my fair one, shine the light over this way." Frowning, Mamma sought out the proper angle for her work, leaning in to clip with her sickle. The moist odor of earth arose, a pleasant remembrance for Jill. This smell was one that she missed while aboard ship. She felt a wistful twinge of longing for her Island, and Mamma's next words increased this feeling.

"Jill, I am going to ask that you put off your departure. Indeed, my dear, I wonder if you can be persuaded to stay on for good." *La matriarca* turned to view the amazement on Jill's face, evident in the warm amber light of the lantern. "Yes, I know you are surprised. You think only of our Giovanni, and making your way back to his arms. But," Mamma smiled in her sideways way, "consider, my Jill, that his loved ones, here, have need of you, too."

"Surely no one could need me as much as my husband."

"Giovanni has needed you, and greatly. You have altered my favorite boy's fate. I think on how your inspiration caused him to become a captain, commanding a ship of his own! Without you, my son would not have reached out to grapple with this ambition. And remember, splendid girl, that soon, thanks to your visit here, Giovanni will reclaim a lost dream. You choose not to bear him children, yet you have made certain he will know his daughter. His happiness will abound, and he need never be alone any more."

"Thinking of his joy to come, Mamma, brings tears to my eyes." Jill's voice quivered, and she pressed the back of her scarlet hand to her lips, holding in her emotion.

"And tears of sorrow fill my own, when I think of you leaving us." Mamma put away her sickle and set down her basket, then made to wipe at her eye. Taking the lantern from Jill, she placed it on the ground and sat down upon a fallen tree trunk within the ring of its radiance. "We all miss our Giovanni. Your presence with us has healed this wound. Hearing your stories gives him back to us. We have only to listen to you, and his life mingles with ours again. You will understand this miracle. After all, you yourself pine for the sons you do not see, and would be so very grateful for news of them, no?"

Jill thought of the letters she'd received from her parents, detailing their lives, and the exploits of her brothers and Curly. Each missive brought a surge of delight, and filled in a chink she'd felt had been empty. "It is true. And I know that my own parents live to hear from their daughter, and to read the news that I write about myself and my boys."

"Just so. Surely, you would not deny your new family this same bliss?"

"I...I know I cannot write to you, once I'm away again..."

Mamma shrugged. "Even if we could receive your letters, we could not read them."

"But what can I do? Our intention was to cheer you with tidings of Giovanni. I've no wish to leave you unhappier than I found you."

"And this impulse is what we treasure in you, my Jill. You think first of your family, and what is best for your loved ones. You are loyal. It is one of the reasons our Giovanni adores you. I know you will deal kindly with us."

Jill recalled Cecco's cautions. Was this woman the artful *la matriarca* now, or was the hope she expressed sincere? Once again, Jill felt the disadvantage of leaving her ship. There, she knew her crew. In some way, she had contributed to their stories. Here, among the troupe who were none of her own creation, she understood that they intuited more about her than she could sense about them. Especially Nico. Full of this doubt, Jill inquired, "What of the *Padre?* Have you consulted him on this question?"

Mamma drew up her fan, to wave it slowly under her chin. "I think you have guessed, my dear daughter; the *Padre* nearly always sees things my way." The woman's smile was persuasive, just like her favorite son's.

Stella's music shifted tempo, to a slower melody. The youngsters joined in, enriching the simple song she plucked with a throaty chorus. This new tune's poignancy carried Jill along in its flow.

"I don't know how to answer you, Mamma. I feel pulled toward the sea. Much as I love the countryside and the people here, I am bound to Giovanni…and I'm pledged to—" Jill blinked and put her hand to her head. As she faltered a step backward, the bells of her anklet jarred upon her senses. The silver sickle in Mamma's girdle reflected a shard of moonlight that stabbed at her eyes. Pain shot through them.

Mamma's gaze sharpened. "Pledged to what? Or…to whom?"

Jill pressed both hands to her temples. The piercing pain eased, but the name she'd been about to pronounce had slipped from the tip of her tongue.

Watching Jill closely, *la matriarca* continued with an edge in her voice that smoothed as she coaxed, "You must take time to think the question through. But I envisioned your destiny, my Jill, that very first day. I foresaw that you would bring change to us, for the better."

"What you said that day intrigues me, Mamma."

"I predicted that you would give me something. This gift, I know no other can bestow."

"I would gladly grant such a gift, if I knew what it was."

"Now that we are better acquainted, the mystery grows clearer to me." *La matriarca* let her fan drop on its cord, then stood to dust the last crumbles of earth off her palms. "But for now, my lovely one, hear the music! Stella's fingertips pluck magic from the strings of her mandolin. A favorite old song. Come, we must dance." Mamma reached for Jill's crimson hand.

The strains of the folk song rose from the camp, with the vibrant voices of the singers filling the air. *La matriarca* encouraged Jill, "It is a song of destiny. Let us free our minds of care, and allow the melody to speak to us." The chords sounded plaintive, pure, uniting strings and vocals in a compelling refrain. Mamma raised her skirts, then pointed her toes to demonstrate the steps. In a hollow, minor key, the song rolled, luring its listeners to move along with it. Jill observed Mamma's motions, and replicated them. Her bells rang out pleasingly now, complimenting the cadence.

Jill and her mother-in-law circled the lantern at first, hands joined, knees up and ankles turning. Widening their play, they moved side to side, then bowed and bent, stepping in tandem. Mamma's movements were graceful, practiced, but not difficult to follow. As the melody swelled and enlivened, the two women twirled. Mamma's earrings bobbled, her hair flew around her. Jill's copper curls flared.

Laughing and looping under one another's arms, the women of the Cecco clan danced.

Although Jill smiled, she felt this haunting tune tug at her heart-strings. This song imparted a sense of freedom, but not without a price. It tasted bittersweet, a chance of release from something demanding, yet something sure to be mourned. As she glided along in the dance, she felt she was poised at a balance. This melody and, indeed, Mamma herself, offered to Jill something new, in exchange for something dear. It was no surprise, then, when Mamma exchanged her hand for a handkerchief, and, with the space between them increasing, the two women reeled freely. Mamma laughed, her fan swinging wild at the end of its cord, until, as the song reached a crescendo, she snatched the fan and snapped it open, to fling it high and low, however the music demanded. At the end of the melody, she stopped to stand suddenly still, fan splayed, her skirts swirling around her, her chin high and eyes closed in reverence.

Jill did the same, breathing hard, shutting her eyes to catch up to her senses. Under the spell cast by Mamma and this gypsy music, her soul ached with fondness and longing. With heightened perception, she heard a whisper on the air. One sentence, in the old Romani, which no one here suspected she might understand...

"You affect the fortunes of not one son, but two."

Standing her ground, her vision muted but her ears listening, Jill waited for more. Through her eyelids she knew the glow of the lantern. Its rays grew cooler. They grew whiter. The beams of the moon. Stella at her mandolin plucked out a new song. A lovers' song. In her crimson hand, Jill still gripped the silk of the kerchief. She felt Mamma's tug, ever so gentle, inducing her to dance again.

Slowly this time, Jill followed along, the steps instinctual now. She danced, and gradually— so gradually— sensed an alteration in the atmosphere. She danced, and only when her curiosity became too compelling did she feel she must open her eyes. The unexpected promise of the night manifested.

The lantern no longer stood on the floor of the forest where Mamma had set it. In its place at the center of the ring lay only leaves in the grass. Moonbeams lit the darkness, and darkened the woodland beyond. Mamma had vanished. The hand that led the dance, the hand commanding the other end of the kerchief, belonged to another.

Nico.

Jill took in the sight of him, stern and striking. The breath caught in her throat.

Yet the music carried them. Neither dancer broke stride. Like *la matriarca* herself, Stella's melody would not be denied. In the Neverland and beyond, Jill had gamboled to the rhythm of her heart. Tonight was no different. Her body followed its own inclinations. And, she reasoned, like an herbalist, one learns when each heart's properties wax the most potent.

Seeping sweetly, Jill's memories of her husband danced into her mind. A gypsy himself, he understood her. He had sent her home, to blend with his people. Under the silver moon, with copper lights in her hair and a vagabond verse in her ears, his wife became one with his heritage. Surely, to mingle thus was his heart's desire.

Moving in the music, Nico slid nearer. He looped the scarf once round Jill's wrist. Then twice. Then a third time. The distance between them eased. Nico wrapped his half of the kerchief around his leather wristlet. With their forearms upheld, connected by the cloth, they swayed together. The forest floor beneath their feet felt springy, easy to navigate. The scent of bonfire tinged the air, the breezes warmed with their vigor. Closer now, the man whose steps mirrored Jill's turned from her side to dance face to face.

He stepped forward. Jill stepped back. Three steps, then she reversed to press toward her partner, and Nico retreated. Like opposing poles of a magnet, to and fro each propelled the other. They took turns at leading, until Nico thrust his bound arm forward, drawing Jill's entangled wrist to her back. He cinched her arm tightly behind her waist. Still, their flesh did not touch; the scarf and the cloth of their clothing kept the two separate, but only just. Refusing to be dominated, Jill led again, this time urging Nico to circle round with her. In his turn, he prevailed, circling in the opposite direction. But when at last he pressed back again, she stepped rearward, one, two, three steps, wide steps, until, steered by his contrivance, her backside bumped up against the smooth, gray bark of a tree.

Stella's love song dwindled, sighed, and died. The night-wood sounds resurfaced, filling the empty air. Stars sparked across the sky. The Mediterranean moon burned above them.

The elder brother stood staring at Giovanni's woman, his sultry, brooding eyes so familiar, his body so near in shape to Giovanni's. So near, in space, to Jill's.

Nico said nothing.

Jill leaned against the tree trunk, conscious of his muscular arm wound behind her waist, holding her firm in his grasp. She murmured, "Tonight, my whip is not at hand."

A night bird fluttered down from the treetops. Nico did not seem to hear it.

"Sir, your silence asks a question."

Like Giovanni's own, Nico's strong jaw was set; his gaze never wavered.

"I am a woman of words, but, this time, I will not answer with them."

He nodded. With his smokey gaze, he seemed to worship her face in the moonlight. Jill imagined that he saw, in its glow, the younger girl who first captured Giovanni's heart. Whatever he envisioned, his earnestness was evident. Here was a gypsy, dark, and handsome, and daring to steal.

Just like his brother.

Withdrawing his grip from her waist, he pulled her arm along with his, by the scarf. He freed his leather brace. He unbound her wrist, too. He held the silk up to dangle between their two faces. Its wine color, like Jill's crimson hand, blanched in this lunar light, as the powers of each appeared to diminish. He watched as she shifted her gaze to consider the kerchief. She knew he could not miss the understanding in her eyes. She recognized the silk's significance. The meaning of this moment was clear to her. In wordless terms, Nico offered a parting, and a joining.

His fingers opened. In silence, he dropped the cloth to the ground.

Ensnared by suspense, Nico allowed himself to bend forward, till their foreheads nearly grazed. He felt his chest swell and fall with his breathing. With both her arms free now, Giovanni's Jill reached back to hold fast to the tree's trunk. Left, right, or forward, he had penned her so that she could not move without touching him. But would she? Was she the flesh and blood woman he wagered, or, like a sorceress, might she turn him to stone? Patience would deliver her answer to his offering.

He was sure of her; he felt his hands shaping the future. He told himself that whether the outcome be truth or be treachery, it did not matter. Either way, he would learn where her loyalty lay. By her own admission, gypsy magic had mastered her, in the past. In the present, in this moment, his own spell worked to defeat the first. He must determine her heart's bent for certain, for Mamma's peace of mind. *La matriarca* agreed on the need to set this trial; beyond that ploy, wisewoman that she was, she left the finale in the hard hands of Fate.

For Bezzi's sake, too, Nico seized upon this chance. Whatever the answer, his brother could not lose by the truth. If Jill failed Giovanni, the heart of Bezzi still beat for him. She, the deserted one, mother of his unknown daughter, deserved to reunite with her lover. Giovanni was assured of his dream of a family, no matter who his faithful mate turned out to be.

Nico believed that any true brother would do as this brother did now. Any true lover would do as he, Bezzi's adorer, felt he must do, tonight.

Pressing ever so close, he tilted his face. Urgently, he offered his lips, to embrace her. He held steadfast and steady, awaiting her answer. He'd learned restraint while handling the mares; he would not cause this beauty to shy. A breeze swept a lock of her hair to brush his cheek, a copper stroke of down. He suppressed a shiver. Slowly, she blinked, and he discerned every strand of her eyelashes. Warm from the dance, the scent of her skin aroused him. Intimate now, and eager, he held his kiss ready, a thumb's width away. The blood rushed in his ears, but, somehow, he thought he heard her heartbeats.

Silently, he counted them. At the sixth, he closed the distance between them. In the very last moment, as her mouth opened to welcome him, when his own lips demanded to press into hers, she surprised him. He had not expected to feel what he felt.

As he intended, she did not shy from him. Smoothly, she turned her head. But she turned her head away. She cast her gaze down, at the forest floor. Like a statue of a goddess, graceful but cold, she held her stance. She refused him. What Nico felt was disappointment.

And more. He was devastated. Realization crashed down upon him. Jill, he now knew, passed his test. She was faithful. He had guessed incorrectly about her...but correctly of himself. The man in the shadows, the dark and dubious stranger who tempted her, was none but Nico. And the man whose name was a weapon? His own name served to sever his integrity. From now forward, his was the name of a knave, synonymous with treachery. Tricks played by fortune made fools of the wisest. Even Mamma had been led astray. Who could have supposed? Who'd have believed that he, brother Nico, would be the one tried, and he be the one who had fallen? With the fresh venom of discovery, he cursed the name of Nico.

Nico was the offender. He was a schemer, plotting to steal a wife from her husband. In the guise of loyalty, he'd masked a will to betray his own brother. This twist was ironic, but telling. He fooled himself in believing that if he possessed this woman, only once— for one hour— in the moonlight— his duplicity signaled a virtue. Loyalty was the trait that Nico Cecco prized most. Only now that her fidelity was proven— for the duration of this wild, shining moment— he coveted Jill not in sham, but in earnest.

Nico fell to his knees. On the mossy ground at her feet, he declared, "Loveliest of women! I know now, with no doubts— you are she whom Giovanni deserves." He seized the hem of her skirt. *"Ti supplico!* On my knees, I offer apology." Still, she stood motionless. On her toes Giovanni's rings shone, and the silver bells of her bracelet hung silenced. He pressed the ruffled red edge of her skirt to his lips, embracing it, fervently. When Nico dropped her gown, the thought pierced him, like the tip of a spear: the law of the cloth remained intact.

He swept up the kerchief, concealing it in his pocket, a sacred object to be revered. As he rose, he stumbled back. He felt her jewel-blue gaze upon him. The sorceress forbore to turn him to stone. Yet— left, right, or forward— he could not move without touching her, if only in his desires. In a cruel curve of Fate, his own gypsy magic had mastered him.

He left her then, a redheaded, red-handed woman— a copper goddess— standing frozen and alone as if he'd set her on a pedestal, in a temple of bright, lunar light.

Supported by the tree, Jill sorted this interchange, wondering at Nico, assessing herself. Without doubt, Nico was a compelling man, and a worthy one. She had delighted in the dancing this evening, as on many another evening, and she savored the romance of Romani life. She could not blame Nico, or even *la matriarca*, for seeking to belay their suspicions. She, too, would have risked as much to ensure her husband's happiness. She would tell Nico so. By tomorrow, the ties that bound this family would prove all the stronger. Neither she nor Nico need bow to shame, nor to regret. As Mamma decreed, Jill was a Cecco.

While she rested, her vacant gaze swept her surroundings. Gradually, within the forest, something summoned her notice. She sensed only that some kind of presence lurked in the woodland. It was foreign, and frightening. At first, Jill's impulse spurred her to flee, back to the camp, back to her clan. In this country, still new to her, courage and curiosity could bring trouble to her troupe. For the good of her family, she'd learned when to set her bravery aside. Yet Jill's feet refused to obey, and she found that she could no more run from this entity than she could run from herself.

As she stared, her trepidation increased. She perceived a figure. Formed of shadow and smoke, slowly, the figure reconciled into silhouette. Measure by measure, this being entered her consciousness. It became human. He was male. Each second, his attributes clarified, as if he drew off a cloak. Tall. Long, dark locks....As his face became flesh, the outline of a brief beard appeared. Black clothing melded this man with the night. Something glimmered at the end of his arm. Seconds passed, and, like a spyglass adjusting to come into clarity, the glimmer resolved into a shape she could identify: a crescent, sharp and barbarous, in place of his hand. Jill gasped.

As her enchantment dissipated, it seemed to bead and drip off, like waterdrops after a rainfall. The reservoir that collected this magic began to fill, with trickles of recognition. As this man's nature manifested, so also did Jill's own. Knowledge returned like a rising tide, as if it surrounded her, inch by inch, spreading its waters to both of their bodies, revealing by increments the twosome that stood in its pooling. She gathered that his was such a power that, in sheer mercy, he revealed himself not in a wave, but a rivulet. When at last he allowed Jill's vision to come to full focus, memories flooded her mind. Her recollections pooled, the ripples smoothed, and the mystical oblivion that obscured her senses sank away, as silt sinks in a river.

The next moment was exquisite. Jill was filled with knowing. She was Red-Handed Jill, of the *Roger*. He was Hook, of her heart.

Her body tingled from her scalp to her toes. Her feet broke free again, and she rushed to him. Claw and all, his arms reached for her, but she no longer ran. She flew. With no shame, no regret, she abandoned her sanctuary of moonlight. Soaring into the woods, she sailed through the danger of darkness to be captured by his black embrace.

Doubled Love

*D*earest wife Mary, my own one, continuing my correspondence…
I now understand why our letters from Wendy arrive so infrequently. It's devilish difficult to hunt down a post box, even on the rare occasion when we pull into port. I shall, however, persist in sending word at every opportunity, and trust to His Majesty's Mail to deliver my missives to Number 14, and into your sweet, loving hands.

I'm pleased to find that I am developing my sea legs. Our voyage has been pleasant, on the whole. Unlike the City's, the weather is temperate. No need as yet to don my greatcoat. Respiring fresh ocean air, I begin to feel fit. I tread the deck when allowed and, with no roof to press me down but the wide sky above me, even my posture has improved. I confess, though, that the example of Doctor Heinrich may influence me there. He is so very proper! I find him in all ways respectable, the more so since he proved his mettle when taxed with the setback we just encountered.

Eager to set eyes on Wendy, we arrived in good condition at the appointed rendezvous spot, where we waited interminable days, or so it seemed to me, who was charged to keep below in my cramped little cabin with the window (porthole) clamped shut. In spite of a quiet room next door which I guess to be vacant, I must share this cabin with the captain's first mate, a chap named Renaud (one doesn't pronounce the final letter d). He's a peculiar lad, spit-and-polished, dour of face, and so lean the sea breeze might tip him overboard. I believe the boy speaks English but refuses to do so, which, despite what one might suppose, serves to make our propinquity less awkward. We have very little in common, after all, and

122

nothing to discuss beyond "What's in the soup?" (I believe it to be some vile form of fish). Once or twice he's poked me in the ribs in the dark of night, startling me wide-eyed with some French accusation or other, which I presume is chastisement for snoring. You know, Mary, that I am not a man who stands on his dignity, yet I do prize my pride. But enough of that for the nonce. I'll not complain when my daughter is in danger.

Anchored off the shore of a rather dull and ill-smelling island, at last we heard the hailing shots of the expected party. Upon their arrival, it turned out to be two parties— two ships, that is. Renaud locked me into the cabin as if I were a child unable to follow the rules. I wasn't allowed so much as a peep out the window (porthole) until late afternoon. I heard nothing all day but the croak of the ship and the nattering of French sailors. The captain and Doctor Heinrich, you see, desired to keep my presence a secret until the most auspicious moment, which was, I must say, when it arrived, quite dramatic, in keeping with Wendy's flair for storytelling. Dullness is banished, but, alas, we are still anchored off the coast of this foul-smelling isle.

I shall explain. When in the fullness of time I clambered up the stairs— a sort of glorified ladder, really— blinded by the light of day, they injected me into a gaggle of French sailors and told me to wait for the captain's signal. This scheme gave me plenty of time to look about while the principals hashed out the details of their dealings. I was so hoping to see our girl. I could hardly breathe for the anticipation, (and the odor of seafaring men), but disappointment quickly gripped me. My dear…she is not here.

Apparently, the parties in question put our girl ashore somewhere, to keep her from her husband. Doctor Heinrich of course presented his case as to his right to reclaim her. While he and Captain LeCrow disputed with the two new arrivals (or rivals ha ha), I got a good, long look at the gentlemen with whom our Wendy keeps company. And now, dearest Mary, to use Wendy's expression, I must caution you: brace yourself.

Listening to their negotiations, I was able to determine that one of the two strange captains postulates that he himself is Wendy's (Jill's, as they call her here) lawful husband. A direct challenge to our presumed son-in-law! Yet I am not convinced. The fellow is not Wendy's type at all, except that he is I suppose exceedingly good-looking, and probably wealthy, and obviously an adventurer. He speaks with an Italian accent. A dark, menacing man, he is muscular in the extreme, which is plainly evident as he wears no shirt but a sleeveless vest. He positively *glows with jewelry— on his arms, his ears, and poured over his head in some kind of gypsy crown. Yes, the doctor has since confirmed that this man— Cecco is his name— is a gypsy, and further, his capture would earn a sizeable bounty from the Italian government. Believe me, at this point I felt quite dazed, but I summoned the lion courage for which you are wont to praise me, for this time was none to give in to weakness.*

And weakness is a tempting retreat when one sets eyes on the other captain. That atrocious claw! I tell you, I shuddered to see it threatening at the end of his arm. He flings it casually about as he speaks, while one wonders in terror when and who he will rend with it. In short, as strong as the impression that man Cecco makes, the Commodore, as I believe is his official title, is dreadful beyond expectation. Tall, fierce, and commanding, this maimed man would be Hook, the legendary pirate Wendy made up, or so our son John would have us believe, and the lothario with whom Wendy ran off to sea in the first place. I am thunderstruck at the daring of our brave, plucky girl!

Although he is clearly an Englishman, one might say much the same of him as the first captain: strikingly handsome, obviously rich, and a swashbuckler. It's the oddest thing, Mary. This buccaneer, this Hook, has the look of some long-lost aristocrat out of his era, something on the order of Charles II., with his antique togs and flowing black hair curling down halfway to his elbows. Commodore Hook impresses one as a person much older than he appears. Our Wendy claims in her letters that she's aged a bit, yet, considering her relative youth, I wonder all the more at her fascination for him. But I am a banker. What do I understand of a young woman's heart? If only she'd stayed home in London, I too should feel less my age!

Well then, as it transpired, Captain LeCrow knew what he was doing when he kept me hidden from sight. The four of them contended in their strange, bantering fashion, (Commodore Hook applied one particular phrase that dropped my jaw and appeared to shock even our Frenchmen), and then, just as LeCrow predicted, once I stepped up to the rail, the tide turned. You could have heard a pin drop, Mary! Those two bold, unbridled pirates goggled at me, and then— they gave in. I am proud to affirm that it is my presence that will fetch our daughter back, wherever they have hidden her. So— well done on the parts of LeCrow and our doctor! And well done on mine, I might say, for venturing forth from our parlor.

I was asked a few questions to verify that I am who I claim to be, and how I came to be here. That man Hook is a shrewd one, aiming those brilliant blue eyes (very much like our Wendy's) and attempting to trip me up. But I know my daughter, and I know at least some of their secrets. It was plain that he himself did not wish to give too much away to the listening ears that surrounded us but, in the end, he seemed satisfied, if irritated.

I then retreated, and a tense and terse conference followed between our son-in-law and the Commodore, an hour or so after which, to our doctor's delight, Hook's ship rattled up anchors and caught the wind, heading wherever our Wendy is concealed. Although our deck is strangely crowded with crewmen for a vessel that isn't going anywhere, I stroll about 'topside' at my leisure now, awaiting our daughter's return with a hopeful heart. That Italian captain hails me, wishing to parley, as I've learned is the term, but LeCrow and Doctor Heinrich steer me away, advising me to keep my distance, until 'Jill' is here to speak for herself.

I've become accustomed to Heinrich's uncivilized visage now, meaning those scars and all, and am given to understand that these marks are badges of honor. Next to those pirates, indeed, he appears wholesome, modest, and tame. I am mystified as to why the other captains refer to him as Doctor Hanover, but changing names seems to be some kind of tradition in the buccaneer community, as our Wendy has demonstrated. Still, I am comforted by Heinrich's concern for Wendy, and his scrupulous handling of a bad situation. Another foreigner, but, on the whole, he does inspire my confidence.

Rest assured that I will write with more news as it transpires. Kiss the dear boys for me, and, soon, I'll kiss our girl on your behalf, too!

Your ever loving,

George

P.S. I heard a ruckus just now and peeked out the porthole (window) and what did I perceive? That Italian captain dropping sails, too, and turning his ship out to sea. All of us here aboard the Lotus *feel much relieved!*

Hook seized Jill in his arms. His lips met hers with force, and any mercy he'd shown as he dissolved her enchantment left him now. Their reunion was too impassioned for restraint, but was by necessity brief.

Bodily, he swept her up and hastened deeper into the wood. He murmured, "Your Romani must not discover me."

As he set her down, Jill declared, breathless, "The news must be wonderful— or terrible— for you to risk coming." He still smelled of stardust. She inhaled the scent of the sky. But she read his intent with her new-restored sense of him, and her smile fell away. "Hanover has dealt us some trickery."

"Indeed. The tidings are dire."

"Someone I love is in trouble." Jill clutched at Hook's shoulders. Beneath her concern, she reveled in the pleasure of touching him. "Did Hanover learn of my marriage to Cecco? Has he challenged Giovanni?"

"How faithful you are to your husband, my dear, in your concern— and in spurning the seduction I was just privileged to witness. One of Cecco's brothers, I presume?"

Jill tossed her head. "Nico was merely testing me. Giovanni's people are as prescient as he claims."

"Then you must apply all caution, now that our thoughts are rejoined. The danger of exposing your duplicity is a risk I had to consider before revealing myself to you."

"But has Hanover injured him?"

"Captain Cecco faces no peril. LeCorbeau was amazed to find him alive, and Hanover was dumbfounded to learn of your wedding. But, stubborn as Hanover is, he persists in the belief that his own marriage to you is the lawful one."

Jill felt relief for her husband but, as she considered, her brow furrowed. "And so, against the revelation that our ceremony was counterfeit, the man comes to claim me."

"As we expected. What we did not expect was his resourcefulness."

"Tell me."

Hook gathered her two hands in his one. "Hanover has found your family."

"No!"

"He rang at the door of Number 14. The good doctor presented himself as a son-in-law. Mr. Darling was persuaded to accompany him to our rendezvous. Even now your father is a guest upon LeCorbeau's ship."

"My plan went awry, then! Father failed to locate the registry in London, to learn of my true union. No doubt Hanover presented the marriage lines LeCorbeau signed."

"Mr. Darling, I find, is credulous. He is as yet unaware that he is a hostage."

"In my letter, I withheld my married name from my parents to shield them should any official inquiry arise. I relied on David to deliver the ship's log to the authorities. But by the Powers, Hook— how could Father be so foolish as to step into the trap of a stranger?"

"You know your father better than I, and you know Hanover better than most. The situation requires quick decision. Shall we suffer Hanover's worst, or shall we surrender to his demands? I warn you, my love, your father's life lies in the balance."

"You would prefer that I stay here, in safety."

"Captain Cecco and I agree. However much we loathe the fact, this choice must be yours, and yours only. For the world, Jill, I would not rule on a question so close to your contentment, yet..." Hook's fine features turned savage. "If I followed my impulse, you'd soon dress in mourning, and live to resent me."

"I cannot hide while Hanover threatens my family."

"Be wary, Jill. Hanover's terms are straightforward: He takes you, or he harms Mr. Darling."

"Poor Father. He has traveled quite out of his world."

"Nor can we presume that Mr. Darling will return to his world— to London and to your family— upon your acquiescence. Doubtless Hanover will keep him as leverage."

"Can we not rescue Father from LeCorbeau's vessel?"

"I have considered every angle. LeCorbeau will not allow us aboard under any conditions. Since his appearance on deck to prove his existence, Mr. Darling will never be free or unguarded. It is no secret that I am a pirate, thanks to your stories. Naturally, your father distrusts me. Even if I held his confidence, I've no means to wrest him away on the sly. I am certain that, pocketed with a lacey handkerchief, LeCorbeau harbors his stiletto. At the first sound of cannon fire, your father's throat will be slit."

Jill's blood chilled, and she shuddered. Yet as she reflected, she found no alternative. She vowed, "Very well. I will return home to the *Roger*."

"Alas, your return to the *Roger* is simply the beginning. Once you choose to cooperate, you shall willingly board LeCorbeau's new ship, *La Fleur de Lotus*. You and your father will be captives of the wealthy and influential Doctor Johann Heinrich. Your 'home' will soon lie in Vienna."

"Worse and worse! With Father to manage, I'll have little opportunity to escape. Nor..." tears of anger burned like pepper in her eyes, "nor might I fly away!"

"Hanover is clever. Even unaware of your powers, he perceives he can shackle you with your sire." Hook's velvet voice lowered, but he could not soften the blow. "Tonight, you must ponder. How much of yourself can you sacrifice to spare your father?"

Determined to fly to her father's aid, Jill had not fully grasped the vileness of her predicament. The truth dawned, and she could not stop her words from wavering. "With Hanover," she conceded, "no half measures will suffice."

"As you have learned to expect, the consequences of our actions catch up to us. With my own ears, I heard you speak the words. You vowed, that fatal day on *L'Ormonde*, that you *would* come away with the doctor."

"In the heat of my triumph! I misspoke as I sent him away. I meant only to mock him." She said, disheartened now, "We face the very fate we strove to divert with my visit to Italy." In her fist, she clenched a colorful fold of her gypsy skirt. "As ever, my stories come true. My own kind of magic. Perhaps I am more Romani than we imagined." Compelling herself to meet the prospect, she stood straighter. "Of course, Hook, you are correct. I must deal with the damage I've done." Their eyes met. "I created the circumstances. I, myself, will effect my father's release."

"We have not a moment to lose." Hook embraced her, but hastily. "Jewel and Tom will escort you and Nibs home in the morning." With a forced, wry smile, he looked her up and down. "I shall advise them to seek out a redhead."

"Speaking of redheads...Nibs requests permission to bring his new sweetheart aboard. She is...her name is Stella. I vouch for her character. Stella is sensible and self-assured, and..." Jill's tone filled with significance. "She is Cecco's own daughter."

"Ah...." Hook lifted one eyebrow. "Your story increases in intrigue. An unexpected turn." Eyeing her, her lover nodded. "In that case, we shall consider the consequence of this new story later. I judge we shall have one day to adapt to this coil. Say your goodbyes, and be ready to fly."

"Jewel has your leave to use fairy dust?"

Hook asserted, "If the girl is in love, she'll find no difficulty winging her way home with Nibs."

Jill looked around the forest, searching for a familiar fairy light. "Where *is* Jewel?"

"I left her with Tom, preparing for the journey. They'll have begun by now."

"But— but how did you find me, without her?"

Hook's grip on Jill's upper arm tightened and, fiercely, he averred, "Do you imagine for one instant that I might not memorize the map of your whereabouts? Before you left me, I knew your dwelling place, and how to find you."

Jill's satisfaction battled with her anxiety. She smiled, half-way.

"You cannot escape from me, my love." Hook shook his head. "Not on the sea. Not on this earth."

The high chime of bracelets broke the still of the night. A whistle came sharp through the darkness, and a laughing voice called, "Sister Jill! We are waiting for a story! Have you danced your way into fairyland?"

"Trinio calls for me." Jill sought his flashy figure in the fringe of the woods. She spoke to Hook over her shoulder. "I come to you, tomorrow." The same nightbird she had heard earlier fluttered among the trees.

When Jill turned again to kiss her lover goodbye, he had gone. She no longer felt his mercy, nor intuited his thoughts, nor sensed even a shred of his presence, and of the first, misty inklings his visit had formed, not even a shadow remained. Yet, this time, *Signora* Cecco could not forget him.

This journal entry is my last from Italy. I do not address it except to myself. I now recall in full who I am. What bliss to be whole again! My life held abundance before, but now, I embrace its true depth.

When Hook flew away, I returned to the camp. I must not exude too much of Hook's half of me, but no way exists to veil the strength that knowing his presence provides me. Mamma's first look at me, the change in her gaze, told me that attempting deception is useless. As I greeted the Padre, *the shrewd eyes under his bushy brows narrowed. His long white mustaches twitched, and he said to me, "I once claimed your boldness was brass,* Signora. *I now see more clearly." His many rings flashed as he pointed his pipe at me. "That red hand is iron." I do honor these canny people. Half of me yearns to remain here. All of me longs for my love.*

Trinio asked for a story. Before taking my place by the fire, I withdrew to the wagon to collect my thoughts. I packed my belongings in my satchel, preparing for morning's departure. Holding up my wedding ring and its companion topazes in the lamplight, I admired their fire. With a sigh both unhappy and honied, I tucked my brass dagger in my sash, hung my whip at my waist, then stepped down the stairs again, into the fragrant night air. My last gathering with our Romani.

I settled on the bench in my usual place, Mamma on my right, Brother Nico at my left. They both held back at first, assessing my new dimension, but a few quick words, and we three agreed. We harbor no resentments. We would each do the needful to guarantee Giovanni's contentment. Nico's only request is that, from now on, I address him as Brother Nico. He wishes to disassociate himself from the man who held doubts of me. In truth, this change is unnecessary, but it soothes the burn of his error, and places a distance between me and the former Nico's new passion. Our earlier scene shapes another story, which, out of respect for him, I'll never tell. Brother Nico remains at my left.

He is drawn to me, and he yearns for Bezzi with years of devotion. Now that I am whole again, I know I'm no stranger to this doubled love. This is the tale I told, my last night, in the firelight, to the troupe of Romani I've come to prize. It is a simple story, requiring few words, and involving the very basics of human emotion. To increase its impact, I told the tale in the old Romani tongue:

"Trinio calls for a story." The people looked to one another in surprise, exclaiming at my choice of language. I raised my crimson hand for quiet. "At the end of my visit, I speak the old words. I find myself to be more tribale *than any of us expected. And so, instead of a tale of the past," I fanned my fingers, "I'll weave a tale of our future."*

"Tonight I met a messenger. With the return of morning light, I too must return, to my home and my husband at sea. I do not doubt that you intuit the bad tidings that trouble my spirit. Yet you also sense that I summon the strength I require to venture into this danger. With Giovanni, and my sons Nibs and Tom, and the sailors of Giovanni's company, I believe we may prevail. Have no fear for sweet Stella. She will be protected. She need not brave the dark seas upon which I must voyage.

"When I arrived here among my new family, Brother Nico advised me that no one should wander this world solo. *I hear you chuckling, and you have good reason. He seems not to heed his own counsel. But the Cecco family is strong; we travel together. We none of us walk in solitary."*

I waved the people back from the center. "Kindly clear a space now in this well-trampled grass, where we've worked and breathed and danced and sung. The trees above bend in the breeze. The fire crackles and the Padre's pipe smoke drifts toward our noses. Here, in our gathering place, I call Mamma Cecco, and Brother Nico, Trinio, Nibs, Stella and Bezzi to come circle round me. Before I must go, we stand all together.

"Trinio, pull out your turquoise scarf. Here is one end for you, and one end for Mamma. This bond is unbreakable. It is the love Giovanni sent along with this cloth; it is the love of my own that I intertwine with its silk as I bind your two hands. Mother and son...you two walk together.

"Nibs, Stella." Nibs adjusted his old orange kerchief. Stella's smile rimmed with dimples. "The family has agreed; you need no longer walk apart. Hold hands, while my own hand, here, bestows my blessings. Should you decide to travel thus forever, you are each no less than your dear other deserves."

I stepped back and addressed Nico, admonishing him. "Brother Nico. I must treat you more harshly." I set my blood-red palm on my whip. "Not that you have caused any harm, nor that you don't deserve company, but because you deny the love of your life." Sternly, I frowned upon him. "Despite your choice, you do not walk alone. No, your partner is Pride." While the people gasped, I loosened my whip, freeing it of its coil. "Like your horses, Brother Nico, you must be herded and handled. As you advised, just a touch of the whip, a mere tickle, can guide a team in the proper direction." I raised my lash. It resounded like a clap as I shot the tip out to snatch and wrap Nico's wristlet.

"I see your indignation at this treatment." The gypsies watched his face darken in a scowl, and they smacked their thighs and chortled. "My lash yanks you in, and...now it drags you toward destiny." I circled him, and soon I'd surrounded Bezzi, too. "The whip wraps you round, the pair of you. As my hands pull it tighter, you both are bound. True, you cannot walk, you cannot wander...but you stand together. As partners, you press close— too close for Pride to fit in between. You conceal stories from one another, truths you've been too proud to share. Together, you've raised a daughter." Stella clasped her hands, her green eyes shining with delight. "More daughters, and more sons, await you. When I take this whip away, when I have flown, the Ceccos' number will not decrease. Another daughter-in-law stands with you, your faithful Bezzi, to match your footsteps along the road." Bezzi, too proud to protest, looked vexed, too, wagging her auburn head, until I freed Brother Nico's wrist of the *whip. His scowl had cleared while I prophesied, his brown eyes turned dusky. He looked adoringly down upon his beloved. He cupped her face in his hands, and, as Trinio whistled and the tribe applauded, he kissed her till she kissed him back.*

I caught Mamma's eye. Her sly smile showed her approval. "So, Mamma," I nodded, "you see that your vision comes true. I do bring a gift, and it is twofold. Red-Handed Jill is the changer of fortunes. I affect the futures of not just your Giovanni— not one son— but two." Mamma laughed in satisfaction, "Brava, brave Jill!" and she flicked open her fan to dance a few steps in the firelight.

I looped the length of my lash. "We have danced, we've heard a story. Come back to the fire and be glad of our company, for tomorrow this night will be memory." I bunched my fingertips at my lips, as Giovanni does so often for me, full of love and fidelity, and I flung my kiss winging among our people. Among our tribe, among our family.

My eyes sting with tears of grief. No matter how far I wander, whether I end in Vienna, or I sink some far day in the sea, I will wish—

"Jill, my lovely one," Mamma whispered as she pulled back the curtains of her bunk.

Startled, Jill stood to spin round and answer, "Mamma! I hope the scratching of my pen didn't disturb you."

"No, no, it is my thoughts that disturb me. I have something important to say to you, before the morning light, before you must leave us."

Mamma slid from her bed to stand in her nightshift, comfortably plump, her long dark hair in a braid. The coziness of the caravan held the two women, its bright colors muted in lamplight, soft surfaces dulling their voices. Rifling the skirts that hung on her clothes peg, Mamma unhooked the cord of her fan. Turning to Jill, she said, "I need not consult the cards to see the peril you must enter. It is that doctor, yes? He it is who menaces the happiness of my Jill and Giovanni."

"*Sì*, Mamma." Jill saw no point in disguising the danger. "I can no longer hide. I began this trouble, and it is I who must fight him."

"With a woman's weapons. Yes, I understand. This is why I offer what help I can." Mamma spread her fan open, displaying its beauty, the little white bird on its branch of exotic flowers, inlaid on a background of crimson. "As I told you, a fine lady once owned this fan."

Solemnly, Jill nodded.

"This plaything is elegant, yet it is also a tool. The lady applied it to hide her emotions, to mask her intentions, perhaps, or to display them— a tap here, and a flutter there. She may have used this fan to seduce, or to bend a man to her will. She exchanged it, this female shield, for the good fortune my grandmamma promised. My *nonna* handed it down to my mother, and she to me. The time has come for me, myself, to bestow this gift upon a daughter." Carefully, with little wooden clicks, she closed the fan's folds, and she kissed it.

"You have witnessed my use of this tool, and I've seen you work *your* wiles, my daughter, my Jill. You do not play a tune like Stella, but if ever a woman might play upon the power of *this* instrument, you are she." Mamma gathered Jill's hands and placed the fan in them, enfolding them in her own warm clasp. "Remember. As women, our power lies in mystery. Keep this fan close to you. I need not look into your palm to know that the news you received tonight, while dealing a blow, also redoubles your strength. From today forward, you make your own fortune."

Mamma's magic prickled in the tips of Jill's fingers. "Mamma, I receive this token, with gratitude. I accept your lesson. We women must work together, to protect one another."

"A wise young woman once told me: 'A cunning counterpart calls for more cunning.' You and I are simpatico." Mamma leveled her shoulders, standing proud, and she decreed, "To your own sons, you are *la matriarca*."

Jill's throat closed with emotion. When, at length, she could speak again, she uttered, "I ask no higher compliment."

"A daughter *will* come to you, perhaps of your blood, perhaps of your spirit. You will know, Jill, as certainly as I know tonight. You will recognize the girl who next requires this kind of tool, this… shelter."

With ceremony, Jill looped the fan to hang from her own girdle, according this heirloom a place of honor against her gypsy skirts. "And now, Mamma, I have a gift to give *you*." From her satchel, Jill withdrew a small crystal vial. She held it up in the lamplight, where the contents caught the flame, the little sharp shards glowing golden. Mamma's face lit up, too, as she inhaled in admiration.

"I bring you magic from my Island. You must keep it with you always, and you must never, never uncork the phial." As Mamma's eyes reflected its light, Jill laid the vial in her hand. "Whether this glitter is hidden or visible, it will act as a beacon. While you possess it, Nibs and Stella will be able to find you, no matter where the troupe travels."

Mamma beamed. She breathed, "Such a treasure! Be assured of it, I will keep this beacon safe."

"I hope one day to make use of it myself, and return with them to tell you new tales of Giovanni."

With her gypsy mystique, *la matriarca* held silence, as handsome and intriguing as ever her sons had appeared, making Jill wait to hear her pronouncement…

"We will be expecting you."

Mamma spread her arms wide. The two women embraced, and held each other tight. More talk was unnecessary. Woman to woman and mother to mother, no words— in Italian or in the Romani— could express their true depths of devotion.

Reflections

At last, the lookouts hailed the deck, with joyous shouts in both English and French. Captain Cecco dashed to the mizzenmast, where he scurried up the shrouds, too swiftly to burn his hands on the hemp and just as agile as in his days as a crewman. He meant to meet Jill at the earliest moment, in her own element, in midair.

She came rushing toward him, her gypsy skirts flailing in her wake, and, as the commodore informed him, her long hair streaming in a bright shade of copper. With her scarlet hand, she saluted the cheering sailors on the *Roger* before circling Cecco's perch on the *Lady*. As she fondly recalled of times past, he extended his arms in invitation, his bracelets chiming with music and sparkling gold in the sunshine. She descended into his welcome. In his warm, loving hold, she felt his chest vibrate with his emotion. *"Ciao, Bellezza!"* So eager was her husband to greet her, he had not heeded the lookouts' report.

The subject of their heralding became obvious to all, as, led by Jewel's streak of blue fairy light, Nibs and Tom escorted a young woman between them. Tom bore two packs on his shoulders, and over Nibs' back hung his own pack and a mandolin. Back at the gypsy camp, once Stella's wish to travel was approved by the *Padre*, Nibs had acquainted her with the circumstances of Jill and Cecco's marriage. The young woman reflected on this eccentricity in her levelheaded manner, attributing it to the intricacies of piracy, with which she was not yet familiar. She would deal with her concern for her father's happiness another day; her first priority was to get to know him.

Besides, to follow a fairy while winging over the ocean made other nonconformities pale in comparison.

Their party approached the ships, floating lower. With a gentle precision, Nibs guided his Stella to touch down on the deck. The brothers supported her as she panted, recovering her respiration with gulps of salt air. The journey had been a long one, but the girl's cheeks flushed with pleasure, even as her feet felt for security on the pitching of the boards. After the marvels of flight, she looked around her, collecting first impressions of her papa's ship and his people.

Nibs allowed her these moments as he shrugged off his burdens and tightened his old, orange kerchief. Jewel sank to alight on Tom's shoulder. She secured herself there with a grip on his collar. Stamping to the gunwale, Tom spat a bug from his mouth, then accepted a mug of cool ale and a grin from Guillaume. Bowing, the French mate offered a feather to Jewel, who jingled her thanks for his gentlemanly gesture, and fanned her face with it. When Nibs judged his beloved was ready, he bent to whisper in her ear.

He pointed aloft. Beneath her wavy bangs, Stella's gaze traveled up the slope of ropes. Her dimples disappeared as she stole her first glimpse of her father. In a rare lapse of poise, the girl dropped her mouth open, and she stared, taking in the near-mirror image of Nico. She seemed unaware that every man aboard these two sister ships— except for her papa— stood gawping at her arrival.

Jill assured herself of the young lady's safe landing, and then, smiling, she cautioned her husband. "Giovanni, you must hold tight to the shrouds." Tenderly, she broke the news. "I have much to say of your family, and I kept a journal to tell you more. But first, I bring to you…a dream come true."

He answered, sadly, "Your presence is my dream, *amore*, and yet we must part again."

"While I am away, here is someone to bear you company. Someone from your homeland. Look down and behold her." Jill clasped his arm against the chance that, with the coming revelation, he might let loose of the webbing and tumble. "My dear…that bright gypsy girl is Nibs' sweetheart. Her name is Stella. And…" She waited for her husband's gaze to meet hers again, questioning her. "She is your very own daughter."

They hung in the sky with the *Lady's* sails furled below them. The mast swung with the waves, side to side, like a slow, steady metronome. The seconds ticked past. Cecco's brown eyes held Jill's, growing ferocious with hope. She nodded. "I speak to you truly, Giovanni."

The next moment, the lookouts jolted at their posts, spinning round to identify a fresh source of commotion. A stream of loud, foreign words gushed forth in a torrent. Restored to her spirits, Stella laughed and blew kisses, for— from his perch in midair, in buoyant, joyous shouts of Italian— Captain Cecco hailed the deck...and his daughter.

The last day of Jill's freedom flew quickly by. After depicting the gist of her visit in Italy, she left her journal with Cecco, with the two private entries cut out and secreted. Jill had addressed most of her pages to her husband, and now that she must be absent, her written record would reflect a fuller picture than time allowed her to paint for him today. The Japanese fan he recognized instantly. Watching Jill snap it open brought a smile to his lips, and memories too numerous to relate of *la matriarca*'s maneuvers. "You see, lovely one, it is as I predicted. My mother and my wife are simpatico."

Jill answered, warmly, "We are Ceccos." She kissed him, and sent a smile to Stella.

Yet she had read the anger in his eyes, the outrage that he could not spare her from Johann Hanover's machinations. He reminded her of points on which he judged she should be wary, and informed her of Mrs. Hanover's plans to travel to Vienna with the surgeon too, and that he'd granted leave to Pierre-Jean to serve as the girl's guardian. Too soon, Jill bid her husband *addio*, leaving him in the company of her sons and his daughter. All four of these loving ones expressed their apprehension at the ordeal that loomed in her future, hoping that, somehow, her coming tribulations would pass quickly, too.

Now, at home again in the luxury of Hook's quarters on the *Roger*, surrounded by candles and veiled by red velvet draperies, Jill was bathed and comfortable. The cabin held the familiar scents of lavender and tobacco. On her tongue lingered the warm taste of rum, shared in the renewal of intimacy with her lover. Wrapped in her sky-blue robe, she stood by the daybed and packed the last of her necessities into her satchel, in preparation for the morrow's parting.

Hook glanced down at the contents. He too wore a robe, maroon in color and fulsome in texture, with buttons like gems. His claw hung on a hook of its own by the bedstead. He had not left Jill's side since he escorted her up the companionway and through his brass-plated door.

Dropping a purse of silver coins in the bag, he observed, "A gown and tunic, lace and linens, Lelaneh's herb tea, and…gloves."

"I am too familiar with Hanover's sensibilities. He will bid me to cover our blood mark. This adventure may be a long one, so I shall fight him only on the matters that most vex me."

"My respect to *la matriarca* for arming you with her fan. I hold a recollection of just such an ornament from my life in London. A thing of beauty, yet its crimson color in your right hand, despite any glove's covering, will indicate your marking. A double reminder, reflecting our dual strengths."

"As Mamma described it, this fan is not just a token of femininity, but a tool for a woman's ploys and protection. Seemingly harmless, its power is wielded in secret."

"A sage lady. And although I cannot envision Hanover allowing your whip, I see you will bear your brass knife. If only the solution to our dilemma were as simple as gutting him, as you practiced to such beneficial effect upon Lean Wolf."

Jill convulsed as she remembered that struggle, the smell of the blood that had covered her, and the assault on herself that led up to it. She set her teeth in determination. "With patience, I shall learn how to deal with Hanover, too. He will lay down the rules; I will try to subvert them. And, perhaps, I might gain access to the doctor's medicines. We have identified his weapon. I may use it first."

"Remember that his pharmacy is only one of his armaments." With a grim look, Hook forbore to elaborate. He knew Jill was aware of the physician's armory— his relentlessness, his wealth, his conviction of his virtue, and, perhaps the most dangerous device, his intimate knowledge of the female physique. "He will still be smarting from the drugging you gave him before we tossed him off our ship. No doubt he will restrict your movements, within and without his household."

"I expect it will be so." Still regaining her sense of the sea's moving surface, Jill swayed as the ship crooned and shifted. "And Austria itself is new territory for me."

"As was Italy, and yet you prevailed. I presume the home he has established is secure, but Heinrichhaus cannot be a fortress. Take your bearings. Look about you for means of escape," her lover advised, "and be watching for a sign, for the captain and I shall undertake to discover some means to extract you, together with your sire."

Indignant, Jill spun to glare at him. "It is enough that I am forced to look after Father. I forbid you to enter territory in which you might be clapped in irons and executed! Do not encumber me with that kind of care."

Hook fixed her with his stare. "Since we have entered the province of forbidding, Jill, I might mirror your words, forbidding you to sail off with Hanover— and your father and his foolishness be damned!"

Her nostrils flared. In a blind fury, she shot out her crimson hand. He caught her wrist to hold her fast, his five fingers digging into her flesh. Vehemently he avowed, "I know you, Jill. I have *not* forbidden your decision. I merely voice the thought that you yourself have churned, over and again, in your mind."

He read her too well. Jill looked away, but now she vented her ire on its proper cause. "I apologize, Hook. I am frustrated by my father. He dashed our plans, falling victim to this monster. And I must pay for his error."

"We are all of us paying." Hook's grip on her wrist slackened. "Just as Hanover schemed it should do, the presence of Mr. Darling causes complications we cannot foresee."

"If not for Father, my Island tigress would soon spring to life." A tinge of green ringed her irises. "My eyes would burn murderous, and I'd slash Johann Hanover's throat!"

"Should that chance offer, you must seize it. Your first kills lie behind you, and the blood-rage will no longer blind you to reason."

"At least I needn't strive to protect Father's life. Without him, the doctor holds no power over me. But," Jill believed in honesty. She refused to hoodwink herself as to the extent of her dilemma. "I myself will live at Hanover's mercy. Until I gain the upper hand, I must do as he wills— and he wills to possess me."

Hook's lip curled. "While I can stretch to Captain Cecco's advantage, I find Doctor Hanover's demands testing my tolerance. Even more now than on the day that we captured him, the role of 'gentleman' he plays disguises the depths of his depravity."

"I cannot think of him as a reality, Hook." Jill shut her eyes, which had returned to blue. She rubbed her temples. "I accept the truth, but I must make believe I am in a story, as I did when a child."

"As we both know, childhood's demise need not be the end of pretend. In this circumstance, in fact, I recommend the use of your imagination." Hook's aspect grew darker. "I trust, however, that you will not employ your narrative powers in search of a solution. Even if Hanover permitted you an audience to enchant, we have witnessed the risks of telling your own tale."

"Indeed," Jill agreed, grimacing at her folly. "My arrogance led me to bait Hanover with words. I have thought through the possibilities, but far too many complications are involved, and I am in no frame of mind to retell my story with safety. It is action that is required. As you advise, I promise to remain alert for opportunity."

She caught sight of herself in the long oval looking glass on the open door of the wardrobe. Cecco's mother kept only a small mirror in her wagon and, although the shade of Jill's hair was accepted unreservedly by Hook and Cecco and the two ships' companies, her reflection as a redhead was still strange to her. And another, subtler change was at work as well.

Again, Hook read her thoughts. He stood at her back, and they both gazed at her image, framed in the glass: her womanly figure swathed in blue brocade, her eyes of forget-me-not, and her pirate king of her tales looming, dark and tall, behind her. "Yes, my love," he affirmed. "Your experience is still shaping you. You are no longer the girl who came of age in my arms, nor yet the young woman who battled so bravely for the captaincy of the *Roger*. A daughter, a sister, a storyteller. Wife, mother, mistress...and murderess. As you observe today, you are a woman who applies her wit and her talent to vanquish adversity. You are she who holds the hearts of many men, and you are the seasoned ideal of their commanders. From blonde to copper, and from innocence to awareness. Changes, in my opinion, that increase my lady's fascination." He clasped her crimson hand, and, with the fervor of his esteem upon his lips, he kissed her palm. His own senses mirrored the excitement his touch roused in her.

As he held her hand in his, she turned from her reflection to admire him. Lifting his hair from his temple, she noted the fine lines at the corner of his eye. Surely they were deeper today than the day they first met? "And yet, we met only a short while ago..."

"You have learned, I think, not to trust in Time." He smiled, causing the creases to deepen. "Yet even as we alter, we are matched. Together, we have crafted a handsome pair."

Jill watched him in the glass as he moved toward the wardrobe. Hook himself receded as his image enlarged there. The flickering light of the hanging lantern illuminated her lover as, with his single hand, he drew a crimson sash from a drawer. Jill recognized that swath of fabric, and felt her heart jump a beat.

Returning to her side, he laid the scarf in her satchel. "Hide your sight beneath this sash, and you may summon me to mind. I will be with you at any moment you require me— in fantasy, if not in the flesh."

Leery of coming encounters with the enemy, Jill felt the effect of his implication course through her being. Following that wave, she felt the heat of relief. "Once upon a time, and not long ago, your magic transformed a love scene. With or without this blindfold, you will work that spell again." She lured him close, her elegant robe no barrier to his body. "I only hope to return home to you, the same woman who left." As he gathered her into his arms, she sighed. Here, within the strength of Hook's hold, was where she felt most secure.

Yet she drew back as, negating the wish she expressed, he shook his head. "Of one thing I am certain. We cannot help but change through our experiences, and neither ever, nor never, will we be the same Hook and Jill who are joined here, together, this night."

A dire premonition seized Jill in its grip. "Time is a trickster, but there is no turning it backward."

"Not even were it desirable to do so. Every moment, we become more ourselves, and the richer for our difficulties. Do not dread the unexpected; we are helpless to prevent it. As with any vessel we happen upon at sea, you must seize the prize it presents."

"Aye. Experience itself is my treasure." Jill reflected on the adventures that had led to this wisdom. It was Hook who had spurred the girl Wendy toward maturity. As she cherished this memory, she was moved to appreciate her lover's appearance in the candlelight, his trim black beard and chiseled cheekbones framed by the flow of his hair. She touched his earring, discerning with her fingertips the intricacy of its filigree. She had removed her own gypsy jewelry, and her wedding ring, and neglected to don the band of emeralds Hook had bestowed upon her. At her ears hung the golden crescents she favored. Her other treasures she left in their drawer in the wardrobe, where these earrings would soon join them. Her pirate plunder. She glanced at the mirror again, to glimpse Hook's head tilting down toward her own glowing face, with the backdrop of the crimson curtain behind them. This sense of intimacy with him, too, she had learnt to value as one of her winnings.

She said, "I've tucked a few diamonds in my bag to employ in extremity, but most of my cache will remain here in safety. After we worked so hard to wrest those stones from Hanover, I should hate to see him reclaim them."

"Ostensibly, as *Herr Doktor Heinrich*, Hanover has rebuilt his wealth and established himself with the nobility in Vienna." Hook cut her a look. "I believe that, at Heinrichhaus, he will keep you in style."

"He will *try* to keep me. He knows my weakness for jewels." Jill shared his wicked smile. "I do hope he intends to indulge me."

As always, the subject of plunder prompted a throb in her vitals. The feeling mounted, and she allowed herself to revel in it, knowing how few moments were left to her in Hook's embrace, in his bed, on this ship she called home. Intuiting her mood, he encouraged her. His sapphire-blue eyes brightened, and he was keen to kindle the flame the mere thought of pirates' prizes inspired in his Jill. Yet they both knew she did not require the sight and the feel of jewelry. All she craved was collected in this rich vision of the man standing before her.

"Indulge me now in yourself, Hook, so that while I'm held hostage, I may hold tonight's memory as my golden trove."

Her encouragement was unnecessary. Already, he was loosening his robe. As she slid from hers, Hook set the satchel aside. He moved a candelabra closer to the wardrobe, the mirror there duplicating its light so that the last of the shadows were banished. Their flesh blazed in the yellow rays. On the fabric of the couch each satin medallion shone, to be doused as they tossed their robes upon it.

But instead of reclining there, Hook guided Jill to stand before the mirror, her beauty fully unveiled to their gazes, with the majesty of his own physique manifest behind her. Bending to set his lips at her cheek, he spoke to her, his words resonating in her ear. As if invoking a magic spell for this parting, too, he incanted, "Whenever you seek me, my love, only look in the glass. Where you see yourself, there will I be reflected." Their eyes met in the mirror, alike in shape and in tint at all times, and, at this moment, alike in intent.

With searing kisses, he roved from her shoulder to her jaw, still watching her reflection as his attentions appeared to make her skin tingle. He raised his damaged arm to caress her, slowly, with the satiny patches of his scar-ridden skin. He traced the seam across her throat, naked now with no necklace, then he circled her breasts, then the soft mound of her abdomen. The indigo ink of his mermaid, another likeness of Jill's figure, swirled in tattoo along his forearm. For one instant, she burned in his flesh as sharply as the day she was impressed there. Jill's arm quivered as if she felt it, too. To steady her, he framed her legs with his own, firm with strength as he braced her body against his, the heat of each rising.

Observing the once-hidden kiss in the corner of her mouth, he accepted its invitation, lingeringly, while he pressed the wreck of his wrist lower, against the point of her pleasure. He listened as, through those lips, she gasped at the touches she'd awaited while away. The room was warm, and they each appreciated how, relaxed at first in the comfort of their quarters, the rose-colored crests of her breasts rose taut under his stimulation, and both lovers felt the onset of her eagerness. His single hand, bedecked with gems, shot facets of color to the glass. He stroked her tresses, a new hue to their sight, but still the same texture to his touch. He pulled a few strands to cascade down her shoulder, playing upon the locks at her breast, setting her nerves all afire. Mirroring his movements, she reached back with her pale hand to tangle in his hair, sleek and shining as it tossed back the light. Turning her head, but not her gaze from their reflection, she shared her kisses with his curls.

She stroked his interrupted arm, from the bulk that shaped his biceps to his stump, until he guided his staff between her thighs. With gentle movements of his hips and his wrist, he urged her with just enough play. In tandem, he and his mermaid applied a steady pulse of pressure for long, melting moments as he moved behind her, until in the fullness of time she trembled and sighed, never closing her eyes but always memorizing this image, this instant, this amity. As her knees weakened, he shifted to uphold her, and the imprint of his arousal at her backside hastened the next rush of her rapture, resurging more forcefully as— indulging her delights— with his eyes, his arm, and his focus, he prolonged it.

While her giddiness eased, their matching smiles became visible in the glass. She stepped to the side to behold the reflection of his body, too, sculpted with muscle, his chest fringed with black. Before hiding his manhood in her hand, she treasured up the sight of him, and then she held him, and caressed him, and knelt down on the cushion of the carpet, and when he angled to face her, they both watched in the glass as he slid into her kisses. Now neither could see her tongue, but both felt it. She pulled his jeweled hand to cup her chin, prompting him to rub his thumb along her lip, adding his own touch to her strokes, intensifying the pitch of his sensation. He and she watched his chest swell as his respirations came deeper and faster, and with his eyes he adored her as she adored him, and with his voice he called her, exhaling her name and spending his treasure.

Together in the glass, they lavished their gazes upon one another while he recaptured his breath. He drew her up to embrace her, face to face. This kiss was an abiding one, deep and desiring, exchanged with open lips and open eyes, with not so much as an eyelid to blind themselves this time, so that in the months to come, each might conjure the other's face, flavor, and touch at any time and any place and any extremity to which Fate brought them while it forced them apart.

Hook swept his prize up in his arms then, and carried her to his four-posted bed, where softly he laid her— encompassed by bed-clothes but unshrouded to his gaze. He stretched out beside her, disdaining to cover her with anything but himself. With his fingers cradling her cheek and her palm at rest on his jaw, the couple bore witness to one another in the illumination of lanternlight, two lovers parting soon, and filling their coffers for recollection.

At home in the luxury of their quarters, surrounded by candles and veiled by the drapery, inhaling the musk of their coupling, Hook and Jill lay bathed and comfortable in their love.

"James Hook…" She spoke low, her clear voice reflecting distress yet to come. "No matter what I must do to survive, I will see you in my soul." She had to blink, but begrudged it. She set her blood-red hand over his heart. "I vow to return home to you."

"Jill Red-Hand," he murmured in that glossy voice that elated her, and soon might elude her, "you are pulled from my hold, but never from my soul." Still gazing in her eyes, he asserted, "You will do what you must, and I will do what I can."

He made love to her again, while the light burned. And then, finally, her vision failed. His handsome, hardened features softened, and blurred. Jill wasn't blinkered by his scarf, this time. It lay packed in her satchel, awaiting her need. This time, her lover's looks were obscured by emotion, for it was the scald of tears that hid his visage. After tomorrow, she could not truly view him until, on some distant day in the future, she came home to him. On that day, their gazes would meet again, and their arms, and their lips, and he would escort...whomever she had become...up the companionway, and back through his brass-plated door.

But for Hook and his Jill— despite the light and the looking glass— that time was unforeseeable. And it was, oh, so far away from today.

Fateful Exchanges

With victory in reach, the anxious figure of Captain LeCorbeau paced the deck in his short, hasty steps. He wished to see Hook and his pirates dwindling in the distance as soon as possible. His intention was to make a quick and insincere promise to meet again in one year, then drop sails and fly.

The *commandant* swiveled to draw a bead on Doctor Heinrich, ensuring that the man was behaving himself at the stern. Applying all his persuasive powers, LeCorbeau had induced his partner to await the bride there, where Olivier de Beaumonde stood sentinel, solemnly pledged to keep the physician stowed behind the mizzen. Enough that Papa Darling was nearly swooning to greet the *femme fatale* he'd begotten. The French captain desired to avoid any spectacle that might lengthen his voyage by so much as a minute.

Next, his jaded gaze sought the *Red Lady*'s dinghy as it rowed his direction to deliver the physician's daughter and a deserter, the fair Pierre-Jean. Disappointed that his beloved Guillaume had not rejoined them at the last moment, the mighty spirit of DéDé LeCorbeau flagged. He drew his hanky from his sleeve to tamp his nose. As far as he could see, however, all other arrangements were in train, and the cocky *commandant* resurfaced to abandon his drowned, bedraggled hopes. Shooing Renaud, he commanded, "Everything is in order, my boy. Now scurry down and prime our, eh…package, for Commodore Hook." With *Le Lotus*' hatch flung open to the lower deck, gaping in expectation, the captain braved a smile again. Assuming an official air, he hailed the *Roger* for his last lie to Hook. That brave smile turned sly. The time of his waiting was stretched to its end.

In due course, Pierre-Jean, sworn to serve, followed Mrs. Hanover and her pale green skirt up the ship's ladder, she sheltering the sling that contained the slight weight of her baby. The young woman was even quieter than usual and, as Pierre-Jean supported her during the crossing, he felt the trembles of her apprehension. Apprehensive himself, he was unsure what attitude to expect from his old shipmates as he boarded LeCorbeau's new vessel. With Mrs. Hanover behind him, he hung back until the few men he knew in this crew met his china blue eyes to grin at him. Clearly, they believed the truth: he'd chosen to sign up with the pirates for this girl's sake. Also obvious was that they believed what *appeared* to be true: he had won the girl, and saved her from slavery. Pierre-Jean was gratified to be entrusted with Mrs. Hanover's welfare. Even so, he recalled the warning with which Captain Cecco admonished him, months ago. The young Frenchman could not credit that this young woman might be the death of him, but he understood that he himself was the one who might be enslaved.

Heartened by his former mates' greetings, Pierre-Jean returned them. He felt relief spring again when Mrs. Hanover's father, the formidable physician, appeared condescending and contented, but made no move from the stern to repossess her. The look in her eyes told her escort that she, too, welcomed this reprieve. Before the *Red Lady's* boat shoved off for home, the young Frenchman saw Renaud drop a leathern bag into it. The pouch chinked as it landed in the boat's bow with what must be the last half of LeCorbeau's tribute, destined to be shared among the pirates. Collecting their baggage, Pierre-Jean and his charming charge trailed after not Renaud whom he expected, but an unfamiliar officer, who would settle the guests into cramped quarters. Just before he jogged down the stairs, Pierre-Jean followed Mrs. Hanover's gaze, sent afar to the *Red Lady*, acknowledging the distant but vigilant hulk of Mr. Yulunga. As a gesture of farewell to his little woman, Yulunga touched his thumb to one of the pair of earrings he wore, the golden set rejoined as the pair of lovers divided.

Aboard the *Roger*, the pirate king and his queen stood on the prow of their flagship, Jill in her full-skirted amber satin and Hook in his leonine bronze. Beneath the brim of his hat, Hook's eyes narrowed. "I see that LeCorbeau has deserted his berth by the islet to lie in open water. He intends to complete our business and escape at the earliest opportunity."

"He trusts us no more than we trust him." In these, her final minutes of safety, Jill cast her gaze across the diminishing distance between here and her future. "His anchor is already catted. It sounds silly, I know, but I am disappointed to find that those few minutes of raising anchor, within sight of you, are lost to me."

Hook turned upon her his full blue regard. "My love, as we determined last night, we can never lose sight of one another. The sooner you sail, the sooner I shall view you face to face again."

Gravely, she smiled. "I reflected upon that principle all evening, and I am convinced of it." Again, she looked to the ship she was destined to join. "Just as you described her, Commodore, *La Fleur de Lotus* is a graceful vessel. And I cannot refute your conclusion. That Englishman aboard *is* my father." Across the way, George Darling yanked his handkerchief from his pocket and waved it with vigor, bright white against his black banker's coat. Upon Jill's affirmation, Hook turned to signal to the helmsman, and the *Roger* continued on her course, ghosting closer to LeCorbeau's ship and to the fateful exchange to be made with her.

Mr. Darling could be seen hurrying down the deck, seeking *Le Lotus'* closest point to the *Roger* as it neared. He cupped his mouth, calling out, "Wendy, dear girl…I have come for you!"

Above the shouts of the deck hands and the screech of island birds as they soared round the sails, she could hardly hear his words, but she recognized his mannerisms. He stopped to stand clutching the rail of the French privateer, his elbows up and his expression as eager as her youngest brother Michael's. Like her mother's before her, Jill's heart bruised to see him looking as brave and as innocent as her pack of Lost Boys. She gazed his way tenderly, and while the ships drew together, she lifted her crimson hand to answer his greeting.

She saw him start. His face turned a deep shade of pink as the full effect of her bloodstain assaulted his eyes. Jill's smile ebbed as she ached with the irony. She had believed she might never see her sire again, yet here he turned up, misguidedly, rushing in to defend a woman who enjoyed all the protection she'd ever need— until he thrust *himself* into danger. Honored and irritated, she slid her red fingers back into Hook's welcoming grip, sending her father a kiss with her unblemished hand.

The commotion of furling sails and clicking pawls filled these last minutes. At length, Mr. Smee stamped across the forecastle and touched his forehead in salute. "The chair is prepared, Sir, and the last crate is ready to hoist." Behind his spectacles, his saddened look alighted on Jill. He sighed with regret. "I'm that sorry to be saying goodbye, Lady. But don't you be fretting. That Frenchy may think he holds the winning hand now, but I'll be seeing to the commodore, and we'll both see you sailing back to us, once you've settled Hanover's hash." Smee smiled his encouragement, and she slipped into his hearty hold, kissing his rough, red cheek in return.

While the *Roger*'s sailors were bustling to haul up the canvas, Jill had closed her eyes to listen to the sounds of her men at work all around her, and the sighs of the ship as she eased off her labors. But now, the atmosphere aboard felt subdued as the chores reached completion and the men wondered what might next befall their lady. Their eyes shifted with unease. Remembering the tangles caused by the privateer and the physician, they mistrusted this maneuver. But, in obedience to the commodore, all arrangements were ready, and their pirate queen conceded to herself that her time had run out.

As Jill seized her final breath of freedom, Hook wrapped her round with his velvet-sleeved arms. They shared a last, lingering embrace. To starboard, the *Red Lady* rolled on the swells, waiting. Jill sought the figure of her lawful husband, and there he stood, reassuring her with a nod and a kiss from his fingertips. She caught up the red fan from the sash at her waist, flourishing it for his benefit. Captain Cecco laid his hand on his heart, and the pirate queen, with a final squeeze of Hook's fingers, turned away from both her true lovers, to make the best of her next adventure, on the voyage toward Vienna.

Smee escorted Jill to the gangway and the bo'sun's chair. He seated her, securing her with care, even in the knowledge that, in any exigency, she could save herself with flight. This ritual of attentiveness was another excuse to loiter by her side, and, he knew, as much a comfort to her as to him. He settled her satchel on her lap, offering her the handle of her little wooden travel desk filled with parchment, quills, and ink. As she had confided to him, she intended to keep a log of her journey and write up her new stories, and even, with luck, to send letters. With the lady and her accoutrements secure, Mr. Smee laid his big, warm hand on her shoulder. His Irish lilt became husky with feeling. "May the wind be at your back, lass." He stepped back, his spectacles glinting in the sunshine. "Safe home."

She held tight to her parcels. Smee hollered out his command, and the cables creaked through the pulleys as the chair rose up above the height of the railing. The yardarm swung Jill over the slash of sea between ships. Her stomach lurched with the lift and the glide, not unlike her first flight, but missing the joy of it. The wind ruffled her skirts and cooled her ankles. Jill watched her own sailors waving farewell, but she averted her eyes from *Le Lotus*. Soon enough, her view would be full of nothing but this new ship. Longing to rejoin her loved ones, she filled her heart with the sight of Hook standing firm on the forecastle, grim but proud; beyond him on the *Lady*, Cecco jumped up on a cannon, gripping the braces as if, in each hand, he strangled a foe.

As her toes touched the dry boards of the French privateer, two of LeCorbeau's men bowed. *"Bienvenue, Madame."* They relieved her of her burdens and assisted her to rise. She didn't search for her second husband. Instead, her father appeared by her side. "At last," he said, his voice strained from the wait, and he took her in his arms. Denying her surroundings for just a bit longer, she nestled her face in his shoulder. With too much to say to one another, father and daughter held silence. Reminders of her girlhood home struck Jill with force. The wool of his jacket, the aroma of his pipe…his familiar grip, both shy and paternal. She wove her arms around his middle, and stayed there. Here stood one burden the French sailors could not lift for her.

The yardarm swung over once more, with the last crate full of lotus petals netted like a pendant, to be lowered into LeCorbeau's hold. After some moments below decks, the block and tackle rose again to sweep home. Jill did not watch, nor did she need to look back to the *Roger*. She felt Hook's regard following her. At this moment of parting, his concentration on her heart was uninterrupted. The echo of her feelings bounced back to her; he perceived the mixed blessing of this reunion with her sire. The ships drifted apart. Men's feet pattered over the boards, orders were uttered in French, sails dropped and snapped. Growing more distant, the communion between Hook and Jill thinned. Still, her heart sensed him, as Hook sensed herself. Until, in an instant, the thread of their netting broke.

Resigned to separation, Jill lifted her head from her father's shoulder to take her bearings. Time, with its inescapable capers, must have passed faster than she noticed. *Le Lotus* had moved well away; the *Roger* floated farther than supposed. The odor of the shore had departed, freshened by the breeze of open sea. The sails of the two smaller ships billowed out full, and beneath Jill's bare feet she felt the vessel vibrating, alive at the urging of the winds. Amidships on the *Roger*, still dormant, the sailors who were not at work in the rigging congregated with their backs to the gunwales. Jill spied Hook's tawny hat among them, and the yellow sparkle of its topaz band. The empty hook on the tackle block swayed. Whatever happened on that beloved ship from here on, Jill's part in it was merely in spirit. The care of Hook's fleet must become his priority. Oddly, she caught a whiff of lily of the valley, and an unexpected image flashed in Jill's mind. She saw a portrait in miniature almost come to focus— was it a reflection of herself?— only to vanish as a commodore's duties diverted him.

Whatever came next, the fateful exchange was made. Jill's father, deceived himself, had lured her to the power of a fiend. Aboard a foreign vessel on a voyage to a strange land, she must deal with the outcome, against the gypsies' counsel, *solo*— all on her own. Like DéDé LeCorbeau half an hour before, she intended to handle her business, and escape at the earliest opportunity.

At the tail of her eye, she spied her false husband approaching. His walking stick tapped on the decking. She released her father, smoothed her satin, and straightened. Spinning on her heel with her amber skirts swishing, Red-Handed Jill confronted *Herr Doktor Heinrich*. She twisted her wrist, flicked open her fan, and, like *la matriarca*, she veiled her intentions.

Mr. Smee frowned as the block and tackle swung back toward the *Roger*. Its net didn't hang limp and empty, as expected. It dangled, pear shaped, with something inside it. Cursing, Smee came alert. LeCorbeau had sent some kind of surprise. Smee raised his arm, cautioning, "Easy, lads, easy! There's no knowing what blasted thing's in there." The crewmen manning the tackle obeyed, their muscles bulging beneath their striped shirts while the rope spun through the intricacies of the pulleys. The gear squeaked as, inch by inch, the hook lowered its mysterious burden.

The object touched down on the grating of the hold while Smee bellowed, "You men, knives out! You on the tackle there, clear away. Drop that net!" The watching sailors armed themselves while the tackle men hurried to unhook the weaving of rope. It fell to the deck. The men stepped back, gasping, and more sailors gathered round, their exclamations rising with their curiosity. Smee goggled, his ruddy complexion deepening, but the fresh curse died on his lips.

Alerted by the commotion, still Hook delayed in pulling his gaze from the final sight of his lady. Letting her go with reluctance, he stalked his way down from the forecastle, his footsteps striking the deck. The men elbowed each other clear of his path.

"Commodore," Smee warned, "that little rooster sent something more than his tribute."

Hook didn't break stride. With his sharp iron claw poised for action, he reached the grating. He stopped dead.

Within the pool of netting stood an antique steamer trunk, with brass clasps in want of polish. Upon the trunk spread the folds of an old-fashioned traveling cloak, flocked in purple velvet and edged with fur. From the fabric floated a faint scent of lily of the valley.

The figure wrapped in the cloak was that of a woman. Forced to trade the remnants of his vision of Jill for this apparition, Hook scowled, and took in the sight of her. This lady sat still and composed, as if posing for a portrait. She held fast to the straps of the trunk, her identity veiled in black lace.

The commodore drew himself up to his full, fearsome height, outraged at LeCorbeau's gall in boarding a passenger without consent. He trampled the netting with his fine, polished boots, stepping up on the grating. Seething through his teeth, he issued his demand.

"Take off that veil, and let me see your face!"

The ship lay at wait in the water, her men hushed, and only the skull on the flag that flapped above dared to grin. With gloved fingers, the woman pinched the lower hem of her veil. Hesitantly, she raised it up and over her head, to let it fall down her back. Violet eyes stared back at Hook, wide with uncertainty. At the sight of her face, Hook's countenance turned savage with surprise.

In the next moment, he remembered his Jill. He closed his mind to her. Instantly, he had absorbed the implications of LeCorbeau's souvenir. Enough that Jill must contend with her surgeon. In good conscience, Hook could not further weigh down his ladylove. This complication was his to handle, and his alone. Or, rather, not alone, but with this woman's complicity.

Hook's one good hand would be full with this arrival. The inferences at work here were twofold: one, that this visitor was owed something; the other, that Doctor Johann Hanover Heinrich had learned far more of James Hook than he ought.

Once again, a chapter was emerging from the storyteller's lore. Agreeable or no, the experience now presenting itself was another filament from the intricate tapestry of Captain Hook's history, as woven— long ago— by Wendy Darling.

Hook wasn't smiling this time, not even half-way. This time, he damned her imagination.

"Johann." Jill lowered her fan, leaving it splayed and pressing it to her bosom. She chose a bantering tone. "I am certain you have rules to dictate. Shall you list them now, or will we pretend for my father's sake that you have not abducted me, as you so handily kidnapped him?" At her back, she heard her father gasp, but Heinrich had prepared for her resistance.

Evenly, he replied in the clipped accent of Austria she so well recalled, "On this voyage to recover our loved one, your father and I have struck an accord, as your pirates would phrase it. Mr. Darling understands the shock you are experiencing. I have counseled him that such a response is to be expected from victims of captivity."

Mr. Darling toddled to his daughter's side, and, gingerly, linked her arm with his own. Jill took this opportunity to really look at him. Still many inches taller than she, yet he seemed to her to be less substantial that when she was a girl. Swatches of gray hair now showed over his ears. Had she been away so long, or was it her own risks and adventures that wrought these changes? Seeing the concern in her eyes, he soothed her, "There, my angel," and patted her arm. "Doctor Heinrich has afforded me the best of care, and will of course attend you just as conscientiously. Together, your husband and I shall do all we can to ease you back into life on the Continent."

Jill's moment of concern for her parent abated at these words, which were so clearly prompted by Hanover, or, as she supposed she must call him now, Heinrich. "Oh, if this is the case, then, Father, please tell the captain to reverse the ship's course." She snapped her fan shut, and pointed it toward the stern. "You'll find my husband in command of the *Red Lady*."

With an admiring smile, the surgeon leaned upon his cane and feasted his eyes on his wife. Her amber gown complimented the flush on her face. Her figure remained trim and vigorous. She now carried an ornamental fan that he suspected would fit very nicely into the salons of Europe. Naturally, the blemishes at her throat and hand could not be erased, and in regard to the alteration of the color of her hair, he must take some time to consider. He also noted a certain gravity of demeanor, betraying the fact that she had grown somewhat older. Yet, he confessed, "Jill…you are even more spirited than I left you. I hate to think what horrors those buccaneers put you through, but the woman I see before me now is more splendid than one year ago. This time of adversity has tempered you."

"If it is temper you admire, Johann, believe me, I hold that trait in abundance to share with you."

"More and more, the challenge of holding you intrigues me."

"As I understand it, your real wife perished from your 'intrigue.' I may resemble the first Mrs. Heinrich in appearance, but I will not be domesticated."

"Nor should I desire it," he countered. "A man who selects a pirate queen for his bride must seek not to tame, but to satisfy her."

"I was satisfied as a pirate queen!"

"And yet, as I described our rich and vivid life to come in Vienna, you eagerly entered my arms."

"*You* eagerly entered the snare Captain Hook and I set for you." She flicked her fan in dismissal. "And your iron pride has driven you to return the favor. No wonder Liza's poor mother perished."

"I concur that, in you, I find what I missed in my first embarkation into matrimony." Seeing that the topic of his previous marriage discomfited Mr. Darling, Heinrich reassured him, "Unlike our Jill, the first Mrs. Heinrich was delicate. She suffered from a condition of the heart."

Jill snorted. "Yes, Father. Marriage to Doctor Heinrich does have the effect of afflicting a lady's heart. Although my own marriage to him is spurious, I know whereof I speak."

Turning her back on the physician, she urged her father toward the hatch. "Come, Father, show me to our quarters. I am impatient to hear the news from home, and I have wonderful stories to tell." She shot a dark look back to Heinrich. "Tales, I am certain, that will rival those lies the doctor administered to you."

"Er, yes, well…" Mr. Darling dithered in confusion, but allowed her to steer him below decks. "Wendy…or, must I say, Jill? I am sorry to disappoint you, but the room I've been assigned is not a private one. I'm with that skinny French officer-fellow, that Renaud."

"Then take me there, please. I would speak to you alone." As she expected, the discreet footfall of soft leather shoes followed them down the steps, which were more accurately described as a ladder with wide rungs and a rope for a banister. The sunshine softened as they descended this passage, and the surgeon commandeered Jill's arm to assist her as she dealt with her skirts.

He advised, "You must understand, my darling, that the cabin space on this vessel is limited. Captain LeCorbeau's carpenter only just finished fitting new bulkheads to cut three into four."

Light fell in squares from the lattice of the upper hatches. No guns armed this deck, and it was filled with provisions in casks, kegs, and barrels. Jill recognized the two crates of lotus so coveted by LeCorbeau as the means to his riches. One's lid was pried loose; no doubt the contents had been inspected before *Le Lotus* took leave of the *Roger*. Heinrich sent a proprietorial glance to these crates, then gestured aft with his silver-topped cane, leading the way down the deck to open one of four doors. "You and I will occupy these quarters, next to your father's." His charcoal eyes kindled as he anticipated, "After all, we were robbed of our wedding night. It is time, finally, that we enjoyed the privacy to which we are entitled, as man and wife."

"As man and *another* man's wife, you mean."

The doctor gave his short gust of a laugh. "Ah, my Jill! Always a story on your lips. You have found harmless means with which to manage your distress."

Executing the habit she remembered, he hung his stick over his arm and gave a brisk tug to each of his cuffs. Jill eyed her *faux* husband, noting the changes wrought by the past year. Gone were the days of the modest ship's surgeon. Now that Heinrich practiced in Europe among a circle of socialites, he was attired in appropriately fine fabrics of fashionable cut. The ensemble he wore today boasted a long, royal-blue coat with wide lapels. Broad at the shoulders and tailored tight to his waist, his suit displayed his athletic physique while maintaining the dignity expected of the good doctor. His shirt was crisp and white, with a brief, simple frill at each cuff. The vest was sewn of silk in a lighter shade of blue, patterned with an Oriental design of waterfowl in flight.

More interesting to Jill, though, was his face, which bore those three scars. The two wounds she and Hook inflicted appeared as healed as they'd ever be. The bloody slash she'd last seen as Heinrich lay senseless in the bottom of *L'Ormonde*'s longboat had faded. It now nearly matched the first of his scars in texture and color, a slight but very visible pucker of pink, in a line from cheekbone to jaw. She smiled as she admired the symmetry of Hook's impression, for, on the physician's right side, that cut was a mirror image of the old dueling scar Heinrich had earned as a student at Heidelberg. The smaller, horizontal mark that Jill delivered topped the first, and turned it into a seven. Looking at this man had always given Jill a thrill; in spite of the flaws in his character, he presented a handsome and manly figure. The thrill Jill felt today was enhanced by her own handiwork, and Hook's. As she gazed at *Herr Doktor* Heinrich, she hid her gratification under the shade of her fan. Now she folded the accessory to tap her chin with it.

"I wonder how you explain your appearance, Johann. Fascinating as these scars may seem to your patients, surely these blemishes point to a dubious past? I am amazed to learn that the Austrian nobility patronize a physician who so obviously owns up to his dealings with buccaneers."

Heinrich shook his head. "My standing as a physician and innovator has come to full flower. Had you been at my side this past year, where you belonged, the situation would now be clear to you. But you and I have been separate too long, and your principles are confused. My professional opinion is that, now that your ordeal is at an end, the trauma may yield illness, or worse. Your condition requires watching."

Heinrich looked to Mr. Darling, who nodded, admitting, "I have agreed to honor the doctor's wish that he himself watch over you. These first weeks, he tells me, are the most critical."

The surgeon pressed Jill's arm. "You needn't fear, my darling wife. I shall not relax my vigilance until we reach our new home in Vienna." So saying, he ushered Jill into their quarters. Mr. Darling followed.

Divesting herself of his arm, Jill declared, "And so, Johann, we come to the first of your rules. I am not to be let out of your sight, even to confide in my father."

"How strict you make me sound!" Heinrich shared a smile with Mr. Darling. "My 'rules,' as you term them, are simply a loving husband's care, and a physician's guidance."

"Of course. You could not explain your dominance any other way." The cabin in which the threesome stood was compact but clean, smelling of newly-shaved wood from the ship's carpenter's rasp. It held a narrow bunk, a good rug, a framed mirror above a washstand, and a small, polished table with two chairs. Jill's satchel and travel desk lay on the bed, upon a down counterpane. Heinrich's sea chest sat at the foot of the bunk, with his medical bag atop it. His clothing hung on pegs, next to a rapier and a saber. Blue and ivory chintz framed the porthole, and, unable to resist the impulse, Jill stepped to it to search for her fleet. Past the curtains and far away, the neat lines of *Red Lady* rode the waves. The *Roger*, though, with her black flag and glinting fittings, was nowhere in sight. Convinced now of the reality of this misadventure, Jill spun to face her second husband. "You may as well lay down the rest of the terms of your 'guidance' now, and get it over with."

"First, a gift." Heinrich hung up his cane. From his sea chest, he drew a velvet box. "Because of the secrecy we were forced to maintain when you accepted my proposal, Jill, I was unable to bestow upon you a betrothal gift. I now offer this necklace." The smile between his scars turned wicked as he revived their old private phrasing, "Today." Jill grimaced. As she made no move to take the box, Heinrich, with his manicured hands, opened it for her.

Nestled within a satin lining lay a treasure to take her breath away: a choker of creamy pearls on a triple string. Set in bars that banded the three strings together at regular intervals, diamonds accentuated the pearls. In the light from the stern window, the precious gems seemed to wink in temptation. The clasp, too, was speckled with clear, sparkling stones. Jill felt the familiar twinge at her loins, the desire that such jewels aroused in her. She didn't fight the feeling. She was a pirate.

"How beautiful, Doctor." Turning her back to him, she tucked her fan in her sash and lifted her hair from her neckline. As the cool beads met her flesh, she trembled with pleasure. At the same time, she understood the physician's game. As she and Hook had discussed, here was Doctor Heinrich's weakness. She pressed the glossy pearls to her throat, then faced the men to show the effect. "Just the right length and breadth to hide my scar. How very thoughtful of you. I see, in fact, that your thoughts are focused not only upon me, but on your reputation. Naturally you wish to disguise the evidence of my experience. But…no matter. I profit by it."

Taken aback, her father exclaimed, "By gad, my angel, how jaded you have become!"

"When you've heard my stories, Father, you'll understand me much better."

In too good a humor to allow Jill's moods to ruffle him, Heinrich continued, "I have kept my promise to you…" He pulled another box from the chest, and, with a flourish, opened it. "Your wedding ring, exactly as you requested— a circlet of diamonds and rubies."

Holding silent, Jill allowed him to lift her hand and slide the ring on her finger. This gift was, perhaps, more dangerous than the first. But it was dazzling, and it was precious…and hers. As Heinrich squeezed her fingers, her pulse throbbed. She licked her lips, and said nothing.

Her father examined the band. "My, my! How very grand." He cajoled her, "Now, this is what I deem a handsome pair of wedding gems, for a handsome wedded pair, ha, ha!"

His son-in-law bowed. "I am gratified, Sir. And, now that Jill has rejoined us…may I refer to you as 'Father'?"

Mr. Darling flushed pink, nodding happily. "Why, yes, certainly. It is my honor." He turned to his daughter. "I know you've been through trying times, my dear, but I'd call this a happy ending, now wouldn't you?"

"Oh, no, Father. I don't call this an ending at all. Rather, our next adventure has just begun."

"That's the spirit, Wen— I mean to say, Jill! I'll become accustomed to your new name in time. I promise you."

"I agree with you, my darling," Heinrich interposed. "We stand at the beginning of our venture into wedded life." Having reached what he believed to be a point of concurrence, he complied with Jill's earlier request. "As for what you so charmingly call my rules, Jill: first, you will wear these pearls, or a similar adornment to cover that scar, at all times. The next directive concerns your more scandalous mark. I must insist that you wear gloves whenever we are in company." He kissed her crimson palm, lightly, sending shivers up her arm. "Fascinating or no, I will not have your damage discussed in polite society."

Arching her eyebrows, Jill looked for her father's response.

"Well, Jill…I have to say that your bloodstain is, after all, quite shocking to view. I understand it to be the result of some outlandish rite of passage on that Island, but, now that you dwell among civilized people again, perhaps your husband *is* correct to wish you to disguise it."

"Again, Father, I have much to tell you that I could not send in a letter."

Mr. Darling emitted a chuckle, not unlike his old, good-humored chuckle, but somewhat constrained. "Your mother would be much amused, I am sure, to see your red hair!"

"Dear Mother! Is she well?"

"She is worried. We must write to her posthaste, and let her know you are safe."

"Shan't we ask permission of our guardian, Father?" As the new rubies on her hand flashed in the sunlight, she solicited Doctor Heinrich's ruling. "Am I allowed to send letters beyond the walls of my cell?"

Unnecessarily, Heinrich smoothed his irreproachable vest. "I am certain Father will pass your messages on to Mrs. Darling."

"Then your answer is 'no.' I may not write, not even to my mother, to allay her misgivings."

"Nor to your paramour." This time, Heinrich's voice held a threat.

Mr. Darling blanched, and cleared his throat.

"Tell me, Johann," Jill inquired. "Just how did you manage the cost of these jewels?" Lovingly, Jill stroked her pearls. She had already adopted them, in full. "I would have thought the loss of your diamonds that day on the *Jolly Roger* set you back."

With a smug smile on his generous lips, Heinrich affirmed, "I was never one to carry all eggs in one basket. I kept a healthy bank balance even as I sailed as ship's surgeon....But, since you ask, Captain LeCorbeau and I believed—" he sobered, "believed sincerely— that Mr. Cecco was a dead man. When we left *L'Ormonde* in Hook's charge, with all his powers restored to him, we were certain that that Italian brute would be murdered."

Jill's expression turned blank. "No."

"Indeed, Captain LeCorbeau was inspired to report Mr. Cecco's death to the Italian authorities. We did so. Happily, the word of two respected professional men was enough to persuade them, and the captain and I collected what I acknowledge amounts to a liberal bounty."

Of a sudden, the pearl choker that ringed Jill's neck became heavy and tight. Had she not known for certain that Cecco lived, she'd have torn it from her throat. "Finding him alive and thriving on the quarterdeck of the *Red Lady* must have given you both quite a start."

"I admit that it did. The deed is done, however. There is no help for it. Perhaps we have performed a favor for your Captain Cecco. As a corpse, he is no longer hunted."

"Allow me to guess your next commandment, Johann. I am forbidden to reveal that he lives— even if I desired to do so… which I do not." Gripping the fan Mamma entrusted to her, Jill appreciated the solid wooden feel of it in her hand, and her spirits lifted. Someday, when she was free again, she had joyful news to tell the mother and son. Heinrich's next words, though, crashed through her happiness.

"On the other hand, my darling, you may tell all the stories you desire about what you call your first marriage. Because, you see, your first husband's death, as recorded by the Italian Admiralty, occurred on the very day you and I wed." As his gaze met the devastation in her darkening eyes, he nodded, supreme in his victory. "Yes, Jill. Judged by the law, as in my heart…you are mine."

The freshly erected walls that crowded so close around Jill seemed to waver. In her ears, the usual creaks and groans aboard ship turned into wails. *Le Lotus* became to the lady just what it was— not a bastion of security on the bosom of the sea, but an insubstantial contraption of planks, ropes, and canvas, adrift on wide water. Like herself, the vessel was controlled by no will of its own. It could but follow its master's steering, and even that course lay at the whim of the winds. Her stomach churned as the sea heaved beneath her.

As the doctor had counseled her father, the shock she was experiencing was the response one expected from victims of captivity. Below her feet she sensed the creatures of the deep, insensible to her dilemma and living by impulse alone. So, too, from this moment, must Jill live, by her wits and her instincts. And, as clear as the water around her, she now perceived the exact nature of this fateful exchange.

From today, Giovanni Cecco owned his full freedom. In return, his wife, his lovely one, his *amore*, was held a prisoner, to be known when she arrived in the circles of Vienna not as *Signora* Cecco, nor Red-Handed Jill, nor even as Wendy Moira Angela Darling. However splendid with gold or silver her bonds proved to be, forthwith the girl who was first nurtured in London and, as a woman, crowned queen of the *Roger*, was chained by the identity thrust upon her by Fate: *Frau Herr Doktor* Heinrich.

She gripped the folded fan in her hand, like a dagger.

Past Baggage

Mr. Smee ventured, "Do you know this baggage, Sir, come here all on her own?"

Hook leveled his stare at the intruder where she perched, wordless, upon her trunk. "I assure you, Smee, between LeCorbeau and Heinrich, this female did not scheme, 'on her own,' to come to me." His stance remained fixed, yet he felt his guard ease as his memories informed him.

Even all these years later, this woman retained the qualities he once demanded of her. As a very young man in London, he'd sought certain requirements that altered well before he entered the Neverland. Her grace and her graciousness, her modesty, her circumspection, all these traits appeared to him, as evident and as advantageous as in the time in which he'd kept her his secret. Eyes of violet, hair of brunette, pinned up in matronly swaths now, but with long curls cascading over one shoulder, the lush locks he used to kiss and caress like sacred relics in his fingers. Her beauty had mellowed with Time, but only just. He watched as her glance flicked away from his claw, and his lip twisted. He determined from the distress in her expression that he, on the other 'hand,' had altered dramatically.

After her first, full gaze at him, the woman would not meet his eyes. The blushes suffusing the softness of her cheeks indicated that she felt awkward aboard this ship, as fully aware as each of the rough men surrounding her that she did not belong here. Although Hook had lingered with this lady in the past— the distant past— he still knew her. He intuited that she would not suffer him to keep her, now. Quite the opposite. She had come to him to be sent away.

Hook determined to do so, and as efficiently as possible. He yanked the pistol from his belt and aimed the muzzle between her eyes.

The woman gasped, jumping up from the trunk to back away from him, her eyes dilating as she clasped her hands to her bosom. The company fell silent. A seabird screamed as if scandalized at the master's drastic action, but, true to her breeding, the lady held her tongue.

"Mr. Smee, search that box."

"I'll be doing that, Commodore, and with a will." Smee bent to spring the clasps of the trunk and throw open the lid. A cedar interior sent up a pleasant, pungent odor. Smee adjusted his spectacles and began sifting the contents.

The sailors watched, shuffling a bit, curious but constrained, edging away from this scene as if they themselves hadn't pillaged in this very way scores of times. Here was a female of an alternate temperament to Red-Handed Jill's. She hadn't uttered a peep of resistance. None of the *Roger*'s men would dare doubt the commodore, nor would they question Mr. Smee, but, in their eyes, the threat of this genteel female didn't warrant the pistol pointed at her head, nor the precaution of the knives in their fists, nor the disrespect so uncommon in the ship's ladies' man, Smee.

The bo'sun's rummaging discovered only gowns of good quality, undergarments, accessories, footwear and books, and one worn wooden case. He hoisted this box by its scuffed leathern handle. As he opened it, he sniffed linseed. Three tiers of trays moved outward on hinges, revealing the instruments of an artist: brushes, pigments, a pestle, and miniature paint boards.

Holding his gun steady, Hook commented, "Knowing Doctor Heinrich as I do, I believe you will find another surprise there."

"Aye, aye, Sir, I'll be rousting it." Snapping closed the paint box, Smee returned to his task, suspicion still furrowing his brow. From one of the compartments built into the arching lid of the trunk, he pulled a flat, oblong package wrapped in brown paper. A glance at the lady brought no sign of further upset, nor of relief. She remained standing, moving only to pull her flocked purple cloak closed. Smee waited for the commodore's nod, then tore open the packet. He stared at it, his mouth slowly forming a sardonic smile. The sailors close enough to view the object widened their eyes, throwing chary looks at the lady. Smee got up from his knees and hastened to Hook's side, presenting the portrait to the commodore's view. "Far from perfect, but not a bad likeness, Sir."

"And not painted by this lady's brush." Hook lowered the pistol. "Escort the baroness to my quarters, and have her trunk brought up, too." At the revelation of the lady's rank, the men uttered their astonishment. Hook turned away, striding off toward the bow to mount the steps of the forecastle, the plumes of his hat waving, his tawny coattails flailing in his wake.

"This way, Lady."

The woman made no protest, but allowed Smee to grip her arm and lead her in the opposite direction, along the deck and up the companionway. He disliked this turn of events. Just the trace of this female's scent, discreet as it was, irritated and enflamed Smee's regret for Jill's absence, and he heard his boots on the boards falling heavy. The woman's high-button shoes made no sound, as if to maintain the silence in which Hook had kept her secreted in his past, with no mention, ever, not even to Smee.

At the entrance to the commodore's cabin, under the gold-painted carving of the companionway, the lady halted to focus upon the shining brass plate officiating over Hook's door. She turned to look back at the man himself. For the first time since boarding, she spoke. Reluctantly, Smee noted that her voice, like her face, was gentle, and of a pleasing timbre.

"He was the young Master James…I should know him anywhere. And yet…he now looks so very solitary."

Smee's musical lilt abandoned him. He blue eyes blazed, and, harshly, he refuted the lady's conclusion. "Well, Ma'am, I can't be knowing what you expected, but I'll tell you this. Our commodore is not *alone*."

As Hook reminded me, and as I accept, I am suffering the consequences of my actions. My storytelling led me on this voyage, and although I see no quick way to reverse the words I too carelessly spoke, I am determined to fight my way back to my lover, and to our life within his world. Knowing no one near who can aid me, I turn again to my journal. Writing helped me to feel less alone in Italy. I shall do the same now, but will employ Italian this time, to confound

intruding eyes. My aim with these pages is to clarify my thinking, and to bolster my spirits.

This cabin scarcely allows room for my elbows, not to mention the rest of me and a man whom I am so loath to touch. I am nauseated by even a glance at the bunk, in which I seem destined to lie all night by his side. Yet I refuse to feel sorry for myself. I have borne worse impositions, and risen victorious. By the time the ship's bell rings for the evening watch, I'll have concocted some excuse to turn my back to this blackguard, and keep it turned. If I'm to wage the sustained campaign I foresee, I must ensure that I have good nights' sleep throughout this voyage.

To my relief, Johann and I spent the early hours of our afternoon topside, strolling the deck. No doubt the good gentleman believes it unseemly to enjoy pleasures of the flesh in the daylight. In this case, I quite agree with him. Soon I experienced yet another of today's jolts when Mrs. Hanover appeared. By my order, she and I have not sailed the same ship nor walked the same soil since one year ago. She emerged from her cabin to breathe clean sea air with poor Pierre-Jean in tow, her charming, blond-braided French sailor. In my judgment, he is blinded by his obsession with her, and he cannot envision the depths of danger in which he wades while within the proximity of the Hanover family. I caught only a glimpse of Mrs. Hanover's child by Johann, but even that glance of the pale little thing pricked my maternal pity. We two women didn't speak; Mrs. Hanover, looking small and dressed modestly, continues to take my old admonishment to heart and today kept her distance. If we did speak, I'd call out her foolishness in trusting her father. I must consider, though, whether as her 'stepmother' I should forge some accord. After all, we shall soon live under one roof. I have yet to solve the riddle of why Johann's pride bends to treat this embarrassing son begotten on his daughter. Yes, I believe I should learn, from the girl's own viewpoint, just what he promised her. This subject is not one to pursue in a sunlit stroll among the other voyagers...on a very small vessel.

Mrs. Hanover's renewed faith in her father is another example of Johann's adroitness in conciliation, whether sincere or not. After my clash with him early in the day, he proposed our walk on the deck together, providing a welcome alternative to remaining confined, shoulder to shoulder in our quarters. Later, we took our tea with Father under a canopy behind the wheel, where, although I was still enraged enough to wish to throw the scalding contents of the teapot in the doctor's face, he was considerate enough to allow the dear man to bring me up to date on the news from home.

Thanks to Johann's machinations, I may not speak with my father privately, but to talk with Father at all is sweet bliss. I see by the moisture he blinks from his eyes that he feels the same way. How refreshing it is to converse with him, asking all those little questions I couldn't fit in my letters. The boys are well on their way to manhood. Mother misses her infants as they mature, but enjoys good health. The house is in order, and the family's needs are provided by Father's industry, and by my good fortune. I shall deal out another share of that fortune to Father when I can slip a few more of my hard and hard-won diamonds into his hands. He promised to send my love to Mother in the letter he'll pen tonight although, as he complains, in the newly-reduced quarters he shares with Renaud he has barely area enough to spread out his paper. How gladly I would trade my Austrian for my father's Frenchman!

In spite of the many assurances I've sent in my correspondence, my mother and father worry over my welfare. I do understand. As a mother myself, I know that a parent never ceases to carry concern. Indeed, after bringing life forth, a mother's first duty is the protection of her children. How contradictory is the fact, though, that through the gullibility of these loved ones I am heading 'home' for Europe, the very circumstance that places the welfare of their only daughter at risk.

As for the ship, LeCorbeau seized a lucky chance with Le Lotus. *She is sleek and seaworthy, although my insides do feel the difference in sailing on a vessel so much smaller than the* Roger. *The frigate flies over every crest and dances a jig in each wind. I observe that the crewmen who remained with LeCorbeau at the loss of* L'Ormonde *are as respectful of their* commandant *as before. His new sailors don't yet know what to think of him. Naturally, LeCorbeau avoids me, not only because of the aggravation that Johann's infatuation causes him, but because, like English ale, any woman is a foul taste in his mouth. I know from our previous meetings he believes females bring bad luck to seamen. Let us hope LeCorbeau's superstition proves correct.*

One man aboard is a fish out of water: the soldier, Olivier de Beaumonde. He took a cup of tea with us, and seems an amusing study. I shall behave well enough to retain my freedom to roam this vessel, so that I may continue our acquaintance to see where it leads. Johann appears to dismiss him. De Beaumonde is devoted to his country, yet I perceive that his fellow countryman, LeCorbeau, dislikes him. To my way of thinking,

LeCorbeau's antipathy is a point in de Beaumonde's favor. The man is strong and good-looking, reputed to be an excellent swordsman. I shall sound him out, for although he is no sailor, he may prove a useful man.

Of course I'd much rather tackle my tribulations with my own scarlet hand. My escape, with Father's, will require a great deal of ingenuity—even more than I'd imagined before this reunion with Johann. As forcibly as the will to murder my false husband goads me, I cannot act. The first moment Father left me alone with him, in the intimacy of our cabin, the doctor encircled me with his firm, sturdy arms, kissed my throat tenderly above my pearls, and, most persuasively, made clear the penalty should I act upon the impulse to kill. His lust inspires my own, although the nature of my desire is much darker. He is indeed a clever adversary, who requires a more cunning counterpart. Remembering Mamma Cecco's counsel, I shall subdue my passions, observe from behind her fan, and seek the scheme to save myself.

Johann's security rests in his pocket. When he released me from his embraces, a self-satisfied smile grew upon his scar-marked face, and he presented a parchment for my perusal. Within this document, he has detailed our voyage upon the Roger. *He identifies the men who constitute her company. He names the ships we plundered, and depicts our abduction of him and his daughter. He calls me a pirate, describing my illicit and willing relationship with the notorious, Most Wanted Captain James Hook. He enumerates the crimes I perpetrated against him at Hook's bidding— kidnapping, seduction, conspiracy, theft, drugging, desertion, and the cut of my knife. Signed and notarized, this evidence is strong enough to have me arrested and tried at the least, and, at the worst, could see me hanged. Further, Johann incriminates Captain Hook as the defiler of Liza. Not content to stop there, Johann names Mr. Smee as Mr. Cecco's 'executioner.' He includes his guesses as to the latitudes and longitudes we sailed, so that the Navy might search our best cruising waters, in hopes of bringing Hook down. When my gaze rose from this vile paper, my fingers flexed, and I longed to put my nails to good use, tearing new scars in the flesh of that face.*

Even now, I yearn to draw blood. As I sit at my writing desk, unable to act, my heart burns, searing my breast as I consider the portent of the physician's missive. I can hardly breathe as I contemplate my position. I know I turned pale after reading it. My knees shook with my rage. Johann seized my waist to support me, but I commanded the strength to shove him away. I whirled to the porthole. As I stretched out my hand to cast this testament to the sea, he caught it. Folding it again to fit in his fine-tailored waistcoat, he still smiled, apprising me that a notarized copy lies safe and inaccessible to all but his solicitor, in a strongbox within Heinrichhaus, in Vienna.

And so, to Vienna I go. No shorter route to escape or to safety exists for me. If I flee, if I raise my red hand to harm him, the doctor's evidence will be delivered to the authorities. Johann, quite coldly, described also the sudden 'fever' that will deal death to my father if I rebel. As long as we stay in Europe, or in European waters, I remain chained to Johann. Except in gentle caresses, I cannot touch him.

I must, therefore, secure an ally to aid me.

James Hook threw open the door of his quarters. As intended, his entrance startled the baroness. She spun from her view of the vista beyond his mullioned windows, nearly spilling the wine Smee poured before deserting her here, half an hour ago. Hook shut the door with a heavy click of the latch.

Her gentle voice shook as she greeted him. "Master James."

"Milady." Hook allowed his tone to hold a touch of deference, but only a touch. Once upon a time, the house of his family far outranked her own. He crossed his luxurious carpets, to pause by the divan and its crimson curtains, where only last night he'd made love to his mistress.

Again, and more thoroughly now, the lady gathered in his appearance. "The portrait I was given could not prepare me. I anticipated, of course, that in place of the youth, I would find a man in full. I was told, but could not envision, the look of a legend instead."

Even in her discomfort, she held the ladylike bearing he remembered. Her cloak, gloves, and veil lay folded upon the cushions of the window seat. The clothing she wore was revealed to be a damask jacket tight to her waist and skirted below it, overhanging a narrow underskirt in linen. This outdated ensemble, tailored for traveling, was brown as mink to compliment the hair of her coiffure, which she had tidied to repair the muss from the sea breeze. Above the high collar of her jacket hung small antique earbobs, with one fine but modest red gem set in the center of each. He watched these earrings quiver as she endeavored, with her lips apart, to return his surveyance.

With graceful fingers, she gestured toward her own chin, and toward one ear, indicating his beard and the crescent of his earring. "You are still the man I knew. Yet you are transformed, from the patrician to the piratical."

At last, he favored her with a smile. "And you. You are the woman I...*knew*."

He watched her blush burn at his inference. No, she had not changed in character. Physically, her body was more slender and her stature taller than Jill's— the point of comparison, now, for Hook, forever and for always. Milady's speech was more reticent than Jill's, still forming words with the elocution drummed into young women by a governess in the schoolroom, in those long-ago lessons before 'coming out.' Beyond doubt, Hook reflected, the woman *had* come out, much further than ever her governess could have imagined, across an ocean to a ship full of buccaneers, and a man so iniquitous under his alias that to reveal in England who he really was would even at this date set the country in a blaze.

Delving deeper, Hook recognized this woman afresh, from the perspective he'd gained since he had discovered the Wendy to be his storyteller. Like Mr. Smee, Milady was conjured for him, a necessary character in the tale. In a magical paradox, she was crafted into existence an age before the girl Wendy herself, and decades before Wendy transformed into Jill, who possessed the mind and the means to satisfy the Pirate King of her dreams. And as the man, Hook, emerged from the girl's consciousness, so too, but more subtly, did his history.

Here, today, Hook's history stood before him, with her violet eyes gazing up into his own. In appearance, she seemed to have ceased aging in her late middle years. Still, as narrated by the storyteller, she was a perfect figure of a woman, designed for his needs when he was a younger lover in search of the appropriate paramour, with her looks, physique, manners, and intelligence all formed to fulfill his requirements. As always, when aroused, Hook felt a twitch at his lip.

His perspective today, though, informed him that, this time, Milady's presence was *not* contrived by his storyteller.

She offered, "You must be wondering how I discovered your whereabouts, and why, after all these years, I dared come to you."

"On the contrary. I do not wonder at all."

The divan where he stood had been furnished by the Wendy, the wooden back carved in the likeness of a swan without flight. It was here that, when the girl herself was struck flightless, he had alternately saved and persuaded her. Doffing his hat, he tossed it to lie with its yellow jewels twinkling on the satiny gold medallions of the daybed. As he shrugged off his tawny coat, he caused a slight reaction in Milady. She shrank back in apprehension, but witnessed the care with which he drew the barbarous point of his hook through his sleeve. He dropped the coat to lie alongside his hat. Next, he shed his velvet vest. He heard her breath catch as he came close, still taking in and, apparently, taken by, his changes. He watched her gaze travel over the mustache that circled down to his beard, becoming to his features but so unfamiliar, his ample shoulders grown to a man's maturity, great gems on his hand and fine lace at his cuffs— and a notorious barb on his arm. Motionless, she too, it seemed, was unable to fly from him.

Concealing his claw behind him, he looked down upon the fading bloom of her complexion. With no distance between them, he saw the lighter tints at her hairline, silver strands held at bay by the same enchantment that lengthened his own years. Raising his hook, he waited for the fresh alarm it engendered to dissipate from her expression. Then, with its tip, he pulled the tortoiseshell pins from her hair. She uttered a soft syllable as they plunked to the carpet. He watched the glossy, dark coils tumble down all round her shoulders. Again, he caught just a trace of perfume, not heady like the scent Jill favored, but a light aroma that suggested the delicacy of tiny white flowers.

Holding the lady's gaze with his own, blue as jewels, he slipped the goblet from her hand. He tipped it up to drain it, discarded it upon the nearest surface, then cupped the lady's head at the base of her skull. Pulling her into his embrace, he pressed his warm mouth to hers, sharing the taste of the vintage in a ritual they devised once, together. Like the fine wine they drank, then and now, age enhanced this rite's performance.

As he drew back for breath, she said, with a tremor, "I did not presume—" but he leaned down again and stoppered her words, sealing her lips with his kisses. He bent to slide his hooked arm beneath her knees, careful to keep her from fearing it, then lifted her up and onto his four-posted bed. She seemed dazed as he lay down beside her, but offered to him no resistance. For old time's sake, he wondered, or desire? Yet he held no real interest in the answer.

He loosened his breeches; he shifted her skirts. Leaning on his damaged arm, he disengaged the fastenings of her jacket. Exposed now, the white ruffles of the chemise beneath her corset framed her breasts. Not as firm as before, her bosom still swelled against this restraint, responding to his lips' stimulation as he covered her breasts with kisses. With his left hand he remembered her pleasures, thumbing the cleft at her chin, slipping one finger beneath the ribbon of her garter, brushing her thighs like a feather. He felt her arms tremble as she embraced him. Pushing aside the silk tulle of her undergarment, he found her body already ready for his, and, without hesitation, he mounted his mark, moving to the delectation of both, now pulling himself over her, into her, out of her, over and over her, until beneath the brocaded hangings of his bedstead, they inhaled as erratically as they'd breathed long ago, in her modest boudoir, sharing the ecstasy of exchange, lip to lip, center to center, widowed mistress to her patron not long past a boy.

As he recovered from his exertion, he fingered her hair where it lay like lace upon the comforter; he felt the play of her hands as she ran them through his black locks, dangling above her, so much longer than when she first, impelled by necessity, accepted the terms tendered by his representative. How greatly he, and she, had changed within those few years of their compact. How much more had changed now. As she stroked his beard, Hook studied how she kept her eyes on his face, still demonstrating the circumspection he had known and exacted from her, averting her gaze from the claw where he laid it to rest by her shoulder.

He didn't tax her discretion too long with the hook at her side. He raised himself up from the bed, restored his breeches to respectability, and collected his clothing to hang it over his interrupted arm.

"Master James?"

"Milady." He swept away to the door and wrenched it open. She blinked as the brass plate shone orange in her eyes, bright with mirrored rays of the afternoon sun. He declared, "You have fulfilled your commission, and may return to your newfound patron. Inform him that you have, successfully and sexually, distracted Commodore Hook from *Frau Doktor* Heinrich."

"Oh— no." With a flurry of clothing, she hurried to sit up on the bed, her dark hair streaming. She clutched at her jacket to cover her corset. "No, please! You mistake me, Sir. You are so very mistaken!"

His piratical earring sparked sharp in the sunlight, while his manners reflected the patrician. "Have I behaved in an ungentlemanly fashion? I do apologize. Mr. Smee will attend you, Madam, and arrange passage to whatever rendezvous suits."

He deserted her, and, against expectation, he didn't bother to slam the door shut.

As the sun dipped in western waters, Jill, garbed in her sky-blue dressing gown, knocked softly upon Mrs. Hanover's door. When it opened, she slid swiftly in, closing the door and ignoring the alarm on the young mother's face. The tiny cabin smelled of books and ointments. The babe napped in a basket in a corner. Pierre-Jean slid down from the hammock that Doctor Heinrich, for propriety's sake, had insisted be hung above Liza's bunk. The young Frenchman touched his forehead in respect. Jill kept her voice to a whisper.

"Quickly, Liza! I have only one moment."

Liza blinked in astonishment. "But the commodore commands, 'Mrs. Han— ' "

"…and the doctor would have us do otherwise. While we live under his influence, I shall call you 'Liza.' You and I must forge a new front, together, if we are to handle him."

Standing in support behind Liza, Pierre-Jean set his callused hands on her shoulders. His gesture was more intelligible than his English. "*Oui*, little *Madame*, the lady words right. You are want two *Madames ensemble*."

"*Merci*, Pierre-Jean. Yes, Liza, we should do all we can to help one another manage in Vienna, but I need one favor *now*."

As Jill had gambled, Liza nodded her willingness. Jill had caught the girl between surprise and desperation.

"What medicine in Doctor Heinrich's bag will upset my stomach?"

The puzzlement upon the girl's face soon turned to shrewd understanding. Unwilling to trust her rusty voice, she seized a book from the stack on her table, rifled through the index, and pointed to the name. Taking a moment to recall her medical reading, she murmured, "One swallow."

"Thank you, and *adieu*. We women," Jill smiled at Liza, then turned her gaze to engage the china blue eyes of Pierre-Jean, "and our protectors, must keep our secrets."

As Liza pledged her silence by pressing her index finger to her mouth, Jill effected an exit, slipping silently back into her cabin. She would be sick soon but, as the ship's bell dinged for the evening watch, she never felt finer.

My dear Master James, and now Commodore~

My single hope is that you will grant this letter your attention long enough to learn the events that returned me to your sphere of existence. I, myself, received no formal explanation, and little choice. You, Sir, if you honor my request to read on, shall be given both.

Please excuse my presumption in employing your own pen to disabuse you. Your Mr. Smee seated me here at your handsome desk, having cautioned me that the exquisite escritoire resting so near to your hand is your ladylove's station, and, like every other reminder of her in your princely apartment, precludes the touch of a lesser woman. I commend him for his loyalty; you have chosen well to trust this man, who, finding me in tears, made his heart large enough to allow to me this opportunity to enlighten you.

I assert here, without reserve, that I have kept the spirit and the letter of our legal agreement. For decades, your agents honored it too. The facts I present I learned gradually, in the few conversations Johann Heinrich conducted with me during our voyage aboard La Fleur de Lotus.

I have come to understand that, in an unfortunate turn, the great-nephew who inherited the office of your original solicitor is proven unworthy, valuing gain above the integrity of his firm. The silence held sacred by generations of his forebears is broken, for, you see, when Doctor Heinrich's inquisitor came calling, armed with your family name, your trusted representative unworthily yielded to a bribe. I shall do my best to elucidate the method with which that name was discovered.

Knowing only that you are an English aristocrat absent from society for some years, the clever doctor described your appearance to a portraitist. He requested that the artist impose upon that image the features of the younger man you must have been. You have now viewed that portrait, which I carry in my trunk. Heinrich instructed his agent to show this likeness to those gentlemen who fill their leisure hours documenting the Peerage. Your face was recognized as a member of your father's line. Even I, when shown your picture, assumed the subject to be your descendant— a noble son, perhaps, or a grandson. Gladness for your sake filled my spirit, for this evidence convinced me that you had secured a new home somewhere in the Empire, and re-founded your heritage.

Even as a youth, you understood the importance of settling the security upon me from your own estate, unknown to your father and independent of his control. You preserved me, better than yourself, against the misfortune His Grace the Duke later caused to befall you and your honorable house. I am forever grateful, but, because your settlement remained extant after that disaster, Doctor Heinrich was informed by the solicitor of our connection, which led him to call upon me personally.

Again, I fear, coins were exchanged, for under Doctor Heinrich's persistence my maid allowed him entrance against my explicit instruction. Distrusting his appearance, with his visage so roguish but his demeanor professional, I remained aloof. When pressed, I denied you. Yet when he unveiled the portrait before my eyes, I could not disguise my emotion. Heinrich claimed to have found you, asking only if I might desire to behold you again.

While hearing him speak of you, I became convinced that Doctor Heinrich had met, not your descendant, but you, in the flesh. For that interchange to be possible, I deduced that you, like me, have been blessed— or afflicted— with some unfathomable longevity. I've been astonished to find myself so long-lived, yet resilient. Before the physician's visit, I believed myself alone in this phenomenon. The new knowledge that you, too, are alive, and that you live vigorously, overcame my reserve. As you always have done, Master James, you fire my curiosity. I felt compelled to learn more— perhaps, even, to solve the mystery of my being.

Heinrich imposed no conditions save secrecy. One reason you sought me out to become your inamorata was my habit of discretion. I saw no occasion to alter that habit. After all, as a penurious baronetess widowed twice, engaged for a role of intimacy with a youth half her age, I exercised strict discretion. Pledged to guard your identity, I conceived the threat Heinrich posed to your confidence, should I refuse to follow him. In my power lay the means to prevent him from exposing you. Long after the day of your disappearance, as a matron who retains too much youth, I retired to the background, solitary for the most part, lo, for an age. To this day, only one has discovered us. I relaxed my tenets not at all to accompany Doctor Heinrich; indeed, I stayed true to them.

One aspect of my nature has changed. I am weary of living. I may not participate in the modest round of society I once enjoyed before and after my mourning. I've kept no deep domestic companionship, discharging my maids every dozen years or so, in order to stop any gossip over my agelessness. Friends I used to cherish have passed, all, away. What had I left to leave behind? My paints I brought with me. My suite of rooms, so lovely and comfortable thanks to your generosity, I closed up with fond recollection, but without remorse. I gave away my furnishings— all antique now— packed my trunk, and stepped aboard the Dover steamer for my very last voyage.

And today I beheld you. I held you. If you are moved to do so, dismiss me sans further ado. But, I beg, do so kindly, for, as reluctantly as I was persuaded to enter into our association, I cannot regret you. I consider that interval, in which I indulged your thirst to learn the secrets of womankind, to be the few bejeweled years of my lifetime.

I congratulate you, with sincerity, on finding love with your lady. I wish you the joy of reunion.

Ever your
Lady J— L—

Smee planted his boots before the ebony desk, where the commodore sat enthroned. The bo'sun stood straight as a ramrod, clasping his hands so tightly behind his brawny back he was sure his knuckles had whitened. His spirit still smarted from Hook's rebuke, along with his biceps. Smee knew he'd overstepped, and he knew he was right. He hoped to hell the commodore would soon know it, too. Smee's eyes tightened of their own accord, but he held off a wince and kept his spectacles aimed at the dimming horizon.

Hook tilted the papers toward the candlelight. Ignoring his man, he read the letter through, then read it again. His aristocratic features waxed taut with the tenseness pervading the ship. He'd ordered no course for sailing, and, stagnant, the *Roger* swayed where her anchor dropped that morning, pinned just off the odiferous isle of her rendezvous with Captain LeCorbeau. With few chores to occupy her crew, they kept below. Restless, they held their noise down as they rattled the dice, gambling and gossiping about the commodore's guest. A solitary man again, and with his mind closed to his Jill, Hook ignored these other men, as well.

Smee ruminated on how, within only hours, this fresh, unforeseen absence of Red-Handed Jill upended the ship's routine. In the twilight loomed the memory of Captain Hook in his long years alone, before Jill and her influence did her best to civilize the 'Lion of the Sea.' She'd been gone just one day. Smee's own ill-treatment was testimony— already Hook reclaimed his ruthlessness. Hook had withdrawn, brooding, from his ship's company, castigated Mr. Smee, and, as the rumor soon circulated, the commodore took a tryst in his bed— in Jill's bed. Although the sailors were inclined to broadmindedness where women were concerned, Smee resented Hook's loose use of the baronetess, if only for Red-Handed Jill's sake. Smee felt his face heating, then thanked the Powers that Captain Cecco had sailed leagues away by now. Jealous of Hook at first, now Cecco would be jealous *for Jill.* In this unpredicted twist of Captain Cecco's priorities, Hook's betrayal of their lady would surely set those two fierce men's claws at each other's gullets— again. Smee's mind wandered through the abyss of this discord.

Hook struck his desk with his barb, a clash of iron on ebony. "I addressed you, Smee!"

Smee startled back to the present. "Sir. Begging your pardon."

"Where have you placed the baronetess?"

"She's in the spare cabin, Sir, awaiting your answer. Tom Tootles is watching over her."

Shoving his chair back, Hook stood and threw down the papers. He angled his jaw, studying his bo'sun. Flatly, he stated, "You are bleeding." He drew his handkerchief from his right sleeve, below the claw, and tossed it to Smee.

Smee caught it. "Aye, Commodore." With the fine linen cloth, he swabbed the cut near his shoulder, stoic. He would stitch up his striped shirt later. And not for the first time. "A hazard of the job."

The freezing gaze of Hook's icy blue eyes was the only apology he'd ever give. Long moments passed in this stare. Of a height, neither man looked down upon the other. Hook never flinched, and the two men, as both allies and adversaries, stood where they'd planted their boots, while the water lapped along the ship's hull.

"Escort her to me." Rolling his shoulders, Hook flexed to ease up his tension. "You had better divest me of this hook first. Fetch my robe, too."

Smee did as he was told. A little later, with the lady in question in tow, he knocked at the commodore's door, then opened it. Gently, he touched the elbow of her mink-brown jacket, urging her to enter. Her violet eyes turned up to him, rimmed with pink from the tears she'd shed earlier. He could tell by her look. She was trusting him. And he had to trust Hook, to do right by her.

The commodore rose from his daybed to stand, tall, unsmiling, his hair black as a raven and full as a mane, a touch of the wilder world in this civilized room. In contrast, the barbarous hook had been banished, and the soft, quilted sleeve of his robe hid the wreck of his arm. The lady hung back, reluctant to intrude again, until he reached out his one hand. His rings flashed as he beckoned to her, and his five fingers curled in encouragement.

In her high-button shoes, Milady ventured one step. She caught a breath, and then she hurried into his arms. He held her, his jaw pressed to her temple, his gaze trained on Smee's. At a further flick of Hook's fingers, the bo'sun was dismissed. Smee held off the wince, and backed off. He shut the door.

Smee had overstepped, and he knew he was right. But, now that he thought about it, which woman *wasn't* he betraying?

Wedded Bias

When she woke, she was the woman in the bed on the ship in the sea, and she used to be Wendy Darling, who dreamt in the bed in the nursery of Number 14.

Now, the heavy arm that protected and confined her belonged not to the man she'd imagined. That man's powerful, handless arm ended hideously, at the wrist. The hideousness, here, was a faultless physique. The nightmare was the lack of her lover, and the imposition of this husband.

Heinrich.

Her eyes flew open to darkness. Still tasting the bile of her sickness, Jill remained motionless, her stomach calmer now and only her temper rebellious. Unwilling to awaken her bunk mate, she lay quiet, letting her eyelids fall closed. The ship moved in time to the rhythm of the sea, and, in Time, her body obeyed her need for sleep.

She dreamt again, the same story she dreamt up as a child, the tale she wove into reality to fly beyond the boundaries of London.

Forget-me-nots. Shades of black. The silver flash of a sickle. A laugh so rich it felt gilded in gold…

And then, he woke her.

Hook was awake. He was always awake when she was. Yet, tonight, Jill was not the lady who saved him from solitude. True to his own code of chivalry, Hook didn't care. He was a man who didn't care about a great many things, and this female's need was unique. He had abused her, then soothed her. This long-ago liaison at last lay at rest under his arm— his gashed, ghastly arm. His one-handed grasp closed more firmly round her body, in which, as a youth, he so deeply indulged. Sleep, tonight, remained out of Hook's reach.

It was Jill who dreamt life into him. In Time, Hook had to hold Jill again. Milady was a paradigm drawn from desire, a widow now wedded to solitude. She should be freed from his story.

Jill had created the lady, dictated her tale. It was Hook who must open the door to her escape.

But the night pressed upon them. And Hook was awake.

In sweet morning light, Johann Heinrich awakened in his bunk with his bride. Through sleepy eyes, he admired her attributes, warming to his victory in possessing her, physically, at last. Almost heaven, it was, to lie with this woman in his arms. With his chest pressed against her back and only the film of her nightdress between them, he and she fit together in that magical manner granted to lovers who slumber. Sweet was this victory, and the spoils, seductive.

To divert himself from his arousal, he examined her with a physician's regard. He determined that the dye applied to her hair seemed innocuous. No damage was visible on the scalp, nor were her tresses less luxurious to his touch. Her pulse was now steady, her temperature cool, the respiration regular. She had taken little to eat in the excitement of yesterday. In his estimation, her face was thinner this morning, her cheekbones sharper and her flesh more pallid— natural aftereffects of her early lack of appetite, and her late bout of nausea. Skeptical that a woman so accustomed to sailing should succumb to seasickness, last night he confirmed the authenticity of her ailment. Employing a physician's indifference to the filth of illness, he inspected the contents of the chamber mug. He diagnosed Jill's malady as actual, not fabricated.

Upon ascertaining this fact, he'd experienced the clammy dread of a crisis that might threaten his plans. Examining her immediately, he quickly determined that she was not bearing a child. A glance at her facial tissues, now illuminated by daylight, showed no glow of pregnancy, nor the maternal mask so common in gravid women who spent time in the sun. A blessing, for, if she were *enceinte*, between those two sea rogues her offspring could be the progeny of heaven only knew which. The thought had been rank enough to delay his desire for her, and, of course, given her malady, he had treated her, then allowed her to rest.

Heinrich felt confident as he looked to the future. In a gracious townhouse within a glorious city, Jill would adjust to this life with her husband. His love was a legitimate one. He was a respected physician and scientist, a man much more able to care for her than any pirate king living by plunder on some reeking, leaking boat. She would suffer no less affection, no less affluence. After all, one year ago she yielded to his suit, accepting his hand and his heart in circumstances far less advantageous.

With a pang of old anger, he remembered the frustrations he endured at that time. Hook had coerced him, then Cecco played on his desperation. The indignity made Heinrich almost as queasy as Jill felt last night. How vividly the good doctor imagined the manipulations that Italian must have applied to Jill, with his musical jewelry and his mellifluous accent. Right under Heinrich's nose, he induced her to enter in to their so-called marriage. Apparently, Jill had rejected the gypsy after Heinrich's expulsion from the ship, preferring the criminal who *first* corrupted her.

And now at last Heinrich had removed her from the influence of that infidel, Hook. She was free to learn again to appreciate the virtues of the man she married of her own choice. He need only remind her of the dear, intimate moments of their courtship. Cheered by his more tender recollections, he chuckled to think how she chose to bait him yesterday— her clever banter, those thrusts of her wit from behind the façade of her fan. He thrilled to anticipate this banter transposed to the bedroom. The physician had observed that, for a female, *making* love was foreplay to *feeling* love. Her thirst for jewelry, too, ravished her. How happily he would indulge her in each of these inducements, and win her whole heart! Heinrich amused himself by resuming their secret code. 'Today,' or 'tomorrow,' his Jill would repay him for all of his trouble.

Yes, he remembered her taste for games. This time, he would humor her. In his own country, his own drawing room, far from her brigands and with the added gravity of her father's influence, he could afford to show patience. Conversely, his beautiful bride could *not* afford to resist her handsome husband. For her own benefit, he had limited the players, controlled the gameboard. In his strongbox, he stocked ample tokens in the form of gems to provoke or reward her participation. Both morally and carnally, his win was her gain as well. With a generous smile upon his lips, he bent to her face, and, in a new spirit of playfulness, he roused her with kisses.

She surprised him again. He had not anticipated that, as he embraced her, her lips would open in this way. That she might turn as she did to wind her arms round his neck, and press her breasts against him. Their kiss grew from just a folly to fervor. He heard the beat of his heart, and felt hers. His satisfaction swelled. Against the play of her mouth, the doctor murmured, "Today. My darling, today!"

Lost in the dream of her lover, Jill threw herself into his kiss. She craved his caresses with her body and her soul, and, by the intensity of his response, she sensed his same hunger. Some nightmare disturbed her earlier, and now relief fueled her eagerness. At the edge of her mind that specter lurked, but she thrust it back with her passion. She made love with the man in her arms until she heard those soft, significant words, articulated in the accent of her adversary…"Today!"

As a sense of her present rushed back, Jill froze. Before opening her eyes, though, a flash of insight aided her. She might use this mistake to advantage. Still recumbent, she recalled her excuses of the previous evening. She renewed her embrace, then withdrew it. Rolling toward the side of the bed, she pretended to gag. "I am sorry," she gasped, her hand to her mouth, "I am not well after all…" With the easing of his hold, the hot perspiration of relief advanced her deceit.

Heinrich placed his fingers on her forehead, assessing her temperature. "My poor Jill, I shall dose you again." He rose from the bed.

"No, Johann. Help me up." He did so, and she sat on the bunk, using the confusion of her gaffe to mask her subterfuge. "There, it is as I told you last night. This ship is too small for my comfort. I am unacquainted with the quirks of a frigate."

"I observe, however, that you slept."

"Only after your treatment. But I feel well enough, as long as I'm upright. In fact, I look forward to a walk on the deck, and another chat with my father."

"I cannot advise you to stir until you are quite fully recovered."

"Thank you for tending me. I feel foolish. I am so rarely ill."

Recalling the first time she made excuse for stolen moments alone with him, he wore a sly smile, and his gray eyes ignited. The sheer stuff of her nightdress was an improvement over the gown and corset that confined her that evening. "Unlike a prior occasion, we cannot blame the tight lacing of your undergarment."

"Oh!" Coyly, she spread her hand to cover her bosom. "Johann, do please give me my robe." How far to carry her seeming submission was a problem she could think about later. This morning, she must deal with her nights. "I believe I have a solution. Let us request a hammock."

"What? You would bunk like a common sailor?"

"Common sailors sleep well, Johann. In a hammock, I may remain upright. A few pillows will help. Such a bed would sway me gently, instead of letting me feel every lurch of the waters."

"You cannot imagine that I would lie with you there?"

"Oh, no. You seem comfortable in the bunk. A hammock can hang just above. I believe this arrangement is what you ordered for Pierre-Jean?" She offered a smile. "Let us try it tonight."

"Very well, my darling, we shall make the experiment. But I shall keep a close watch upon you."

She looked down, demure. "Yes, Johann. I am beginning to feel the benefit of your care." Unable to continue this charade, she raised her gaze, defiant. "Do not mistake me, though. I have no intention of forgiving you so easily. You have taken most dreadful advantage of my father's credulity."

"I see that you have recovered, indeed, Jill. Dress now, and we shall take breakfast in the galley."

"No, thank you. Have the chef send me baguettes. And hot water. I shall make my own tea."

Not displeased with the progress he had made with his wife this morning, Heinrich acquiesced.

As he turned from her, Jill received the full view of his ravaged back. She had told the gypsies how, for the physician's transgressions against her, Captain Cecco with his notorious knife engraved her name in his hide. She had watched with satisfaction that day. 'Today,' with a glow of gratification, she memorized the markings. *JILL*. Smooth and pink, the letters invited her fingertips, desirous that their namesake might touch them. She experienced that kind of lust that her pirate side provided, whenever she entered into revenge.

Heinrich dressed in his royal blue suit with his usual care. He tied back his sandy hair with a ribbon, tugged his cuffs into place, then took Jill's hand to press his warm lips to her palm. "I shall collect you after you have breakfasted. Do not neglect to don your pearls."

She raised her ruby fingers to the blemish at her neck. "Ivory pearls, to cover my scarlet character. And tell me, Johann. How shall you cover *your* guilt?"

He stiffened.

"Your child; your grandchild. Liza is now my stepdaughter. I ask for her sake."

"I see you still believe in your buccaneer lover."

"Hook has never betrayed me."

At Jill's testament, Heinrich burst out with his brief but vehement laugh, exhibiting a certitude that upset his wife's stomach, again. "I promise you, my darling. Hook will not waste one day in repining over your absence. While in London I learned a great deal about him. One of his lady friends, in particular, desired to—"

"You are cruel to laugh so."

"Perhaps. The truth is often cruel, as, for example, you read in my sworn statement yesterday. I accuse Captain Hook of the rape of my daughter. I hoped to spare you this pain, Jill, but I saw him, with my own eyes, in the very act of Liza's violation— and not once, but two times."

"You did the same to me as I slept, on the night I imbibed your potion…when I'd trusted in you as a gentleman!"

"And I married you, thus restoring your honor."

"*My* honor."

"Because I *am* a gentleman, I shall respect my lady's sensibilities, and never refer to these unpleasant incidents again." With a scowl on his scar-ridden face, he commanded, "Nor, *meine Frau*, will you." Curtly, he bowed, and left the room.

Jill sighed in exasperation, throwing herself backward on the bed. The cabin seemed to spin around her, and, for that moment, she really did feel the pitch of the sea. She articulated soft, significant words, cursing the ascent of her adversary.

As Jill's husband, Captain Cecco found it difficult to let go. He and Hook agreed before she sailed with LeCorbeau that the *Red Lady*

would follow *Le Lotus*, for a time. In the face of her determination, nothing the pirate captains could do would dissuade Jill from her departure, but at least her loving spouse could keep an eye on her voyage, if only for a while. Because of the bounty on his head, Cecco would tempt Fate if he entered European waters. To be captured himself would be no use to Jill. At first light, and through most of the morning, he watched the stern of *Le Lotus* beneath the French flag, rising and falling in the brine, and wondering what ordeal Jill had suffered in the night. Unhappy as Cecco felt, he also felt the extreme opposite, and it was difficult, too, to let go of his daughter. He held her now, one strong arm around her shoulders, while they continued to become acquainted.

Stella's mandolin lay in her lap, the strings vibrating under her fingers with an old Romani song. Nibs sat cross-legged on the rug, in front of the father and daughter as the two nestled together on a settee, alike in features, and likewise in their vivid gypsy garb. The light, Mediterranean mood of Cecco's quarters, with gold curtains and azure-blue cushions, made Stella feel she had come home.

Nibs had won permission from the commodore to sail on the *Lady* until the two ships met up again. He was part and parcel of this family through the bonds of what he considered to be blood-ties, and love. His brother Tom held the unenviable position of remaining on the *Roger* as bo'sun's mate to Mr. Smee— and the next in line to wait upon Hook in whatever mood Jill's desertion brought upon him. Nibs couldn't help but feel guilty, but one look at his beloved banished remorse.

Below the pretty ringlets on her forehead, Stella's eyes glowed. When her tune was finished, her melodic voice thrummed with happiness as she said, "Red-Handed Jill's stories brought you back to the tribe, Papa. Her visit reunited us, the next best thing to having you home."

"And for me," Cecco replied, his white teeth flashing in his smile, "you are the next best thing to being home. A reminder of the sweet incense of Italian air, and the tangy taste of the vineyards. I have had to neglect you, with the business with LeCorbeau, and then making ready to sail. Now, all my time will be yours." Still, his smile faltered, as he dealt with his loss.

"I peeked out with your spyglass to get a look at that doctor from Vienna. Poor Jill. He is not nearly as dashing as you, Papa!" A frown wrinkled the girl's brow. "And such a bad man, to deserve what you did to him. *Bravo*, Papa."

Cecco gazed into the distance, his hand falling to the knife in his sash. "A satisfying moment. But I should have killed him."

Nibs reminded him, "By the rule of ship's articles, Captain, you could only discipline the man. He was one of the company then, an officer. Jill had her chance to slay him, but her love of treasure got in her way." The line between Nib's eyebrows deepened, and, savagely, he pulled at the knot of his kerchief. "She regrets her choice now."

Distressed for their sakes, Stella encouraged her menfolk. "Jill will surely face troubles, but I believe in her. She will find a way to escape him."

"And we will find a way to help." Nibs turned his dark eyes toward Cecco, for reassurance.

The captain nodded, grave, but emphatically enough to set his gold earrings swinging. "*Sì*, my heart is set on it, and my mind is at work on this problem." He turned once more to his daughter, his stern expression softening. "As we begin our life as a family, little Stella, I want you to know. If I had not been transported far off to Gao, I would have celebrated your birth, and raised you by Bezzi's side."

"I never doubted, Papa. I understand, though, that although you have suffered, you found your true love. In spite of the difficulties, you make your home with Jill." She glanced at Nibs, her dimples in play, "And Jill brought me Nibs."

"I cannot regret the events that carried me to Jill's part of the world. Yet I am sorry you were cheated of a father."

"Nibs can tell you, he saw how Uncle Nico and everyone else cares for me. I enjoy the blessings of family that you yourself miss. And now that they know you are married, Papa, Nico and my mamma at last are together. Jill saw to it with a marvelous story! I know they will be happy. You need not fear for your Bezzi."

"And what will make my daughter happy?"

Nibs' swarthy complexion showed just a tinge of red. "I'd like to take on that duty, Sir. I asked Stella to be my wife." Remembering the manners Jill taught him, he added, "If I can have your approval, of course."

Cecco gazed intently upon him. "I have known you, boy and man. I witnessed your courage and your loyalty, even when these traits led you and me into, shall I say, uncomfortable circumstances?" He looked to his daughter, her face flushed, her green eyes sparkling. "A good man wants you. What is your answer?"

"I will give my hand to Nibs— both hands, gladly, Papa, if…"

Nibs held his breath. Cecco asked, "If?"

"If we can spend part of each year with our gypsies."

Nibs jumped up to pace the cabin, unsure whether to shout out in happiness, or hang his head in despair.

"I cannot speak for the commodore." Cecco shrugged. "It might be arranged. Certainly, when you two begin bringing up a family, a pirate ship is not the safest place for *bambini*. Hook does not care to have children underfoot, but Bezzi would welcome your babies in Italy. Still, Mr. Nibs swore his duty to the *Roger*, while I want you sailing with me, here on *Red Lady*. You cannot be three places at once."

"Four," Nibs stopped in his tracks to interject, "I want Stella to learn to love the Island, as well."

"Ah, yes, the Island! The magical place I found Jill. Many wonders await you, my daughter. Let us enjoy one another's company in this time Jill is absent, and, when we celebrate her return—" Cecco broke off, sickened to his core to own to himself that he'd almost said 'if.' He sighed. "When my lovely one returns, she can give us her counsel. She may intercede with Commodore Hook on Nibs' behalf."

"Aye, Papa— isn't that how you sailors say 'yes'? Aye, we shall make the best of our time, for what else do we have? Only the present, and one another."

"And the music of your mandolin." Kissing her fresh, youthful cheek, her papa affirmed, "Jill is correct. You are a wise young woman. Whenever you must leave me, I will find it a trial to let you go, and, I see, so will your betrothed— who will please show us the civility of ceasing his roaming and sitting down? But, Stella, tell me now all about my brothers, your uncles. Trinio was young when I left him, but I well remember his outrageous ways!"

Stella took her cue, warming to the subject. The rest of the day passed in this pleasure, and in the pain of Jill's lengthening distance.

Her husband was loath to let go.

Substitution

Curious to get a gander at the new woman in the commodore's
quarters, Cook himself brought up the breakfast, with a tea
towel over his shoulder. He placed his ear against the door, just above
the brass plate. Hearing nothing, he balanced his tray on one arm and
with a ham-fisted hand, managed a mere, modest tap. With no delay,
Hook answered, "Come!" Cook smoothed his apron and obeyed, not
daring to guess what to expect as he stepped in.

The stern windows were hung on their hooks, wide open to invite
the ocean air, brisker now that the ship had departed from the islet
and gotten under way. The *Roger*'s wake foamed and fizzed in the green
sea behind her. The four-poster's bedding was tousled; the divan, on
the other hand, was tidy, barren of pillows or blankets. Draped over
the back lay the lady's nightie. Her traveling trunk gaped open in the
corner by the bookcase.

The baronetess perched on the window seat, fully dressed in a
quaint kind of gown, wide lavender skirts and belled sleeves, a low
neckline veiled with a filament of black fabric, and indented at the
waist like an hourglass, all highlighted with shiny jet beads. Hook sat
beside her, half dressed but shaven and shod, his claw at rest on his
thigh. He pitched his jaw to an angle while the baronetess waited on
him like Jill or Smee would do, her two hands beneath his chin as she
pinned a gold and gem brooch at the collar of his blouse. The lady
paused her task when Cook entered, her wide eyes upon him. With
loose fingers, Hook gestured to her to continue.

"Sir, Mr. Smee said you was primed for breakfast."

Hook jerked his head toward the table.

"Aye, aye, Sir," Cook said, and laid his tray there, setting out the dishes, keeping their pewter covers in place to prevent the release of their heat along with savory aromas. The teapot held an ordinary blend this morning, not Red-Handed Jill's special recipe. Cook was proud that Jill knew she could count on him to brew it right for her. He stood straighter, a man who was trusted by the queen of the fleet.

Glancing round again, he spied an empty goblet on the sideboard, and a tumbler lined with dregs of rum. Also on the board was an item that did not belong there: the commodore's tricorn, with a colorful blue jay feather spearing the brim. Hook hadn't worn this hat since their last, brief visit to the Island. Cook left it where it lay. The commodore's clothing was Smee's dominion. He piled the glassware onto his tray for a washup. Before speaking again, the wary cook eyed the commodore, gauging his mood. The weather looked fair enough. "Anything else I can get for you, Commodore? Or for your, uh— your new lady. Beg pardon, Ma'am."

Hook's silken voice held its edge. "Begone."

Cook had misread the weather. With his meaty paw, he touched his forehead, and quickly departed.

All a-tanto, no damage done, and no surprise to find the commodore still testy, given the absence of Red-Handed Jill. Everyone missed her. Was it good luck, or ill, that the cocky French captain smuggled this former lady friend aboard? At worst, she might be a spy. At the very least, the commodore had a companion. Still, Cook reckoned...she seemed a bit strange when you thought about it. Pretty, aye, and an air about her. He'd like to see that shiny brown hair let loose down round her backside. Compared to Jill, though, this woman was a ghost. Willing enough, she seemed, but when you came right down to it, not enough flesh and blood for a man to set his teeth into, so to speak. Not a working girl, nor a matron, quite. She was a blue blood, maybe that's what the trouble was. If only Jill was here, she'd bring this lady to life with a story.

And then, she'd end it.

With a crooked smile, Cook tucked up his apron and descended to the galley. Their pirate queen had flesh and blood aplenty to offer a man as forceful as the commodore. And a temper to match him. Cook didn't dare guess what to expect, once *she* stepped back into her quarters!

The two took breakfast together in the lavish, padded cabin on the ship Hook called home. Here upon the sea that freed him of his past, he hearkened to older echoes. For the sake of his 'new lady,' as Cook had so blunderingly phrased it, Hook concealed the raw wound of Jill's leaving. With only a hint of irritation, he offered, "Were we back in England I should say, 'Are you feeling quite recovered this morning, Milady?' "

Her lavender gown accentuated the hue of her eyes. Sunlight bounced from the sea to the ceiling, illuminating them, making highlights in her hair, and the room glowed in silvery waves all around her. "I should reply, 'Yes, my health is improved. I thank you, Sir.' "

"And I would consider your maxims: 'Does her gaze linger upon you? Is the tone of her voice pitched for your ear alone?' You see, I have forgotten nothing. Now, as is only proper, will you accept the honor of pouring?"

She smiled, and picked up the pot.

Hook's voice flowed more silkily than she remembered. " 'Take note of each motion, take no gesture for granted.' " He did these things as he spoke, still following her counsel.

She paused with the spout above his cup, the belled sleeves of her gown floating gracefully. "I am flattered that you remember. Two sugars, no milk, as I recall?"

"Now it is I who am flattered."

She held the full cup and saucer out to him. Through its swirling steam, she reminisced, her tenor light and mocking, " 'What did you think of the play…of the races…the book?' "

Hook took up the cup, and her banter. "Then, 'Let us withdraw to the boudoir.' " This last phrase to be spoken, though, only after hungry months she spent extending his patience, dancing him through subtle steps to seduction. *The drawing room is a threshold to the bedroom; every nuance of one's demeanor nudges the door.* Even after he crossed that delectable threshold, she insisted upon honor, esteem, and etiquette, all agreeable to him as a man of his taste, and his class. *This, Master James, is the game I am engaged to provide. As a gentleman, you will find that a gentleman's ways work your will.* Words of power, whether she whispered them in tangles of lace, or pronounced them over her teacup, as now. Drunk on passion as a youth, still, he'd imbibed all she offered.

She'd been proven correct, and not only in intrigues of intimate intention. Ever since their liaison, where the fairer sex was concerned, the slow, steady pressure of a man of manners served James' every need. After England, when forced among much rougher company, his deportment engendered welcome from women, and envy from men. If no female on whom he'd turned his charm said him nay, his successes were due in good part to Milady. Joined with the authority born with him— and his share of his forebears' fine features— Milady's prompts served his purpose among the masculine, too.

With his half-smile, he revealed, "Your young Master James could not foresee how very valuable your influence would prove, and for the whole of his lifetime. In those days, I sought what every boy seeks in female affections. Experience first, expertise at the last."

"Your handicap then," Milady's cheeks reddened as, realizing her mistake, she darted her gaze away from his gleaming hook at its ease on the end of his arm, "your difficulty, I mean, was your rank. I sensed how you felt the gravity of your position. Scandal must be avoided, and you were much too fastidious to indulge in low company. Looking back, I judge that your instinct was correct in pursuing a lady of status for your mistress. Considering the formality of your station as a youth, you benefited from my more gentle companionship."

"That boy assumed that, in good time, he'd put the edification you granted him to practical as well as pleasurable use." Young James had intended, after this liaison served and surfeited him, to choose— and to keep— for his wife, a woman of title. "Ironic, is it not, that my mother proved to be the very model of the dilettante spouse I sought to avoid." Only after his mother's *faux pas* and the violence of his father's retribution did young James fully comprehend his own wisdom.

"As I once told you, Sir, you were never as young as your age."

"Nor were you. I came to know you well enough to wonder now; how is it you put your trust in a man like Johann Heinrich?"

"Of course I did not trust him. I merely expected certain things of him. I expected him to ignite the old embers of your household's scandal if I did not assist him. And, I believed, he would take me to you. I was curious, you see. So many memories, and no word of you from any quarter— not one— in all these long years."

"My alias, then, has proven successful."

"No one ever imagined who you became. The revelation shook me to the marrow."

"After the quiet life into which my attentions forced you, you desired to emulate me? To throw it all over and venture to sea?"

"When I learned from the doctor's description that you were yet alive, my heart compelled me. Come what may, I wished to see you again."

"Milady," Hook said, more tenderly than he'd spoken to her in, quite literally, an age. He slid his hand along the table, so that his fingertips touched her own. "As deserving of love as you are...ours was never an affair of the heart."

Even so, her heartstrings vibrated at this, his lightest of touches. "I have known it, always, and accepted your terms. After all, as fascinating as you have become, when I knew you then you were merely a man in the making."

"I was a boy." He raised his hand and his hook to the level of his eyes, to compare them. "At that time I held, in a whole and healthy right hand, a future I now would not wish to reclaim." He returned his gaze to Milady. "I was the gentleman Heinrich only professes to be."

"After listening to him, I understood that it was my connection to you that so strangely preserved me. On this, my final voyage, that quiet life I led may come at last to conclusion."

"And so, it is as I anticipated. You came to me to be sent away."

"I learned long ago to place faith in you."

"I see the time has come for me to tell more of Jill."

"Your ladylove."

"Our storyteller." Hook sat back in his chair. "Cast your thoughts to the past, to the beginning of our tale. How do you remember it? Pray, do tell me." Ever so slightly, he opened his mind to his Jill, and old echoes.

Milady looked puzzled, but, ever obedient to him, she gathered her memories. Slowly, she summarized, "Out of nowhere, or so it seemed to me...at the opera, a young man arranged for an introduction to be made to a lady. She had shed her mourning that season, for a second time. She recognized him; how could she not? She did not flatter herself that he looked for affiance. Her rank was too low for the young heir of a grand family, and her marriages yielded no children. He seemed fully informed of her circumstances, appeared to have learned all about her. Handsome he was, tall for his age though still a scholar, with black hair and blue eyes like dark blooms of forget-me-nots. In the few moments he conversed with the lady, those eyes never left her. Within a day, his man of business called upon hers. An offer so discreet, so generous, her distress might be banished. He was a youth of breeding. To him, this lady of lower peerage presented the ideal alliance, each to feed a need of the other. He and she never spoke; their solicitors bandied the terms. After much resistance, and at great cost to her dignity…she agreed.

"I was selected to share intimate secrets. I then guarded his. Time ticked by, weeks, months, a few years, punctuated by the hours in which he called upon me. When his own distress struck, a family scandal, I, like everyone else, was aghast. He vanished from academy, from London, from England, and I sympathized. I thought never to see him again, until, at long last, a strange and strange-looking gentleman appeared, bearing a portrait.

"And now, my dear Master James, you owe me nothing, and it is nothing that I ask. For, you see…you owe me merely an end."

He said it softly. "No."

Weary now, her eyes appealed to him.

With his hook, he gestured toward Jill's escritoire. "There is where you will find it. One day, when she returns to me, she will set it in ink, in her elegant lettering."

Milady looked upon the deserted desktop, and sighed.

Take note of each motion.

"We must, both of us, employ that patience you recommended." Another glance at the escritoire, her quills, her pillow. Then Hook took his mind from them, concealed the wound of her parting, and filled his eyes with the sight of Milady.

To give her hands something to do, she did him the honor of pouring.

Take no gesture for granted.

"Were we back in England…" But he ceased speculation, and anchored himself— in the very pleasant present.

The sky turned iron-gray. With a clapping sound, the wind whipped the *Red Lady*'s sails. Nibs had dressed in dark colors. Poking his orange kerchief in his pocket, he shucked off his boots. He had maybe half an hour to accomplish his errand before the storm made flight impossible, and less time before nightfall would blacken his path. Captain Cecco stood by, his face as overcast as the weather.

Both Nibs and Cecco were determined that he make this attempt, risky as it might be. Tonight was their last chance. After weeks of trailing *Le Lotus*, they were sure to lose her in the gale.

Although Nibs knew his instructions by heart, Cecco repeated, "Waste no time, but ask her my questions. She will have learned more of her situation by now, something, anything, to help us help her."

"Aye, aye, Captain. Keep those lights burning."

At Cecco's signal, Nibs clamped his knife between his teeth, bent his knees, and shoved off into the atmosphere. The air beat at his chest as he pushed his way through it. It forced itself into his nose, almost too thick to inhale, and smelling of rain. Stella had woven his hair in a pigtail that flapped behind him as he soared high, and higher. Best to keep aloft, where *Le Lotus'* lookouts wouldn't be watching. Nibs shivered as he approached LeCorbeau's vessel, but not from the chill. He knew what Tom would say about this gamble. To be caught in the *commandant's* clutches again could be fatal, or worse. One voyage under the Frenchman's thumb was more than enough for both brothers. This stunt was lunacy…but Tom would love the adventure.

As he closed on the ship from above, Nibs surveyed the watch, determining where he could sink to the hull without being spotted. From this height and straight down, the men looked like mice running over the deck, battening hatches with mallets, and belaying cables. With most of *Le Lotus'* sails furled for the bluster, Nibs got a full view of the frigate's narrow deck. Sure enough, LeCorbeau ruled from the quarterdeck, flapping like the cock of the roost in his shiny green coat.

No sign of Jill, though. Nibs and Cecco reasoned that Jill wouldn't be allowed on deck in this weather. Nibs watched for his chance, and dove. He let the ship pass him by, then latched on to the rudder as it bucked in the waves, wet wood firm in his fingers. From there, he made his way through the cold of the spray to the portholes along the stern, his best guess as to where Jill would be quartered. Knowing the doctor, Nibs figured a corner cabin as his choice, with a mite more privacy than those in the middle. And he'd have chosen the one closest to the quarter gallery jutting off to starboard. The loo. He hoped Heinrich was stationed there right now and out of the way. Clinging to the sill, Nibs swiped the drops from his eyes, then, slowly, raised up for a peek.

Right in one! In the tiny space through the window, Jill sat by herself at a table in a swinging pool of lanternlight, a pen in her hand.

She wore her blue robe and a set of pearls around her neck that must make her woozy. Well, she deserved them, and that sparkling ring, too. Nibs snatched the knife from his teeth and tapped on the glass.

Jill startled, she stared, then she jumped up and ran the two steps to the sash. On second thought, she rushed back to the cabin door to throw the lock.

. "Nibs!" she whispered as she pulled up the window.

Nibs wedged his elbows in and spoke low, just audible over the gale. "Captain Cecco asks what information you have for us? Where will you be? And…and are you all right?"

"I am managing. Pierre-Jean looks after Liza, and I look after myself. I've no hope of disillusioning my father about Heinrich. I'm not allowed to write letters, not even to Mother. Perhaps you can send word to her, tell her Heinrich is *not* to be trusted, but that I'm watching over Father, and we may be trapped in Vienna some while. But listen, my dear. Here is the number and street for Heinrichhaus— it's not far from a canal off the Danube." She rattled it off, spelled it for him, and made him repeat it. "And, Nibs, most importantly— Giovanni is no longer hunted! The doctor and LeCorbeau reported him dead, they collected the bounty." Jill had time for only a dash of bitterness, "They exchanged my freedom for his."

Nibs' damp, dark eyes opened in astonishment. "Then…Captain Cecco could go home again!"

"Yes, it is wonderful. But you must fly now before this squall rises. I have no more news." She kissed Nibs, tasting the sea on his cheek. "My love to Giovanni, and to Tom, and, when you return to Hook, tell him—" All at once, Jill's eyes lost focus. Her eyelids fluttered and she uttered, almost at random, something that came into her mind again, the faint hint of voices she had heard days and days ago, "…make an end to her story."

"Jill! Has the damned doctor drugged you?"

She blinked and aimed her gaze again, on her son. "No, thank the Powers. I simply miss you all, and terribly. Now go!"

Nibs fixed the steely knife between his teeth and wiggled free of the sill. As he floated backward, his face dwindled into darkness. Jill waved, once, then lowered the window and wondered.

"My love, what was it that I overheard?" She searched her soul for his answer, but saw only the iron-gray of his hook.

The sky had cleared. The roiling of the sea, which surged for days, was reduced this morning to great, rolling swells. Jill stood at the stern of *Le Lotus*, her amber skirt blown against her legs, one gloved hand firmly grasping the taffrail, the other holding tight to her fan. With her copper hair tamed in a twist, she scanned the horizon, left, right, and back. As she had supposed, the *Red Lady* no longer followed. The storm finally parted their ways. Jill sighed in tandem with the sound of the sea. The ache of homesickness invaded her insides, exacerbated by her brief meeting with Nibs. She'd held no illusion that Cecco could come to her aid here at sea but, in the weeks since she left her happiness behind, his nearness had cleared the clouds from her spirits.

Jill felt the loss of her husband's vigilance all the more because of the lack of Hook's. Of her lover's thoughts and emotions, usually so intrinsic to her soul, Jill sensed very little. She could guess at his reasons, but, absent her uncommon connection to him, she could confirm none of them. No doubt Hook suffered as she did. He would hardly wish to burden his Jill by doubling her pain as his heart reflected the turmoil in hers. Whatever he concealed from her, Jill intuited that he acted out of consideration. He meant to spare her. If, however, his silence covered something new, something dreadful, Jill was warned. Resolute, she braced her feet against the pitch of the deck, damp and clammy under her soles.

Even before the fury of the storm, Jill managed to keep Heinrich at bay. While she endured his embraces, her success in evading his bed made his lesser attentions a small price to pay. *No,* Jill admonished herself. She might prevaricate with the voyagers on *Le Lotus* to escape from Heinrich, yet she must remain honest within her own heart. She *enjoyed* his ardor. Hook's recommendation to hide her eyes and substitute himself in the clinches— compounded by the pirate pair's thrill in winning— lent attraction to such amorous adventures. The cuts she, Hook, and Cecco carved into Heinrich excited her. As she professed in her very first tryst with the surgeon, she was a passionate woman to begin with. Now, having marked him, she felt the old blood-rage that stained her hand scarlet. It spurred a Fury of her own, mimicked by the winds.

Not long after dirty weather hit, Heinrich learned the virtues of abandoning the bunk. He ordered another hammock strung beside

Jill's. He succored Mr. Darling, whose land-based constitution proved unfit for the frigate's tantrums, and whom Renaud, in a spate of unflattering French phraseology, had lashed to the bunk. In the end, it was Heinrich's vial of sleeping draught that put to rest both Renaud's complaints and Mr. Darling. When finally the Englishman awoke, much restored, he touted the physician's skill and stowed the vial against future squalls.

From her limited communications with Liza, Jill understood that Heinrich called at his daughter's cabin twice daily, fair weather or foul, to roll up his sleeves and attend to the babe. In spite of his care, the child's health showed no improvement. Pierre-Jean never left Liza unaccompanied, most especially during the physician's visits. The sailor crossed his arms and held his ground, refusing to be sent out on Heinrich's errands, the trick the doctor used to employ on the *Roger* when maneuvering for privacy with Jill. Jill and Liza each felt relief at Pierre-Jean's stubbornness. In the scarry face of the physician, that sweet, fair-haired sailor demonstrated his dedication to Liza's welfare. Young Pierre-Jean presented a force that, like the waters, Heinrich proved powerless to manipulate.

For Captain LeCorbeau, now installed on the forecastle inhaling the change of atmosphere through his overlarge nose, the storm had given vent to his petulance. Gesturing orders to Renaud from under canvas, he'd avoided shouting himself. Such effort didn't suit his temperament. When the galley fires had to be extinguished, he grieved at the start of his days: no hot chocolate. Jill too felt the inconvenience, but, now a veteran of sailing, she steeped her tea over a spirit lamp, and imbibed it before it turned cold. This morning's more properly produced draught had, however, immensely refreshed her, as did this view of her surroundings on her first visit topside.

"Ah, *Madame!* Allow me, *s'il vous plaît.*" Olivier de Beaumonde strode toward her, whipping his blue capelet from his shoulders to drape it over hers. "You made a promise, and I would not have you take ill before you keep it."

Jill found a smile for the French soldier. She knew him by now. He was just a big boy in uniform. "Indeed, *Monsieur*, I will keep my promise, if I may borrow a saber for our practice?" Jill allowed herself a pout, emphasizing it with a flick of her fan. "My *faux* husband refuses me the use of his own."

"The more I hear of *Monsieur le Docteur*, the more I despise him! Hoodwinking your father, misleading that girl— he is no gentleman, if what you tell me is true. *Mais...bien sûr*, I do not doubt you." As the wind ruffled the short whorl at the peak of his forehead, de Beaumonde drew his sword and offered it to Jill. Red and gold cords dangled from the hilt. "Is the weight to your liking, *Madame?*"

Jill let her fan hang from her waist as she balanced the saber in her hands, testing it. "Yes, I thank you. Shall we meet on the foredeck tomorrow afternoon? I believe the sea will have calmed by then. Oh, I am so eager to hear the clash of metal, to feel the beat of the blade, engaging in swordplay again!"

"I, also, although I would prefer to make more than *play*." Snapping to a salute, the soldier threw his gaze up to the glorious tricolor of France on the mast, flailing in the aftermath of the storm. "As I told you, I and my saber defeated the Austrian before. He sued for mercy! Another insult, and I will trounce him."

"Please," Jill pleaded in her clear, storyteller's voice, "I did not intend to tell tales. Johann, too, is proud of his homeland. You mustn't hold his birthplace against him."

"Why not, when he holds my love of *la France* against me?" Suspiciously now, de Beaumonde looked Jill up and down. He squared his substantial shoulders. "But, my lady, you hide something! Tell me. What outrage has your *Herr Doktor*, the stinking abductor of women, uttered now?"

Jill gasped at his vehemence, then whirled from him to run alongside the rail. Stopping short, she lowered the sword and raised her folded red fan to press against her lips. She shook her head in refusal. The deck shuddered as the strapping de Beaumonde, in his military boots, pounded his way to her side.

"*Vraiment!* The lady's silence speaks all!"

"No, *Monsieur*...my dear Olivier! I will not have you place yourself in danger. I warn you, with a blade in his hand, the doctor is lethal."

"I know my duty, *Madame*. If this swine insulted my country again, I must hear it."

Jill laid her fan on his arm. "Do not make me say it. Do not make me speak such vile sentiments."

"This time, he will die for his lies!" He stretched out his hand. "My sword, *s'il vous plaît.*"

Holding it back, Jill sent him a look of anguish. The ship surged again, and she stumbled. The soldier caught her, and, skillfully, relieved her of his saber.

"My apologies, good lady. Of course you must not speak the foul words, nor do you need to. *Je comprends tout!* The doctor is a dead man." He pivoted, his sword upheld, and he dashed up the deck in search of *Monsieur le Docteur*, to challenge him.

Jill watched his retreat. At the fore of his ship, LeCorbeau observed, also, before swiveling his beady black eyes toward Jill. For once the French captain forbore to shoot a look of venom her way. Instead, his thin lips curled in a smile. He soon drew his lacey hanky, to cover it.

After her back was turned and she gazed at the sea again, Jill smiled, too. The coastline she spotted earlier, as the clouds cleared away, loomed off to starboard. Even before now, Jill smelled the greenery. This ship was too small to stage a true, virulent duel. How fortunate for the honor of *la France*, to find a port so handy to host her defender.

On another coast, cloaked and hooded, Hook strode down an alley with his man Mullins at his back. The dark lane smelt of the shallows off the shore— damp sand and seaweed. At the rear entrance to a tavern, Smee's hardy frame separated from the whitewashed wall where he'd been leaning. He slipped the cloak from the commodore's shoulders and opened the door for him. Smee stood against the wall again to wait, his ears pricked for trouble.

Hook, too, raised his head to listen. With his black hair clubbed like any other sea captain's, a smallish gold ring on his lobe caught the starlight. His ear caught only the bark of a stray, and shreds of music from a bawdy hall by the docks. Dressed inconspicuously in chestnut brown, Hook stepped over the threshold and along the hallway. He delayed going farther as he inspected the premises. Flagstones beneath his feet, the ceiling ribbed with beams like a ship. The place was a typical seaside inn— brass, plaster, and taps. A cautious look about the serving room showed it half full with diners and loafers. Hook kept his claw cloaked in his pocket.

At a wooden booth toward the back, Tom Tootles felt the power of the commodore's presence before he spotted him. Hook's subdued attire couldn't alter his authority. Tom was sitting with Milady, his hair slicked back like a gent, and remembering to keep his elbows off the tablecloth. The light was the usual glow of yellow from candles in chandeliers, obscured over the settle at the fireplace by the loungers' pipe smoke, a local blend that smelled peppery. The clientele here, though, was not the familiar sort in Tom's experience, since this establishment catered more to merchants than to merchant sailors. The gentlemen at the bar wore reputable cravats and wool coats of quality, their hats and canes hung on hooks by the door, and they ordered port wine in glass goblets. A stairway led upward, but Tom's hopeful gaze found no women waiting, leering and teasing. There were doors up there, all right, one of which he'd secured for Milady, each numbered in brass, shut, stolid, tight-lipped and silent. On Hook's approach, Tom half rose, but recalled his orders. He settled down on the bench again, to keep watch. Mr. Mullins remained standing guard in the shadows of the back hallway, his beefy thumbs tucked in his belt. Hook bowed his respects to the lady, swept his coattails back, and seated himself at her right.

He bent toward the baronetess, awarding her his full attention. She looked delicate, Tom thought, in her lavender gown with her figure-eight waist and twinkling black beads. A black lace shawl draped the alluring lines of her bodice. In the light of the candles, Milady appeared younger than Tom guessed she was. The man Jill had raised Tom to be felt concern that she'd have to stay at this inn unaccompanied. Her brunette hair was lustrous, pinned up in intricate loops that any young miss might envy, with long cylindrical curls lying over one shoulder. Hook spoke in her ear in a way those girls would envy, too, with a low voice that Tom couldn't hear over the buzz of the customers. Milady cast her gaze down, her smile a modest one, her soft cheeks gaining color at his closeness.

The covered meat was already laid on the table, carved bite-sized on Tom's instruction. The waiter scurried over, wiping his hands on his apron, and he poured the wine, his white sleeves secured by black garters. He raised the platter's lid, but Tom seized the spoon to serve out, dismissing the man with a wave and a grin. Tom's stomach rumbled at the smell of some species of roast fowl, potatoes, gravy, steamed greens, cheese, cherries, sauces, butter, and the dream of all seamen— soft, warm, fresh, fragrant bread. He was lucky to be the newest member of the crew, unknown to the law and, thus, the unlikeliest of Hook's men to attract unwelcome attention. Tom's job was to order a feast, escort the lady to her inn, keep a weather eye on the door, eat, and pay out the bill. Even if this jacket Smee found for him pinched the bulges of his shoulders and itched at his neck, he couldn't wait to gloat about this treat to Nibs.

The action moved so fast once Jill got back from Italy that Tom and Nibs hadn't had time to talk. Nibs was away on the *Lady* when *this* lady descended to the commodore's deck. The men on the *Roger* were divided about hosting the baronetess aboard. Tom reserved judgment. It was plain to him that while in Vienna, Jill wouldn't behave like a nun. She might have little choice in grappling with Heinrich, but Tom knew her tricks. She would use whatever tool— or whatever fool— came to her red hand to defeat him. He remembered, vividly, the bloody job she'd done on Lean Wolf back on the Island. She seduced him to death, no regrets. Tom didn't feel any sorry for Heinrich, but, on some level, a man who really knew Jill had to pity her enemies. Her hand wasn't stained crimson for nothing. So far, though, Jill's feminine foes walked away.

As for Hook's presumed dalliance in her absence, Tom witnessed what seemed like betrayal on Jill's part back when Cecco came to the captaincy. Nibs had been riled about her relations with Cecco, but look how well all that bother worked out. No, Tom wasn't as worried as Nibs might be. He held not a drop of doubt that Hook burned for Jill, could not live without her, and Tom agreed with the half of the crew that saw Milady as a handy salve to Hook's temper. Once the commodore got over the jolt of her boarding, he allowed her to soothe his savagery. But odds bobs! The decision wasn't up to the sailors by any stretch of imagination, so all their talk didn't matter one whit either way. And now that Hook accorded Milady a permanent shore leave, Tom didn't have to worry how she might get *un*hooked once Jill flew back home.

While Tom chewed on his thoughts and his meal, the commodore entertained his guest. She ate daintily, and Hook ate with relish. He poured more wine; she sipped, and he quaffed. As the diners around them kept up a hum of conversation, Hook's words blended in; his claw never came out. The party of three enjoyed a leisurely meal, then Hook filled Tom's glass again, and sent him off to take a stool by the bar.

Hook turned the conversation. "Our provisions are aboard, Milady. Tomorrow we sail. 'Tis a pleasant port town, and this, a respectable inn. Mr. Smee has seen to your dunnage, and I to your funds. You will be comfortable here, and safe enough while you inquire for a proper companion."

"It is not only I who require companionship."

With just a touch of umbrage, Hook agreed, "I existed alone for too long, indeed. You, however, may return to your life in London. I cannot."

"My time in London stretched long, every day like a link in a chain. I knew not where its end lay."

"Then I suggest you remain in this city, free of that chain. No one knows you here. You may begin life anew."

"You must believe me this time." Her violet eyes held his own, startling in both color and honesty. "I have lived my life quite long enough."

"By your admission, you came to me to be sent away. I merely honor your wishes."

"I came for nothing. I came for…" her gaze drifted away, "nothingness."

His voice fell like velvet, as inducing as she remembered it. "What matter, then, where you find it?"

Milady held no bitterness. She spoke with simplicity. "If by my dealings with Doctor Heinrich I have done you one, final, good turn, then, Master James, my purpose is fulfilled. I discarded pride long ago. I am not wounded that you've no more use for me. I beg you, please. Before you leave me, release me."

"I will not pretend not to know what you mean."

Her head tipped back against the booth, and the black lace at her breast rose and fell with her sigh of relief.

"Yet I shall not act."

Her shoulders sagged, and she hesitated before asking, "Then, I must wait for her, still?"

"My intention was never to harm you. The story unfolds."

"Will she be kind?"

Hook shook his head. "She was not kind to me."

"In the beginning, she provided all you required. I learned to be content as I gave it you. Perversely then, she caused you to suffer great loss. And in solitude."

"The blindness of a child. I exacted my vengeance." Hook placed his one, heavy hand on her own, his rubied ring reminiscent of the blood he drew, on the night he brought Red-Handed Jill into being. He said, hardheartedly, and with a *soupçon* of triumph, "The Wendy is no more."

"And yet the tale she laid upon us lives on." Milady was aware how openly her face showed her emotions. Almost desperate, she looked about at the room's other occupants to gauge their observance before daring to gaze at her escort again. Only one looked her way: the man who commanded her— then, and today. Tonight. Tomorrow. "Can you not sway this story's ending?"

In the depth of his pocket, the claw masking the gash of Hook's wrist jerked. He set his teeth against the sting. He knew how deeply the rule of Jill's truth could cut. Jill herself was not safe. Even so, Hook didn't flinch. As a curtain is thrown open to morning light, all at once he'd envisioned the pattern of this lady's existence.

"Milady, you have persuaded me."

She felt the grip of his hand, so strong in its singularity, as if to make up for the absence of a counterpart. His dark blue gaze locked upon her with an intensity to match his grasp.

"The reason you came to me has naught to do with the doctor, nor any wish of our own." He lifted her hand. He felt her shiver as he pressed his lips to her fingers, and he went on. "All those years ago, with a pen in this hand you agreed, signed and sealed, to be my creature, whenever and however long I have need of you. Naturally, the girl was incapable of conceptualizing the consequences. I know the woman she since became. She accepts culpability. Was she kind, or was she cruel— cruel even to herself? In either case, the answer rings true."

"My dearest Sir…" This lady could never refuse him. "You have need of me *now*."

With the authority he could not cloak, Hook concluded, "Jill is gone, and you are here." If his ears were pricked for trouble before he entered this scene, he heard danger sing to him now, like a siren. Sweet music, and an old, favored refrain.

Swiftly, Hook pushed himself up from the table. Remembering not to cause unwelcome attention, he bowed to Milady. Like a gent, he assisted her to rise from her seat, and, courteously, he ushered her up the stairway and handed her into her chamber. In an ungentlemanly breach of manners, however, he stepped over a delectable threshold, and entered in after the swirl of her skirts. He closed her door.

Staring after him, Tom gaped in surprise. He slid from his barstool. Upstairs, Milady's door stood stolid, tight-lipped and silent.

Tom recalled his orders. He settled down on the stool again, to keep watch. He wasn't as worried as Nibs might be. But he came pretty close.

Champions of France

"We know the rules of dueling, the so-called, eh, Code." DéDé LeCorbeau strutted across his cabin, the breeze from shore bearing the scent of fertile earth as it stirred paisley hangings. The room, opulent but petite, dwindled further with the presence of the two duelists. Each sat uneasily in LeCorbeau's stylish but spindly chairs, their very beings swollen with their pride. The *commandant* halted before the opponents, his chin hidden in the plumage of his cravat. "Doctor Heinrich, I offer you the opportunity to avoid this conflict. You may apologize to *Monsieur de Beaumonde*. Shall you do so?"

"Absolutely, no. I would never befoul my mouth with the insults he attributes to me. By this accusation, *Monsieur* disgraces not only my character, but his own."

Olivier de Beaumonde leapt to his feet, remembering just in time to duck to avoid a clash with the ceiling. "*Bien!* We shall fight, then!"

LeCorbeau held up his two shapely hands. "Please, *Monsieur*, I beg you will sit down. You are much too huge for this cabin, and, if I may say, so is your violence."

With a grunt of dismissal, de Beaumonde declined to be seated. He remained stooped beneath the beams, spoiling the lines of his blue and red uniform. "It is truth! This ship itself, she is not enormous enough to contain my enmity. Let us to the shore, and we will resolve this matter with swords."

"Well, eh, the choice of weapons is, by custom, up to the challenged party. What do you say, Heinrich? Sabers, rapiers, or pistols?"

"Sabers." Heinrich stared coldly upon his challenger. "And as soon as may be."

"Oh, very well, then," LeCorbeau's nonchalance was belied by the glitter of his hawkish eyes. He was as eager as de Beaumonde to get on with this duel. All three men exuded such impatience that the formalities concluded almost before they began. "Renaud, are the boats lowered?"

"*Oui, Monsieur.* All is in readiness for the contest."

"*Eh, bien!* My dear de Beaumonde, whom do you appoint for your second? I am afraid we have no man of equal rank. One of my officers must suffice."

"I shall be pleased to accept *Monsieur* Renaud, if he is agreeable."

Renaud clicked the heels of his shining black boots, jerking in a bow. "But of course, *Monsieur.*" He aimed a thin, haughty look at Heinrich. "I consider this service to you to be a service to *la France.*"

Beneath the hair overhanging his brow, LeCorbeau's eyes rolled. "Well, eh, *mais oui.* I am sure France agrees with you. Now, Doctor, whom shall you appoint?"

Heinrich pulled his gold watch from his pocket and rubbed it with his thumb. He pursed his lips as if debating, then said, "I will have Pierre-Jean, if his loyalty to '*la France*' will allow him to serve in this role."

"I must caution you, Doctor," LeCorbeau's nostrils narrowed, as if he smelled vermin. "Pierre-Jean, as I can most painfully attest, is a traitor, a deserter, a mutineer!"

"I understand your feeling, Captain, yet I have reason for believing him to be my best choice for this office."

LeCorbeau snorted. "Perhaps, now I am thinking of it, Pierre-Jean is most fit to second the man accused of disgracing his country. Protocol is satisfied; we may proceed. Fortunately, we have plenty of daylight, and need not wait for morning. Being anxious to resume our voyage, I should not like to dawdle on this coast."

"Do not fret, *mon Commandant*," offered de Beaumonde, jutting his militant chin. "In no time at all, I shall vanquish this slanderer, and we will hold our heads high again, sailing home beneath our valorous colors."

Riffling the air, LeCorbeau shooed the soldier's enthusiasm, like a flock of pesky geese. "*Oui, oui*, we shall certainly do so. Now…Renaud, escort *Monsieur* de Beaumonde to his boat, and I myself shall see to *le Docteur* and his man."

Renaud and de Beaumonde stalked from the cabin as if their boots disdained the deck. LeCorbeau spun to Heinrich, his accents now confidential. "We have no time for the argumenting. We both know you will defeat de Beaumonde. What I need to learn is that you will kill him."

With an offended frown, Heinrich planted his watch in its pocket. "Once again, I reject your amoral code. Of course I will defeat the man, but I will fight him with honor, or not at all."

"You do not consider it honorable to pay your debt to me? I, who have made all things possible for you, even to restoring your elusive spouse to your arms?"

"If you have made my contentment possible, you have only done right. You and I formed a partnership, acting to our mutual benefit. To murder a misguided soldier boy is not, in any way, in my interest."

"You pain me, Doctor. I, who believed in you, who sailed to the ends of the earth— and back— to uphold the terms of our association." He shrugged. "*Alors*, I see you are determined to live by your conviction, no matter the consequence for me. Let it be so. I shall press you no further."

"It is good of you to say so, LeCorbeau. You made such ugly threats just a few weeks ago."

"Did I? Well, eh, that was before events took such a fair turn for us. Now that Hook is behind us, naturally, I am a much more happy man."

"Then, may I be relieved of my fears for my wife and my daughter? Your *petit ami* will not slip from its hiding place, to harm them? Nor, I hope, might the ladies stumble and fall into the brine?"

Smiling, LeCorbeau patted the pocket where his stiletto resided. "*Non, non*, Doctor! Only vow to me that you will strike the man. Draw his blood! Then, I will feel the satisfaction for my grievances against de Beaumonde, and I can forgive you this error of conscience. We will sail on in harmony, to pursue our so-profitable business."

"Here is my hand upon it."

"And mine, *Monsieur*." The two men stood and shook on this agreement, all amity. "I will send my second officer to collect your saber, Doctor, together with de Beaumonde's. Your weapons will be waiting when you and your Pierre-Jean— that rascal— arrive upon the shore."

"Thank you. And now, as to the grounds, I believe I have right of choice." Shading his eyes from the sun, Heinrich pointed through the portside window and said, "See there, a flat plain with shrubs at the edge, rather high above that river where your men are filling your casks."

"Yes, yes. It is the spot I should have chosen myself. And," LeCorbeau dismissed the doctor's next question, "my men have strict orders to keep watch on your women, and the man Darling. None of your party shall disembark from the ship, to run off."

"I am glad to hear this promise in regard to *Frau* Heinrich. She has not quite adapted to her good fortune. As for my daughter, however, I intend for her to accompany us to shore. Liza can serve in my role of surgeon, in the event that I am wounded. As you know, she is studying the science of medicine."

"A female underfoot! Heinrich, you tax me. But if she deserts you, Sir, it will be only a fair exchange for my Pierre-Jean!"

Confident that the day was going his way, Heinrich gave his gust of a laugh. "Indeed! A strange fellow, though, that de Beaumonde."

The *commandant* turned a crafty look upon his so-predictable partner, gazing steadily upon him. "These fanatics, sometimes…they play right into our hands."

"I can't think how the boy got it into his head that I insulted your homeland."

"Can you not," came the dry reply.

"It is of no consequence. I look forward to a vigorous exercise… and, I admit, I will enjoy some satisfaction for offenses I myself have endured." He tugged his impeccable vest. "After all, as de Beaumonde claims, this ship is not enormous enough to contain my enemy."

Ever the suspicious one, LeCorbeau peered over his nose at the surgeon. " 'Enmity' is what the boy said, I believe. You have misquoted him, with your 'enemy'."

Heinrich looked across the bay to the green heights in the sunshine. He crossed his arms and stood his ground, like young Pierre-Jean in his valiant act of protecting Liza. "Either way, I agree with him."

Dear Mrs. D or my grandmama,
Captain and I have followed Jill my mother your daughter as far as we can. I got in a few words with her and she says to you she is looking

after Mr. D grandpapa and that they'll be in Vienna maybe longer than you'd think.

She couldn't tell you names before but would have if she'd known you'd mistake that doctor for her proper husband. Try not to worry, she's clever and we're aiming to get her away again.

I'll print her house number out at the bottom. I know she'd be pleased to hear from you, also Mr. D who must miss you too and by the looks of him is no proper sailor.

To my brothers John Curly and Michael, What ho and a little less noise there.

Your grandson Nibs

"*Êtes-vous prêts?*"

In chorus, the two gentlemen answered, "*Oui, Monsieur!*" The adversaries posed opposite one another, with one knee bent and sabers extended straight out at eye level. Their fingers loosely gripped their hilts, their wrists weighing for balance.

The dueling ground was acceptably level, with no stones to trip the opponents. Wildflowers cast off a sweet scent, and bees buzzed at their work, ignoring the human aggressors. A grove of palm spread up a slope to the north, the ship wallowed in the waves to the south. At the end of the field, a hedge speckled red with berries edged the steep wall of earth that dropped to a river. A vista of palm fronds and lush, rounded mountains graced the farther bank.

LeCorbeau flourished his foil and dropped the point to the ground. "*Allez!*"

In a clash of steel, the duelists struck out to engage. Employing his bulk to begin, de Beaumonde barged forward. Like a bull enraged, he made his first thrust a stab to send Heinrich staggering. Above the ringing of the blades, the gush of water beneath the cliff could be heard as the river rushed toward the sea.

The gentlemen's seconds were stationed on opposing sides of the grounds. Renaud held de Beaumonde's capelet. Pierre-Jean clutched the doctor's vest. When the swords began swinging, Pierre-Jean, with Liza behind him, spread his arms and gently pushed her back to a place of greater safety. She stood on tiptoe in her anxiety, wearing a gray gown that matched her eyes, bibbed with a white apron. In support of her father, her brown hair hung long, as he now preferred to see it, and her bare toes sank into the softness of grass, a change from the planks aboard ship. In her arms she cradled the surgeon's medicine bag.

For this brief space of time, Liza held no fear for her child, or not directly. Jill was tending the boy in his mother's absence. At this moment, Liza's apprehension about the babe was tangled up with concern for her father. Liza held conflicting emotions in regard to her sire. Handsome and masculine, he looked a hero today in his loose shirt and close-fitting fencing breeches, his sand-colored hair bound back in black ribbon. When near to him, she trusted her own desires less, perhaps, than she trusted his. Often, her heart filled with gratitude to Pierre-Jean for distracting her from her unsuitable impulses. However awkward her alliance with her father, she found she could not turn away from him. Without Doctor Heinrich, little chance remained for her child's survival. Liza bit her lip, reminding herself that, although de Beaumonde's fury was formidable, this combat was not intended to be a duel to the death, at least, not openly. She bolstered her spirit by believing that, whatever degree of hostility his challenger brought to this battle ground, her sire was sure to prevail. He had just once failed to do so. Only one gentleman bested him— one man with no second to support him, and no second hand.

The soldier, de Beaumonde, bore his badge of loyalty at his shoulder. There, the blue lilies of France danced with his movements, and the crimson stripes down the seams of his pant legs accentuated his height. Like a baited bear, de Beaumonde applied his size to bully the doctor. He and his wrath pressed Heinrich to break ground and back down the field. Heinrich caught sight of the clump of red berries and knew the ravine to be nearer now, the precipice some few yards behind him. He ducked under de Beaumonde's arm in an avoidance, reversing their positions. Their white sleeves belled in the breeze, rising up and then descending as their blades clicked and hit in their cadence.

As he thrust and he parried in this quest for redress, Heinrich understood that if this contest was one of brute strength alone, *corps à corps*, de Beaumonde might predominate. But subtler skills were demanded of the combatants, all of which the surgeon mastered many years before. His days at Heidelberg taught him more than his medicine. The long, ugly scar he'd won at university was the result of the bungled stroke of his opponent, dealt after Heinrich's final flick incised a neat line on his foe. Both that bout and today's were gentlemen's disputes. As LeCorbeau pointed out to young de Beaumonde in an effort to reduce the man's zeal, their object was to mark, not to murder. Satisfaction was the prize. Heinrich's hands would not be stained by the blood of an equal. No, not even today.

Summoning his force, de Beaumonde beat the doctor's sword down, then pressed it into the grass. With a smirk, he stamped on the blade, securing it under his boot. Heinrich let go of the hilt. With his own shoe, he ground down de Beaumond's blade, so that the weapons lay crossed on the field. With neither a victor, each man raised his hands and spread his fingers, then they backed off, to bend down and seize each his own saber again. The Frenchman's glance was lethal.

A glimpse at the seconds showed Pierre-Jean's wide, Gallic smile and Renaud's pinched look of scorn. Liza had set down the medicine bag to twist her fingers together in front of her apron. LeCorbeau, dressed in his best coat for the occasion, an embroidered mantle of auburn and brown, refreshed himself by sniffing at a flower he had plucked from the grass.

As the parties engaged again, the doctor put his dexterity to work, nipping in and back, his body light and lithe in comparison to the soldier's. Like the bees in the field, he set his sword buzzing with vibration, darting about his foe's face, pricking here and there, seeking the chance to cut into his cheek.

That chance was not yet apparent. Body blows were prohibited by the rules, but certain tricks might be tried. Frustrated by the relentless motion of the surgeon's sword, de Beaumonde forced his mass forward almost to meet it, then, daringly, hooked his elbow over the weapon to command the blade, pulling the flat of it to his chest. Outraged, Heinrich glared. He yanked his weapon back. He hoped to see a trail of crimson staining de Beaumonde's shirt, but the soldier had detached his grip. Taking advantage of the doctor's surprise, he charged again, redoubling his blows. Heinrich had only just time to raise his saber, angling it sideways again and again, parrying to stave off the jolts. Once he regained his stance, the blades swished and shrieked. Both opponents breathed heavily now.

At LeCorbeau's hail of *"Arrêtez!"* the combatants retreated to rest. Unruffled, LeCorbeau smiled, remarking, "An amusing spectacle, *Messieurs*." He nudged Renaud with his toe. "The flasks, *s'il te plaît*." As directed, Renaud produced two flagons and offered the drink to the principles. Heinrich accepted his and, as he sipped, grateful for the balm of cool water, he strolled to the brink of the ravine. A glance informed him that the cluster of berry bushes hid the ship from his view. He corked the container and tossed it into the grass, in their shade.

Again, the two swordsmen took their positions. LeCorbeau gave the signal to commence. Heinrich set his jaw, feeling the cuts that had carved the three old scars on his face, cold and sharp, as if they were freshly stricken. Leaning into his stance, he held his blade raised at shoulder height, pointed at his challenger. With a look of determination, he stared down the shining steel of his saber and into the fire of de Beaumonde's belligerent eyes.

De Beaumonde eyed him back. He blinked. The next moment, a tiny red line erupted upon the Frenchman's cheekbone. After that came the sting. One second later, Heinrich had caught the crossguard of de Beaumonde's saber with the point of his own, and dashed it down to the sward. Olivier de Beaumonde stood empty-handed and incredulous— dismayed, disarmed, and marked.

The company gasped, then sighed in admiration. LeCorbeau crowed, *"Touché!"*

Applause burst forth. Pierre-Jean let out a whoop, his china blue eyes alight, while Liza sank to her knees in relief. All the men, including the much disgruntled de Beaumonde, shook Heinrich's hand. Renaud draped the soldier's cape on his shoulders, received his saber, and escorted him well away, to cool his wrath on a camp stool. LeCorbeau bestowed a wily smile upon the physician. *"Félicitations!"* He cut a bow, then turned away to soothe the loser's wound— not the prick of the blade, but his pride.

Victorious, Heinrich saluted his daughter. She rose up and came to him, but kept her distance. Undiscouraged, he gave a curt nod. "Well, Liza, you see that your father has not lost his skill while you have been away. Come, fetch me that flask, and I'll drink again, more deeply now that the contest is won. Pierre-Jean, if you would?" The three ambled toward the edge of the drop where he'd tossed the flagon under a berry bush. Liza presented it to him, and he drank.

"Monsieur?" Pierre-Jean asked, his expressive hands indicating a donning of the vest he held.

Passing the flagon to Liza, Heinrich answered, "No, I must clean my sword first. You may set my vest down in the grass. Just there." The sailor turned away and bent down to lay the garment out, the long blond pigtail for which he was much adored by the ladies dangling down his back. Heinrich rolled up his sleeves and looked over the field, to locate the captain and his first mate. The two hunched together above his seated antagonist, apparently tending his cut. With a wound so discreet, the defeated man had no need of Liza's ministrations, nor was he in a frame of mind to accept them. When Pierre-Jean stood again, Heinrich said, "Now, you will please receive my saber."

"I am honor." His English depleted, the Frenchman finished, "*Une grande victoire, Monsieur.*"

"Thank you, Pierre-Jean." Heinrich set his hand on the boy's shoulder. "But my victory comes only this moment." He drew back his sword and swept the point across the young sailor's neck, like incising a patient with a scalpel. With this, his second satisfaction of the day, Heinrich noted that the seam was neat and clean. The boy gurgled, the blood seeped from his throat, and soon it began leaking through his teeth. In desperation, his expressive hands clutched at his gullet. Liza rushed to her father to tear at his arm, pulling and snatching at him, fighting against Fate, but it was too late; blood pumped from the surgeon's incision.

Poor Pierre-Jean turned his horrified gaze upon her. Wilder than she'd ever witnessed them, those china blue eyes froze their last image, like ice, right into her soul. Helplessly, she watched the life dim from them. Yet, as her father had gambled, at this time of his triumph Liza was incapable of shaping a scream.

With one gory hand, Heinrich shoved his daughter's guardian. He sailed his last voyage, over the brink, and into the ravine. Heinrich watched the body tumbling, down, and down, to splash into the river. The current gathered him up, his legs loose, his French blue jacket turning dark as the water saturated it. His beautiful blond braid dragged out behind him as the stream rolled him coldly along, lifeless and limp. "He will end in the ocean. An appropriate burial for a seaman." Heinrich moved away from the ledge.

At last, his daughter uttered a cry, one deep, grief-stricken sob. Paralyzed with desolation, she stood three feet from the verge, staring down at Pierre-Jean. As if propelled over this cliff herself, she plunged into horror, remorse. Devastation raked her face.

"I am sorry there must be so much blood, Liza." Heinrich had needed Pierre-Jean to die, and die silently. "As you study to become a physician, you must accustom yourself to such sights."

Gazing down, she stepped closer to the verge.

"Come away, Liza."

The girl did not move.

"What you are feeling is shock. It will pass. I will help you. Come, Liza, look at me."

Slowly, she raised her head. The vast landscape beyond framed her in her sorrow, with palm fronds and shadings of green.

"That's right. Now turn to me."

With a vacant gaze, she turned around. Blankly, she viewed her father's hands.

Heinrich, too, looked down. In his right hand, he gripped his saber. Pierre-Jean's blood smothered his left. Liza crept another step back. Toward the clifftop.

"Now, Liza." He judged the distance. If he reached to seize her, she might shy and slip away. His clipped accent softened, to persuasion. "Come toward me. Come."

Her gaze met his. His eyes were gray like her own. Gray like her son's.

"Yes, Liza. Good. Now, step this way."

She picked up her foot. She set it down…and stepped backward.

"You do not need that boy. You need your father."

Liza dragged her stare from his face, to turn her head and look over her shoulder, downward, and into the gully. The wind tugged the tendrils of her hair, tugged her toward Pierre-Jean. Again, she inched backward.

"No, Liza. This way. This way, please."

He reached out his hand to her. The breeze pulled her skirts back. The air smelled of blood.

"Liza."

Below her, the river rolled. It murmured; it called to her. The water spoke in a language of its own…like Pierre-Jean. He seemed to be whispering to her.

Heinrich still offered his hand. "You are in danger here."

The urgent note in his voice stirred her. She turned her face to him.

"There now, my little one. This is the way." He continued to tender his hand, bathed scarlet in the life of her lover.

"Come. I will take you away from here." He beckoned now, he and her lover. Somehow, the two men were merged. Liza blinked, but said nothing. Pierre-Jean's life force was here, yet his body lay far behind her, washed clean. Once again, she edged his direction.

"Remember, my child. You have a child of your own."

She frowned at his fingers. Red, and wet, and waiting.

"Together, we will tend to your boy. If he survives our voyage to Vienna, he will receive the finest treatment. But now you must let me tend to *you*."

She felt her toes in the grass, the breeze beneath her heels. She felt light as a bee's wing. She swayed.

"Your baby, Liza. My son." Her gaze flicked up to his. "Yes. I acknowledge him. I do this for you. Now, Liza, do this for me." He reached out farther, his blood-red fingers bending to beckon, closing, opening.

Her mind cleared at length, and she focused on his fingers. She imagined their feel. His touch would be warm, and slippery. But, slippery or no, she understood that her father's grip would be binding. Moving as if in a dream, she raised her hand. She tried to make a decision, and, in time, she knew only one choice remained, between oblivion or obligation. Death, or indenture.

Her hand slid into her father's.

Her guess had been wrong. His touch was sticky. She closed her eyes to shut death away. She felt the pull on her arm as he yanked her from the brink. She felt his arms cage her, smelled the sweat of today's efforts. Too late now to run, too late to fall. Now came the fresh feel of grass beneath her thighs, and cold water poured over her fingers.

Her father called, "Pierre-Jean, where are you? Pierre-Jean!... LeCorbeau, how right you were. The boy has run, he is gone." Heinrich huffed in disgust. "A deserter!"

Liza opened her eyes. Deserted.

Heinrich shrugged on his vest and tugged it into place. His sword had been wiped, his fingers rinsed. The flask lay empty on the grass. As intended, his hands were unstained by the blood of an equal, unsullied even today. Weighing for balance, Heinrich felt that his grip was secure. When it came to handling his daughter, quite simply, the doctor's equal did not exist.

He took Liza up in his arms, her face near as gray as her gown. Hers was a light weight, but her body sagged slack, and her spirit seemed drained. Gently, he carried her toward the others. "*Monsieur* Renaud, if you would please collect my things? My daughter has had quite a shock..." He halted in surprise. With one hand, he hurried to press Liza's face to his shoulder, shielding her eyes from the sight. He gaped at yet another scene of devastation, and this one, for him, unexpected.

Renaud knelt beside the overturned camp stool, crouching at de Beaumonde's side. The French soldier lay in the grass, thrashing. A few drops of blood beaded on the thin red line on his cheek, a cut not two inches long. LeCorbeau stood over both men, smoothing his lapels and observing.

Still larger than life, de Beaumonde's energy was boundless, tossing him from side to side. His boots scraped the earth, tearing the soil, his body bucked. Renaud tried to hold him down, his skinny face filling with panic. De Beaumonde's eyes glazed, white lather bubbled from his lips to splatter his uniform. Through clenched teeth, he tried to speak. Even in his extremity, this soldier of France pledged fidelity. *"Vive...vive la—"* The only sound that remained was his struggle.

Renaud murmured, *"Vive la France."* De Beaumonde's body seized again, then he collapsed on the ground, to lie still. Renaud crossed himself, hanging his head. LeCorbeau straightened. He turned his beady black eyes upon Heinrich, his features arranged in an expression of innocence.

He asked, archly, "What was that you said, Doctor Heinrich? That rascal Pierre-Jean has run away?" He brandished his foil. *"Alors!* It is a good riddance."

Liza's shoulders shook as she started to weep, and the surgeon held her tighter to his shirt. Her hot tears wetted his chest.

"As for this one, eh, his country's dishonor seems to have proven too much a shock for him. *Une tragédie.* The man's defeat at your hands has provoked an unfortunate fit, so you see."

Heinrich's face paled with anger, his triple scars reddening to prominence. "Yes. So I see." He saw quite clearly. The surgeon knew precisely what nature of poison LeCorbeau applied. No doubt Heinrich himself had just wiped its remains from his blade, mingled with Pierre-Jean's last blood. Equally probable, a drop or two lay secreted in LeCorbeau's pocket, on the tip of his *petit ami*— on the chance the wrong man won the duel.

The time was too late to save Olivier de Beaumonde. But the doctor had saved his daughter. He sent the *commandant* a look of begrudged understanding. As the French soldier's body stretched dead at his feet, Heinrich, in his curt Austrian inflection, conceded to LeCorbeau, the victor of this day's contest.

"Touché."

Poignant Pens

Monsieur le Commandant,

You believe me to be a lying, scheming, greedy female. You are correct on all counts— except one. Even Johann Heinrich admits that I use truth as a weapon. I wield that weapon now.

At stake are my father, my freedom, a young mother's sanity, and our very lives. Once the horses' hooves clatter upon the cobblestones of Heinrichhaus and the doctor's fine carriage draws within his courtyard, iron gates will clang closed upon us. We shall be prisoners, mere puppets for the doctor to play upon. Even you must admit— a man with the brazenness to murder two men in one day would not blink at betraying, or slaying, a woman.

According to Heinrich, he holds the beating heart of Vienna in his two skillful hands. His character among the nobility is established; no one will question him: But no man knows him as well as his longtime partner, DéDé LeCorbeau. No other man has toiled as you have toiled, Captain, to raise him to such heights of glory.

Yet you cannot know this man quite as well as I. Since the day of the duel, Doctor Heinrich is conceited enough to trust me with his own type of truths. I now understand that, once this voyage lands him safely in Europe, the good doctor will cast you off. Engaged in new and influential connections, he boasts that your partnership is no longer needed. He confides in me, for you are unlikely to acknowledge, as truth, any word that falls from my lips.

Beware, Sir. Letters were posted from our recent port of call. Too soon, you will be betrayed. You have more to lose than this beautiful ship and the fortune you so cleverly accrued. When next you set foot on your beloved French soil, les gendarmes *will stand ready to arrest you. Vengeance will visit you— from no lesser force than* Le Baron *de Beaumonde. Olivier's father will see you thrown in a stark, stony cell for the cold-blooded killing of his son.*

What may we each gain by this warning? You are shrewd enough to see. In return for our sworn statements affirming your innocence, I ask you to deliver us from Heinrich's power. I dare, even, to request one further favor. S'il vous plaît, Monsieur, *accept the bountiful reward for our ransom, which, as you know, I and my* confrères *can well afford to lavish upon you. Set us free in Tangier, Sir, and this scheming, greedy woman will ensure that the truth will be told. You may yet escape the foul fate our mutual enemy designs for you.*

Quickly! You say we sail closer to European waters. Any hour, the horizon could bring a ship of la République, *and any moment your capture.*

Unsigned, yet sincere.

▲

Chère Madame~

Mon Dieu! *Were I an admirer of women, my heart would lie vanquished, utterly in your thrall. Excepting myself of course, I know of no man who compares in mettle and intelligence.*

Je m'excuse, *I do know of one. Given your talents, perhaps you will one day return to him.*

Forewarned, I shall disguise La Fleur de Lotus *and sail past our landing at Marseilles, to make port upon the Italian coast. I will learn by my partner's behavior. If all you say is the truth you proclaim, he is but a corpse with a pulse.*

In this event, I shall strike the colors. The victory, Madame, will be yours, and the bounty belonging to me.

~LC

▲

Dearest Mary, hoping you soon receive the letters I posted last week,

This interminable voyage, I'm told, is to stretch on a bit longer. The captain announced (not so I could understand him, that is, his nasal accent is impenetrable and the doctor has to translate) that we will not land in France, after all, but shall sail on to Italy. Funny to think that

~~Wendy~~ Jill only just left the Italian countryside, and there she'll find herself again. She reports that the sky is beautiful there, enough to tug on one's heartstrings, and she describes how bracing it feels to dance beneath stars to gypsy violins.

There'll be no dancing for me until I regain my land legs, and then it's on to Vienna. Our girl is pestering her husband to make a stop in Heidelberg first, to show us his old stamping ground at university. Seems that, like her gypsies, she is reluctant to settle down. Can't stand the idea of living the high life in an opulent townhouse in the shining city where East meets West, with servants and a housekeeper and carriages and ropes of pearls to wear and a box at the opera, to boot! We've known a long time, though, that our daughter is an adventurer, have we not, dear? Why, she'd rather waltz barefoot with the moon than attend the grandest ball in all of Vienna.

She's become increasingly restless, wandering the deck with her hair blowing wild. Rather magnificent, really. One night I spotted her up in the rigging, and, speaking of the East, she was dressed like an Eastern Rani, in some kind of outlandish trousers. I know I'm prattling like a fond father, but, I must say, she's a beauty. I've quite gotten used to her tinted red hair, but will I ever get used to her growing up? Mary, I tell you, if I did not know the year she was born, I'd swear she was old enough to be your sister. You may take that as a compliment to yourself as well, my darling Mrs. Darling!

I'm still having trouble with the novel name for our girl, mixing up the old and the new. She herself is a mix, after all. I'm too old a dog to learn new tricks. Ha! It is comical— the last few days I was *back in the doghouse,* (but not literally this time), for ~~Wend~~ Jill let loose her temper on me for respecting my promise to Doctor Heinrich. I am proud to be a man of my word, you know, Mary, and as such I was honor-bound. Upon sealing my correspondence, I was incapable of slipping in her notes to you and to various other parties who shall be unnamed by my pen. Of course I gave you her love, and do so again now, but our son-in-law knows best. While he judges that the nervous affliction she suffers after so much time among reprobates is improving, he does not yet feel comfortable in allowing her to circulate her stories abroad. He prefers that she retain them in her collection, which everyone knows is pure fiction anyway, instead of confusing people by swearing the truth of them.

Tragedy struck not once but twice while we lay at anchor at our last landing. Mary dear, I won't grieve you with the details, but that big

French soldier I told you of— excitable chap— dropped dead. At the very same moment, the young man I called Goldilocks in my last letter, who was charged with the duty of chaperone to the doctor's daughter, ran off! These foreigners, so flighty and unpredictable. Give me an Englishman every time. One knows where he stands, and one can understand him. Ha, I am droll this afternoon! But I own that I am feeling cheery, in spite of the Frenchmen's bad luck, for, by their absence, I have gained a cabin to myself. That Renaud had become quite insufferable. Some nights, he didn't even sleep in our room at all, that's how much he detests me. Frequently he stumbled in about sunrise, reeking of some foul perfume. I'm beginning to wonder if perhaps a young miss of questionable repute is stowed in the hold. I should hate to think it, but one puts nothing past these Continental types, and what could be worse than such a liaison?

I did broach the subject with Doctor Heinrich, but he became so stiff and proper that I could see how even the suggestion of such blatant debauchery disturbs a man of his principles. I shall keep future doubts to myself. I've noticed a distinct cooling in his relations with Captain LeCrow. They used to be quite cordial together, but in recent days they have begun to eye one another as if the Franco-Austrian War were still raging.

The sailors keep busy, never saw such an industrious bunch. They're painting the keel (or is it the hull?) even though the boat is fitted out in shipshape condition already. The vessel's name has changed. As I mentioned before, to alter one's appellation seems a tradition in the seafaring population, but still it seems odd to me. I must admit I am what's called a 'lubber.' There's a French word for that and Renaud applies it constantly, the cheeky cove. In any case, without packing our luggage or stirring a step, we are now aboard the Mary Rose, and, most auspiciously, sailing under the good old Union Jack. I gather that's allowed.

The little mother, Miss Liza, is taking the loss of her friend very hard. ~~Wen~~ Jill moved into her cabin to console her, and to help look after the babe. By the looks of him, he's not got long to live. Our girl is quite kind to the doctor's daughter. Always was the nurturing type, and always will be! Even close by in the cabin next door, I hear the girl weeping, yet I catch mere mews from his little lungs. The doctor dotes on him, does all he can but, with the sorrow you and I can well understand at the loss of a child, he confides to me that the boy's days are numbered. Oh, Mary! How fortunate we are that our little ones came home to us! All but Wendy, of course— she shall never come back.

I may be pardoned, I think, for longing for our darling little girl…

I pick up my pen again to apologize for becoming maudlin. The result of venturing so far from home, and so far from my beloved wife and sons. Do kiss them all for me, Mary. I shall stay in Vienna as long as Doctor Heinrich feels I can be of any use to our daughter. It is a great comfort to me to know that her future rests in such capable hands. Two hands, if you catch my meaning. I wag my head as I write this. Dash it all! Every moment we two find the least bit of privacy, she does harp on the man with a hook. Claims she has to get back to him. Some kind of foreboding, she says, some story or other needs fixing. Says she can't explain what she means, even if we did have the benefit of more time to talk by ourselves.

With a woman's intuition, ~~We~~ Jill tells me that by the time we arrive at Heinrichhaus, letters from you will await us. Of course she doesn't really know, but she quite seems to know, which would inspire any man's respect. In any event, it quite cheers me to think of you sitting down at your dear little desk, perhaps at this moment, where in olden days you'd sit drawing your dreams of our babies' faces instead of totting up household accounts. This time, you will be thinking of me. My own one. I send my dearest, darlingest love.

George

◄

Mother,

I hope by now you've received word from Nibs, to whom I entrusted a message. Father and I are, indeed, held captive by Doctor Johann Heinrich, and sail toward his home in Vienna. I regret to alarm you, but Heinrich is a most dangerous man. Masquerading as my husband is his least offensive crime.

I have every confidence that your intuition cautioned you against believing in him. I also know how headstrong Father can be when he supposes his duty calls. His primary purpose is to protect his children.

As mothers, we cannot fault his instinct. As women, we must rescue ourselves, and our loved ones. I am making every effort to ensure our escape. Due to various circumstances, however, I cannot convince Father of our peril. If he were to hear the truth from you, I could enlist his aid.

If you receive this note, I have succeeded in my attempt to fly from the ship in the nighttime, to post at the port where Father mailed his own letters. If only Father could fly, we might be home in your loving arms this very minute.

Take heart, Mother. My friends now know how to find me. We have only to seize whatever opportunity offers.

I shall write up this story, too, once its ending is clear. This jaunt may be Father's greatest adventure.

All love,

Your daughter

Dearest, my darling George,

I am quite beside myself. I write to you urgently, with warning. As you will be living under Doctor Heinrich's roof by the time this news reaches you, please try to disguise the shock it delivers.

I have received correspondence from Jill, and from her son Nibs, who confirms that we have been duped. Do not trust Doctor Heinrich!

You swore to aid in our daughter's escape, George. My dear, you must do so, and at the earliest chance. Do consult with her, and lay your plans— together— to come home to me!

Remember what she wrote to us. She meant this sincerely: "I believe in you. Believe in your Wendy."

I believe in you, too, George. Set loose your lion courage on this task, and bring our dear daughter home. Where she goes from here is her own choice, but, my darling, she must have that choice.

Mary

Meine gute Frau Lieber,

I am pleased to send notice that you may expect our party to arrive in town within a week's time. You have my instructions. My plans are unchanged.

As anticipated, the party consists of Frau *Heinrich,* Fräulein *Heinrich,* Herr *Darling, and myself. I know you will have the household in order, and our rooms prepared.*

Frau *Heinrich will require an urn of piping hot water by her bedside each morning, as she prefers to brew her own tea to imbibe before breakfast. As you are a woman of tact and taste, I trust you to know what pretty touches should adorn my bride's suite upon her homecoming. On a similar note, I concur with your suggestion that it is too soon to hire a lady's maid. While* Frau *Heinrich becomes accustomed to her new position, your own attendance will be preferable. You shall receive a rise in wage reflecting this additional function.*

Instruct Karl to disable the locks on Frau Heinrich's doors, from the inside only. You will keep the keys.

J. Heinrich, Dr. med

Ma,

I think you know I try to abide by your wishes. You brought me up to respect my elders, and for sure I honored Uncle Edmund. He was a decent and hardworking man. When we was in need, he took me aboard the Unity *and showed me the ropes of seamanship. I can't repay his kindness in helping me provide for you and the younger ones, but the least I owed him was obedience. That's why I'm ashamed to learn I disappointed his hopes.*

Mother, after Uncle's death, my orders from his officers were to deliver his log to the shipping office. I was proud that, even with the storm bashing us about, and the cabin wall stove in and the ship getting sucked down so fast, I fulfilled my orders. But today I got a sharp reprimand for turning the logbook in incomplete. As it was a chore of great trouble to keep that book safe and dry through all my misfortunes, it is pretty hard to take, being reproached for fiddling with it.

You know what I'm guessing? I think you was afraid for me. You wanted to protect your boy. But Mother, it's true. I've met with some pretty bad men. As the good man you raised me to be, I can take care of the consequences, whether I done bad or good myself. I hope I've done good. If not, I'll face my duty, like always.

It's my duty now to ask you to abide by Uncle Edmund's wishes and bring that page to the shipping bureau. He would be proud of you, and I will be too.

Your son, and Uncle's nephew,
David (Davy) Appleton, Able Seaman

Mr. Hodgson,

You will kindly accept this correspondence as my formal instruction to your firm. I wish to direct the income from my holdings to that worthy hospital which has previously benefitted from my charity. I hereby relinquish all rights to my properties in that institution's favor.

I have taken up residence abroad. With no intention of returning to England, I release your offices from my service except to execute this, my final transaction.

Cordially,

Lady J— L—

If I ever swore to a truth, it is this one, and it is bitter: excepting the day I learned the truth about Pan, I've not experienced such an appalling hour. I take refuge in my journal, for this horror is beyond the scope of my father's faculties, and no one else aboard this ship can be a friend to me.

Liza's child is dead. Such a cruel twist, when we are so close to setting foot in Italy. With the boy having struggled thus far, I began to hope he might survive long enough to receive the help Johann promised from his colleagues.

Liza is devastated. Losing Pierre-Jean, only nine days ago, makes this blow doubly difficult for her. I fear for the girl, not only because of her grief, but also because this child wrought such a change. For the first time in her life, someone brought out the best in her. She became a woman too soon, and a mother too young— and yet the role of mother bestowed upon her a heart. I hope for her sake she will recover, and that when she can raise her delicate head again after this most ghastly of tragedies, she will be the better, not the worse, for these heartbreaks. While Liza dwells under the influence of her father, however, I can only dread for her future.

A much darker deduction abides in my mind, which I will spare Liza if I can. May she never suspect as I do. The timing of the babe's death is too convenient, the opportunity too ripe. I mistrusted Johann's willingness to risk his indiscretion in the city of his success. His paternity was easy to see. Over his physician's oath, above his daughter's well-being— beyond even the bare bones of decency— the doctor is driven to preserve his reputation.

I can find, however, no advantage to Johann in the death of de Beaumonde. LeCorbeau could not contain his disdain for the man, and now that his benefactor's son has met an honorable end, he can run his business unfettered by oversight and unencumbered by a volatile fanatic. Of this death, therefore, in spite of my lies to LeCorbeau, I absolve Johann.

In the case of Pierre-Jean, though, I must question if it was simple coincidence that the man charged to protect Liza and her child ran off before the baby's demise. The boy was loyal, unlikely to desert at any time. Liza has again adopted the silence her father imposed upon her when we first encountered her. She won't tell me what happened after the duel. Yet, as I listened to the sobs that wracked Liza that day, I imagined a betrayal, perpetrated upon the most faithful of sailors. I am ill, thinking of this possibility. Pierre-Jean was a jewel, so young, so devoted to the girl he loved. Alas, I fear that his affection for her was the death of him.

That young French sailor was sent for Liza's protection. Now his burden weighs upon me. The pride of Doctor Heinrich's profession is the obligation of its practitioners to preserve life, yet I must suspect Johann of not one, but double murders. And if he could so much as ponder the smothering of an innocent child— and to do so would require only the half of a minute with that manicured hand upon a wee face— then Liza and Father and I dwell in more danger than I imagined.

As I work toward deliverance, all on my own, my efforts founder. Although fired with fury, de Beaumonde was not the swordsman he claimed to be. As I feared, Captain LeCorbeau sidestepped my gambit to shake his faith in Johann. I've tried my best to prevail upon Johann to delay our journey to Vienna. I'd hoped that an excursion to Heidelberg might lead us to some old enemy who could serve my purpose. I feel called to that city somehow. Perhaps the reason will come to me as we enter the territory.

Recalling Hook's motto, I've identified Johann's weapons and examined his weaknesses. My scarlet hand itches to act, yet I live under the threat of that secret document. Johann's written word holds me hostage; words, perhaps, may prove my best weapon against him. How I miss my champions and allies— my Lost Boys, my crew of buccaneers, my husband, and, most cutting loss of all, the man of my soul. How much more deeply I feel for his long years of suffering in solitary— years that I myself imposed upon him by my storytelling. For one of those stories, I now pay the price, all alone. Solo.

Tomorrow we take to a coach, and our road to Vienna unfolds. In two days, we expect to set down at Heinrichhaus. To toast the end of our voyage, Captain LeCorbeau hosted us in his quarters this evening. His auburn coat shone iridescent in the candlelight, like a prize cock's feathers. The swirls of paisley cocooning this quirky little man, together with my failure to fool him, made me seasick. I had to hide my feeling behind my fan. The commandant *inhaled the wine's bouquet through his copious nose, then raised his glass to me. Still sly, his smile held none of the revulsion I am accustomed to reading there. Surprised, I folded and lowered the fan, in token that I accept our* détente.

"Je regrette, Madame," *he opined, "that the fruit of the friendship we sowed may wither on the proverbial vine. But do not desperate. I do not name you a liar. Truth, she is a goddess. Like any deity, you may worship her, you may serve her. Mais…she may not serve you in return."* *He shrugged. "To one such as I, the truth, she is, eh…so-flexible."*

I swallowed his counsel along with his wine, surprised not to find it taste bitter.

My love,
You well know I rarely put pen to paper, and for what reason. I lost that part of myself that your presence returns to me.

Another hand addresses this message so that, innocent in appearance, it may find deliverance into your own hands at Heinrichhaus. Innocent or otherwise, that story is one to finish another day.

Today, know that I remember you endlessly. I am wherever you go.

I will not sign, for every wretched letter of this script bespeaks my identity. I am the man as you made me.

Je t'aime. Ti amo…

…Ich liebe dich.

Vainglorious Portraits

Milady was learning to lay down the strokes of her paintbrush quickly. To keep a fairy stationary long enough to pose was impossible. Between rays of sunshine bouncing off the waters, the golden glow of the creature, the smell of linseed oil, and the heady taste of mead, the commodore's cabin this afternoon was transformed to an artist's ideal.

"Never have I rendered a more lovely subject."

Her tones fell softly upon Jewel's ear, in congruence with the velvet on which the fairy curled in her fairest frock, trying to keep her peacock blue wings from wiggling. Every few minutes, Jewel scrambled up and zoomed to perch upon the artist's shoulder, to inspect the work in progress. She felt Milady's shiver as her wings wafted breezes to her cheek. Jewel was overjoyed at this new kind of homage to her beauty, better even than the mirror the Twins had crafted for her boudoir. She really, truly tried to cooperate. To stave off another leap, she tried staring at the lady the way the lady was staring at her.

Milady's green dress was reminiscent of the Fairy Queen's, but less majestic. A classic style, not modern like the younger sprites' dashes of fabric. She had hair the color of cherry tree bark, dark brown, and wore it both up and down as if she had plenty to spare. The fairy liked her perfume. It was the same scent as her own— lily of the valley. Her eyes, though, were different than most of the people's Jewel knew. They were eyes that seemed to view the end of an adventure, rather than looking forward to starting a new one. Her eyes reminded Jewel of the violets blooming in the Fairy Glade.

When Jewel flew in through the cabin window this morning to report back to her master, those two violets looked as if drops of dew still pooled in them. Jewel was surprised as she watched her master caress the drops away with his thumb, but then he'd turned to welcome Jewel and her news, and the care creasing his face transformed to his beautiful smile. He made his hand linger on the lady's cheek, though, as if it was important to hold her down, to keep her from flying off somewhere. Jewel knew the lady wasn't sprinkled with fairy dust, but still, the woman's eyes said she might jump without it.

Her voice pleaded softly, awakening Jewel to the fact that in her musings she'd been drawn toward the painter's shoulder again. "Please, Miss Jewel. I shall never finish if you insist on abandoning your pose."

The fairy chimed, and Hook looked up from the window seat and the book he was reading to intercede, "Calm yourself, Jewel. A work of art as unique as yourself demands time for its creation. And, as you know, we require not one, but two of these precious portraits."

Jewel flew back to the window and onto the wispy surface of his book. She bestowed a squeeze upon his thumb, which had dried by now, then she zipped to her pillow to primp her flossy hair back into place. She had hardly been able to contain her pleasure when her master had sworn, solemnly, to bring one of these miniatures to the Island where Jewel could admire herself in her niche in the hideout under the ground. But she had positively glistened when he told her of his plans for the second. Her image was to be kept and treasured, framed in a locket that her master vowed to carry with him, always. Because, as he'd said, exuding admiration, "What use is a gem locked away? I shall wear your beauty as I bear my lesser jewels, upon my own person."

He now poured another drop of ambrosia for her in the thimble Mr. Smee dedicated for her use the very first time she entered her master's quarters. "To settle you, Jewel." As she imbibed a sweet sip, he removed his coat and, with a flash of silver, tucked a knife in his boot. Next, he slipped the letter in his pocket. Jewel preened again. This missive was addressed in Milady's artistic script with the address Jewel memorized, meticulously, from Nibs' dictation. "Now," her master promised, "tell me where I will find the *Red Lady*, and once your image has been captured— I speak these words, admittedly, as if any imitation could come close to your reality— you may dash off to the Island." It might have been the effect of ambrosia, but Jewel beheld a rainbow around him.

Jewel had to blink a bit first, but then a musical conference ensued, full of the notes and gestures that master and servant had refined to a pleasant and productive means of communication. Milady listened as she worked, enchanted by the melodious language, but she jumped when a knock struck the door.

Tom stepped in less loudly than usual, *sans* his beloved boots, in bare feet. He wore no jacket. His weapons were stowed at his belt. "Mr. Smee says our Jewel's come back, Sir." He nodded his acknowledgement to the lady who all the ship's company now knew for certain was sitting where Red-Handed Jill should be sitting and sleeping where…well, likewise. Catching sight of Jewel poised on her green velvet pillow, he beamed. "Many's the time Jill's painted your picture in words, Jewel, but this'll bring even more life to your legend."

Inspired by Milady's creations, Jewel felt her little head packed full with an idea for a new pastime to share with the Lost Boys. Ringing with delight, she signed to Tom that soon the Neverland would play host to the arts, too, with its rocks and its driftwood so abundant for canvas. Peter would be sure to leap into this game, which offered myriad methods for his expression. Jewel predicted that the hideout under the ground faced a future, for a few days at least, as a studio. Tom laughed, Jewel tintinnabulated, and the two circled in a sashay, remembering the old days ashore.

"Ahem," Milady cleared her throat in the most respectful manner, and Jewel plumped herself down again. A cloud of golden dust rose up around her, its slivers glinting in sunlight.

Hook looked askance at his young sailor. "Perhaps I erred to bid you leave off your boots." He drew a crystal vial from his vest pocket. With a sweep of his hand, he gave it to Tom, who, sporting a sheepish grin, uncorked it and brushed up the residue of Jewel's fairy dust.

He returned the vial to Hook, topped up with glimmering granules. "I'm set to go when you are, Commodore. I look forward to talking to my brother again."

"I shall do the talking, Mr. Tootles, and none of it will refer to our guest."

Milady blushed, but she kept her focus on her painting.

"Sir?"

"I have two reasons for keeping our ships geographically separate. One is that we will be sailing closer to Europe than is comfortable. I prefer to avoid naval vessels seeking a fleet of two ships, having been, perhaps, tipped off by LeCorbeau. Another reason is to ensure that Captain Cecco and Mr. Nibs remain in what is aptly called blissful ignorance. They need not learn of the presence of the baronetess."

In an automatic reaction to trouble, Tom felt of the scar at his temple. "But Sir, they're sure to hear about Milady sooner or later. Isn't honesty the best policy?"

"Certainly. And I shall become the model of honesty, once Jill is returned to us. We must work all together to save her, and I have no patience to contend with a husband jealous for her sake, and a son loyal to a fault." Hook's blue eyes narrowed, and his voice dripped like the mead he had poured for his fairy, "Or, shall I say, *two* sons?"

"No, Sir! But won't Nibs be rejoining us here on the *Roger?*"

"You and Mr. Nibs will be our means of messaging between ships, as we determine our course for Jill's rescue."

Tom's face cleared, and his old veneration pushed his doubts down. "Aye, aye, Sir. Right you are." A chance to prove his usefulness again loomed on his horizon, and relief for Jill dawned there, too. Jewel saw that look in his eye that was missing in Milady's. His barrel chest expanded. "It's sure to be an adventure."

"Indeed. Now we shall fly." Hook rose and strode over the carpets to lean over Milady. He drew the brush from her hold and set it down. Nestling her hand in his own, he appraised her work on the miniature. He murmured, "No lovelier subject. No more gifted hand." Like a knight accepting the boon of her token, he kissed her fingers, and then, less chivalrously, her lips. He bowed to Jewel, called Tom to action, and the two men departed the room, to take wing to where *Red Lady* lay waiting.

The fairy and the woman watched after the commodore. Jewel gave out a grace note, and Milady sighed. Each was eager to hold him stationary long enough for the next portrait she'd paint. With his dark, carved features and his adventuresome eyes, James Hook was an artist's ideal.

The air on the Continent felt crisp, almost sharp in Jill's lungs. Autumn had just begun touching the leaves. She had traveled so far away, so long upon the sea or in tropical climes, that this weather now seemed exotic. Her earlier visit to Italy was in summertime. The change in her circumstance matched the fading of the days, and the approach of the cold.

Jill took a deep breath of Italian air, and launched into her strategy. "If you refuse to take me to Heidelberg, Johann, you might at least relate your adventures there."

Heinrich reached for Jill's hand, and she yielded it. For the duration of her life in Heinrich's household, she would exist side by side with him. If she were to prevail, she must subdue her suspicions about his role in the deaths of Pierre-Jean and the child, along with the repulsion her misgivings stirred in her. She prepared herself to grant a great deal to win her way, and the less she understood with certainty of recent tragedies, the easier her act should be to maintain. As the coachman whipped up the horses to convey Heinrich's party from this port on the Italian coast toward Austria, she intended to question her *faux* husband only so far as the events of his youth. His more recent dealings she knew, or knew these dealings must be ignored.

He smiled, willing to indulge his new wife. "I will not pretend that there is little to say of my university experiences. Most of them, however, have to do with academics."

Jill studied his very first scar. "Most, but not all." Lifting her finger to his face, she traced the mark down his cheek. He was pleased, and he pressed her hand there. She felt his response not only through his gesture, but by way of the electric connection she'd hoped her storyteller's instinct would grant her so close to his native soil. As Nico's story revealed itself to her in his home in the countryside, so, she believed, Johann's would open to her here, upon his own familiar ground.

This port hosted ships from all over the Earth, too many to count when the party disembarked from the *Mary Rose*— soon, Jill presumed, to be returned to her true name and French colors. At the harbor, Heinrich arranged for the two crates of lotus to be shipped by dray to his laboratory where, through the magic of his formula, he would transform the flowers into his elixir. Sailors swaggered along the docks and into streets noisy with mule carts and vendors. Tall, rectangular, multi-colored dwellings stood crammed shoulder to shoulder. Their shutters were propped open as if to welcome the world.

Jill felt her apprehension swell as she left her own wooden world behind, her life at sea. Exiting the city, the coach rolled along, entering too deeply into Heinrich's dominion. Liza, tucked under a coach rug, still clung to silence. Apathetic to her surroundings, she let her gray gaze wander anywhere except toward her father, who sat opposite her. Mr. Darling, in his black banker's coat and bowler hat, had settled in next to the girl. He assumed a paternal oversight of Liza's welfare, and every so often he patted her knee or adjusted her wrap. At Heinrich's elbow, Jill sat wrapped warm in a stole with her hands in kid gloves, her scar disguised by her pearls. The road was smooth, the horses well behaved in their jingling harness, and the scenery no less than magnificent. In happier circumstances, and with her true husband, who was born in this country, Jill would have enjoyed the journey.

She ventured, "Tell me of your student days, Johann. Where did you study?"

"Ah, I took rooms in a respectable house of cut yellow stone, a block or so from the library. I lived on the second level, looking out upon the garden. On pleasant days, I would set my desk on the covered balcony, where hung the scents of the vines and flowers that climbed the garden wall."

"An idyllic setting."

Heinrich looked into the memory. "A tree grew over that wall from the footpath, twisting and twining, as if it too grasped at the knowledge I was acquiring there in my books. That garden was a quiet haven for me, shutting out busy boulevards, and tucked away from the rowdy boys in the *Biergärten*."

"I imagine you as a young man, dedicated to study, uninterested in the antics of the more affluent young men. No doubt your ambitions soared above those of most of your fellow scholars."

"How well you understand me, my Jill."

"I shall understand you even better, as…" her scarlet hand was hidden beneath her glove. In its stead, she pressed her fan, open just a few inches, on Heinrich's thigh. Closing her eyes, she allowed inklings and insights to seep in, from the man, to the red fan, to her red hand, up the long run of her glove, and into her being, "…as we make this journey, together."

When Jill opened her eyes, she saw that Liza focused now, upon the Storyteller. The girl knew her father, and she knew Jill.

Expectation entered her gaze, and just a touch of curiosity. Jill nodded to her, pleased to see the girl taking an interest in something more than her sorrow.

Mr. Darling also felt the change in atmosphere. "My angel, I haven't seen that look upon your face since before you left home. But...never quite the same look as today." He readjusted in his seat, leaning forward. "I suppose your mother would say that the difference is that your stories have grown up."

Not yet wary, Heinrich indulged his wife. "I once discouraged you from revealing my history. I no longer demur. My past is, after all, not nearly as fearsome as your story of Mr. Yulunga." He smiled, glancing at his daughter to catch her reaction to the name of the former slave, her former enslaver. Liza winced, but, reading the empathy in Jill's expression, seemed undeterred about learning more of her father's background. Liza appeared to understand, as did Jill, that knowledge could be power.

"Heidelberg..." Jill mused. "I can see it in my mind's eye." With her fan still resting on Heinrich's thigh, she placed her other hand on his handsome blue coat, in the crook of his elbow. "Red roofs nestle in a valley mothered by green mountains. A row of evergreens marches up the hill behind the university, trekking toward a castle that still stands, broken but robust. The town is both homely and bold, a world unto itself between river and castle. Enter a young scholar from Vienna, determined to make the most of his intelligence, one who yearns to shape his future with the skill of his own mind and hands."

"You are most perceptive, my darling. I always thought of the buildings of the university as upright and square-shouldered. They seemed to me, in my idealistic youth, to house the ancient virtues of our Germanic peoples."

"I see them, Johann, just as you describe. And two round, white towers topped with pointed helms host the riverside entrance, offering welcome only to those who are worthy. When morning illuminates this gateway to Heidelberg, it is like the sunshine of enlightenment. A good omen for you, Johann, an appropriate setting for your sense of order and propriety." She sat back. "Yes, I see it all. You belonged there."

"This, I admit, was my vision as I entered those halls of erudition. I soon became aware, though, of the disruptive element of boys thrown together, learning to become men."

On this topic, Jill was an expert. She encouraged him, "Some of these boys never do mature, do they? Others benefit from a mentor. A guide."

This suggestion ignited the spark Jill was seeking. As Heinrich cast his mind back to a more specific memory, her cognizance followed. "Yes," he affirmed, "a mentor, such as my dear old professor."

Jill peeled off her glove, allowing her ruby and diamond ring to lend luster to her inspiration. She placed two fingers on Heinrich's generous lips. "Allow me to speak for you, Johann. Let me recount your tale as you yourself would voice it."

He kissed her fingers, and trapped them. "As you wish, my darling. After all, we will have few secrets between us now that we are wed, and, at last, together."

Jill twined her fingers in his. She turned her gaze toward the landscape where it sped past the carriage, and she began. Effortlessly, her words mimicked the cadence of Austria.

"My most respected professor— he excelled in teaching the chemical arts— was an old bachelor devoted to his calling. His sister had died and, kindly, he took his niece into his care. Katje, he called her— his little kitten. Katje and a maid kept the house for him. They dwelled quite happily together in a townhome set into a courtyard, through a vine-covered archway off an avenue. Away from the university proper, the bespectacled uncle and his bright, petite niece worked another kind of chemistry, distilling the purest of elements— a home.

"I would pay visits there to discuss texts with him— he was an excellent fellow, and a clear-thinking tutor. I'd look up to the terrace as I entered the courtyard, and there she would stand, as if awaiting my arrival. Katje, with a copper can in her hands, would be watering the planters. They bridled with deep pink and white geraniums. She'd lean in to inhale their unalloyed scent, and, when she saw me, she would curtsey and smile. Never a forward girl, she behaved shyly at first, opening gradually, like one of her blooms. Slowly, we grew better acquainted. Perhaps, when Katje sat with us, working at her embroidery, my own thinking was not always as clear as the don's. But he was a good-hearted man. He trusted his students, and, when necessary, he kept us on task.

"As was proper, we two sweethearts never met beyond the presence of her uncle. I was circumspect, as befitting a hopeful medical student, and she, the essence of discretion. She was fine-boned and pretty, her pale hair swept up and tied with a velvet ribbon, to hang in ringlets down her back. Her neck was delicate, and white as swan's down. These features were much admired by my fellow scholars, although out of respect for gentlewomen in general and for our professor in particular, no one discussed her in any manner but that of a gentleman. Naturally I was in no position to ask for her hand at that stage of my career, yet we allowed an understanding to develop between us. She would wait for me to earn my degree and establish my practice, either here in Heidelberg, close to her uncle, or in Vienna, my own home.

"Over many a congenial dinner with her uncle, and, if the weather was fine, walks along the bridge or in the wooded lanes above the River Neckar, the three of us would converse, agreeing in temperament and in philosophy. For our future family, prospects appeared formulated for contentment.

"Regrettably, as you already know, I was an earnest young man, unschooled in the art of flirtation. When another student began to call upon the professor, one who knew how to flatter both uncle and niece, an unwelcome chill settled on my heart.

"Schuler was an adequate pupil, but not so serious as I. He too studied medicine, yet with an eye not for service to his fellow man, but only to social standing. He dressed well, his suit always topped with his green corps cap, and he spoke openly. Yet he'd no bent at all toward research, the passion of our professor. It was another passion, altogether, that motivated Schuler's visits. Once he wedged his foot in the don's door, he took advantage of his opportunity to study, not chemistry, but Katje.

"I watched, in increasing distress, as her smiles warmed to him, as his hand found moments to come to rest upon hers. I witnessed him whispering in her ear when her uncle wasn't watching. To see Katje mesmerized thus became torture. Kind to me still, yet she seemed fascinated by this clever boy's daring. An innocent himself, our professor suspected no guile. Once or twice, I hinted to him that, perhaps, Schuler might be less interested in science than in the fairer sex. Awkward as the subject was, I dared not offend my mentor by expressing my fears in more direct fashion. To correct his niece myself was not yet my place.

"The evil day came. One late afternoon, on a bright autumn day like today, I called at the professor's home. Katje's copper watering can stood on the terrace, but her smiling face did not appear over her geraniums. The maid answered the door. Denying me entrance, she shook her head, the ribbons of her bonnet trembling, and she mumbled that the household was indisposed.

"Filled with foreboding, I postulated a suspicion. Discreetly, I made inquiries around campus. I found Schuler at the *Biergarten*, sitting with a stein in his hands and his green corps cap askew. Appalled, I heard him boast to his circle of friends— our classmates— about the texture of a delicate neck white as swan's down, and the sleek feel of pale ringlets in his fingers. Worse, he shocked me to my core, describing the blushes that followed his kiss, past that white throat and all the splendid, swelling way down to her breasts. He named no names, yet to those who were acquainted with our professor and who admired his niece, his evidence was empirical.

"I challenged Schuler on the spot. At the strike of my glove on his face, his cap tumbled to the ground. I may not have mastered the art of flirtation, but no man may mistake the demand of my honor. I called him out for a cad. We met at dawn the next day. The man was inept in all tests but defilement, and the proof is this scar. Any swordsman will tell you— at Heidelberg, the duelist seeks to draw the first blood, taking pride in his skill to cut the neatest of marks. And so I did. Schuler's face, if he yet breathes, carries a line on his cheekbone, two inches in length. But, at the burn of my blade, the fellow failed to drop his sword, as any honorable duelist is obliged to do in defeat.

"He lashed out again when I could not expect it. His saber laid bare this mark, carved from my cheek to my jaw. Compared to my astonishment, the pain was as nothing. In the end, though, I felt the balm of gratification for exposing him and his ungentlemanly deeds. Around the university, Schuler's behavior became known, and reviled. Even so, the man showed no shame. In that silly green cap, he laughed, and held his head higher. Thenceforth, however, only his foulest mates had to do with him.

"Had he one ounce of decency, he might have redeemed himself. Yet, in a blow lower than I could imagine, he discarded my Katje. The poor girl was used, and cast off. Her uncle, a wiser man now, took me into his private study and spoke frankly to me. He regretted his carelessness. In hindsight, he understood the warnings I'd couched in discretion. He requested of me, if I had ever loved Katje, to marry her…to save her, as he worded it. With what delicacy I could garner, I refused. After all, the girl was ruined. Her slip of character was known among our associates, and I was obliged to consider my future. Unlike Schuler, I aspired to a life of integrity.

"My respected professor bowed his bespectacled head and nodded. He understood; he could not blame me. I believe, rather, that the experiment raised me in his estimation, for he knew how deeply I had loved his niece and he recognized how the loss of her hurt me. He followed the only course left to him. He resigned his illustrious position at Heidelberg, and carried Katje to Switzerland. I never saw her sweet face again, nor should I know it, so altered must she have become in her degradation. It is just as well. After the duel I fought for her sake, my own appearance was despoiled. To view her own shame on my face, each time she looked at me, could only be torment.

"I am fortunate that my mark is one of honor, unlike the scar of disgrace that she bears, hidden deep within her body. I had not believed her to be foolish, but so she proved. I have always wished Fate had been gentler, that she had seen Schuler for the tempter he was. My vanity is comforted by my thinking that if she had preserved her virtue and become my wife, I could have guided her to a worthy womanhood. Her uncle taught me a great deal about chemistry. Once an element is debased, it cannot be purified. It is a pity he could not teach his niece more of the world, before the world and its wantonness sullied her."

As Jill ceased to speak the surgeon's story, the travelers sat silent, considering the tale's implications. The coach trundled on, Heidelberg to the north, Vienna a long way ahead. The horses' hooves beat out their rhythm, and the wooden wheels spun on in unending orbits. After some moments of meditation, Heinrich dissolved the silence. He filtered Jill's fingers in his own. "Just as on that day you guessed my true surname, you amaze me. You render my history with accuracy. I could wish, however, that the lady's name had not been mentioned."

As a father, Mr. Darling's wish was that he might have protected the girl, and he did what little he could toward that end now. "I am certain none of our party will ever mention her, Doctor. Have no fear of her further embarrassment. As for your narrative skill, my angel,

I am impressed. I…I begin to understand what you meant, some time back, when you mentioned that I must listen to your tales." While he gazed at his daughter, only she noticed his uneasiness. He was beginning to believe in her again. As a genuine gentleman, though, he declined to cause discomfort to the rest of the company by imposing his opinion.

Heinrich spoke, more brusquely, to his own daughter. "Perhaps, Liza, this tragedy helps you to comprehend my anxiety. While we were held hostage by ruffians, my worst fears for you came true. I am home now, a free man once again, and I am determined to watch more carefully over your welfare."

Jill inquired, "What plans do you hold for Liza, Johann? Shall we send her to school, or shall we hire a tutor?" Persuasively, she coaxed, "As her father's daughter, she inherited a quick and brilliant mind. It would be shame to waste that intellect."

Liza stared down at her knees. Mr. Darling patted her blanket.

The physician replied, "You are good to concern yourself with our daughter's future, my darling. Liza needs time to convalesce from her grief and ordeal. I shall make no decision as yet. Perhaps some schooling, one day."

"Or maybe, even if you feel you must hide her history, a suitable suitor?" At Jill's question, Liza closed her eyes. Jill persevered. "Do you not wonder, Johann, if, as you believe in Liza's case, your former sweetheart was coerced? It is possible she did not consent to what you call her ruin."

"In either case, she became unmarriageable."

"And yet, you married me."

Heinrich stiffened, but riposted with a smile, "And see how much trouble you have caused me." He kissed her cheek. "I do look forward to showing you the sights of my beautiful city."

"And I look forward to walking on dry land again. Assuming, that is, you will allow Liza and Father and me to venture out while you call upon patients and work in your surgery?"

"Liza and Father have my leave to stroll in our neighborhood. Our home faces a fine little park." Heinrich's gaze upon his wife became sharper. "With you, my Jill, I reserve the honor of walking out with your arm in mine, and showing you off." Noting Mr. Darling's gasp, and no less the ire in Jill's eye, he attempted to smooth the waters, "As for Liza, you are quite correct. We two together shall strive to find an occupation worthy of her heritage."

"Naturally, Johann. Just as you did at Heidelberg, you must act according to your code." Saucily, Jill went on, "A girl's fate is, after all, dictated by convention, and consequences must be met with fortitude."

"What are you thinking, my darling, to sound so playful? I hope you are simply cheerful, anticipating your new life in Austria."

"Oh, yes." Now Jill's tone was not satirical at all. "I look forward to a change there." With her father's new insights and her own fortitude, she would deal with upcoming consequences in Austria. Here in Italy, though, through the weapon of the words she'd just employed with his story, Jill felt a change in her circumstance. She let her wrap fall loose about her shoulders. An alteration occurred, that might overpower the approach of the cold.

"Remind me, Johann. What is the name of our housekeeper?"

"*Frau* Lieber. And we employ Karl for the grounds and the heavy work, a groom for the stables, and of course a cook and a scullery maid and several housemaids."

"Of course. I presume that the women of our household wear suitable uniforms. Black frocks, aprons…high collars?"

"Certainly. The staff of Heinrichhaus are required at all times to behave and to appear with propriety."

Jill still envisioned the girl in her story, even if her false husband could not. A chemical experiment was a-brew. Not alchemy perhaps, but, in Jill's judgment, pure gold. When the carriage rolled through the gates and bowled up to the grandeur of Heinrichhaus, a sweet face might greet her new mistress. A proper high collar could hide a neck white as swan's down. No pink and white geraniums would bloom on a terrace, but Jill did expect to find— planted there in suitable shoes with a copper watch pinned on her bodice— *Frau* Lieber, a woman unloved, but in love. With that thrill of distilling true stories, Jill felt sure she would soon behold, by her door, the older but wiser guise of young Katje.

Suite of Secrets

"**F**rau Heinrich, now that you have seen the rest of the family settled, I welcome you to your suite."

Frau Lieber opened wide the doors to a high-ceilinged, white and gold sitting room. Plush armchairs and a dainty divan bid Jill to rest within their comforts. A writing desk with spiral legs stood by a window, illuminated by sunshine to display a decoration of inlay and ivory. By the other window stood a hand-painted table for cards or for meals with scenes of the Austrian countryside rendered in yellow, azure, and green. The windows themselves were works of art, etched panes set in long doors that opened onto the air, half filled with wrought bronze railings to ensure a gazer's safety. Another set of double doors opened upon a bedchamber and, set into one end, a dressing room and a bath. Underfoot, a parquet floor beneath soft woven carpets in tints of gold and bronze completed the luxury. The room welcomed its mistress, a comfy, feminine refuge from the wider world through which she had traveled.

"I hope you find these rooms comfortable. If not, please ring— the bell pull is just here. *Herr Doktor* has ordered that I arrange all to your satisfaction."

As Heinrich stated, *Frau* Lieber was garbed in a long black gown and a high white lace collar. And as Jill predicted, a copper watch hung pinned to her bodice; her feet were shod in dependable shoes. Her housekeeper's keys dangled from her waist. *Frau* Lieber's voice was muted and diffident, speaking English with a slight accent of Switzerland. Under small, tinted spectacles, the color of her eyes was not obvious, but Jill could see that her face was fine-boned. Jill also discerned, beneath the subterfuge of *Frau* Lieber's uniform, a figure attractively shaped. She wore her pale hair up in thick braids beneath a small net lace cap. Nothing in the woman's demeanor indicated a more personal knowledge of her master than was appropriate, nor did she communicate on any level a sense of hurt or entitlement. Clearly, in the years since her heart was broken in Heidelberg, the lady had accepted her lot. Whether for good or for ill, Jill reflected, *Frau* Lieber's new mistress was about to disrupt her comfort.

Jill turned to survey her quarters, so spacious that her wide amber skirts with petticoats beneath swished about without hindrance. With a pang of homesickness, she missed the confines of her quarters on the *Roger*, which, to her, symbolized the closeness she felt there with her lover. Informed by Heinrich's story, Jill designed a scheme *en route* to Vienna that should make her time here more tolerable. She intended to use that time working toward her return to her more buoyant life upon the waters, and reunion with her pirate king.

Jill toured the rooms, sniffing the autumnal bouquets *Frau* Lieber had arranged to bring color to the suite. She opened a gilt music box to hear it plink out the strains of a waltz, then listened to the tick of an enameled clock beside it on the mantel. As she admired a bowl of grapes on a glass and gold-plated table behind the divan, her thoughts ran off to Italy, and the picnic with Nico by the vineyards. From the third level of Heinrichhaus, the view from her windows looked down upon the front. The shaded street was paved in cobblestone, and across it lay a small enclosed green, reminding Jill of the park near her old home in London. Were her father housed at Number 14 where he belonged, she would slip over these curlicues of bronze and fall into the air, to wing her way back to him and her mother, a family safe home in their rose-colored parlor.

In the bedroom, Jill glimpsed her reflection in the mirror of the vanity. She stopped to tidy a stray strand from the pretty French twist in her hair. Finding a small package before her on the dressing table, she pulled its green ribbon and unwrapped it to reveal a cut-crystal flacon of cologne. The bottle was incised with a design like hoarfrost, with shades of color graduating from clear to emerald. She pulled the knob of the stopper and dabbed it behind her ears. The liquid felt cool, the scent was like roses. Not too strong, not too sweet.

Without thinking, Jill moved to pull off her gloves, then stopped, remembering her false husband's rules. In spite of his restrictions she assumed a smile, speaking to the housekeeper as she returned to the sitting area. "These rooms will do nicely, *Frau* Lieber. Only one thing does not suit me." Jill pushed shut the double doors of the suite, then faced the housekeeper. "You will call me Madam, rather than *Frau* Heinrich." Aiming her gaze at *Frau* Lieber's innocent eyes, Jill announced, "And I will make it a rule *not* to address you as Katje."

In an instant, the composed housekeeper transformed to a grief-stricken girl. The healthful glow of her cheeks turned ashen. Her left hand clutched at the watch on her bosom— a gesture that was sure proof of a longtime familiarity with Heinrich. She stuttered, "Madam...I— I shall give my notice immediately."

"You will do no such thing. I see that your service is satisfactory, and I feel certain of your discretion."

Frau Lieber tottered. For balance, she leaned on the desk. "He... *Herr Doktor*, he confided in you?"

"No, he failed to recognize you. Even if he had, his honor as a gentleman forbids him from speaking of the incident. My own intuition informs me. You will find that I am perceptive. I believe, for instance, that throughout all these years you have remained faithful to him." Jill gentled her voice, "Your love for him lives, does it not, *Frau* Lieber?"

Some moments passed before the woman could answer. Finally she murmured, her head bowed, "*Meine Frau*, there has been no one but *Herr Doktor*. He is the finest man I have ever known. It is why, after the death of my uncle, I followed him here to Vienna. I never approached him, but I venerated his progress from afar. He went abroad, eventually, and established a practice there, even married an Englishwoman. But because he once fought for my honor, I waited here, hoping in some way, some day, to serve him."

"You rose above your heartbreak, and that act is a commendable one. What did you do here?"

"I was hired on staff in reputable houses, earning my references. When I learned at length that *Herr Doktor* Heinrich intended to return home again, I interviewed with the agency staffing Heinrichhaus. I believed enough time had passed, since my disgrace, that the doctor must have forgotten his poor little Katje." She produced a snow-white handkerchief and, raising her tinted spectacles, wiped her eyes. "I am both pleased and pained to find that he *did* forget me." Her words wavered. "Forgive me, Madam. I am reluctant to speak of subjects so personal."

"I understand. I have shocked you with my recognition. But you should feel no shame for loving him. The disgrace belongs to the rogue who distracted you and your true love from happiness. Indeed, I think you and the doctor would have made a fine pair." Jill tried not to burden herself with wishing, with imagining, how different her own life might be at this moment if Katje's love for her Johann had prevailed over his principles. "Here, a drop of cologne will revive you. Give me your wrists. There now, isn't the scent refreshing?"

Frau Lieber held out her wrists and stared at them. "Yes, Madam. I am pleased you approve. *Herr Doktor* ordered me to select a scent especially for you."

"Have an empty vial sent up to me, and I will decant a measure for you. I want you to enjoy this cologne you took the trouble to choose for me. You must put on a drop, every day."

Hesitant, *Frau* Lieber acceded, "As you wish, Madam."

"I see that you require time to recover. I won't insist upon your attendance as lady's maid this evening. Hold no doubt that I will keep your secret, and, soon, I will exchange it for a confidence you may keep for me. Let us talk in the morning. Come to me here, after breakfast." In her most winning way, Jill smiled. "I will pour you some tea."

Dazed, *Frau* Lieber dipped in a curtsey, then, in her suitable shoes, made her way to the door. As she neared the more familiar territory of the hallway, she corrected her posture, reassuming the poise her dark housekeeper's garb granted. She opened the doors. "Thank you, Madam." Finally, she met Jill's eye, prepared once more to carry out her duty. "*Herr Doktor* bid me inform you that he wishes you to settle into your new home at your leisure this evening. He has much business to attend reopening his surgery, and he will rejoin you at dinnertime. The doctor instructed me to emphasize…'Tomorrow.'"

Jill greeted the physician's final word with silence. With a nod, she dismissed *Frau* Lieber. Disconcerted by Heinrich's message, yet she felt relief wash over her as she realized she was solitary at last, and would remain so the whole of the evening. She pulled off her gloves, then unclasped her pearls. Once again, she strolled through her suite. The sitting room, soon to be her writing room; her boudoir, garnished with white and gold damask curtains on four sides of the bedstead; her dressing room, already furnished with a promising jewelry box, dresses and cloaks, gloves and stockings and undergarments in drawers, even shoes with a soft bench for donning them, and, also, Jill noted with satisfaction, a cot for a maid. She returned to the boudoir and bounced onto the bed.

After weeks of sharing quarters with one Heinrich or another, she reveled in the peace of an apartment granted all to herself… until nighttime. At least she could count on this one night alone. At that moment of her exploration, Jill realized that she was staring at yet another door, painted white with gold trim like the rest of her suite. As an autumn breeze blew in from the window, she felt gooseflesh rise up on her arms. That door, she surmised, must open onto Heinrich's own suite. Quickly, she got up and stepped toward it, reaching for the latch.

There was none. Only a doorknob. Jill might be alone tonight, but she could not ensure that she stayed that way.

With even more sympathy than a moment before, Jill considered *Frau* Lieber's forlornness. Today, Jill had given her perfume. 'Tomorrow,' she'd receive something better. Madam looked forward to their talk after breakfast, and, later, to providing a kind of feminine refuge for Katje, a similar victim of *Herr Doktor*'s principles.

A soft rain had been falling since late afternoon. The effect was a smoothing of the waters. The ship lay at anchor far from any coast, less restless than most of her nights. Her beams didn't speak to her commander as they usually did, in low groans and agreeable squeaks. The wind had died and the brocaded drapes of his bunk hung unmoving. His bed felt strangely still. Moreover, his bed felt strangely vacant.

He reached out for his companion, but she no longer lay by his side. Hook roused himself, opened his eyes, and scanned the lantern-lit cabin. His chest swelled as he inhaled, scenting rainwater, wet wood, and her paints, then he rose and found his breeches. With his hair untamed and his feet bare, he opened his door to look out. Down on the main deck, Milady's hands clasped the rail, and she stood on tiptoe in the pattering rain, staring down at the sea.

Hook jolted, his body primed to fly down and catch her, but, this time, she showed no inclination to move. His pulse slowed again. He hoped he had curbed fatal cravings, insisting with sweet words or severe, as required, that the woman honor her covenant. As his level of wariness fell, he determined to order Smee to caution the lookouts as they stood watch and watch.

To avoid the attention of possible vessels on the horizon, the ship burned only dark-lanterns, but the white dressing gown separated the lady from the night. Her robe was so damp it clung to her figure. Her hair lay loose down her back, straightened by the water. Hook snatched up a blanket and hastened to her side, the deck saturated under his soles. The longtime lovers came together, side by side, like drops of rain on a windowpane.

Throwing the mantle over her shoulders and his, he chastised her, "This conduct is unlike you, Milady, venturing out into the weather." With his arm round her waist, he cupped her hip, fingering the gauze of her night attire. "It is true that only a brace of men is on watch tonight, but stories are sure to be told in the morning."

"Stories," she said, her smile halfhearted. "I tell my stories in paint. When I look out at the sea, though, I feel my little works are not sufficient. My world has enlarged of late."

"As did my own domain, after I left you in London."

"What used to fit into my miniature paintings might now require a full framing."

"An excellent idea. Why not portray what you've seen of our wider world?"

She answered mildly, "I hold no grand schemes. For most of my very long life, I've felt content to dwell within my small sphere of interests."

"This trait is one of the attractions that drew me to you. Despite your difficulties, you displayed a restful self-possession. I sought someone at peace, devoid of grasping ambition."

"Yet now that my self-possession seems at an end, you are still satisfied to possess me yourself."

He turned her to face him, and laid his one hand on her jaw. With a hint of hostility he said, "How artlessly the artist speaks." He thumbed the cleft at her chin. She closed her eyes, then kissed his fingers as, contrary to his tone, he caressed her. The rain drummed the deck in a steady, primordial rhythm while the darkness yielded no relic of a realm around them. The couple stood entwined under their mantle, exposed to the elements and at the mercy of nature. Hook felt a surge of protectiveness, some ancient impulse of man for a woman. This sensation was nothing new to him. He had denied it in the past in order to force the Wendy to think for herself, but Hook felt this impulse for his Jill every day, every hour. On fire to do the same for Jill, he pulled Milady's chilled being closer to the heat of his core. He kissed her wintry lips. Cool droplets pelted their scalps.

She wasn't Jill, but like her, Milady had been thinking for herself. Once again, Hook experienced the paradox created by wishing for a thing, and receiving it. *A fearless woman is difficult to defend.* Deliberately, he stepped back. "You are as wet, if not as warm, as that afternoon we bathed one another in your claw-footed tub."

She blinked the moisture from her eyelashes. "When my maid inquired on her return why the tub stood half full and the rugs were soaked, I lied to her. I told her I'd given the kitten a bath." She smiled, rueful now. "It seems that kitten grew into a lion."

"Hence you spoke no lie after all." He looked up to search the sky, the raindrops beading his mane. No sign of the moon or the stars was visible, nor a foretelling of change in the weather. "As you can attest, we must beware the truth. Reality manifests without warning."

"I have been pondering you, and your famous legend. What makes Captain James Hook so dangerous?"

"Although I am declawed at present," he raised his stump, "the obvious answer is my hook itself."

"Yes…" As always, the lady shied away from his mutilation, "But not only your weapons. Your will. You yourself snare the people you need, whether by rewarding means or through more ruthless methods. I've learned enough of you, here on your vessel, in your world, to see your determination to do whatever you must do, to win."

"It is that determination that keeps me here, playing at tea parties, instead of joining battle for Jill."

"A most difficult decision, but you chose the practical strategy. Other men may most effectively wage that battle."

"I must trust her rescue to delegates. She will look for me, and not find me among her champions."

"Master James, this point is the very one I am proving. Adaptation is your power. You may grind your teeth, but you alter your course, to succeed where most men would falter. You lost your home, your inheritance, your right hand, and you overcame those disasters. Look at us now— I, your past, a burden to you, your ladylove far away in another man's dominion, with no certainty of her return. Yet you find a way to embrace all that befalls you, even to seduce it." She added, quietly, "As you do to me."

"I seduce only what I desire."

At his assertion, the heat rose through her blood, countering the chill of the atmosphere. "It is no wonder you require the love of a storyteller. Only she who contrived you might be your equal. On that count, I fear her."

"We talk of truth, and its dangers."

"Weary as I am of perpetuity, it is also for the dread of her reckoning that I entreat you to end, with this single hand," she gripped his hand, pressing it to her throat, "what she began."

"You may believe yourself craven, but I see courage in your request." Hook's countenance had turned grim as he listened to Milady. Her neck felt so slim, so delicate. The one hand with which he stroked her could wring the very breath from her body. To deal with Milady before Jill's return was a temptation. The kind of protection Milady begged of him met his own notion of chivalry, yet, selfishly, he did not wish to part with her. He dropped his hold to her waist. Any day, though, like this drizzly weather, a change could appear in the heavens. In the meantime, he intended to make use of her, and make use of her gifts. To divert her, he returned to the most innocent of them.

"I should like to see you paint a full rendering. I will have my carpenter build you an easel."

"But...I have no canvas."

"My dear, I command a sailing ship. Of all things, I possess an abundance of canvas."

She blushed, but the night wouldn't show it. "Of course. If you wish it, then, I shall try my hand."

He gave a low, rich chuckle. "You see, you have altered your course, and without even grinding your teeth." Hook threw off their mantle. "And while we are enlarging the scale of our experience, let us eschew the tub, and plunge into the font of the sea."

"What? No, Master James, you cannot mean to—"

Before she could present further protest, he bundled her into his arms and pushed off to fly from the deck. He leapt lightly down into the water, inserting himself like a seal. The cool of the rain on their flesh turned to cold. Water filled their ears, gurgling, and pulled at their hair. Now he forced her lips to meet his again, not only wet, but salted.

Earlier, his arms had felt strangely vacant. Full again with the frantic flails of his burden, his hold still felt incomplete. Yet, like the beat of the rain on the sea, the primeval pulse of a protector vibrated within him, a man who held her alive with his will. Her laughter, so rare to hear, came bubbling up by his ear. He believed that, as the wind might do tomorrow, in his embraces she might revive. And tonight, the lady alive was a thing he desired.

After *Frau* Lieber's retreat, Jill found a letter tucked into a compartment of her inlay and ivory desk. No doubt the housekeeper was so shaken by Jill's revelations that she forgot to mention the post. Jill had been hoping for a note from her mother, but the hand that addressed this piece was unfamiliar. She couldn't guess to whom it belonged, only that it was a woman's. She found a cloisonné opener and slit the seal. When she unfolded the parchment to reveal Hook's left-handed scrawl, Jill's troubled heart almost burst with her joy. Tears sprung to her eyes, hot and smarting, but she blinked them away, eager to read his love letter.

Warmed by his words at first, she felt the jab of his hook in his final affirmation of love, which he'd expressed in the Austrian language. *Ich liebe dich.* She recognized that barb to be a communication of his frustration, and she shared it. This chastisement was no less than the Storyteller deserved for landing them in this dilemma, but the essence of the letter far outweighed any censure.

She sat for a time in the quiet of her suite, basking in his care. Later, as she unpacked the few belongings she'd brought with her, Jill lingered over Hook's scarlet scarf. Fingering its silky texture, she gazed in the gilt-edged mirror that stood in her boudoir. She pulled the pins from her hair, allowing her long copper locks to fall on her shoulders. She saw his face in her own, his fine-cut features, his sapphire eyes, his identical smile…and the last time he'd made love to her. All these elements of remembrance reflected there in her glass. Citing his letter, she whispered to herself on Hook's behalf, "I am wherever you go."

As meaningful as his message was, and as poignantly as she was stricken to read his painstaking script, Jill considered the deeper mystery at which he hinted. The address was inscribed by the hand of a woman whom Hook respected enough to trust. Jill's own hands were full, here at Heinrichhaus. As Hook informed her, 'innocent or otherwise,' the story of that circumstance was one for another day. She understood at any rate that he was preparing her for something, or someone, and, as before, she intuited that it had to do with some story her imagination devised in the past. He was considerate enough not to burden her with a fresh concern, yet whatever that concern proved to be was weighty enough for him to offer a portent.

Jill comprehended his impulse on principle, but also because she felt it within her own heart. She, too, had something to hide. On no account did she wish to open her mind to her lover, not tonight, nor tomorrow.

Jill lit the gold and glass lamp and made herself at home, in one sense at least, at her writing desk. For comfort as well as for inspiration, she opened her red wooden fan to the full, and laid it before her. Her fingers loitered upon its familiar feel while she thought. When she picked up her pen, she brushed the feathery tip on her lips, considering LeCorbeau's goddess of Truth. Jill smoothed her parchment, dipped her quill, and wondered if that deity might be as bendable as the French captain believed.

Johann, husband of tomorrow,

As you know, I am always more comfortable in the role of the storyteller. I write, therefore, as if one step removed from our reality, knowing full well that, after tomorrow, that step will have vanished.

Our good housekeeper conveys that you are occupied this evening, so this lady commits her feelings to paper. She shall slip this missive under your adjoining door. It carries a wish that its promising contents will allow you good rest before morning, when you resume your professional endeavors.

She finds she must thank you for the care you show in arranging for her contentment, here in Heinrichhaus. Although you both know she would feel more at home on the high seas, she is appreciative that, dwelling under your roof, she may manage your domicile as your wife, and as its mistress.

She anticipates your expectations of her, publicly, and privately. Because of your clever contrivance, she holds limited options. What suggestions she does have, she hopes that— out of your ardor for her— you will find effortless to grant.

As you consider the two who will join together tomorrow night to be man and wife, let us not shy from the subject of their intimacy. You convey the understanding that you expect affection, and, if not given, you will command it. During the journey, time gave of itself for reflection. If you will humor her wishes, the lady is prepared to indulge you— without restraint. Indeed, the terms offered here will not deter, but will instead enhance your enjoyment, and hers.

Only once has this writer imbibed your famous philter. It is even more inspiring than you claimed. Before you unite as husband and wife for the very first time, please prepare a small draught for each of you. Your potion will reduce the lady's inhibitions, so that her pride may be overcome by her passion. Knowing that you, also, undergo your elixir's effects will allow her to stand on an equal foundation. From the freedom this kind of equality endows upon a woman, whether high or humble, believe when you are assured so, you will both benefit.

Because of past clashes, she hesitates to reveal herself to you. As an act of submission and mystery, she will make love to you in darkness. Tomorrow, and every night you come to her, no light will shine in her bower. A further practice of blindfolding can be your stimulant. You may explore one another with touches, rather than sight. You've gazed upon one another so often, let you each reach out now with your hands and caresses, and, from this day forward, as befits a wedded pair, seek to reach each other's souls.

One other concern remains, and she will be the first to confess that this matter reflects her vanity. Since you last laid your talented hands upon her, she has grown older. You may recall that you recently remarked upon this phenomenon yourself. Be kind, Johann. Do not expect to enfold in your arms in these nights the miss you once admired, but, rather, a woman, and one who has sailed the seas of experience. You will find that the change in her physical form brings no loss, but adds to the reward…now solemnly pledged to you.

You once advised that an intelligent woman knows when to be silent. In the approach of this intimacy, your directive is taken to heart. She shall hold her tongue. After this letter, she will have run out of words. She can promise you— if you are the lover your physical history together leads her to believe, she'll not remain mute for long.

And so, Johann, you cause even this lady to blush, as she ravishes herself on your behalf with her thoughts. Doctor, her pulse now pounds, and she fears a fever.

Does she now long for your consummation? Her lips, awaiting your kisses, keep silence. Ask her not today, but…tomorrow.

The following day grew lengthy with expectation. As the light faded from the Viennese sky, *Frau* Lieber fastened the long windows of Madam's suite and pulled the drapes. Her shoes made no sound on the carpets as she closed the bedroom doors and came to the dressing table, to offer her service to the lady of the house. Quiet already permeated this room, the setting for the welcome *Herr Doktor* Heinrich anticipated, in the arms of a silent wife. Nothing remained for her to say, anyway.

Jill observed both women in the mirror of her vanity. Above the brush, the powders, the decanters, and her fan, the two faces displayed there belonged to ladies linked indelibly to Johann Heinrich. Both reflections showed somber eyes and sober faces. Each woman faced anxiety in her image, but for very different reasons. She who must give of herself this evening sighed quietly.

A gossamer peignoir drifted onto her body. Her beautiful hair was unpinned and let down, the lush, wavy locks brushed smooth. The heavy tiers of pearl settled onto her throat, where she stroked them, revering their feel. The jeweled wedding band glowed on her finger. As a drop of cologne met each wrist, and a dab touched near her heart, the scent of roses bloomed as if rooted in the room. Last, a sip from a green-stemmed glass. Rhine wine of golden tint, crisp and dry, disguising a dram of precious, potent potion. She drank it down.

The comforter was turned down, the curtains pulled on all but one side of the bedstead. She slid between the sheets, the feel of fine linen a blessing. When presented with Hook's red silken scarf, she took it into her hands, closed her eyes, and tied it behind her head. The rosy glow of the room lasted only a moment, until the lamps were dimmed to darkness. She heard three gentle raps, soft steps retreating, and the closing of a door. She swallowed, still tasting his wine.

Subtly, its effects pervaded her body. She felt warm, slightly hungry. Another few moments, and she felt a fire beneath her belly. Her legs began to move, her heels to dig into the bedding. She lay back, more apprehensive than a bride on her wedding night, and waited for another portal to open, this one not only physical, but emotional. This night, this act, had been delayed a long time, but, it seemed, was after all strangely inevitable. Although she lay mute and blinkered, her breast swelled with too many sensations— reluctance, disbelief, determination, desire— and then she heard his soft slippers step in.

A moment or two, then what must be his robe was laid down on the comforter. The mattress accepted his weight. She sat up, unsure if she could follow through with her promises. The bed curtains slid closed, surrounding the couple— and their coupling— just like the darkness. As his hand felt to find her, his fingers, so adept at handling instruments, were gentle, assuring him that she, too, wore her blind. Then, those fingers moved downward, firing a path over her cheek, her throat and his pearls, and her bosom. He surprised her, not pulling her peignoir at once, but caressing her body through the sheer fabric, and she felt the sensation thrum through her flesh, more sensual than if he had stroked her in her nakedness. She felt her nipples crown, and leaned into him.

Emboldened by the dram, she now allowed her hands to roam his body in return. His shoulders, honed and muscular, his arms, shaped by his swordsmanship, and his back…those smooth, curving scars inscribing the name of a woman who seemed to elude him, only to find herself here, in his household, providing his pleasure. Did he find this seduction worth all the suffering? From his fervid response to her fingertips' tracings there, she read the answer as if it, too, had been written into his skin.

Arriving at the pride of his manhood, engorged by his lust and his drug, she felt the blood rush to her head. The stimulation of the potion, of his potency, of her position, was too much to hold back. Both parties drained of patience. He pressed her backward on the bedding, kissed her lips fully, forcefully, until she was dosed by the doctor almost into oblivion, and he pushed himself into the welcome of her warmth. Her fingernails dug into his arms and, forgetting her vow of silence, she gasped, and she nearly cried out.

This incursion, she found, was only her introduction to this gentleman who so long pursued her. With no words between them, no light, and some little love, the next hours passed passionately in unbridled ardor. No respite, just a desperate intertwining, an ardent assault with all features of their figures— her fingers delineating his skin, her thighs unfolding to his fondling; without illumination, their hands brought to light one another's bellies and buttocks and breasts. With his lips he discovered her intimately, everywhere, even their teeth bit and pulled, and their more sensitive apparatuses of pleasure were teased and tasted and tested to their physical limits. In the blackness their bodies twisted and turned. The foot and the head of the bed became lost to their reckoning; the lovers clutched at turns, too, to dominate, and to defer. When, at last, he rolled sated away, fatigued but triumphant, he pressed a kiss to her palm to bid her his silent good night. He swept up his robe and retreated to his suite. In the rose-scented air, the promise of many more lightless nights in Vienna was unheard, but was surely delivered.

The lady lay, panting in the wreck of the bedding. She tore the scarf from her eyes. Clutching her peignoir, she covered her nudity, not repentant, but not quite approving her actions. She believed she should feel shame, but she could not. She felt exultant, she felt redeemed, she felt…happy.

A wedge of light glowed as the dressing room door opened an inch or two. The lady lying in the boudoir parted her lips to speak, breaking the secretive silence of the suite. In a slight accent of Switzerland, she said, "If you please, Madam…you may come in."

Jill pushed the door open fully. On her arm, she carried a flannel robe to the bedstead. She smiled with relief, wrapping the shaking frame of *Frau* Lieber within its warm folds. She sat down on the bed, offering her service to the keeper of the house. She held Katje closely. She murmured, "Take as much time as you need, my dear. I will watch over you." And then, the two women sat silent. There was no more to say, anyway.

The Happy Home

*M*y own one, a first posting from the city of Vienna...
As Jill foresaw, your letter awaited me here upon our arrival
at Heinrichhaus. While it was heavenly to hear from you, your news has,
indeed, shocked me. Mea culpa. *You know my nature, Mary. Whatever
I do I have to do in excess, otherwise I soon give up doing it. Well, I fell
excessively under the spell of the doctor. By my blundering, I lured our girl
into his trap. There never was a more humble man than the once proud
George Darling. Now the spell is broken, but it is too late. We are trapped
in paradise.*

*I may credit myself for beginning to understand my mistake, just a
little, before your warning fully opened my eyes. As we jostled along the
long road from Italy to Austria, our girl related a most revealing story
of Heinrich's past. It seems he holds all the breeding and instincts of a
gentleman, but loses the spirit of the law within its letter, so to speak. I
quite sympathized with a former sweetheart of his as Jill told her story,
and I pity his daughter of today.*

*How Jill knows what she knows is nothing less than magical.
Heinrich himself, being unaware of her powers, confessed himself amazed
at her intuition of his history. I see now— too late!— why he solicited
my company. I am the anchor that keeps her moored in Vienna. Yet even
he doesn't realize how cleverly he tethered her. While she herself might fly
away, I am earthbound. It is I who keeps our bird locked in her golden
cage. Mea culpa, mea culpa!*

*In different circumstances, I should find Heinrichhaus a pleasing
abode. Although placed on a corner, it's wedged in among other brick*

or block residences. Appointed with taste, the doctor's house reflects the affluent but sober character of its master. When we new arrivals passed through the double front doors, which are heavy great wood carved in impressive and intricate designs, we had to halt just to wonder at the foyer. Paneled with dark wood and marble, the entranceway is lit with a chandelier. A basin and tap are installed, decorated with shells and mermaids and sea creatures that, as our Jill says, caused her a surge of nostalgia for her home on the waters. Once we passed the foyer, we walked between marble columns to see looming ahead of us a stone stairway covered in an indigo rug, shining with carpet bars at every joint, with bronze railings that curled their way upward toward the living quarters.

Heinrich's surgery and laboratory occupy the main floor, the second level holds the common living and dining areas, and the third hosts the bedrooms. Servants' quarters occupy the top stage, and the kitchens and workrooms fill the lower level, where there is even a room outfitted for Doctor Heinrich to perfect his fencing. Quite a grand place, Mary, just what we'd have wished for our daughter, if its master were truly her husband of choice.

Once settled into Heinrichhaus, Jill and I seized our first chance to talk privately. The doctor's daughter and I bunk in comfortable chambers, but Jill is granted a luxurious suite, where we two held pow-wow. I urged her with all my heart to leave me here and flee. Twenty times I insisted, but she'll have none of it, she thanks me.

She assures me she's thinking up a plan. As it turns out, she's been working against Heinrich all this while, staging one clever scene after another to thwart him— feigning seasickness, provoking duels, even penning a poison letter. One day while we toured a cathedral, she contrived to slip from Heinrich's side and nip into one of those cubbies in which parishioners of the Roman persuasion hide to confess their failings. She sought sanctuary, in a way. I don't know how they educate these mystics, but the frocked fellow on the other side of the screen couldn't understand the King's English, although I am certain she spoke perfectly slowly for him. So, no luck with any of her maneuvers thus far but, by gad, she is defying her captivity, laying schemes to seem as if she is happy, while plotting means to loosen Heinrich's hold on her. Playing make-believe again, she is the affectionate wife, all the while a rebel at heart.

The doctor's daughter seems in a bad way. She lost the sailor friend, as I told you, (whom I am more and more suspecting was the father of her infant), and just before we made port, the aforementioned baby boy died. I was rather staggered to hear her father imply, in her hearing, that due to the pirate's life she'd been living, she may be unmarriageable. In my opinion, the right kind of husband would work wonders for her, a few years from now. She's a pretty young thing, with bonny brown hair she bundles into a net, and large, soft, gray eyes. As far as I can see she is quite intelligent. I'm doing my best to be kind to her, as her own father seems too involved in resuming his practice to pay much attention. It is rather nice to take a girl under my wing again. We two are exploring the doctor's library. Since the French boy ran off, she won't speak at all, but the child is quite able to express herself with gestures. She gave me to understand that it was our Jill who made sure she learned to read and write, back on the ship. Odd, that, with such a learned man for her father.

I take her walking each day, in our quiet, genteel neighborhood, to try to get a bit of color back in her cheeks. A small park lies just across the way, full of good-smelling flowers, green grass and trees, birds tootling and whatnot. A few streets away is a canal feeding into the Danube. We navigate our way down the steps, then sit there on the embankment and toss crumbs to the ducks, watching the carriages pass over the little bridge of the street above, and the boats gliding by underneath it. Being close to the water seems to cheer her a trifle. By the longing in her eyes, I guess she wants to traipse all the way to the river, but I don't dare wander too far from the manor. Very often, I catch sight of the doctor's houseman or stableman, keeping an eye on us.

Jill, too, keeps an eye on Miss Liza, feels a conscientiousness toward her so-called stepdaughter, although the two aren't what I'd call chummy. Jill ordered the staff to address the girl as Mademoiselle, *which brought a wan smile to the child's face. Jill is filling in gaps in the girl's schooling, recommending books and calligraphic exercises. We all encourage her to speak, hoping for the best. The stableman, a rather dignified groom, is a fatherly sort, too, and lets her pet the horses. When the doctor isn't looking, he sheds his livery and leads her about the courtyard on the back of a mare.*

On one of our outings, I thought I'd seized upon a solution to our predicament, but no luck. Before our last jaunt to the canal, I pulled a few pounds sterling from my money belt. I craned my neck to ensure that the coast was clear, then waved my hat and hailed one of the boats as it passed. Making signs, I asked if I might purchase passage down the river. The fellow in charge, a great brute with a gnarled, knitted fisherman's hat, quite annoyed me with his disdain for my money. Good

British pounds, Mary! He pushed the cash back into my hand. Turned his nose up. I inferred from his guttural gibberish and from Miss Liza's gestures that he demanded his own foreign currency. Once again, my best laid plans fall to ash. It is too much, it is really too much. As a banker, I'd believed the King's pound ruled the world, or at least all of Europe.

When Jill, who never does things by halves, learned of this disappointment, she forbade me to try taking to my heels on my own again. To hear her tell it, you'd think me a mere boy, unable to find my way home. Seems I'm to be treated as a cypher in her house. She demanded I produce the diamonds she slipped to me aboard ship, and took them back for safekeeping. I don't know how she knows what she knows, but it had been in my mind to go back to the canal with the gems and try my luck again.

Heinrich, to his credit, is showing us the sights of the city, full of gardens and stained glass and statues and oddly-dressed folk of all countries. He won't let Jill out of the reach of his arm, but he portends to be quite liberal in our diversions. We've enjoyed a play and perused a museum stuffed with mummies, even descended into a dusty crypt beneath that church I mentioned to view a ghastly pile of medieval bones rotting away. Soon we will drive out to see what passes for Parliament here, and an adjoining park where everyone goes to show off. I'm told an enormous, gold-helmeted idol of the goddess Minerva rules there, which shows that although these people are foreigners, they are not devoid of a classical education. Why, I heard the doctor prattle away in Latin with his colleagues at a dinner party the other night. Curiously, the primer of the Austrian language Jill requested from him so that she may learn the local lingo has yet to be delivered.

Seats have been reserved for the opera next week. I'm to have a new formal suit, top hat, and cape for the occasion, courtesy of the doctor and his tailor. Heinrich pledges that once we decide which of the several fine opera houses we prefer, he'll arrange for a box of our own! Indeed, he spares nothing when it comes to our entertainment, which effort, I note only privately, allows him to exhibit his accomplished and comely wife, (whom he adorns with jewelry to display, too). I myself am not inclined to attend the salons held at bluestocking residences, but I deduce that at her first appearance Jill made a radiant addition to that round of company. In what I see as a nod in my honor, Heinrich hosted a gathering at an ornately decorative coffee house with cathedral ceilings and gilt-edged everything. He invited men involved in high finance here in Vienna, whom he consults for investments, and whose conversation, as a humble banker, I found most edifying.

Except for the fact that I am here under constraint, and you are (fortunately) not at my side, I am rather enjoying myself. Fear not, Mary dear, I shan't let this luxury go to my head; the scales have fallen from my eyes. Jill and I are now in agreement. We are determined to set the golden glory of the Austrian Empire behind us and fight our way home to you.

I know what your mother's heart would advise, were you here. You'd be concerned that Jill should not overdo, that she should eat well, and rest. Those evenings when we all are at home, we spend pleasant hours as a family in the drawing room, and most days we take luncheon and dinner together, the four of us. With all the worry our daughter endures, I do at these times take upon myself the responsibility of looking after her health, just as you would feel it your duty to do.

I hope this letter's complete picture atones for its tardiness. I have now learnt the Viennese postal system, and shall not trust my script to the doctor's houseman Karl but will mail my correspondence myself on my outings with Miss Liza. Looking forward to your soonest reply,

> *Your own devoted,*
> *George*

Relieved of her duties in the boudoir for the time being, Jill took every opportunity to appear as much of a loving wife by day as by night. Weeks passed in this effort as she plotted schemes of escape. Some days, like today, she found difficulty in presenting herself as a cheerful helpmeet to her 'husband.' The strain of awaiting the result of her most recent strategy to break away frayed her nerves. Yet, in the solitude of her sunny sitting room this morning, Jill believed that the succor for which she had petitioned might be imminent. Hoping for a permanent relief from her wifely obligations, she snatched up the letter opener and slit the envelope that had just arrived. In her scarlet hand she held a communiqué transcribed in perfect penmanship on official, gold-embossed stationery. She may have imagined the whiff of bureaucratic air that came with it.

With no means to directly appeal to the British Embassy, Jill had predicted that some chance of communicating with that office might present itself. In the round of music, theatre, dinner parties, and strolls in the highstreets and public gardens of this capital city, she believed her odds of crossing paths with an official from England lay in her favor. As anticipated, her opportunity arose, at long last, at a crowded salon to which Heinrich escorted her.

Jill enjoyed talking with the interesting men and women who clustered for such occasions in the elegant homes of the intelligentsia. Heinrich took pride in introducing his brilliant and beautiful wife, simultaneously lowering her credibility by proclaiming her talents as a storyteller.

In a rare moment in which Jill could manipulate the situation under Heinrich's watchfulness, she had once managed to take one of the ladies aside for a tête-à-tête. Speaking low, she'd put forth her claim that she had been kidnapped by Heinrich, and that she required the listener's assistance to escape.

The woman in whom she confided seemed to understand Jill's English words, displaying fascination in the face beneath her plucked brows. The *Frau* tapped Jill's arm with her fan, insisting that she found Jill's narrative so exhilarating that she looked forward to reading *Frau* Heinrich's stories once they were published. When Jill pressed her appeal as a genuine plea for support, the woman offered to host a salon at which Jill might be featured as the speaker, to hold her audience spellbound with such tales. Jill found this lack of belief in her ordeal frustrating, but the idea of a performance was tempting, and Jill thanked the lady and set her intellect to work on just how such an event might be turned toward her rescue.

Last week, however, she and Heinrich attended a salon that augured more hope. This conclave was held in the book-lined library of a professor and his wife. Jill felt at home in this erudite environment, running her fingertips along the leather spines of learned tomes. All topics were welcomed at these meetings, from politics to schooling. The day's discussion tended toward international policy, as some of the guests were members of foreign consulates... including an attaché from the office of the English ambassador. Jill's interest in this gathering took on a deeper dimension.

She contained her exhilaration, partaking of the discourse as well as she might with the members of the company who spoke English or even Italian, since Heinrich seemed bent on preventing her from acquiring an Austrian primer. But the moment she singled out the attaché and caught his ear, the plea she'd rehearsed against just such an occasion sprang to her lips in an eloquent statement in their native tongue.

She could still feel the wilting grip of the man's handshake as she made his acquaintance. Even through her glove, his fingers left a chill. Determined not to be put off, she met the small eyes of this gangly fellow-countryman in pinstripes and tails, and spoke over the hum of conversation concisely and quietly so that only he could hear her case, put to him, of course, in the corner of a bookshelf, behind the screen of her Japanese fan. As her candid manner demanded his attention, he wrinkled his nose, and with a thumb and forefinger, adjusted his pince-nez.

"Sir, I am a citizen of Britain. Doctor Johann Heinrich, who is seated next to our hostess, abducted me and my father. Heinrich holds a false marriage certificate, but I am *not* his wife. I beg you to speak with the ambassador on behalf of myself and my father, George Darling of London. Through your official channels, we hope to regain our freedom." Into the attaché's clammy hand she slipped one of the calling cards *Frau* Lieber ordered to be printed before her mistress' arrival for use in her social rounds. "Suspicion arose regarding the death of Heinrich's real wife, in Bath. Here, Doctor Heinrich is influential and dangerous, yet I have every conviction that you and the ambassador, as English gentlemen, will concern yourselves with our welfare and act swiftly on our behalf."

She turned away from the man's awkward gawp behind the pince-nez, to reengage in the buzz of discussion. She hoped Heinrich was too absorbed in the company to note her quick aside to the attaché. Her blood beat fast with the satisfaction of her accomplishment, and, as she observed that her *faux* husband seemed unaware of her briefing by the bookcase, her spirit dared to soar.

Today— now— as she unfolded the embassy's response, the hope generated by her conference with the attaché rose inside her again, like bubbles from a swallow of champagne. One half minute later, with an exclamation of disgust, she threw the paper down to the parquet floor of her sitting room.

Dear Madam,

Per your request, my subordinate apprised me of your desire for guidance from His Majesty's consulate. I myself was invited to the meeting at which you communicated your message. I regret that I was kept to my own hearth by an inconvenient condition, with my foot upon a stool, wrapped in gauze and bandages.

While I am distressed to learn of your complaint, our legal counsel advise me that, without tangible evidence of his crimes, the Government can bring no action against Doctor Johann Heinrich while he remains in his Austrian homeland, nor might we discreetly arrange 'freedom' from your illicit liaison with the gentleman. To do so would be irresponsible on our part, with consequences for the standing of all His Majesty's representatives, extending potentially even to the Crown itself.

If Mr. George Darling will visit the embassy to present convincing substantiation, we may proceed with the handling of your case. We are especially interested in further facts in regard to the death of the first Mrs. Heinrich, whom we find was a British subject, and whose demise occurred upon English soil.

Herr Doctor Heinrich, as you are aware, enjoys a sterling reputation in Viennese society and within professional circles throughout Europe. He is, in point of fact, the only physician outside of England who has been able to lessen the virulence of this official's own painful battle with gout. I am now up and about, and comfortably ensconced in my office, where, nevertheless, we stand disposed to admit Mr. Darling at any time for further consideration of your accusation.

Your servant,
The Honourable Sir Morgan Montagu-Murphy
His Majesty's Ambassador to Austria

His Majesty's Ambassador, it seemed, was bound in both the red tape of his bureaucracy and the white wrap of the doctor's bandages, as thoroughly as Jill was bound by Heinrich's black lies. Nearly spitting, Jill hissed, "Yet another gentleman who fails to live up to his title."

She ground his letter under her heel.

Another letter to Jill, one that might never reach her hand, lay on Captain Cecco's blotter, in composition. With quill in hand, he bent his broad shoulders over the parchment that he would seal, then stow gently away in a slot of his desk, to lie abandoned there.

Bellezza,

I have read and reread the pages you wrote to me, penned in my mamma's caravan on those lonely nights under the fragrant, star-strewn skies of my homeland. My heart is touched so deeply that tears try to cloud the paper before me. I will prevail over them, as, my Jill, I know you are striving to do even now in Austria.

Although one half of your memories had to be hidden even from yourself, I sense the sincerity of your sentiments. Given free rein of those recollections, I know you would have written much the same to our commodore. Long ago, I ceased to question the divide between Hook and myself, and I learned to celebrate our accord. No other lover can pull you from my heart. You love me; I love you. It is enough.

My highest hope is that you will find adventure in Vienna to bring safely home and recount to your sailors here on the sea. You are unhappy, I know. Yet, in the end, your experiences will enrich all our souls. Bring those treasures home, Bellezza, I beg.

I cannot commune with you at present. The delivery of this love letter must await your own deliverance. Nor can I foretell whether we shall, in time, reunite. But wherever I go and wherever you stay, you will know and you will feel that your loyal 'company of gentlemen' are working, every hour, toward your rescue.

Amore mio, may you feel the kisses I send winging your way, tossed from my fingertips into the wind. May the Fates protect you until we might meet again, my lovely one.

Your husband,
Giovanni

With equanimity refreshed by time and patience, Jill resumed her outward air of contentment in her circumstances. Each miscarried effort to thwart Heinrich did have the effect of lowering her spirits, only to generate an upsurge in her mettle as her determination grew. *Frau* Lieber's secret sessions with her unknowing lover relieved Jill tremendously. So too, abetted by a generous flow of gems from Jill's keeper, grew '*Frau* Heinrich's' ability to play the good wife.

This afternoon in late autumn, she and her *faux* husband strolled between two palaces, arm in arm along a long, tree-lined walkway. Mr. Darling ambled behind the couple in a new but subdued suit of gray, with Liza at his side in a flattering yellow skirt and a short, crocheted jacket. Other families enjoyed the sun-filled afternoon, also, resting on benches by the fishpond, or lounging upon the shaded lawns. A brass band played in a pavilion in the distance, performing the famous waltzes that gained fame here. The city showed off her finest this afternoon, and Heinrich strutted in his high collar, brown coat, and tan satin vest. He sported a brown silk top hat, and smiled down at his divine wife in one of her new Viennese gowns.

Under his admiring eye, Jill wore her hair up in a coil with a few tresses falling loose, exhibiting the pearls and diamonds that so thrillingly lay their weight upon her throat. Burgundy silk rustled around her in a slender skirt that gathered at the back, the dress covered in an antique lace overlay. Her kid gloves rose to meet puffed, half-length sleeves, and a velvet stole kept her shoulders warm as the season cooled. She had her choice of hats in her dressing room, but she would not settle for the styles she'd seen everyone else wearing. She insisted that Heinrich take her to a milliner's, and there she ordered a ladies' version of his own headwear to be created for her— a felt topper in brown with a cream-colored band and cream and burgundy feathers, diminutive and daring, to reflect herself and her temperament. As always, she carried her crimson fan. And as on every outing, today she watched for signs of the help Hook and Cecco had promised her, and she remained alert for any opportunity she could seize to help herself and her father elude the vigilance of Heinrich.

The acquaintances who stopped Heinrich in the park were fellow physicians and their wives, prosperous patients and, next, a pair of well-dressed men approached, the older gentleman flourishing his gold-topped cane in greeting. "Doctor Heinrich! Good to have you back in Vienna, Sir. I've been meaning to stop into your surgery. And is this your family? English, I believe?" The man's companion was a younger fellow in a brown British bowler, and they both raised their hats to the ladies and shook hands with the men. Introductions and pleasantries followed.

"Are you interested in firearms, Heinrich?" asked *Herr* Frohmann, the elder gentleman, leaning on his walking stick. "Davies here is a collector, as am I. He has imported a fine set of guns for me, this trip."

Heinrich admitted, "I am not proficient with pistols. For sport or for honor, I prefer my saber and rapier."

"If you look for a new pastime, Davies is the man to consult." Having dispensed with his social obligation, Frohmann took Heinrich aside and, in the bane of all off-duty physicians, initiated a detailed discussion of some ailment he suffered. Heinrich bent his ear to his patient, but kept his eyes watching over Jill. In his usual mannerism, he fingered his watch.

Mr. Darling, recalling Jill's instructions for any occasion in which she might speak confidentially to a gentleman, retreated to a bench, steering Liza with him. The fountain of the fishpond spattered merrily upon the surface while Mr. Darling unwrapped a napkin with pastries he'd begged from the kitchen at Heinrichhaus. He then produced a bag of crumbs, and the two companions nibbled the sweets while they indulged their hobby of feeding the birds, an occupation that soothed and suited them both as the weeks turned to months in Vienna. A flock of pigeons descended to surround their ankles, flapping and cooing, while the man called Davies smiled, taking advantage of his chance to engage the remaining— and engaging— female. He couldn't determine whether the scent of roses wafting his way belonged to those still blooming in bountiful numbers at the borders of the garden, or to the lady's perfume.

"Mrs. Heinrich," the gentleman said in a familiar accent, tipping his bowler again, "I too am a stranger to Vienna. Like you, I hail from England." He had wavy blond hair, a clean-shaven jaw, and a fair mustache that he had cultivated to a curve at the ends.

"How refreshing to meet a fellow countryman, Mr. Davies. But I beg you not to call me Mrs. Heinrich. I tell everyone I meet, but no one believes me..." She smiled in Heinrich's direction, but followed the smile by opening her fan and raising it to hide her lips from her spurious spouse. She spoke earnestly, to draw the man into her confidence. "Doctor Heinrich misrepresents himself as my husband."

Taken aback, the gentleman blinked. "I see. Or, rather, I don't see. Do you mean to say..."

"I mean to say that Doctor Heinrich holds me in his home against my will, as his concubine. But please, give no indication of the astonishment you must be feeling."

Immediately, he reconfigured his features to a more placid expression, but he whispered, "Egad!"

She lowered her fan to her bosom, to indicate her sincerity. "I am married to someone else. Regrettably, my husband is out of the country and cannot come to my rescue."

"But you are a British citizen. Why should no one believe you?"

"I write stories." Slowly, Jill fanned her face, to give an impression to her observant overlord that this discussion concerned only the weather. "Making up tales is my calling, but I am well able to discern truth from fiction. My father there can confirm my claims."

"Why, of course you are telling the truth."

"In fact, Father is outraged, and craves to challenge the doctor on my behalf." For emphasis, she stilled her fan and, with her sapphire eyes, she arrested the gentleman's. "I won't allow it."

"I am gratified that you feel you may confide in me."

"You are generous to say so." Jill sauntered a measure further from Heinrich and his patient, and Mr. Davies accompanied her to a spot where they might better view the glass palace at the end of the park. It was an extension of the royal building, with arches of copper that had oxidized green, supporting glass panels in the place of walls and a ceiling. Jill tilted her hat to a fetching angle, saying, "I only burden you with this information because you are an expert in firearms."

"Indeed, it is my profession to collect them, and to instruct others in their use."

"Perhaps you would be so kind as to instruct *me*."

The boyish look of his face turned more manly. As if in accord with his amazement, the band at the pavilion ceased tooting music. "Dear lady, I would never allow a woman to fight her own battle. Not an Englishwoman, by any means!"

"I see no reason why, upon insult, I myself should not challenge my offender."

"I shall give you a reason. I offer my service in your stead." He bowed.

"Mr. Davies," she folded the fan and laid it upon his shoulder, not coquettishly in a way to attract Heinrich's suspicion, but sincerely, as if she valued his opinion on the architecture of the glass palace. She kept her gaze upon the building. "I could not ask you to place yourself in danger. After all, we have only just met. If you'll not teach me, perhaps you would consider instructing my father."

Davies looked askance at mild Mr. Darling with a muffler wrapped round his neck, licking sugar from his fingers and dispensing breadcrumbs to a swarm of bobbling pigeons. He confessed, "I mean no offense, but your good pater looks more like a clerk than a duelist."

"How perceptive you are! He is a banker, and he has no experience at all in the art of defense. I have to hold him back, every day, from attempting to avenge the damage to my dignity. He is humiliated to see his daughter handled like a jade by a man of status…but what can we do?"

"Have you contacted the authorities? The police, for a start?"

"I am not allowed to leave Heinrichhaus on my own to request the aid of the constabulary. I might write to them, but the staff inspect the addresses of our outgoing letters. My only friend and confidant is our housekeeper, and I dare not ask that worthy lady to perform a task that can only end in her dismissal! I regret that Father has not the command of the language necessary to lodge a complaint of such a delicate nature. Why, our jailor has gone so far as to forbid the staff to help the two of us learn to speak Austrian. In any event, Doctor Heinrich has made so many friends of people in high places here in the city in which he was born that all my attempts to expose his vices prove useless."

"And our British Embassy? Surely our consul would hear you out?"

"Alas, I met the consul's attaché at a salon, and just barely managed to send a message through that channel. I held high hopes, but, not long ago, I received the gentleman's response. As it transpires, our ambassador is a grateful patient of the doctor. Heinrich has miraculously relieved His Majesty's representative of a painful bout of gout."

"Madam, this lack of action on the part of my country's officials almost makes me ashamed to call myself an Englishman."

She sighed. "Until my father and I find another way to escape, we must remain in a foreign city, subjected to Heinrich's debauchery."

"I will not stand for it." Davis squared his shoulders and smoothed his handsome mustache. "Mrs.— I'm sorry, I am afraid I don't know your real name."

"My name is Jill, and you may call me so."

"I could not presume. But I do presume to challenge your oppressor, on the spot." So saying, he began to remove his right glove.

"No, please, Sir." She restrained him not with a touch, but with her gravity. "If you challenge Doctor Heinrich, he shall have the choice of weapon. Due to my cause he has already killed a man with his saber. If you are sincere in a desire to defend me, you must provoke him to offer battle to *you*, so that you may fight him with your own weapon of choice— pistols."

Mr. Davies considered, then restored his glove to his hand. "I agree, Madam."

"I must ask. Are you confident of your skill? Can you prevail? Truly, I wish no harm to come to you."

"I *am* confident, and I can best him."

"Can you kill him?"

Davies opened his mouth to answer, but stopped to think. His honest face clouded. "Your situation is one with which I have too much familiarity. I shall name no names, but someone I hold dear once required just such a champion. I take pride in the fact that I came to her aid."

"Sir, I am sorry to hear of this sad circumstance, but on the lady's behalf, I esteem your action."

"Do you swear, Madam, by all you hold sacred, that Heinrich is the roué you portray him to be?" He searched her eyes for sincerity. "No stories?"

"I swear by my love for my husband, who would trounce the man if he were here."

"Then, my lady, I will do battle for you."

"And might your business suffer if you take such a stand?"

"Believe me, those who require my services won't hold a contest of arms against me. In fact, I may win more interest in my armory!"

"I do hope so." Jill smiled her gratitude. "As we may not be granted another chance to speak, I must thank you now."

"It is my privilege, Madam. But acting the cad is foreign to my nature. I should be chagrinned to take liberties. Such behavior would place me on the same level as your abductor."

Jill solved his dilemma. "I am quite good at pretending." Hooking her arm in Davies', she wandered behind an oak, where the broad trunk stood between them and Heinrich's observation. In the speckled light beneath autumn leaves, she granted him the token of her handkerchief, and blew him a kiss over her glove. Jill watched him tuck her token in at his breast, then she raised her clear, storyteller's voice in indignation. "Mr. Davies!" She struck his face with her folded fan, leaving a red stripe on his cheek. "I shall leave you this instant! Johann!" Her false husband came striding to her side, tearing off his right glove.

Clutching the crimson fan with her hidden red hand, Jill stepped aside to allow the ensuing conflict to evolve. In a whirl of wings, the flock of pigeons fluttered off as Mr. Darling and Liza jumped up from their seats.

During the customary commotion of male pride and posturing, Jill made a more thorough examination of her new champion. He appeared intelligent, and in manner had proven his chivalry. He was not tall but held his frame well, and with decorum. Something in the fact that he was a fellow countryman brought Jill comfort, but, confident as Davies avowed himself to be, she felt compunction at allowing this stranger to place himself at such risk.

Before she grew restless enough to tap her toes, a time was appointed, weapons decided, and a place of contest named. *Herr* Frohmann, asserting faith in each of his associates, agreed to act as judge. Davies' second would be another acquaintance among his arms enthusiasts; Heinrich found a volunteer in a fellow physician who had rejoined him upon overhearing the fracas.

When the other gentlemen's backs were turned to retire, Heinrich linked Jill's arm in his, hustling her homeward with her silken skirts susurrating. She set her concern for her defender aside to continue her charade. "My heroic Johann," she flattered him, "you are keeping your word to me. You predicted, long ago on the *Roger*, that on many a misty morning here in your homeland, you would call the gentlemen out to defend me." Heinrich slowed his pace, then he stopped. Free now to act the coquette, Jill fluttered her fan and caressed her pearls. "We are living that rich, breathtaking dream that you promised me." Her eyes invited him.

He smiled down upon her, and his two dueling scars made him dashing. Amorously, he held her face in his hands. "As I recall, I said, 'I have pleased you now, haven't I, my lady pirate?' " And he kissed her, right there in the park, between two palaces. In her brown chapeau with white and burgundy feathers, the lady returned his embrace.

With vengeance in her sights, a strong, savage surge of Red-Handed Jill's retribution fired her blood. Upon releasing her victim, she adjusted the angle of her hat— the fabrication of fashion that reflected herself and her feeling. She was hopeful, diminutive, and daring.

The two wanderers had made a long journey. Dusty and hungry, they smelled the smoke of the fires and heard the murmur of conversation. It was dinnertime, with the sun's light sharpening as it sank. A few more paces, then Nibs and Stella dismounted from their ponies. Rubbing the aches from their thighs, they scanned the camp to find it much larger than last summer's site. Stella rejoiced, "See, it is as I hoped. It is the autumn gathering time, and all the clans are assembled!" Before thirst could be slaked and supper sought, she and Nibs had news to deliver.

Nibs stowed the vial of Jewel's fairy dust in his pocket, sparkling heartily now that it was so near to its twin with the gypsies. He pulled the orange kerchief from his head and stood tall, waving it. *"Ciao! Saluti!"*

The dogs began barking, and whistles shrieked as the tribes were alerted. Men, women, and children whirled in surprise, then the many Ceccos ran to amass round the travelers, all talking at once in their animated Italian. In a circle by the fire with other headmen, the *Padre* sat back in his rug-covered throne, his pipe in hand and a smile beneath his flowing white mustaches, exposing the gap in his teeth. In a flurry of colored clothing, Mamma and Papa Cecco hurried to embrace the newcomers, and Nico took command of the two ponies. Bezzi arrived with her auburn hair blown, her skirts swirling, and her lungs out of breath. She said nothing. She simply enfolded her daughter in her arms. Trinio in his flashy garb laughed, raising his voice above the others' chattering.

"Welcome home, lovebirds! Are you here to build your nest?"

Stella's dimples didn't disappoint him. *"Sì,* Uncle. Nibs and I have come home to be married."

Her mother squeezed her waist, smiling. "My daughter. I am pleased you are come in time for the gathering, so that all our family may celebrate with you." Bezzi's new wedding band glowed on her finger as she placed her hand on her abdomen. "I, too, have good news to share." Her smile turned shy, and Stella beamed, kissing her, but the young woman sobered as she turned to face the dark form of her Uncle Nico.

As Stella's foster father, authority sat square on Nico's broad shoulders. His look and his manner waxed stern. "And have you won the blessing of your papa?"

Now the cadre of Cecco brothers stood together, six strong gypsy men, their hands on their hips and their wide sleeves flaring in the evening breeze. By their very bearing, they insisted their little Stella's nuptials be conducted according to custom. Nibs returned their stares, and the crease showed again between his eyebrows. "We have his blessing, and we have something better."

Standing next to her beloved, hand to hand and no cloth to diminish the feeling between them, Stella felt tears sear her eyes. She shed one in gratitude for her family. Even if she'd had the words to express herself, she couldn't speak. Only music might do, and, right on time, it chimed in.

A ringing of jewelry sang out at the edge of the clearing, followed by a huff from a horse's nostrils. Heavy hooves struck the earth. From the russet and gold of the autumn woodland, leading a coal black, satiny stallion, a man in brown boots strode into view, crowned with a headdress of medallions blazing under the sunset.

The clan gasped. *La matriarca* leaned for support on the sturdy bulwark of Papa Cecco. If she'd still held her fan, she could not command the composure to use it. In any case, her feelings couldn't be covered. Her face lost all her beguiling wiles, and she pressed her lips together, holding back the tide of emotion.

Giovanni Cecco spoke low, to his mother. "*Ciao*, Mamma. I have come home to you."

The wanderer had made a very long journey.

Existence on the Fringes

Heinrich forbade Jill to attend the duel, so she insisted her father go along the next morning to witness it. He had little heart for such an escapade, but for her sake he agreed. After riding some way past the city's boundary, he, Heinrich, and Heinrich's second stepped down from the carriage onto soft country turf. The second, also a physician, was meant to serve as medic in case of injury, and he carried his bag. Not normally a man of violent inclinations, Mr. Darling on this occasion rather hoped this physician's instruments would prove necessary.

A thin fog hung in the autumn air. The rural setting smelled of dead leaves and loam, reminding Mr. Darling of secret haunts in the park where his three boys used to drag him to witness their adventures, employing sticks and bravado in their play. A wood bordered the field of honor, shielding it from view from the road. Mr. Darling had learned from the doctor that dueling was discouraged but, in a society built on privilege and pride, it was a tradition allowed to exist on the fringes. The sky was a pewter color just before dawn, and ducks could be heard calling on the lake. Mr. Darling expected that, before long, the air would thunder with pistol shots. He bunched his greatcoat more closely around him and waited by the carriage, stamping his feet to keep warm, like the horses.

Frohmann's coach pulled up with a grinding of carriage wheels on the gravelly path. He and Davies stepped down, in company with Davies' second, a rotund and respectable merchant, also a collector of firearms. Once the door snapped shut and the grooms gripped the teams' halters, the scene recovered a quiet that Mr. Darling felt as oppressive. The principals did not behave with hostility, but neither gave indication of greeting save the required formality of a salute. Soon the duelists had shed their coats and prepared to take up arms. Heinrich wore Hessian boots. His sand-colored hair was pulled back in a ribbon. Davies' blond waves were combed away from his face, his trousers fastened with red suspenders beneath his waistcoat. Behind his mustache, his bearing was calm, but alert. Heinrich, too, looked composed but, as he tugged at his cuffs, a murderous glint lit his eyes.

Frohmann leaned on his gold-topped cane to announce in a formal voice, "At this time, either of the principals may withdraw, with apologies, and no honor lost. Will you take this opportunity to shake hands and retire from the field?"

"I decline, Sir," came the brisk Austrian accent.

"I refuse," attested the Englishman.

"The seconds will proceed with their duties, then."

Davies' second stood next to Heinrich's colleague as they both inspected the weapons, then, with scrupulous care, loaded them. After laying the guns in a velvet-lined box, each presented his principal with the proper pistol. Confidently, Heinrich took up his gun and gripped it. With equal competence, Davies handled his own, running his fingers up the smooth muzzle, then balancing its weight. Both men felt the firm assurance of woodgrain and brass, inhaling the scent of gunpower.

Frohmann positioned the combatants back to back. There they awaited the signal, and the count. A rook cawed overhead, flapping its way between treetops. One of the horses shook out its mane.

"Gentlemen. You may ready your weapons."

With ominous clicks, the principals pulled back the hammers and cocked the two pistols. They pointed their weapons up toward the sky.

"Walk on my mark: one…two…three…" Frohmann beat out the count with his cane, and, finally, as the observers held their breaths, "…ten! Turn, and…fire!"

One shot exploded, giving rise to a spume of smoke. Simultaneously, another shot popped. Ducks flew flapping from the pond, and a cry rose up, too, echoing through the woodland. Davies' ball was spent before it could burst from the muzzle. Heinrich's had hit his mark. Davies dropped his gun to stagger, clutching his head.

"Gott im Himmel!" Aghast, Frohmann bellowed, "A misfire!"

Heinrich's colleague hurried to attend to Davies, whom the second stood supporting. He dragged the man's bloodied hands away to examine the wound. After inspection, he pulled gauze from his bag and held it to Davies' ear. Turning to Frohmann, he reported, "The injury is not serious, but it bleeds. The ball shot off part of the ear." Davies leaned on his sizeable second, wobbly, but still able to stand.

"What say you, Heinrich?" Frohmann inquired. "You hold the right to fire again, but Davies does not." Like a man who knew his duty but dreaded it, he resumed, "Shall you continue, or do you declare yourself satisfied?"

Mr. Darling propped his weight against the carriage, chilled to his bones and unable to exhale. A tang of metal lay on his tongue.

Still looking lethal, Heinrich narrowed his eyes and asserted, "I wish my opponent to understand that, had I aimed another inch to the center, he should now lie in the grass, a cadaver."

"...Davies?"

The Englishman breathed hard, his ear burning like fire as he clutched at the cloth. Finding it difficult to respond, he spoke through his teeth, his jaw unmoving. "I deny the accusation of ungentlemanly behavior," he stopped to draw an agonized respiration, "but I must yield." He closed his eyes in pain, then opened them to speak again. "I request Doctor Heinrich to inform Mrs.—" Davies' face had drained white by now, the shoulder of his shirt blooming with blood, "...to convey to the lady my apology."

"If I mention your name to my lady ever again, I shall excise my own tongue."

Having expressed this malevolence, Heinrich spun on the heel of his boot and stalked to his carriage.

Mr. Darling looked about the clearing, wide-eyed. He felt that thunder was about to roll, but the sun peeped over the horizon and the early birds began to chirp as if this morning were like any other. Catching Davies' eye, he raised one finger and nodded his thanks, thus assuring the English hero that his message would be delivered to Jill. Mr. Darling felt nearly as nauseated as Davies appeared. Jill's champion had fought for her freedom, but, unlike these little birds that tweedled in the woodlands, she was still restrained from her flight.

When the horses jogged homeward, Mr. Darling ventured to ask, "Heinrich, do you mean to say you intended to shoot off that man's ear?"

Vindicated in his rights, but still smoldering, Heinrich stared in his father-in-law's face. "In fact," he stated, "I am not much of a marksman. I aimed for that reprobate's heart."

Mr. Darling was reminded again of his boys, staging duels with branches and bravado. He determined that, if he and Jill ever returned home to them, he would stand like a man and abolish this barbarism, even if it existed only in the park, on the fringes.

Soon after daybreak, Hook jolted awake to a clap of thunder. The ship rocked in a fresh wind that whipped up the sea. A stab of despair shot through him, and he rolled to his side. He thought he smelled roses. Wiping a drop of rain from his face, he frowned at his fingers, wondering how it had gotten there. He didn't wonder long, because as he came fully conscious, the truth dawned like the day, and, like the day, it was clouded and bleak.

Jill, too, lay awake. She was suffering.

"I'll not stand for it any longer." He threw off the bedclothes. "It is high time to fly to her."

A soft hand clasped his arm, and a gentle voice admonished, "Master James, you cannot."

Milady rose to her knees to wind her arms around him. She pressed herself to his back and laid her head on his shoulder. Her hair fell to tickle his arms. "We must believe in her, no matter how long she is gone." Her scent, of lily of the valley, now occluded the roses.

"I believe in her, and I believe in her need for me." With his jaw set, Hook freed himself of her arms and reached for his harness. She helped him as he thrust his stump into his wooden cuff and strapped the leather over his shoulders. In his anger and frustration, he appeared like a wild man, naked and unashamed, armed with a scythe and ready to lash out in his hurt.

She shrank back into the warmth of the covers, but said, "To endanger yourself with arrest and imprisonment would do no good for your Jill. Were you to re-emerge in Vienna, from oblivion, you should only augment her distress."

He flung on his robe and strode to his shaving mirror, searching for Jill's face in his reflection. The storm was a mild one, but the deck moved beneath his feet. "She is strong. She is resourceful. And yet she remains in her cage."

"How many times have you told me over these months, Commodore, that we must trust her to deal with her lot?"

"As I have also told you, you need not address me as Commodore. Now that the fleet has dispersed, I am a captain again."

"Yes, Captain. And I am grateful we've returned to sail in safer seas. Being so near to Europe made everyone tense."

Hook said with venom, "A happy crew is not my objective."

"And my objective— the reason I am yet alive— is as we discussed. Your lady provided me to you for relief in her absence, long before she knew the full story."

Still, he stared into his mirror, as if willing Jill to walk through it.

"Very well. I see the time has come." Milady rose from the bed and donned her white dressing gown. She had learned to adjust her steps to the restlessness of the deck, and did so now as she moved to all sides of the cabin, pulling open the drapes to let in the light. It revealed several examples of her artistry, leaning against the hull to dry or hanging where, in the past, the captain's swords had been displayed. She ended at the stern windows, where an easel stood secured to the planking. "Come, Sir, and see if this does your heart good." With reverence, she furled the cloth on her canvas. She turned to witness his wonder.

Hook viewed the image in his mirror first, almost believing his craving came true. Jill's eyes, so like his own, looked back at him, jewel-blue, intelligent, amused. Slowly, he turned to behold the painting straight on, or, more truthfully, face to face. He drew nearer.

"If my ladylove were not already caught, I would say you had captured her." He himself was captured by this creation. "And the *Roger*…like Red-Handed Jill, my ship comes alive."

Milady had rendered a concept of Hook's ship that he had never yet envisioned. On the canvas it floated in a cerulean sea, white sails winging like seabirds, and the gilding of fittings ablaze in the sun. Creamy plumes of froth rose along the hull as the vessel plunged through the water. The *Roger* was depicted from the bow, not quite head-on, her mass diminishing in perspective as the graceful slope of her lines slid back toward the stern. Instead of linseed oil, the scent of seawater hung about the picture.

On the prow, where she had sailed ever since her master commissioned her to be sculpted in the medium of wood, rode the figurehead. His mermaid, as he'd seen her in his dreams. Yet this icon was no longer carven. She was flesh and blood, the real, breathing image of Red-Handed Jill. Her eyes looked to the viewer as if to the horizon. Her right hand upheld a silver sickle, her left beckoned, *Come aboard.* Her hair, in sumptuous copper locks, flowed over her shoulders and curled round her breasts. Her scaly tail, no longer the dark brown of aged wood but a brilliant, iridescent, peacock green, looped along the hull, to dangle her flukes in the water. On her throat she bore her opal and diamond necklace, sparkling in an array of colors just below her red seam of scar. Her smile was royal, inviting. Seemingly real, yet the woman was inseparable from the vessel. This Jill would go nowhere without Hook's ship, guiding his course, and his ship sustained her in turn. A pennant flew above the sails, displaying the ship's colors. On a white background, two blood-red handprints stood out, left and right, male and female: Hook, and his Jill. That flag, although rendered in oils, seemed to bend and to blow in the breezes.

Moving toward the canvas, Hook continued to stare. He reached out to touch the water, as if to ascertain if it felt wet, but drew back again, not wanting to know. He inhaled, and then he sighed. "You have brought her home to me."

Milady's gaze shifted from her masterpiece to her master. She watched him, gratified. She too sighed, in relief for his calmer demeanor. "Like all inspirations, she brought *herself* home. I am the illustrator, but she," she admired the canvas again, "she dictated the work to my hand. She is a dream. She is truth."

In time, he turned his eyes to the artist. His rapt expression waxed shrewd. "I have found you out, Milady."

Her violet eyes opened in unease. "Sir?"

"You and my fairy. You think to hoodwink me."

"Master James…" She stepped back.

"An innocent look won't exonerate you. You have taken liberties with my generosity."

Her lips opened. Her heart skipped, and threatened to stop.

"I am not a fairy-master for nothing. I know every trick that pixie perpetrates. And you…" He seized her in his arms, and she gasped aloud. "You allowed it." He squeezed her mercilessly, his powerful body pressed against hers, shoving the air from her lungs. Only when his goodwill manifested at his loins did Milady recover a shred of her nerve. She saw his lip twitch beneath his black mustache.

When he allowed her to breathe again, she wheezed out, "Jewel is a force of nature. I should be less than human if I resisted her."

"And she dropped a few grains of her dust in your pigments." He threw back his tousled head, and guffawed. As they stood so close together, his belly laugh vibrated throughout Milady's being. Even with the half of him absent in Vienna, this male's life force, to a female at the end of her time, overwhelmed. She drooped in his arms, and he upheld her.

He gazed upon her image of his mermaid again, and he embraced the artist who conjured her. Jill's smile didn't alter. She watched him. She knew him. Whether here or with anyone else, she was his. He was hers.

Although weary, Milady understood. "She demands nothing of you now, but she is counting on you to be here upon her return."

"Aye, Milady." With his hook, he disciplined a lock of her hair. Charily, he queried, "And to what other use have you put my fairy's favors?"

She found a tired smile. "For shame, Sir, to demand a woman tell you her secrets."

"I believed myself aware of them all, but I see I shall have to apply my imagination."

Another rumble of thunder shot through the sky. The sea pitched the ship, sending the two tumbling toward the cushions of the window seat. His hook grazed her ear, and she cried out in pain, clutching it.

"By the Powers, Madam," he declared, "I apologize." He snatched up the canvas' draping and tamped her wound with it, then strode to the door to summon Smee. As he turned back toward the window, the painted portrayal of Red-Handed Jill filled his vision again. She had, in fact, never left it.

"My love," he murmured to her image, "it is high time you fly home to me."

Frau Lieber awakened Jill early that morning with a soft tap at her outer door. When Jill called permission to enter, the housekeeper's keys jangled, then she snapped open the lock of Jill's suite. Upon entering the boudoir, the woman showed a distress natural to one in her position. She stood in her dependable shoes, fiddling with the copper watch pinned at her bodice and answering the questions her mistress asked eagerly about the outcome of the doctor's duel.

Jill rolled over then, aching with disappointment and unable to keep her longing for Hook and home at bay. She lay in her bed, a tear or two of frustration seeping into her pillow, and finding no comfort in the downy nest of the bedclothes. Disheartened that she must begin her machinations all over again, she allowed *Frau* Lieber to steep the morning tea. When the curtain rings rattled under the housekeeper's hands, morning light found its way into the white and gold room. The sunshine danced on Jill's jeweled wedding band, but her outlook, so hopeful last night, had turned gloomy.

Now the ladies of the household sat at Jill's quaint, painted table. Its depiction of the countryside was evocative of this morning's field of honor and honor's defeat, but the fine china tea service set out on the design emitted a warm and welcoming aroma. As they shared the brew, the two women discussed the day's violent events. *Frau* Lieber perched upright, not at her ease while sitting in the mistress' presence, but, as they talked woman to woman, her posture gradually lost rigidity. She had succeeded when tasked with creating the ambience of this suite. The cushioned furnishings and clean, decisive lines formed a haven for the two women, encouraging a sense of coziness and excluding elaborate distractions— both being qualities that led to clear thinking. When she deemed it suitable, Madam allowed her to partake of these comforts. *Frau* Lieber had come to understand that the relationship between this mistress and her domestic would never be a conventional one.

Frau Lieber, too, was affected by the duel that caused Jill's gloom. "May I ask, Madam, what would have become of us if *Herr Doktor* had been killed in this contest?" Her tinted spectacles obscured the color of her eyes, but not the lines of anxiety upon her visage. Not only was her livelihood at stake, but her longtime love for the master of the house was taking its toll. Although the physician had only once employed his philter as their stimulant, the frequent and furious nights in his arms had increased his lover's ardor for him, even though he could not know who he, himself, was loving. While the master's behavior in the bedroom belied the purity of his youthful pretensions, the effect on the woman who used to be little Katje was mixed. She saw the irony, and she modified what was formerly worship to a more realistic view.

After that first night, she and Heinrich had foregone the blind-folds. With both the window curtains and the bed curtains closed, full dark prevailed in this room, and the cloths were unnecessary. Now, freed of the blindfold of her preconceptions, too, this woman, so long abandoned and ashamed, had blossomed under the hedonism of these meetings. To hide this change she took care to powder her cheeks, and to appear more severe in her black woolen gown, in the stricter repression of her pale hair, and in her deportment.

Jill, in contrast, dressed more alluringly, to keep up the pretense that she found making love with the doctor irresistible. Her robe was a sheath of violet velvet, falling in graceful folds around her curves, and warm enough for the fading of the fall season. Unbrushed as yet, her reddish hair tumbled about her shoulders in unruly curls. These two women, so similar in passion and proportion, contrived to appear in Heinrich's eyes as near opposites. *Frau* Heinrich always wore the jewels he bestowed, tastefully strewn, while *Frau* Lieber bore only the copper adornment of her watch pin. The most marked difference, though, was unplanned. The blood-red color of Jill's right hand could not be hidden from a lady's maid, and, when revealed, had come as a fright to *Frau* Lieber. But as Jill came to know this woman, as she watched her adjust to new information and altered circumstances, she gained confidence in *Frau* Lieber's ability to handle the truth. This trait in the housekeeper made all the difference in Jill's plans, and today's setback made *Frau* Lieber's equanimity even more valuable.

"Indeed, *Frau* Lieber, I think of little other than the eventuality of the doctor's absence. I attest to you that I have planned the arrangements necessary for the benefit of the family and staff."

"Yes, Madam. I am sure you spent this long night considering. I, myself, have been wondering. *Herr Doktor* Heinrich should feel himself to be the most honored of men, with his lovely wife and his family. Why is it that he seems so jealous of your company, even among the ladies? I observe that he will not allow you to call on women of your acquaintance in the traditional social circles, nor attend the salons about town without his attendance."

"No doubt before my arrival, Doctor Heinrich seemed eager to present his wife to his associates and friends in Vienna. I expected such engagements, for he promised me the full round of society. In practice, as you see, he permits only those appointments at which he can remain by my side and monitor my conversation."

"Exactly so. Now that you are here with us, he accepts fewer invitations, even to dinner. Of course I never question *Herr Doktor*, but may I know, please, Madam, why he insists upon locking your suite each night, and keeping you confined here whenever he is away from Heinrichhaus? In my experience, this precaution, like the others you mentioned, is not customary. Has he some fear for you of which I should be aware, from someone inside the house, perhaps?"

"The only member of the household whom I dread is Johann Heinrich himself." Over the sweet-smelling steam of her teacup, Jill studied the housekeeper. "I declined to tell you why I asked you to take my place in the intimate duties of his wife. Has the time arrived to enlighten you?"

"Although the situation is a strange one, I admit I grew eager to agree." In spite of her powder, the housekeeper flushed a deep pink that surely must have tinged the celebrated white neck beneath her high collar. "But I have not felt it my place to inquire about your reasons. I supposed you must have fallen in love with another gentleman, and wished to remain loyal to him."

"I do love another, and I desire nothing so strongly as to return to his arms." In opening her lips to speak at last of her lover, Jill felt a swell of longing, both physical and emotional. She covered her eyes as Hook took possession of her. She saw him so clearly, and her visualization stirred her so powerfully, that she wished to snatch the housekeeper's tinted spectacles to dull the ache of her vision. *Frau* Lieber seemed to sense her emotion, because she picked up her teacup to drink and, tactfully, gazed out the window while the lady suffered and then composed herself.

This morning was not the first time Jill felt grateful for the housekeeper's discretion, and she appreciated it as she tamped down her yearning and recovered her train of thought. "In spite of my apparent enthusiasm for our lovemaking, Doctor Heinrich knows me too well. He can guess my intentions. He orders my door to be locked at critical times so that I cannot run away from him. I've no wish to shock you, and to jar your faith in him is unpleasant, but I will do you no favor to lie."

"Madam, I hope you trust me enough to be truthful. After all, my own welfare is tied to his household."

"As you wish, then. Although Doctor Heinrich assumes the title, he is not my lawful husband. That honor belongs to another man."

"What? How—?" The docile voice of the housekeeper turned sharp with alarm. "But…this kind of behavior is beneath a man of the doctor's principles!" Another illusion abandoned her.

In sympathy, Jill placed her hand on the woman's black sleeve. "I can find no way to reconcile his behavior with his principles. I am sorry to disenchant you. Ever since— and including— the day he deserted you, Johann Heinrich has justified the most atrocious of actions with his faith in a virtuous outcome." Jill squeezed her arm, to comfort her. "Had he married you, he would be a better man today."

Frau Lieber removed her spectacles to wipe sudden tears. Holding her hanky over her face, she bowed her head. "I, too, believe I would have provided an influence for his good. How often I have seen a fine man— when unsupported by a loving woman— swayed by greed, or by a desire to succeed." She blew her nose, then sniffed. "My heart breaks to think that my Johann…my innocent young admirer…has fallen so, into wickedness."

"And yet you believe me?"

"Since my disappointment, I have understood that women, despised as lowly creatures, are presumed to be unable to rule over our passions. All the while, we are no worse, if no better, than men." She gave a hopeless shrug. "Look at me. I was raised within a genteel household to be a virtuous person. As a girl, I once— and only once— gave in to infatuation. If I could make such a mistake, how much more must a man, with power and privilege at his fingertips, feel the lure of temptation?"

"My dear, as my mother-in-law told me, we women must support one another. You have come to my assistance, and I am grateful." Jill had considered the consequences of confiding in *Frau* Lieber long before doing so this morning. Believing her to be trustworthy, Jill also held the security of *Frau* Lieber's cooperation in deceiving the doctor. Having overstepped the bounds of her station so egregiously, the housekeeper was not likely to make any move that would risk exposing the secrets the two women shared. "Whatever I can do in return, I will do. In fact, this very day I shall compose a letter of recommendation, so that if you should lose your position at Heinrichhaus, you will be able to find a new post."

Frau Lieber smiled, although weepily. "Madam, I should be most grateful." The spectacles lay forgotten on the tabletop, and Jill could see her eyes clearly under the tears, a light and mild shade of hazel.

Jill asked, "How fares my father? This morning's contest must have taken a toll upon his tender heart."

"*Herr* Darling called for his tea, and padded straight back to bed, I believe. He did appear shaken."

"And *Mademoiselle* Liza. Has she been about yet today?"

"She watched at the door for the doctor's return, then ran away to the library before he could greet her. I cannot blame the little girl, Madam. He appeared quite ferocious." Again, *Frau* Lieber pinkened, "And handsome."

"I am pleased that Liza makes the library her refuge. Although she carries on with her medical reading, she has no formal schooling. I wrote up a list of books for her, feeling that, as her stepmother, I must encourage her education."

"The young lady benefits from your guidance, I have no doubt. As you directed, I and the staff offer her every occasion to communicate with words."

"Have you...have you witnessed any odd exchanges between the doctor and his daughter?"

"None at all. In fact, *Herr Doktor* instructed me to allow *Mademoiselle* access to his suite at any time."

A wave of revulsion sickened Jill. She thought carefully before speaking, but decided, for Liza's sake, that she must. "I will not burden you with the story, but please alert me whenever she and her father are left in privacy together."

"It seems unlikely. I have noticed that he pays her little attention. I attributed his absence in her daily life to his busy schedule, and to a man's usual preference for a son over a daughter."

"Have you really noticed nothing between them?"

"Well," *Frau* Lieber reflected, "I had not realized...but yes, I have seen him express too much impatience with her."

"I have known him, when angered at her deportment, to strike her. To beat her, even, with his walking stick."

The housekeeper gasped. She clasped her handkerchief to her mouth.

The lady prodded, gently, "And, what else have you observed?"

"On the other hand..."

Jill waited, counting the ticks of the clock upon the mantel next to the music box, until the housekeeper continued, haltingly, "At times...*some*times, his gaze lingers upon her in a way he used to...the way my former beau Johann used to gaze at me. Sometimes he will stroke her hair in a manner I shouldn't expect, but…"

Jill said, with delicacy, "At times he may behave more like a paramour than a parent."

"Oh. Oh, my."

"Liza owns no defenses against him. Quite the opposite; if he paid her the least compliment, she might forget his mishandling, and kiss his manicured hands." She granted Heinrich's loving partner a moment or two to absorb this unpleasantness. "But we both know how seductive our doctor can be. Liza is young, and not strong in self-respect. He wields his power over her— and over each of us— according to our individual inclinations."

"I see, Madam." The housekeeper wobbled in her seat, as if woozy. "I believe I hold now a better understanding of what you mean when you advise that we women should help one another."

"When, in time, I am able to leave Vienna, I will be relieved to know you are here to look after her."

"I would do so, if only for the sake of the young man I used to admire."

"As I told you at the start, you should feel no shame for loving Johann. Equally, you should feel no disgrace in simply desiring him— or desiring any, more worthy gentleman." Jill pronounced in a bold tone, "Because of her upbringing, Liza committed dreadful offenses against me. But I am a mother. If it came down to necessity, I would submit myself to her father's domination in the protection of that child, as I should do for any other." As she voiced this affirmation, Jill realized that, as had occurred in her girlhood in the Neverland, she had grown— and grown wiser— yet again.

Frau Lieber wondered at the lady's courage, then determined to emulate her mistress. "I commend you, Madam, on your care for this awkward young lady. You have my word that I, also, shall pursue every prospect to assist her."

The women sat silent for a while, in mutual respect. Finally, *Frau* Lieber asked, "Madam, why do you not ask me for the key to your suite?"

"The key I require is the one to the doctor's strongbox." Jill kept her timbre even. "I don't believe you carry that one?"

Frau Lieber looked wary, and shook her head.

"When the time is right for me to leave, I will find means to do so. But I will not endanger your position. Were I to leave by unlocking the door, *Herr Doktor* would believe you'd betrayed him." Jill drank the last drop of tea, and set down the china cup with a chink. "I do not ask you to hurt him. Make love to him, and I will manage the rest."

Frau Lieber, too, set down her cup, but more quietly. She positioned it precisely in the ring of the saucer. "Yes, Madam. Thank you. And…do you really believe I am not disgraced by desiring him?"

Jill finally smiled. Her outlook, so gloomy early this morning, had turned hopeful again. She picked up *Frau* Lieber's spectacles and, gently, replaced them over her eyes. "My dear Katje. You were made for him. Love him as long, and as lustily, as you please."

Father tells me, Keep silence. Jill says, Practice your letters. She writes stories. She gave me this empty book and I keep it hidden. It is my story.

I cried over Pierre-Jean. He loved me and I loved him. I hear his throat bubble and I see him all blue and red in the water sometimes and I have to shut my eyes and think him alive, and feel his callused hands on my skin. If I could I would sail back to Mr. Yulunga and it is hard to think about him, because I want to touch his body and I miss him so much. He hurt me but helped me.

Father says come to him if I want.

I want.

I won't.

It is easy to be quiet as Father commands because I spoke just for the sake of my baby. My milk stopped dripping, back on the ship. I felt sore for a while but not much because Baby took so little anyway and Jill looked up in my medical books how to bind my breasts. I came all this way for my son, but he is gone and I am here now. I could have stayed with Mr. Yulunga and kept Pierre-Jean alive and loved both of them, but I did not, and now I cannot belong to Yulunga and the others are dead. I did not give my baby a name and there is no stone for him anyway. He is in the ocean, a tiny little thing in all of that space. He has Pierre-Jean to swim with him. I cry but I will not write about them anymore, just like I will not talk.

Mr. D. is funny and good to me. Father told the servants he is kind of addled so they would watch us. He buttons up his big coat and takes me out of the house like a lady on his arm, for fresh air and sunshine. He acts like he likes me. I think he does like me. We feed pigeons and watch them strut around our bench and they make chortling sounds. He tells me stories about his sweet, pretty Mrs. D. and their boys. One of those boys was Jill's before he was theirs. At the park across the street it used to be just us two, now children run to him on the bench and he plays games with them. So do I and I feel odd. I was a mother, now I am not. He treats me like a daughter. But, not like Father.

I read books and I am learning. The library is sunny and cushy and quiet. I hear carriages on cobblestones and winter birds squabbling. I hear the servants prattling Austrian while they work, and in the stable the horses crunch carrots from my hand. Their whiskers tickle my palms. When the boats row through the canal the water slaps at the walls. It is cold water now. The clock in the drawing room tocks and dongs and downstairs people open and close the doors and I watch them walking in past those hard marble pillars to consult Herr Doktor *Father*. Or he takes his bag and the groom drives him in the carriage and he pays calls to his patients. Those times are when Mr. D. and I must stay home and Frau *Lieber* locks Jill in her rooms. Frau *Lieber* tries to look after me, and so does my stepmother Jill. Something has changed between us but it is not me and it is not Jill. I hear the change in her voice. I overhear everybody so I have learned Austrian.

I do not hear Jill's voice when she and Father are alone. I listen in the dark at the door from his room when Father is in Jill's boudoir with her. I don't hear voices but I hear those sounds I heard on the ship. I miss those sounds and even more I miss making them, and making a man make them. I look at his room and it is dark brown woodwork and smells good like him, like our cabin on the commodore's ship. I found his strongbox but it needs a key he keeps in his pocket. I won't go in his room when he is in there. The Indian ladies taught me how not to make another baby. So I can go in with him but I won't.

He says he does what he does for my sake. He kept Captain Hook chained for my safety. He cut Pierre-Jean for my freedom. I don't feel much free and I like feeling bound. He said before it was a mishap when he killed my mother, and I watched that, too. Will he kill me if I do not obey him? I should go to him in his room to be safe maybe. Or not safe but excited at not safe. Now as I write it, I feel the pulse down there in my vulva. I want to go but I won't go.

If I could listen to his voice when he lies down with someone, maybe that would be all I need. But it is always gasping and panting and *movement, like when Jill made love to her handsome captains, each of them, when I watched, except that then she moaned too. If she won't moan out loud for him he might come for me. He does not tell me Keep silence when he loves me. Instead he just stops my mouth. I should not think it anymore. Those memories make me dampen my nightgown.*

I want to care for a child again but more healthy. I will keep at my studies to be a physician. The laboratory is locked where Father makes his potion from lotus but I go in his surgery where I can learn and examine the instruments. It smells like medicine. He keeps his remedies in a glass cabinet. I can see them. I can read their labels. I cannot get them, they are locked in.

I am locked in. I am safe and not safe. Glass walls can be broken, and that makes a sharp sound and a feel like my needles. Needles don't scare me, and I want to make that sharp sound. Will I?

Instead of those feelings that make me go in his room with him, I might maybe think how I feel about breaking. In her new voice Jill says I can fill this empty book, and maybe rewrite my story.

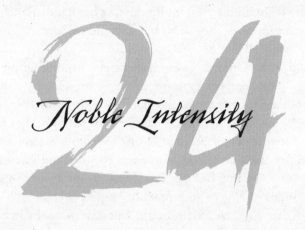

Noble Intensity

The season deepened. All of Vienna seemed lit up on the night of the ball. Coaches, whether sober in black or gilded with coats of arms, lined up at the gates of the palace, dispensing the city's citizens in their finest garb, all laughing and chatting in eagerness for the grand event of the year. The palace glowed mellow with gold light inside and out, and Jill marveled at the showy rows of arched recesses below, interspersed with statuary, and countless pairs of columns above. The palace wings curved, spreading open like arms to welcome her people.

In its turn, *Herr Doktor* Heinrich's carriage, one of the more sober vehicles, rolled up to the entrance. As the doctor's driver pulled the reins and the horses' hooves ceased to strike the pavement, a bewigged and liveried groom opened the door, bowing. Heinrich stepped down to offer his hand to his lady, his exhalation frosty in the chill of the air. He wore an opera cloak lined in gray satin, and Jill was enfolded in a cape of emerald velvet, trimmed all down the edges and lined with soft fur. The cold had set in, if not yet the winter, and everyone looked forward to a night of dazzling chandeliers and galleries bedecked with velvets and tapestries, and, of course, the waltzes that would warm the halls as well as their spirits. Even Jill, accepting the arm Heinrich proffered, looked forward to this party, despite the fact that she'd rather be a guest at the Fairy Queen's ball with no sober elements at all, on the arm of her one-handed pirate.

"I am proud to show you off to Vienna, my darling. You have never looked lovelier." Heinrich uttered these words adoringly, admiring her with his eyes, his lips kissing her hands. "Such festivities are useful to my advancement, but I would be content just to dance with my wife, all alone."

"And you, Doctor, give a supremely striking impression this evening." She kept her gaze upon her escort as they walked under the elaborate doorway, twice as tall as the door of their household. With a loving look, she began her next effort to find her way out of the picturesque pen of Vienna. "Don't feel you must amuse me every minute. You have important prospects to woo, and you know I can manage in company. Besides, if I appear as lovely as you say, I shall attract more patients to your practice."

Together they entered a bright but cavernous hallway, echoing with the voices of the assembly. Heinrich presented his invitation, embossed and engraved. More liveried servants took their wraps, and the servants stopped to look twice as her gown was revealed. It was specially designed for this evening, peacock green that shone like a mermaid's tail, a casing of fabric cinched at her waistline, then emphasizing the curvature of her hips. The dress widened out under a flare of pleats above her knees, and, as appropriate for a mermaid caught in a snare, from her shoulders to the 'flukes' below, the gown was covered with a netting of pearls. Having viewed portraits of the Empress when young, Jill decided to wear her hair swept up in intricate twists and braids, all beaded with pearls, with a long tail down her back in a whorl of unruly ringlets. A series of tightly curled wisps cascaded at the sides of her face. All she lacked to complete the effect of a siren was a mirror in her hand, instead of her fan.

The many guests climbed the white marble steps toward the ballroom. *Herr* and *Frau Doktor* Heinrich followed, his arm supporting hers, her scarlet stain hidden within a single gold satin glove. Her left hand was free, displaying her wedding ring. Her long green sleeves hugged tight to her arms, coming to a point at the base of her fingers. A swath of gold overhung her shoulders. The swath dipped to a daring decolletage in the front, and down to show her bare back behind, with a string of pearls clasping the two sides together across her shoulder blades.

Jill wished for the opal and diamond necklace Hook had bestowed upon her in token of the colors of the Neverland. The necklace wasn't the only memento of her Island that she longed to hold, but, in its absence, she wore a gold ribbon over her scar, dangling a cameo of mother-of-pearl. Her ensemble, she felt, not only flattered her figure and her sapphire-blue eyes, but brought her close, in her heart, to her home on the sea. She'd had a dream, recently, that inspired this costume. As she slept, she thought she looked into a mirror only to see the figurehead of the *Roger* gazing back at her. At first this dream filled her with joy, but it soon reminded her of her captivity. The scent of seawater came to her, and, upon fully awakening, she'd shed a saltwater tear in regret.

Unaware of Jill's dreams, Heinrich indulged her design. He himself wore a cutaway tailcoat of black, nicely fitted to his athletic form, with a tall white collar round his neck and a blue-green cravat. The knot was pinned with a jeweled stick Jill had given him, her first gift. She chose an emerald, confiding in her 'husband' that it matched the eyes of a certain tiger on her Island, with whom she felt an affinity. In both his tie pin and her attire, Jill sought on this special night to revive her ties to her home. Oblivious to the predatory implications beneath her tiger-smile, Heinrich had humored her as he received her token, appearing touched that his love moved her to this generous gesture. His sand-colored hair hung long, the way Jill preferred it, brushed back behind his ears. His liberal lips curved in pleasure. Wherever he met new people, Jill observed, his scarry face startled his observers, then interested or repulsed them, and then, sometimes, enthralled his acquaintances. Tonight was no exception, and she in her beauty and he with his marks of honor arrested attention wherever they walked.

The orchestra swelled with the chords of stringed instruments as the couple stepped toward the floor of the ballroom. The chamber's marble tiles were laid in a pattern of *trompe l'oeil* geometrics. Opulent chandeliers hung halfway from the heights, dispensing the sweet scent of beeswax, and, looking down upon the dancers, painted angels floated on the ceiling, as if watching from heaven with cloaks and clouds swirling around them. Heinrich guided Jill into the center to join the other couples, his swordsman's arms enveloping her as he took the lead for a waltz. Portraits of royalty on the walls observed, as did the flesh and blood Emperor's family. Posing like the pictures on a dais at the end of the hall, they looked majestic in their regalia. Their guests mingled and sipped at their drinks. The attendees were numerous enough to dull the resonance as the musicians played, but the dimensions of the ballroom allowed for the twirling of skirts.

Among the people who received the Heinrichs were the physician's noble patrons, fellow professionals, and acquaintances. Heinrich greeted those whom he knew, and asked for introductions to those with whom he held hopes of connection. Always, the men marked his scars, and the ladies admired Jill's attire. Less obviously, the ladies eyed Heinrich behind their fans, trying to make up their minds, and the gentlemen, their minds already made up, dropped their monocles and sought an opportunity to take Jill in their arms for a turn on the dance floor. The evening waltzed pleasantly on.

In a high-ceilinged dining room, a sumptuous buffet tempted their appetites. As she and Heinrich strolled in, Jill suspected this decor inspired *Frau* Lieber's choices for her suite— white panels and gold trim, although in a much more elaborate motif, and the parquet floor hosted no rugs to soften the crowd's conversation. They nibbled the offerings, until, coyly, she fed Heinrich a last tart bite of apple strudel. As they discarded their serviettes, Jill's curiosity was piqued by the merriment of a party on its way in, loudly jesting and laughing. They spoke in French, and soon surrounded the table. Most were young men, all were dressed in aristocrats' coats and frills, but, as she surveyed the newcomers, Jill truly took note of only one— superlative— sample of these gentlemen.

She had to spread her fan to hide her reaction. As she watched him, her jaw slipped open, and her breath was plucked from her lungs. As yet unaware of her, he was filling a plate with pastries. She followed her impulse, and flicked the fan. This movement among the company caught the gentleman's eye. Upon discovering her, he broke off in mid-sentence. He set down his plate. The man abandoned his companions and hastened to the lady in the ocean-green gown. Jill felt his interest as though she were a delicacy at his buffet.

The Frenchman knew how to dance his way around etiquette. "*Madame, Monsieur.* I believe we have had the pleasure...?" Although a giant of a man, his accent was subtle, his delivery smooth. Clearly, he was used to winning his way without volume.

Heinrich bowed. "I am sorry, *Monsieur*, I don't believe we have met, but I do not deny it to be a pleasure now."

The gentleman reached for Jill's hand and, hypnotized, she surrendered it. He bent over her fingers, merely skimming her skin. She had granted him her left, the hand *sans* a glove. As lightly as she felt his touch, it caused her whole arm to tingle, as it had done when her diamond and ruby ring first slid onto her finger.

"*Monsieur*. A pleasure indeed." She smiled, then raised her fan to draw it, closed, across her breast. She held it limply then, away from her face, a welcoming, an almost surrendering, gesture.

He no longer held her hand. She held his gaze. "*Pardonnez-moi, Madame*, if I blunder. I must have confused you with some *other* bewitching beauty."

When he smiled at Jill, his eyes lit up, a blue so pale and transparent they looked like tropical waters. His face was lined by life, both distinguished and droll, and his whole being seemed bright and alive. Dressed impeccably, he wore a powder blue coat resplendent with ribbons and medals, a red sash dashed across his chest, and epaulettes gleamed golden at his shoulders. His hair was thick, a pure silver pulled back into a club, while a single shining lock escaped at his forehead. Although his body was big, he was well-proportioned. He was obviously strong, but no longer young. His smile claimed Jill's heart with his frank, and Frankish, charm.

Having quickly and unabashedly pressed his effect upon the female, the Frenchman turned to the husband. "And I have taken you, *Monsieur*, to be another bold champion of a man. I see you are a veteran of dueling, Sir."

Inclining his chin, Heinrich acknowledged the man's deduction. "Doctor Johann Heinrich, at your service, Sir. The bewitching beauty is my wife, *Frau* Heinrich." He touched Jill's arm.

"But no!" The Frenchman goggled. "This cannot be! We are both mistaken, *Monsieur*, for we *do* know of one another, although we have not met until tonight's most fortuitous event." With another bow, a flourish of his hand, and a turn of his foot, he announced, "I take the liberty of presenting myself— Victor, *le Baron de* Beaumonde."

Jill gasped, and the muscles of Heinrich's face hardened as his jaw clamped. A moment later, Jill collected her wits. She gravitated nearer. "Your Lordship, I should have known! Your son Olivier carries the noble bearing of his fine sire. Johann, what an honor is bestowed upon us by The Right Honorable Baron."

"So, you are the famous sailing physician whom DéDé LeCorbeau celebrates. But, I believe, you have retired from the sea?"

"I have established a practice and surgery at Heinrichhaus, here in the city of my birth."

"Ah, and I am certain this haven of health lies in a fashionable quarter."

Not eager for the patronage of this gentleman, Heinrich named the neighborhood and changed the subject. "Captain LeCorbeau informed me of the patrician family from which our young companion sprang, but I did not expect the distinction of meeting Your Lordship. I welcome you to Vienna, Sir."

Le baron kept his eyes on *Frau* Heinrich. "I am finding Vienna more welcoming that I anticipated."

Jill let herself drown in *le baron*'s blue gaze, and Heinrich cleared his throat. He asked, "Have you news of your son, Your Lordship?"

"LeCorbeau waited upon me in Paris to report on your voyage. I am led to believe that Olivier deserted *La Fleur de Lotus* at some island off Africa."

"Indeed, the boy departed on a whim. I was astonished."

De Beaumonde batted the air. "No doubt my Olivier ran off on some campaign or other. LeCorbeau's guess is that he has joined the Foreign Legion, to march about kicking up sand and looking for trouble. I am not worried. The young puppy will come home when he needs a new sword. The boy is always charging around, defending *la France*." He sighed, the long-suffering parent. "If only he were a philanderer, fighting husbands instead of enemies! *Mais non*, he must be a patriot."

One of the fashionable young Frenchmen surrounding their patron offered him a flute of champagne. Without removing his gaze from the lady, he put out his hand, accepted it, and drank it down. Another quick minion's hand relieved his fingers of the glass and, seeing that they were intruding, the hangers-on melted away. In the ballroom, the music strummed again, a vigorous tune. De Beaumonde offered his elbow, saying, "If *Madame* will be so kind as to humor an old man, I should enjoy to encircle her in my embrace… for a dance." Merely seeming to seek permission, he spared a glance for her husband.

Heinrich's nod was curt. "Of course, Your Lordship. Only do, *s'il vous plaît*, bring *Madame* back to me…before Yuletide." He smiled at his jest, and watched his wife swept away by the larger than life form of Olivier's father, sea green and pale blue alternating as they rotated out of the door and in time with the tune. Realizing that he held his back more stiffly than usual, Heinrich shot his cuffs and attempted to slow his pulse, much accelerated by the shock of this encounter. He drew his gold watch from its pocket and fondled it.

He and LeCorbeau had discussed the delicate question of how the baron should be informed of his son's disappearance. Heinrich reproached himself for feeling unprepared. The young man was buried at sea, his belongings tossed overboard, never to resurface to provoke awkward questions. Liza had been in no condition to comprehend the transgression committed in de Beaumonde's demise. Jill must have divined LeCorbeau's culpability but, while regretting aloud the unfortunate event on the day it occurred, Heinrich had not invested her with possession of the facts. If he or LeCorbeau should be accused of perpetrating a murder, the claim could be refuted. The single requirement was the loyalty of Renaud. In this instance only, Heinrich approved of the tie binding the young officer to his captain, but the relief it delivered did not stop the doctor from cursing LeCorbeau.

This fête was useful to his advancement, as were the attractions of his wife. In light of his encounter with *le Baron* de Beaumonde, however, Heinrich believed he would be more fortunate if he had declined the invitation. Now his Jill, like a mermaid fished from the Danube, might become trussed in the net of the nobility. As Heinrich considered, he adjusted the emerald head of his tie pin. This gift was further evidence that, since submitting to her husband— and not just consenting but returning his lovemaking with ardor— Jill appeared to be acceding to her role as *Frau* Heinrich. But how far could he trust her? He learned long ago to beware of her words as if they were weapons. Might she sing suspicion into the ear of her escort? Her choice of a siren's garb might be a sign of her slipperiness. While Heinrich's patrons held high places, if he were positioned against a man of *le baron*'s stature he must be as clever as ever was Jill. She dwelt here now, in his household, and although she was his, he must find the means to further entangle the woman he called wife in a net of his own design.

The orchestra performed without cease; more company crowded the table. Pouring a glass or two of champagne, Heinrich swigged it as he cogitated, oblivious to the brisk taste. After reaching a startling conclusion, he determined his course of action, and he rose to begin his recapture of Jill. He intended to retrieve her from the baron's grasp and enclose her in his carriage. He had succeeded in showing her off in Vienna. Now what he wanted was to dance with his wife, all alone.

In the powerful hold of the baron, Jill felt him pull her bodily to the center of the floor. The music swelled in the triple time beat. Flowing with silks and with flowery satins, couples revolved all around them, creating a breeze of cologne. Adroit in the dance, the nobleman whirled her. He said no word but smiled from his height down upon her. He directed her, with inexorable force, toward a corner. The portraits witnessed in silence as the baron's men shooed a gaggle of guests from an anteroom. The pair swept between two of his entourage, one on each side of the doorway, and they twirled together right through it. The panels of the door hushed shut behind them. Before even she'd hoped, Jill found herself alone with her escort. Close in the quarters of this overly ornate chamber with a royal blue rug underfoot, they hardly noticed the music was muted. The party they'd left behind dulled to a hum. Jill swayed in the arms of the baron, panting, surrounded by blue brocade couches, and gazing up at those island-blue eyes.

His accent held authority, even when he didn't already know her answer. "*Pardon, Madame*, it is my policy to ask. Does my Olivier know you intimately?" Reading her surprise, he guessed her reply. "*C'est bien.* Of course I would not object, but I make it a practice not to tempt my sons' mistresses."

Wondering how she might respond to this assertion, she ventured the first questions that came to her mind. "Have you many sons, and have they many mistresses?"

"I fathered four sons. I leave the rest of the counting to them."

"I see, Sir. So it follows you must possess a wife?"

"I possess a most darling wife, but I lose her from time to time. Or, she loses me." He shrugged. "It amounts to the same."

Although they no longer followed the steps of the waltz, the baron declined to release Jill from his arms. Another kind of dance took its place, one that made her heart jump and her flesh tremble. With reluctance, she drew back to extricate herself from his hold, spreading her fan to use it for its basest, most mundane purpose— to cool her cheeks. She felt heated, and not just from the exercise. "You seem to have lost sight of *la baronne* tonight. May I ask what brings you to Vienna?"

"What force impelled you, lovely Lorelei, to swim from the river onto this shore?"

"How sharp you are, Sir. I did come from the water, and I *was* compelled." She stilled her fan, smiling half-way. "But I asked you first."

His chuckle rolled mellow and low before he answered. "In celebration of our anniversary, the baroness ran away with a Russian count. I am *en route* to Odessa, pursuing her."

"This desertion must distress you."

"Quite properly, you offer your sympathy, but there is no need. My wife and I adore one another, and we find to stage these little intrigues keeps our love vibrant. My Margarette bore to me four sons and two daughters, and still, at fifty, she is sought by the laureled heads of East and of West."

"You take pride in her liaisons, then. How very…noble of you."

"Of course I take pride in her conquests. She is more beautiful to me now than on the day I seduced her. As to my visit to Vienna, I am allowing the dear lady time to indulge in her romance. When I arrive in Russia to claim my baroness, we shall return merrily to Paris, even happier than before." Jill realized at this point that he had long ago closed the breach she'd created between them. He placed his hands upon her shoulders, heavy, but tender. No fragranced fop like LeCorbeau, de Beaumonde exuded the musk of a man. The bulk of his masculine presence loomed over her. "It is my hope that you, too, my river nymph, will make me happy."

"Your Honor, you waste no time." She wasn't protesting.

"Like me, *Madame*, you are a clear-sighted observer. You already know we are matched, as romantics. You told me so, in the language of your most eloquent fan."

"I see you are fluent in several tongues! But I seem not as clear-sighted as I'd believed. I should have known you immediately for the father of your son." She reached up, affectionately, to wind his curl around her finger. "Olivier has a lone lock of hair, just like this one. If I may say, however, I much prefer to see it in silver."

"To offset your brilliant tresses of copper! But, *hélas*," he drew her hand from his hair, and pressed it against his chest where she sensed his heart beating, "I am humiliated, to find a son of mine ignored such a woman! A woman not only stunning to view, but one in the beauty of her maturity, so evidently, and so intriguingly, experienced."

The man made her so warm she felt she might melt. Jill recognized the level of his cleverness, though, and, among the desires she felt, she did *not* wish for the too-astute baron to see her thinking. Jill broke from his hold and turned her back to him. He seemed to read her like a storybook. Would he see her misgivings about Olivier's death? And if he did not perceive them, should she hint her suspicion? This man might be the key to unlocking her cage. Yet, the Storyteller had learned to beware of consequences, whether seen or unforeseen. Needing time to deliberate before acting, Jill pushed her plotting to the back of her thoughts— and she rid herself of this burden with pleasure.

She had been living this lie in Vienna for months, scheming, pretending. Tonight, so precipitously, *le Baron* de Beaumonde presented a chance to cast her troubles aside. Her father, *Frau* Lieber, and Liza slept all at peace under their feather comforters, and, for a handful of hours with this beguiling man, she might indulge in the needs she'd neglected. She sensed de Beaumonde moving closer behind her. One large, warm arm encircled her waist, and he swept her hair aside. She stood shivering, and anticipating. Soon his lips lightly touched her bare back, rising from her waist and up her spine, in a slow trail of gooseflesh, to brush across her neck— the very point of her weakness. She closed her eyes and allowed him to love her, thrilling to these sensations. Happily, the first phase in feeding her desires coincided with her grander scheme, and, with a clear conscience, she pursued it.

"My Lord—"

"Good lady," he interrupted, murmuring into her skin, "we shall never get anywhere with My Lord and Your Honor. Dispense with these distinctions, for, from tonight…" his voice dropped low, "I am your lover."

She sighed, yielding her body. Yet her mind still engaged with one single piece of information. With difficulty, she broke this delectable moment, twisting in his hold to face him. She caressed his forearms through his blue silken sleeves. "You inquired what tide bore me here to the banks of Vienna. As you guessed, I came unwillingly, and we may dispense with another distinction. I am not *Frau* Heinrich."

De Beaumonde's face displayed his every emotion; she delighted in his winning, if disingenuous, innocence. At her declaration, though, a look of horror spread over him. Jill was mystified. Surely, this man who so blithely talked of mistresses and seduction could not be scandalized by an unmarried pair. When she felt his hands slide from her hips, she inched backward. A jab of disappointment speared her spirit, but she had to press on. "Like the mermaid you see in me, I would slither from the physician's fingers if I could find a way home."

"*Mais alors*, I am not often mistaken! I perceived you to be a woman made in heaven for me. Like my dear wife."

Still confused, Jill asked, "You appear to be a man made for me, *Baron*, but what word have I spoken to alter your opinion?"

"*Quel dommage, Madame*. It is a tragedy, yet I may not betray my principles."

Jill widened her eyes. "Exactly which principle do I offend?"

"*Madame la Baronne* and I limit our dalliances to those previously entangled. As you must see, this policy prevents complications." His liquid blue eyes appeared in danger of overflowing. "Yet tonight, I confess to you, I grieve." Hand on heart, he breathed a shuddering breath. "I grieve most desperately."

Jill's sentiments, along with her more corporeal parts, ached in tandem with his. "But *Monsieur*, if this rule is all that prevents our entanglement, you need not disappoint me."

Resignedly, he shook his glorious head of rich silver hair. "I cannot make love to you. You are not espoused."

"But yes, I am."

Silver, copper, and now mercury. The man was as volatile as the element itself. As hope reignited his eyes, he drew up to his zenith, spreading his capacious arms. "Then, delightful Lorelei, I must embrace you!" Eagerly, he stepped toward her.

As unpredictable as he, Jill raised her folded fan. Like a baton, she held it firm against his chest, stopping the man in his tracks. With a severe look, she admonished this Gallic Don Juan. "On the contrary, Sir. I arrive at the opposite conclusion. You must *not* embrace me."

The span of his shoulders drooped. Even his epaulettes hung dispirited.

"It is I who must embrace *you*." Jill threw down her fan, seized his collar, and hauled his face down from the heights to her own. On her tiptoes, she thrust her lips upon his, dishing up her kisses, and devouring his with relish. Her first view of him at the buffet had stirred her hunger. Ravenous now, she suppressed not a scrap of her appetite.

In his big, strong arms he enfolded her. He embraced her boldly, madly, until her lungs burned as if underwater, and she had to pound at his shoulders, pleading for air. Even then he did not release her, but poured his kisses all over her throat, pulling her body into his until she felt she'd dissolve in his generous, plentiful passion. All the dry, dreary days without touches of love sank away as Jill plunged in the depths of her longing, alive again, enticed again, and enticing. *Le baron,* with his clear-sighted, island-blue eyes, saw the truth all along. He and this water nymph were matched, kiss for kiss, as romantics. Both intense, both untameable, each of them longed for their lovers. Adapting to the depths again, Jill swam free, re-immersed within her own element.

The blue brocade couches stood waiting, but so did the doctor. On the other side of the doors, the strum of music merged with the tap of some secret signal. With lavish profanity in elegant French, de Beaumonde let his merwoman loose. Efficiently, he straightened her gown and recovered her fan, presenting it to her. Gracing her with a smile of the worldly-wise, he fingered her long, red-gold curls. "When can you come to me?"

"Tomorrow night. *Where* can I come to you?"

"Enchanting creature of the sea," he bowed with a flourish of salute, "I shall restore you to your native habitat. A boat will await you near the stronghold of Heinrichhaus, at midnight, on the canal."

Abundant as, in every way, this gentleman was, he managed to vanish behind a panel, so that when his man opened the door, Jill could saunter out alone, tapping the tip of her *brisé* fan to her mouth, yawning. "Johann, I wondered where you had gotten to." She linked her arm in his as, perplexed, he looked over her head to inspect the anteroom before escorting her off.

When the couple rejoined the company, Heinrich asked with a dash of agitation in his quick syllables, "Did the baron discuss Olivier?"

"Only to express his disappointment."

Relieved on this subject, he inquired, half amused, half distrustful, "And shall I be fighting another duel for you?"

"I shouldn't think so. The man is infatuated with Margarette, *Madame la Baronne.*"

Willing to smile again, Heinrich gave his brief burst of a laugh. "A rare Frenchman, then. He and I hold something in common: infatuation with our wives."

He pressed a kiss to her cheek, and Jill smelled the champagne he'd downed in her absence. She asked, lightly, "May I join your fraternity? I am infatuated with my husband."

Alert for her double entendres, he endeavored to believe she referred to himself— but since she abided within his control, he judged the question to be academic. "What, then, did you discuss as you danced?"

"Contrary to your supposition, the baron is a true Frenchman. He harped on just the one subject." With a rattle of slats, Jill flicked open her fan. "His passion."

"Perhaps it is past time to take you home, my darling."

"Why, Johann? Waltzing in the arms of my darling this evening was exhilarating. Do I look fatigued?" Keeping the fan low, she allowed him to view the invigoration she felt on her features— courtesy of her new lover.

"Quite the opposite, in fact." In spite of her assurances, Heinrich's disconcertion persisted. The intrusion of de Beaumonde in Vienna made him restless in more ways than one, and he was eager to make a start on his strategy. While toying with his watch in the dining room as Jill danced with the baron, the scientist had analyzed his emotions. He had come, unexpectedly, to a fresh postulation. To his amazement, he discovered that his wife no longer held him in thrall. He loved her for her strength, her intelligence, her resourcefulness, and he desired her, carnally. Her hypothesis was proven correct. Casting their coupling in darkness had, for both partners, opened a new dimension of daring. As he indulged in her flesh in their nights in her boudoir, his desire for his wife had compounded to the proportion of the unquenchable.

Yet, now that he subjugated her, her allure was just that: an unconscious, animal drive. Upon deeper reflection, Doctor Heinrich discovered it was his power over this female that he celebrated. She herself was a power; she worked with her own feminine measures to master him, too. He found the potency of domination to be more heady, even, than the climax of consummation. If he were to concoct a drug to achieve this feeling of mastery— as his lotus potion induced physical love— he might dose himself to excess, and end, no doubt, in insanity.

Descending from the summit of his ruminations, he answered her question in the most earthbound manner. "You know you are breathtaking, and all the gentlemen here find you too beautiful."

He cinched her arm tighter as she rested it in his, directing her, inescapably, homeward. Jill might have felt cause to guard against this false husband and the grasp he maintained upon her, but she only smiled to herself. For the rest of the night and throughout the next day, all she could feel was the powerful hold of the baron.

Haunts, Hunts, and Hungers

*C*aptain H., Sir— *The enclosed letter arrived for my daughter at Number 14. Circumstances being what they are, I took the liberty of reading it, believing it may be of urgent interest. I will apprise her of the contents at her current address, and I now forward the letter into your hand at the usual postal box, in the event its import may be critical to your protection.*

Godspeed her home to us, wherever her home may lie,
Mary Darling

Dear Mrs. Cecco:
As your marriage was recently recorded at Westminster, we duly received information regarding the sailing ship Jolly Roger. *The certification lists your husband as Captain. Unfortunately, the officer who performed the ceremony and his crew are now deceased and are thus unable to enlighten us as to the situation of said ship. The single survivor of the merchant on which you were married, the* Unity, *suffered a loss of memory during his ordeal. As you may know, the vessel captained by your husband was notorious under the command of one Captain James Hook, Most Wanted, for whom our Navy has been searching for some time, seeking to detain and try him for acts of piracy.*

While we are relieved to learn that this man Hook is no longer the ship's commander, we seek confirmation of his whereabouts or demise. Your husband's station placed him, and, by extension, yourself, in a position in which you may be able to provide such intelligence.

Captain Cecco was a citizen of the Italian States but, as you are a British subject, I am certain you understand that we consider it your duty to reply with any and all information you may hold regarding this manhunt. In addition, it is the Office of the Admiralty's hope that you might provide us a picture to further illustrate the disposition of the Jolly Roger, *now that James Hook no longer serves her.*

Our condolences, Madam, upon the passing of your husband.

Yours very truly,

Frederick D. Bedford

Assistant Under Secretary of the Admiralty

Whitehall

With timid steps in her high-button shoes, Milady entered the vaulted hall of the postal bureau. Walls of reddish stone soared upward. On the left, a high desk lit by gas lamps loomed, staffed with clerks waiting on a few customers; to the right stood official-looking columns of locked metal boxes, stacked in orderly rows. The walls, like other examples of architecture in this town, were thick enough to retain a cool temperature despite the warm climate. The air hung still, pervaded by the smell of brass polish. Even with her black veil draped to hide her face, Milady held her breath, afraid someone might question her identity. Red-Handed Jill had visited this bureau on only a few occasions, but, having learned of the impression James Hook's partner and paramour left on those who beheld her, Milady was certain the woman's features would be remembered, and those features differed from this lady who, trembling, inserted the key in Jill's post box.

The lock clicked and turned, and the metal door opened to her hand with the resistance of humidity and infrequent use. Several letters leaned against the side of the box, seeming dispirited, weary of waiting to be delivered. Milady collected them to drop in her basket. Leaving a coin in their place, she snapped the box closed, and locked it. She sighed in relief, then turned to make haste of her exit. Just as Tom Tootles opened the door for her and her foot found the threshold, a reedy voice behind her called out, and she froze.

"*Signora!* A word, if you will."

Tom didn't hesitate. He pulled Milady through the door and gave her a push toward the docks. That done, he charged into the bureau.

The clerk had left his desk to overtake the lady, but Tom's bulk blocked the doorway.

"Ahoy, there!" Tom bellowed, his voice echoing to break up the stillness, "Where's a sailor to get a drink around here?"

Brought up short, the clerk tried to dodge around him, his wavy hair plastered to his head and his Adam's apple bobbing. "*Scusi, scusi, Signore...*"

Tom lurched left and right, stymieing the man's efforts to waylay the lady. "Sorry, mate, can't understand a word that you say." He hiccupped. "What d'you want with her, anyway?"

"Please, *Signore*, official business! The Miss, she is watched for, on the Governor's orders."

Stumbling, Tom bumped the clerk's shoulder, nearly knocking the little man down. "*Scusi*, yourself, mate!" He gripped the gentleman by the scruff, setting him upright. "Well, if it's that important, I'll help you out."

"You know this lady, Sir?"

"I know any lady who catches my interest, sooner or later. Buy me a drink, and tell me about her. If I like what you say, I'll help you out. I'm on leave, I've got nothing but my thirst and my time."

Peering through the window, the clerk glimpsed the woman in her slim, mink-brown traveling ensemble, disappearing down the street. He gave up the pursuit, and, realigning his coat on his torso, he considered Tom's offer. "Very well. We have been waiting for months for Miss Darling to return, and the Governor is most insistent."

"Buddy, today's your lucky day. I'm insistent, too." Tom threw an arm around the diminutive man's shoulders, and hauled him, with little difficulty, out the door and up the street, in the opposite direction from Milady. "I bet there's a pub up this way."

As he continued his pretense of unsteady steps, the two men followed brick paving up an incline toward a tavern. Tom's gaze rolled up the tall, rounded hill that crowned the town. Palm trees swayed, and puffy clouds floated in a paradisical sky. The scent of orange groves wafted on the wind. At the peak of the rise, the beauty of the place came to a sudden stop. A stark, stone fortress blighted the hill. Balmy as the air felt, just looking at that edifice gave Tom the chills. Holding back a shiver, he asked, "So that's the prison, is it?"

"*Sì, sì.* A dark place in our sunny port." With a nervous gesture, the clerk pressed his mat of wavy hair flatter to his scalp.

"Anyone ever escape?"

"Only one, years ago. We have heard now that he is dead."

Tom's eyebrows shot up as if this gossip were news. "Dead, you say?"

"The Governor, he was notified that the bounty was collected. This is why he desires to interrogate the lady."

"Here's a place." Tom maneuvered the man into a bistro. "Let's get something to wet your gullet. I want to hear this story, and how that lady enters into it."

"Oh, the lady does not, but, the Governor says, the convict may have married her. He hopes to learn that the gypsy, Giovanni Cecco, died in agony."

"Now you've got my attention, mate. She's a widow! Tell all."

Settling in for the afternoon, Tom listened to the tale, his ale tasting a bit more bitter than it should. He counted the minutes until the ship could shove off from this quaint Venetian outpost of Gao. Red-Handed Jill had visited this bureau on only a few occasions. He had a hunch that any new letters delivered to her here would lean against the wall of that box, waiting forever.

Madam, Mrs. Darling,

I am in receipt of your correspondence. Be advised that the postal box through which you communicated is no longer of service, and you shall be informed when a new location is established. Contrary to appearances, the husband thrives, although he no longer sails.

The net tightens around us but, pray, do not be distressed. To such as we, these moves are all part of the game.

My thanks for your kind concern. For all our Storyteller's skill, in her portrayal she failed to do you justice. I discover you to be Grace personified.

With confidence in the respective recoveries of our Most Wanted beloved ones,

H., Captain

Appraising her appearance in her mirror, Jill assured herself that she looked fit to fill the eyes of her lover. For the first time in Austria, she wore her woodland-brown trousers and forest-green tunic, trimmed at sleeves and neckline with embroidery. Her hair flowed free, her sapphire eyes sparkled. She left her wedding ring on the vanity and ignored the perfumes. Gloveless tonight, and without a necklace to cover her scar, she felt her true self again. Her only ornaments were a pair of earrings, dangling leaves of jade. As always, her counterpart's features reflected from the glass.

Also as ever, she felt the convulsion of her heart as it surged with her yearning for him. In *le baron* she did not search for a substitute for Hook, but, rather, she sought a path back to herself— to her joy, her sense of play, and a renewal of her spirit. That her bodily self, also, would benefit, was a bonus in which she intended to indulge as deeply as she dared. Another glance in the mirror revealed her impatience.

She had received no further messages from Hook, but the portent of his only letter lingered in her soul. His love endured. Jill sensed that whoever addressed the note also remained with him. Had this woman of mystery moved away from him, Jill believed she would receive Hook's presence in a more immediate sense, rather than at the distance at which he set her since her last sight of him. Whatever his situation, the old curse of solitude had not descended upon him, and nor would she allow that scourge to afflict herself. No further justification was required by, or for, either of the partners in their loving liaison. Hook and Jill were wedded more closely, she knew, than even *le baron* and *la baronne*. When she thought of that sharp-witted, silver-haired, vivacious soul, Hook's Jill smiled. Within her mirror, Jill's Hook smiled back to her.

Jill thought of her husband as well. The memories she made with him had sustained her in Italy as his family harbored her there. Even before they learned to trust her, Mamma and the tribe held her close, and tended her well-being. To remain faithful to Cecco was no challenge then. Then, she had been enchanted to believe he was her only lover. Her husband had proven to Jill, over and again, that he would do anything required to secure her safety, and to ensure her contentment. Already pledged when she succumbed to him, and in mourning for Hook when she married him, she was sure Cecco, with his sultry brown eyes, clearly viewed her loves and her loyalties. Were he here with her now in Vienna, Jill's involvement with de Beaumonde would be just a flirtation.

Both of her buccaneers were, however, many, many miles distant, unavailable to prevent Heinrich from handling her, or to tend, themselves, to Jill's longings. Not one nor the other would wish her this isolation. Both would rather he be the man in her arms, and, barring himself, preferred the rival he deemed worthy. And neither need suffer for her decisions here. All would be reunited, loving more intensely, more sensually, when she returned home to their life on the sea. *If* she could return…

She prickled with another sense, a slight feeling of unease. Scanning the vanity, she inspected the bottles and brushes. She'd had a notion when she sat down at her dressing table that something was not quite in place. Nothing was missing. Upon opening a drawer to check her jewel case, all appeared as it should there, too. Her fan waited for her, and she knew her journal was locked in a drawer of her escritoire, to which only she held the key. Widening her inspection, Jill found the room all in order, and she shrugged, attributing her disquiet to butterflies stirred by her imminent escape and adventure.

After the ball last night, Heinrich surprised her with his directive to slumber. She had presumed, by his possessiveness, that he would demand to lie with her as soon as they returned to Heinrichhaus. Instead, he told her to expect his attentions tonight. In what Jill perceived to be some form of perversity, he sensed her excitement and chose to force her to suspend it until it suited his will. Like the baron, Heinrich had appointed for his tryst the hour of midnight. *Frau* Lieber lay on the cot in the dressing room, prepared for Jill's absence and resting before the assignation. Jill recognized a firmer determination in her *faux* husband, and, judging by that insight, she believed the housekeeper would enjoy a rousing night with him. The thought made the vicinity of Jill's feminine parts pulsate, and she became even more eager for her own love affair to commence. No matter what Heinrich commanded, she would not slumber tonight.

She rose, checked the hour on the clock, and drew on a pair of gloves, not to hide her hand this time, but for warmth. Throwing a cloak over her shoulders, she tapped at the dressing room door to awaken *Frau* Lieber. "It is time, *meine gute Frau*." She listened as the lady answered, but declined to open the door to permit a view of her garb. The less the housekeeper knew of Jill's activities, the easier it would be for her to fence any questions Heinrich might put to her. As far as *Frau* Lieber knew, Jill was secluded in the sitting room while, in darkness, her 'husband' made love to his housekeeper.

Jill closed the door of the boudoir to step into the adjoining room, where she turned down the lamps and opened a window. Straddling the wrought bronze rail, she shivered at its chill, pulling shut the curtains and the panels behind her. She considered before taking flight. Certainly, *le baron* inspired an abundance of happy thoughts on which to take wing, but she tested her emotions first. Anticipating her rendezvous, she closed her eyes and brought the memory of last night's intrigue to mind. She felt herself become weightless, levitating a few inches above her perch. Invigorated, she slid over the railing and sailed up toward the roof. Above the house, she looked down to see its chimney stacks puffing, gaslit streetlamps glowing saffron in the frosty night, and only a few carriages hurrying past the leafless trees that lined the avenues. From here, the sounds of wheels and hooves came faint but clear through the cold of the air. She secured her hood, wrapping her cloak more tightly, then turned toward the river, flying high enough to become invisible in the ink of midnight.

A few blocks to the east, Jill waited for a wagon to rumble over the little bridge, then she floated down into the shadows to land on her toes. A small boat waited at the foot of the embankment, the tricolor of France at the stern hanging stiff in the winterlike weather. It was manned by one sailor, who squinted, scanning the street above for her appearance. Jill stepped from the dusk cast by a tall, engraved marker at the end of the bridge, and, treading lightly in half boots, she descended the stone steps to the level of the canal. *"Bonne nuit, Monsieur,"* she hailed him, and he greeted her in kind, offering an arm to help her climb down to the dinghy. He wore a boat cloak and, on his hat, the powder blue rosette of the house of de Beaumonde.

The boat beneath her feet rocked, and Jill found that this motion elated her. To balance upon the water again brought a feeling of freedom she had missed all these months on the shore. She alighted on the bench in the stern, taking pleasure in the simple acts of seamanship her companion performed, casting off, unshipping oars, swiveling his head to get his bearings, then leaning forward and back, plying the oars in capable hands with long, even strokes. She smelled the scent of water as it whirled round the paddles, freshwater this time, and she listened to the trickling. As the little vessel gained distance and the canal emptied into the river, the watery world that edged the center of Vienna opened up to her. When the current took the boat up on its shoulders, the sailor guided the vessel with a single oar, like a rudder. Soon the dinghy lay alongside a two-masted schooner emblazoned with the name *Le Paradis*— and named quite rightly, for it was as close as Jill could come tonight, to heaven.

Victor, *le Baron* de Beaumond, leaned his bulk over the rail, his silver hair catching the starlight. His low voice held an ocean of affection. "Lorelei!" Jill tried to hold herself back as his sailor hooked on to the craft, but, once she set her foot on the schooner's ladder, she couldn't resist the boost of flight her rapture granted her. Effortlessly, she ascended to be swooped up by the arms of her lover and bundled into his embrace. The strength of his hold was now familiar to her, and felt, although heavenly as she'd predicted, so very substantial.

The baron welcomed her with his wise but waggish smile. *"Bienvenue au Paradis, ma petite amoureuse."* Wasting no more time tonight than he'd wasted last evening, he kissed her with eager lips, and carried her down to his cabin. When he set her upon her feet again, Jill sensed the flow of the current; instead of rocking with the sea, the boat bucked mildly at anchor as the water pushed past, stem to stern. Jill slipped off her wrap, listening with nostalgia to the sound of the river rushing down the hull, and to rhythmic squeaks of the boat's timbers. Judging from the lack of footsteps and voices, a minimal crew attended the schooner. The wide waters of the Danube received *les amoureux* to her full and flowing bosom.

As before, the baron cut a dashing figure but, unlike his attire of their previous encounter at the palace, he wore few layers of clothing. As soon as he secured the cabin door, he swirled his cloak from his shoulders and tossed it to a chair, revealing a frilled shirt and French blue trousers, striped red down the sides like Olivier's. His hair was tied back in a club, but, Jill determined, those shining locks would soon flow free, and run like thick silk through her fingers. She reached for his curl and caressed it, but he soon captured her hands in his, and held them to his chest. There, his heart beat in triple time with hers, as if they still waltzed at the ball.

His first attempt at conversation failed. As he opened his mouth to speak, de Beaumonde stopped to absorb her beauty with his pale blue, translucent eyes. His surveyance engendered a surrender to impulse. *"Ma Sirène.* I do so adore you." He lowered his face to hers and kissed her, not once, but infinitely, devoting the first few minutes of their precious time to this sport. As Jill clutched at him, her bones turning to jelly, he remembered her need to breathe, and he was no less impetuous, but a trifle more considerate than during his initial advances of the evening before.

At length he resumed the use of language, his French inflection exquisite. "You have not the armament of your fan to protect you?"

"I believe it accomplished its purpose. I signaled surrender."

"And yet we engaged in no skirmish! But it was not your so-adroit handling of your fan that first summoned me to your embraces. That sweet service, *Madame*, was accomplished in a single glance…" he caressed the corner of her mouth with his fingertips, "the moment I saw these wanton kisses that hang on your lips, entreating me to partake of them."

Again, this man astonished Jill with his perception. Hook himself had set her kiss free from hiding, prompting it to multiply. Like Hook, de Beaumonde now answered the call of those kisses. She felt herself lured further into the fantasy she and he initiated. Some full moments later, he resurfaced to continue, "As promised, I have the pleasure of returning my little sea creature to the waters. Together, we shall undertake other pleasures. But first…I have learned more of this man who pretends to be your husband."

"Must we discuss him?" Jill laid the back of a hand on her brow, feigning faintness. "I am dizzy from your kisses." Slyly, she smiled. "I need to lie down."

With a chortle that rumbled in his throat, the baron humored her, guiding her to his bunk. She shucked off her boots and her trousers to draw up her legs and bask in his sky-blue gaze, like a mermaid under the Neverland firmament. The surroundings were conducive to the intimacy she anticipated. The bunk was large enough for two, wedged into the corner of the cabin, with porcelain-handled drawers built into the base. Set in dark wainscoting, every available space held matching cabinets and niches for storage. Three sets of round portholes lined the walls, where the night obscured Jill's view of the river. Lit with lanterns and candles shedding genial rays, the room was petite, holding an oblong table, a pair of stuffed arm chairs, and a sideboard with an enclosure filled with books above it. The bed and chairs were covered in a gold and blue damask with tassels, a matching carpet padded the deck, and a decanter of wine waited to be tasted, companioned by two cut crystal glasses. This tidy lodge belowdecks was a masculine room with a manly scent. With Victor de Beaumonde's generous presence at the center, the cabin felt not cramped, but complete. He held his head at an angle beneath the low beams until she beckoned him down to her level, where, with large, warm hands, he slid her naked legs aside, and reclined on one elbow.

His fingers swept her thigh, thrilling her skin, then he toyed with the embroidery of her neckline. "The wine, it is from my own vineyard. Soon it will have respirated, and we shall pour, whetting one another's palates with its viscous liquid. And yet," returning his attentions to her thigh, he predicted, "our wine will be merely the foretaste of a grander fare, fit for our regal appetites." He leaned closer. "Now that, at last, we lie together in comfort, my question. Like the scars upon his face, reports come to my ears to indicate that your Doctor Heinrich is a man in the habit of dueling. Need I watch over my shoulder?"

The idea of provoking another challenge had, of course, occurred to Jill, but the baron was much too valuable to her happiness to place him at risk. "You must guard yourself if only for my sake, Sir, but I assured him of your passion for your baroness. I will make no move to engender his suspicion."

With that urbane attitude that won her heart, de Beaumonde displayed his penetration. "I know what you are doing, *Madame*. You recruit champions to fight him, to find a way to break free of his chains. No," in his endearing custom, he batted a hand to wave away her objection, "I do not suspect this to be your plan for your man, de Beaumonde." He cocked his head. "And yet, I think, you wish to confess to me."

This mix of patriarch and paramour appealed to Jill, right down to those vibrating heartstrings that tied her to Hook. "You are wrong. I do not wish to confess...but I shall. I *did* provoke a duel for a certain de Beaumonde." Debating this morning whether to tell her beloved baron the truth, she found she could not do it. She felt a protectiveness toward him. Where Hook had been toughened by trial and seasoned by disappointment, Victor was different. His was such a jocund spirit, his soul so exuberant, that Jill had no heart to condemn him to grief. What good would such suffering do? She had no proof of Olivier's murder, and mere suspicion could not rid her of Heinrich. Her best benefaction to this sweet *bon vivant* was the gift of ignorance. Yet, in another trait he shared with her pirate, the baron was acute; he intuited an intrigue on Jill's part. To conceal the duel would not be possible. Only a half-truth would do. "I found your son Olivier to be so valiant, so strong a swordsman, that I believed he might easily relieve me of the physician."

A jovial soul with this limited knowledge, he laughed from his belly. "Ah, *Madame!* I knew it! My boy cannot resist a clash of arms. And from your continued confinement I can tell who prevailed. Also, the scars upon your jailor's face are not recently carved."

"I am sorry to confirm that Heinrich triumphed. If you were to see Olivier, you might admire a neat cut upon his cheekbone."

"*Alors*, he will be even more conceited than before. An insufferable puppy!" The baron had not, however, forgotten his lady's distress. "But, *Sirène*, I do not jest at your troubles. Together with my youth, I laid aside the game of dueling. If you seek a champion, I shall appoint one of my entourage. I would do anything for you, dear lady…except, *naturellement*, to abandon my darling wife."

With relief, Jill beamed at his benevolence. "I return your sentiments exactly. For you, I would do anything but the impossible: forswearing the *other* men I adore." She allowed her hand to roam over the hulk of his shoulder, saying more seriously, "Another time, let us discuss our designs to break me free. In this place, at this hour, this mermaid is content to be captivated, by *you*."

"And I by you! But first, *Madame*, do you guard yourself against… issue?"

"*Mais oui, Monsieur*. Of little de Beaumondes you have created a plentiful supply. I, too, have raised my family. I am grateful for your consideration, but do not hold yourself back from me for this reason— or for any reason at all." Peeling off her left glove, Jill tossed it aside, but looked *le baron* in the eye before revealing her crimson palm under the other one. "And now, Sir, you become one of the few in Vienna to witness a secret I am commanded by my imprisoner to keep. As men may wear their wounds of battle the way you exhibit your medals, I display my own." She drew off the remaining glove. "Do not be concerned," she soothed him as the creases on his kindly face deepened. "Although painted in blood, the color does not cause me pain. Only pride."

Belying their size, he let his fingers touch her bloodstain with delicacy, then he stroked the seam upon her throat. "This too? Another such trophy, *ma bien-aimée?*"

"An award of experience." New experiences were about to occur, and his touches heightened her anticipation.

"And as we speak of your trials," he said, adding another touch, and this one of diplomacy, "I hear also that Doctor Heinrich claims he rescued his lady from a ship full of sea rogues?"

" 'Rescue' is not the term I would apply."

The clever baron caught her implication. He joggled his silver brows. "The husband then, he is a buccaneer?"

At his question, Jill didn't flinch. She gazed at him, and returned only silence.

"But of course, who would mate with a mermaid, other than a free, wild man of the sea?"

Bringing her scarlet fingers to his lips, he kissed them, one at a time, sending a current shooting up her arm toward her breast. She set her other hand on his cheek, appreciating the weathered texture of his skin. She drew him close for a lingering embrace. Whispering in his ear next, she divulged her second secret, "Victor, you are *le Baron*. I am a Queen."

For the first time, she gave him pause. She watched his open face as he weighed his position against his desires. Yet, as Jill had informed Heinrich, de Beaumonde was a true son of France. "I make confession, also. Although you have hidden these honors from my sight, I sensed your acquaintance with life. I knew you immediately, intimately, as an untamed creature— a woman created for a man such as I." With agility strange to see in a man of his size, he bounced up off the bed. "But enough of discussion. We have entered a land of fantasy, in which we shall revel! We are Peers of the Realms of Water and Wine. In royal fashion as befits us, let us love!"

He dispensed the wine, and with the mellow, woody taste on their tongues, they dispensed, too, with one another's garments, to begin their acts of love with their eyes. Quickly, Jill fell again under the spell of his island-blue gaze. As he admired the full figure that her tunic had cloaked, his eyes were charged with the same light as at the moment he met her. "You are like my wine, even to the color of your hand, and, shall we say, your more delicate parts? Not so young as to taste raw, and aged only to," his smile turned guileful as his gaze dropped again to her breasts, "points of perfection." With a sip of wine between his lips, he met hers, and the potent aroma intoxicated them both.

He, too, was a visual feast. He bore his enormity with a back straight and proud, a solid man with not too much gut and a pair of symmetrical, imposing shoulders. His chest matched his hair, flossed with silver like a fox of arctic climes. He wore a jewel-studded medallion of a saint at his throat. The emblem rose and fell with his lungs as his intake of air kept pace with his enthusiasm. He bore no battle scars save one, a slice from a saber, white now with age, at the juncture of his shoulder and breast. Jill laid her crimson hand upon the mark, another link to join them in lives lived to the fullest.

Looking lower, Jill inhaled as her vision encompassed another form of fullness. "My Lord," she breathed.

He tutted, admonishing, "Have I not decreed that we must dispense with the titles? We are equals in nobility, on a valiant quest to conquer love, *n'est-ce pas?*"

"That was no title. I exclaim at your— as you might say— *less* delicate parts." She gloried in the sight of him, already impatient for the touch of her lips on that firm wedge of flesh. At her declaration, he gave a mellifluous, good-humored laugh, and her ears drank his sound. The hunger she suffered last night seized her, and she salivated. She had jested about feeling dizzy. At this moment it was true, and the composure of this queen was eaten away with her eagerness. "But... equals, Sir?" Still staring, she shook her head. "I fear that you have none."

When she left the *Roger*, Jill expected to be forced to couple with her captor. Hook prepared her, with an incantation, to blind her sight with his scarf, relying on the memory of his mirror to place herself close to him, and at a distance from Heinrich. With the revelation of Katje, half of Jill's dilemma dissipated. Last night, with the discovery of *le baron*, her needs while in Vienna were completely fed. She had starved here without her partners, and her body ached to be filled. Grateful that her senses were not dimmed after all by a blindfold, she found her memory in accord with reality. Her heart thumped, her frame shook, and, in the recesses below, she prepared, as de Beaumonde promised, to supplement his wine with fare of royal proportions. With a half-smile stolen from Hook, she heard an echo of his incantation, and understood that, once again, a spell had been cast. She and her baron dwelt in a new land of make-believe, apart from every world they'd ever known.

With her blood-red hand, she drew her new lover down to her and, soon, he enchanted her. She found him as adept as she in charming his listener with storytelling. As he teased her in terms of the legends of Chivalry, she followed his charge into a foray. On his knees, he proclaimed in the heroic tones of a *chevalier*, "I, thy Knight, have thundered astride my noble destrier, across the breadth of these lands, to gallop over the moat of thy stronghold. I importune thee, my Queen, to let down thy drawbridge." He laid his length upon her, heavy like armor, weighty and satisfying. She set his majestic mane free to flow through her fingers. His mouth tracked his plan of battle as he murmured, "I ascend to lay claim to the turret of thy throat; I mount, Fair Maiden, to the crenelation of thy jaw…" He pledged his fealty to her ear, nibbling there, then, moving down, "I lay siege to the bastion of thy breasts." With little moans and less resistance, Jill enjoyed every invasion of his hands, his mouth, his tongue on these sensitive vanguards, while he offered no clemency. Heralding a new maneuver, he slid his bulk lower. "And, now, shall we, perchance, prepare for the old-fashioned battering implement? Or shalt thou open and allow thy *Seigneur* in…" he set himself to feast, like a king, "…at the portcullis of thy passion?" Knavishly, he smiled up at her face. His hands cupped her backside, his knees splayed her own.

Her clear storyteller's voice had forsaken her. Like a princess long imprisoned within too tall a tower, she whispered, "I yield to thee, Sir Knight. I am thine."

With his silver locks trickling through her fingertips, she lifted her hips to him, offering wine for her champion to draw from her chalice, until she lost all restraint, and, unlike any Lady, her lust and this Lord made her cry in capitulation, as she blissfully ceded the citadel.

"Forsooth," she panted at last, pressing her palms to the bedding and trembling throughout her limbs, "Sir Victor, thou art truly well-named." Her head fell back on the pillow as she thanked the Powers she would not need to walk to make her way home. "Like unto thy Lorelei, I have not the use of my legs."

"Although I deem thy legs admirable, I shall not require them." He rolled to the side, and, tenderly, drew his lady atop of his body. "*Votre chevalier*, thy nocturnal Knight, hath stormed the castle for thee, regal Queen." With his bright, vital being beneath her, he positioned her, his capacious hands on her hips. He smiled like the proverbial fox and proposed, "*S'il vous plaît, Madame*, do take the throne."

This giant with gentle intentions proved to be a fairy tale Lord for her daydreams. Happily— though not for ever-after— Jill trod this path through an unforbidden forest, hand in hand with her hero, sharing his divine sense of play with a joyous renewal of spirit. This game of pretend aboard *Le Paradis* was purely adventure, in which to revel tonight, and to chase through again as the months of captivity kept the Fair Lady chained— alas— in the depths of the dungeon of Heinrichhaus. Thenceforth, the Queen of the *Roger* and her storybook Baron indulged in their make-believe, as deeply, and as frequently, as they dared.

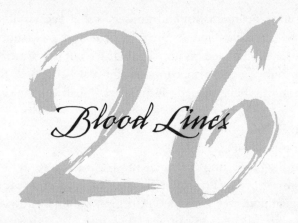

Blood Lines

A discreet tap at the *Gästehaus* room door, and *Herr Doktor* Heinrich was admitted directly. A manservant bent to him. With a double take, the physician determined that the sneer on the face of this slightly seedy man was not intentional. Diagnosing a harelip, Heinrich set this information aside to suggest a treatment, perhaps, after attending the master. He presumed this retainer to be a valet, and allowed the ungainly man to guide him toward the sitting room of the suite.

Although this hotel was known as an expensive and venerable place of accommodation, another impression struck the doctor right away. The room was shaded and stuffy, its tasseled curtains pulled and the shutters closed against the glare of a snowy day, barring out the more salubrious air of outdoors. On the chairs, blankets lay scattered. Medicine flasks and half empty goblets dotted the surface of the table by the filigreed settee. As the manservant indicated the patient's presence there, a smell of stale wine filled what air was available to breathe.

"Monsieur," Heinrich bobbed his head in a professional greeting, then moved to set his bag on an armchair. He was thwarted by a none too clean basin.

"Churl!" rasped the Frenchman to his minion, "Prepare a seat for *le médecin.*" A small but graceful gentleman, the patient made up for his stature with an imperial bearing. Unlike the valet's, the sneer this man wore was genuine. "And light a lamp! *Veuillez m'excuser, Monsieur.* I am plagued not only by ill health, but by ill-natured retainers." He lay on the settee in a nightshirt and trousers, a shawl across his shoulders, his yellow hair disheveled. As the valet lit a lamp, pale stubble became visible where it dappled his jaw. The manservant performed his chores with his look of malevolence increasing.

The master remembered his manners. "Shall you take a *demitasse*, Sir?"

"No, I thank you."

"A drop of wine?"

"Nothing." Setting his medicine bag at the ready and seating himself by the patient, Heinrich got down to business. From his long acquaintance with DéDé LeCorbeau, he knew how the French could make curlicues of his professional time. "What seems to be your ailment, *Monsieur?*"

The Frenchman filled his lungs to complain, "What is *not* my ailment! *Alors*, for weeks I am troubled by the shortness of breath, the palpitation, the headache. Today, this *crétin* feeds me broth that upsets my stomach! I long to return to my chateau on the Loire, but cannot travel until you cure me. See." With a firm-knuckled hand, he yanked open the shawl and the nightshirt, exposing what looked to be a chest in robust health. "My heart. She skips like a ballerina." He stared at Heinrich, and, impatient, began a rapid blinking of his eyes. "Well?" He tapped his upper ribs. "Listen to her!"

Doctor Heinrich pulled his stethoscope from his bag and rose to remove his coat.

"Adelphi! Hang the gentleman's *manteau* for him, then begone. I do not wish to be ogled in my nakedness by the scurrilous likes of you. When I want you, I shall ring."

Wordlessly, the man Adelphi did as his master bid, arranging the coat on a hanger in an open wardrobe, then withdrawing, with bad grace, to an anteroom.

Heinrich rolled up his sleeves. Having reached this peak in his career, of routine he came to swift and efficient conclusions. He underwent the motions of taking the pulse, pressing his ear to the tube of his stethoscope, depressing the tongue, laying hands on the glands. This Frenchman suffered only from hypochondria.

Reaching into his bag, Heinrich retrieved his lancet. "I believe a bleeding will relieve some of your symptoms. Shall you bare your arm for the procedure, or will we ring for your man?" He reached for the basin.

The blood drained from the patient's face as if the treatment were being performed. He clutched at the cushions of the settee. "*Non, non,*" he said, queasily. "I think I should feel rather much better if I decline."

"Very well." Brusquely, Heinrich summarized as he replaced his instruments, "I shall send medicines from my apothecary. You will follow the instructions on the bottles, and I do not expect a recurrence. Within the week, you may travel to France." Again, he tipped his head in a bow. "*Bon voyage, Monsieur.* I will settle my bill with your man."

"*Vraiment!* You Viennese physicians are not only disciplined, you are miracle workers. Perhaps I should not vacate from Austria after all." He snatched a handbell from the table, then thought better of ringing. "You are sure you will not take some refreshment?"

"As you say, I am disciplined. I have more calls to pay." With an intuition that he would only be wasting more of his time, the doctor decided against discussion in regard to the harelip. "I suggest you imbibe a little less wine, regulate your temper, and let in some fresh air. These precautions are healthful practices to adopt, whether one is subject to sickness, or resistant."

"*Bien.*" The patient shook the silver bell with vigor, and its peal rang clear and sharp through the muted atmosphere of the room. After the briefest of delays, Adelphi slunk in.

While the physician rolled down his sleeves, Adelphi held his coat, then helped him to don it. Automatically, Heinrich patted his pockets to be sure of his possessions. He left the suite, bag in hand, wealthier for the fee but poorer for the minutes. A discreet word to the *Hausmeister*, and he arranged that he should not be bothered by such spurious calls to this establishment in the future.

The next day, soon after *le médecin* left the house for his rounds, *Frau* Lieber answered a ring at the door to receive a parcel. The courier was a seedy-seeming man, his bearing inelegant, and he wore a knitted scarf that concealed his mouth. When he asked if she was the housekeeper, his words were misshapen. Upon comprehension, she answered in the affirmative and he handed over the package to slink away.

In elegant script, the packet was marked, *À Madame, et rapidement.* *Frau* Lieber lifted her skirts and hastened upstairs to Madam's sitting room. Circumspect, she delivered the parcel to the lady's hands, and retired.

As Jill held the packet, her heart flooded with happiness. If the contents were jewels, she could not be more pleased. She pulled off the string and tore away the wrap with the brown paper crackling, to toss them into the fire. The next layer was a wooden box, plain and unlacquered, that smelled like timber. Lifting the lid, she found a pale blue rosette— an emblem of noble blood, the symbol of the house of de Beaumonde. Wishing this ribbon could be cherished as a keepsake, Jill fingered the satin, knowing she must feed the fire with it too. But first, she inspected the gift that lay beneath it. Not gems. Something, at this point in her life, much more precious.

The key!

She exulted in the pleasure of the moment, and in the emotion that inspired this favor that helped heal her heart. But soon, her elation ebbed. In her hold, she clutched only one half of her freedom. *Le médecin* retained the other, in his bloody, manicured hands.

As she had vowed to Hook she would do, Jill watched for signs of deliverance. When out in the town with Heinrich, she observed the people around her, at the parks, the theatres, the galleries, hoping for a familiar face or some sign of a friend. Not knowing what to expect, or whom, or when, she felt the weeks slipping by, but she kept up her vigilance. Now that winter had closed in, she spent more time at home in the daylight hours, where she went about her duties and her diversions, keeping watch out the windows, setting her sights near and far.

She could not expect to see her pirates this far inland, nor might either vessel of Hook's fleet sail up the River Danube. Only Nibs and Tom could venture ashore in Europe, unknown, she hoped, by authorities. Yet both of Jill's boys could be easily identified by Heinrich. If he spotted Jill's sons, he would summon the law, and, accusing, he'd be believed. Even Cecco, as a 'dead' man, would dare too great a risk to show himself here. Try as she might, Jill could not conceive of a way for Hook's envoys to enter Vienna, much less pluck up and carry away herself and her father.

Since arriving at Heinrichhaus, Jill was able to communicate in full with Mr. Darling. Closeted in her sitting room over cakes and tea, or sometimes a schnapps that made him cough, the two discussed their situation with candor. Since Mrs. Darling had enlightened him it was a relief to Jill that he comprehended their peril. The months of travel and touring had wrought changes in him. The hair at his temples still showed the gray streaks she and her brothers occasioned by their adventures, but his walks with Liza and his newfound amusement in entertaining the children he met at the park made him livelier. He was slimmer, and stood straighter too, and, although he could not take wing with Jill, if the opportunity arose to escape with her he might be spritely enough to be saved. Under the circumstances, though, with Heinrich restricting Jill's freedoms and the servants watching wherever Mr. Darling walked out, she had yet to conjure the form their liberation might take. Further, she questioned if either she or her father would recognize such an opportunity before it dwindled and disappeared.

In due course, Jill had put pen to paper to compose the letter of character for *Frau* Lieber, and she made other arrangements with the housekeeper as well. If Jill departed, Liza would be looked after; Jill's writings would be hidden and handled, and even a few of Jill's diamonds were set aside for the two left behind, just in case. Or, perhaps more desirably, if she managed to render Heinrich harmless, similar safeguards would come into play.

Grateful to her caring baron for the key to Heinrich's strongbox, to date Jill could devise no plan to employ it. Acquired by a member of de Beaumonde's retinue who delighted in staging the scene, the key was made from a wax impression of the original. Heinrich was unaware of his temporary loss when a locksmith masquerading as a valet slipped the keyring from, and returned it to, the doctor's coat pocket at the *Gästehaus*. Yet, even after the destruction of that damning document, Heinrich would still hold control. Not only did he carry a copy of the affidavit upon his person at all times— which paper, had it been stolen at the hotel, would have created suspicion— but, having destroyed the original, Jill must commit an act of aggression immediately. For, once he discovered it missing, Heinrich must compose another— and subsequently punish her.

Jill realized how cleverly Heinrich had acted in this defense. The doctor's evidence endangered not only herself, but all of her buccaneer company. By running away without assailing his person, Jill would leave her pirates open to his vengeance in the form of advising the authorities of the fleet's disposition. Jill knew none of the brotherhood would wish her to suppress Heinrich's information at the cost of remaining a hostage but, if she could protect them by destroying it simultaneously with Heinrich's copy, all the better. In any case, the key must be used only in an interval when both documents could be secured. She considered the possibilities until her mind grew tired, but a practical solution eluded her. The gambit by the baron's minion gave Jill a tool to unlock the box, but not the luck she required to use it.

Although ready enough to kill her abductor and take possession of each of the affidavits, Jill restrained herself in this impulse. Liza, Jill believed, had suffered too much trauma by witnessing violence. To murder the father practically in front of the girl went against Jill's maternal instincts. Even if Jill could procure a phial of sleeping draught to render him senseless, Heinrich proved himself too wary to swallow any liquid she poured for him. She had gone so far as to test this theory, only to see the man refuse from his wife's own hands cups of tea, coffee, drams of liqueur, champagne, and even good Austrian beer in a stein with which she had gifted him, painted with a picture of Heidelberg. For Jill, to use *Frau* Lieber in such a maneuver, thereby subjecting her to Heinrich's wrath, was unacceptable.

Further, whether Heinrich was dead or just deadened, the question of absconding still loomed. The groom and the houseman adhered to their instructions to follow every move Mr. Darling made outside their living areas. To distract one might be possible, but dodging both was a puzzle. And, once broken free, even after managing a meeting with the baron's hirelings and boarding a waiting carriage, a further question was how to flee Austria itself, while possibly hunted by the constabulary. It seemed to Jill as she pondered her predicament that Heinrich had fortified his home like the castle Jill and her lover envisaged. This adversary proved to be cunning, indeed, in his own homeland. Hence, the best course was to focus on some other solution for escaping his stronghold.

Because this quandary was multifaceted, she and de Beaumonde, while tasting delectable repasts of his chef's cuisine and sampling his vintages, had yet to complete any of the schemes they dreamed up to solve her difficulties. Some days, Jill felt her plotting functioned only to help her look forward, instead of sinking down without hope. Now that her affair with the baron spiced some of her nights, her bland days were much easier to bear, and the Austrian winter felt warmer. But, also in due course, one day, and soon, he must follow his baroness over the snows, his devotion to her pulling him eastward, toward Russia.

Every time her lover greeted her aboard the lovely *Paradis*, Jill scanned his eyes at the very first moment, searching for the sorrow that parting would bring to the telltale landscape of his face. Thus far, unlike the skies, his pale gaze remained cloudless. She shivered whenever she thought of that day when his vast, affectionate presence must desert her. She knew the truth, and she must accept it. She would not set sail with her paramour upon *Le Paradis*. And, once he left her behind, she could never see him again.

One twilit evening, as she stood by her window dreading the coming *adieux*, Mr. Darling caught her looking wan and forlorn. He'd put his arms around his daughter, patting her back. Jill took comfort from his stolid, English stance, and she returned his consolation with an equally loving hug because, while keeping an eye on her appetite and recommending that she slumber, he, too, was missing his beloved. Yuletide had come and gone for him, without Mrs. Darling. Many weeks further on, while Jill braced herself for the loss of her sweetheart, she encouraged her father to look forward to his reunion with his family at home. She took refuge in hopes of her own of rejoining Hook and Cecco on the free, rolling waves, however long those dreams may be delayed. She felt homesick for her sons, too— those aboard ship, and those on the Island, not to mention her pining for the *Roger* itself, where not she, but only the carven image of herself, greeting the sea on the prow, remained sailing.

Another image of herself, and one Jill considered a false one, was taking shape under the brush of a Viennese portrait painter. Heinrich had hired the artist to capture his family, and now at least one afternoon each week was devoted to posing in the formal parlor of Heinrichhaus, with the doctor ensconced in an opulent armchair, Jill in her finest gown seated upon a dainty stool and resting one hand on his elbow, and Mr. Darling and Liza posted on either side. Heinrich in his depiction appeared prideful and pleased, the scars upon his face softened by brushstrokes, but no matter the coaxing from the painter, Jill would not offer a smile. The portrait remained under a cloth on an easel from session to session, awaiting completion. While frozen in her pose under the eyes of the artist, Jill filled the time with fantasies of altering the image, substituting the primary subject with genuine loved ones— her mother, her brothers, her sons, or her lovers.

The days dragged on. Sighing, Jill set down the pen with which she'd jotted a greeting to her mother. Of late sometimes, after writing, her hand cramped or her fingers felt sore, and as she gazed again from her window, she massaged her scarlet hand. A crust of snowfall lay on the street, marked with parallel carriage tracks. In the little park across the way, the trees held their arms up to the sky, as if to show off their mantles of snow. A few little yellow-gray birds with orange faces flitted from branch to branch, making Jill wonder why they didn't choose to fly off to warmer regions, as she would surely do if set loose. As brave as the birds, apple-cheeked nurses helped their charges roll balls for snowmen, and Jill had written a description of these activities to remind her mother of the old days with her brothers on the green across from Number 14. While she watched, listening to the shouts and laughter of the young ones muffled by snow and the glass, Jill's eye was drawn to one of the nurses, who wore brilliant colors unsuited to her role. She looked like the winter robins.

The woman wore a short jacket, wrapped round with a cherry-colored shawl that stood out against the white of the snow. Her skirt was layered in yellow and orange above what appeared to be riding boots. Surely, this lady could not be a governess after all. She was different, too, in that she wasn't minding a child as she kept watch upon her bench. Instead, between exchanges with the other women, she surveyed the windows of Heinrichhaus. It was too chilly to sit outside without a head covering, yet, as Jill watched, the woman let her shawl fall down for a few moments, shaking out a tumble of lush, curling locks...of auburn. Jill gasped.

She jumped up, nearly overturning her chair. Pressing her nose to the cold of the window, she blinked to clear her vision, and stared again. She spun away to slip on her boots and grab up her gloves and her cloak, fleeing from her suite, skipping down the stairs, and rushing toward the drawing room, where the rest of the family was gathered within wallpapered comfort to while away a Sunday afternoon.

Slowing her pace in order to keep her secret, still, Jill startled the others with her entrance. In a puff of rose-scented perfume, her blue and white striped skirt swished round her ankles, and the three looked up from their various occupations. Beneath the pendulum clock counting time on the mantel, the fire's flames leapt from their bed of coal. The heat toasted Mr. Darling's toes as he stretched his slippers toward the grating. With a small knife in his hand, he was whittling a toy horse. Liza's gaze rose from her book to look on Jill with surprise. As usual, her brown hair was constrained by a net, and her lips remained closed. Heinrich lowered his newspaper, smiling at his wife. Pulling his watch from his pocket, he remarked, "Jill, what brings on this flurry? Have you quite finished your writing, my darling?"

"Yes, Johann, and now I am restless. Fresh air will fix me. Please, take me for a walk in the snow."

He sat up to look past looping curtains to the winterscape outside the window. Checking the time on his watch against the clock, he conceded, "A walk will be pleasurable before we take tea. But you must dress warmly. I shouldn't want you to suffer from chill."

"Certainly." Jill slid on her gloves. "Father, please come along. A walk will do you good, too. The winter has made you too sedentary. When was the last time you ventured to the canal?"

As he snapped his timepiece shut and tucked it away, Heinrich interposed, more sternly, "I cannot recommend that we go quite so far. Let us just stroll a while in our little park. But do join us, Father."

Disinclined to enter the wintry world, Mr. Darling remembered his pact to be ready for any eventuality, and he answered his daughter, "As you wish, my angel." He forced himself to perk up. On further thought, Jill's eagerness sparked his optimism. He'd been away from home far too long. Perhaps Jill had seen the sign she awaited. "I shan't be moment, Doctor. I shall just exchange these slippers for boots." He set aside his whittling and hoisted himself up, speaking kindly to Liza. "Miss Liza? Won't you come along?"

Liza shot a glance to her father. He was marching from the room, giving no indication he required her company. She looked next to Jill, who signaled the negative. A clever young woman, Liza perceived the undercurrents of Jill's relationship with Heinrich. Her stepmother confided only as much as necessary to assure Liza that plans for her welfare were in train, but Liza had learned to trust in her. Seeing that Jill wished her to remain in the house, Liza answered Mr. Darling by hugging her arms as if shivering, then she moved to the warmer seat he had vacated and took up her reading before the glow of the fire. Only a flush on her face indicated her hunch that something exciting might occur this afternoon. Once left on her own, she would be sure to watch from the drawing room window.

When all were bundled up snugly, the party passed outward through the foyer and its contrast of dark woodwork and marble. Jill felt the frigid breeze hit her face, but, along with the cool, she felt a sense of liberation. She empathized with the sea creatures that decorated the foyer's basin, frozen there instead of splashing about in tropical seas. But at long last, Jill, at least, might return there. She set her boot on the top step of the entranceway, knowing, or perhaps only wishing, that this time was one of the last she would walk through the artfully carved doors of her prison.

Heinrich had summoned the houseman, Karl, to don his fleece cap and come along, ostensibly to lend his hefty arm to Mr. Darling on the slippery street. Whatever adventure the family met at the park, no escape would occur today. Heinrich himself took Jill's elbow, to steady her steps on the stairs and lend his warmth in the weather. Of late, he had become more solicitous. Vigilant, he often gazed upon her with an eye not only for his wife's well-being, but with hunger, as if to fill his eyes in the daylight with the vision denied him in the ardor of their nights. This trend was not unwelcome to Jill, as she guessed his increasing attention to be a sign that, not only was he thoroughly satisfied by his assignations in her boudoir, but he was gratified by the vibrancy she did not attempt to conceal, the result of her own assignations aboard *Le Paradis*. Though the air felt sharp in her lungs, Jill pushed her hands into the fur muff *Frau* Lieber fetched at Heinrich's insistence, leaned on her escort, and inhaled an atmosphere fresh with potential.

They passed through the bronze gate of the fence that bordered the park and onto the pathway alongside the bare trees. The tiny birds twittered, and the children hollered at play. As had become their pattern, the little ones broke from their nurses to surround Mr. Darling almost as tightly as the woolen scarf at his neck. A man upon whom they could depend, he drew from his pocket his newest carved animals and the usual bag of crumbs for the robins. Jill took the opportunity to point him to the bench placed next to the one where she'd spied the gypsy. "Here, Father, sit down and get it over with. The children won't leave you alone, you know, until you do your duty by those birdlings." Gesturing to the other bench, she said, "I'll just settle here to wait, and then we'll go on."

As she and Heinrich approached the young woman, Jill greeted her. "Hello, Miss. Might I sit with you?"

The girl smiled back at Jill, and dimples deepened in her cheeks. *"Guten Tag, Signora."* She scooted down the seat to make room for Jill, who alighted next to her. Now that she had drawn Jill from the house to her side, she pulled her shawl more closely around her auburn locks, for warmth. Jill caught a whiff of wood smoke, and felt a surge of nostalgia for the gypsy camp.

"Please," the girl continued in broken English; Nibs, apparently, was not as skillful a tutor as he was a student. "I tell fortune, lady?" Holding out her hand, she pointed to her palm, and Jill, always attracted to jewelry, sighted her wedding band. "For coin, I read pretty palm."

Jill smiled widely, at both Stella's sudden appearance and the evidence of her handfasting. "Oh, yes, I should be charmed to learn what lies ahead." Jill pulled her hands from her muff as Heinrich, who stood guard over her, stiffened. "You don't mind, do you, Johann? Have you a coin for the fortune-teller?"

"You will offer the left hand, if you please, my darling." Relaxing as his wife obeyed him, he went on, "And yes," he reached into a pocket, addressing the girl in a manner that left no doubt of his wishes, "but I hope that in my lady's future, you will find nothing but happiness."

Quickly, the girl tucked the silver piece in her sash. She grinned up at him. "Yes, Mister, much happiness for lady, sure, with kindest husband as you." Her voice was melodic, even through her imperfect wording. Taking Jill's left hand into her own, she studied it. Jill could barely control the trembling her excitement brought on, but Stella held her hand steady so that Heinrich might not notice. If Stella had an opinion of the ring of diamonds and rubies there, she made no sign. With her thumb, she smoothed the skin of Jill's palm and followed the mounds and the lines. Her strokes moved down to Jill's wrist, across, and up to her fingers. Jill delighted at the touch of her stepdaughter and, observing her face, remembered her features with fondness. Stifling her urge to ask about Nibs and Stella's wedding, she compressed her lips, keeping the rush of words she wanted to say at bay.

"You enjoy to home here, in city. Fine house, good husband. Papa loving, too…but lady miss somebody, a journey away…Mamma, maybe?" Stella peered more closely at Jill's palm, and her brow wrinkled. "You will dance, you hear music."

Jill asked, laughingly, "Will I waltz with a tall, dark stranger?"

Stella's green eyes met Jill's. "You will be adored, always."

Each woman felt the pang as she quoted Cecco's own words to Jill. In what felt a long time ago now, he himself read Jill's palm, and romanced her with this phrase as he prophesied their entanglement. Plainly, with her heart bounding, Jill heard the message he sent to her today. But Stella must now press for information.

"Husband bring you where, er…violins, many bright lights… songings…"

Speaking slowly to ensure Stella understood, Jill offered her the options she seemed to request. "Indeed, we do enjoy waltzing at the winter balls. We like to attend salons with string ensembles…And the opera."

The gypsy's eyes sparkled. "The grandest of music!"

"Johann," eagerly, Jill turned to him, "is this prediction a sign that we might attend the opera house again soon?"

Stella had been watching Heinrich, and now she declared, victorious, "Ah! Mister keeps surprise hiding, yes?"

"Ha!" his laugh burst out. "You surprise *me*, Miss! I had thought my plans were inscrutable."

As she heard this complicated word, the gypsy's bright face dimmed with confusion until he said, "As it happens, I have secured a box at the opera next month. I did mean to surprise you, Jill, but our little friend here has spoiled it."

"Johann! Your thoughtfulness isn't spoilt in the least. I *am* surprised, and you've made me happy. May Father come too? You know how he likes to snore in harmony with the strains of a baritone."

Mr. Darling retorted through a swirl of birds, "A little less noise, there!" But he smiled and laughed at himself— and with his rising hopes of home.

Jill's fingers moved to her throat, where her mother-of-pearl cameo lay beneath the cloak. "I shall wear my finest jewels! What night shall we go, and to which theatre?"

Heinrich named the place and the program, to Jill's enjoyment and Stella's edification. As if rejoicing in the news, Jill repeated the date and location, to be certain Stella caught it. Then, as if in perfect contentment in this foreign place and her Austrian husband, Jill leapt up in elation and kissed his scar-ridden face. Heinrich enfolded Jill in his arms, covering her lips with his and returning her fervor, while the gypsy looked on.

Stella's expression showed nothing but cheeriness. In her spirit, though, she quailed. As Jill prepared to leave her, Stella shook Jill's crimson hand, disguised as it was in a glove, and accepted her thanks. She watched the family shoo off the birds and the children, to walk on to stroll over the grounds in the winter and chill. The train of Jill's blue and white striped skirt trailed behind her in the snow, as if she paraded the banner of some other country.

As Stella slipped through the gates of the green to disappear in the city, her heart bumped uneasily against her ribs. She was pleased to find Jill, and joyful that Jill had observed her outside Heinrichhaus and even succeeded in speaking to her. The ploy had worked even more smoothly than all parties had hoped. Now that Stella had completed this rendezvous, though, a fundamental element had changed.

Although she had been shamming, Stella, like her father and grandmamma, understood the art of reading hand lines. She was charged with the task of alerting Jill that she need make ready for a departure, and to learn from Jill when and where she and Mr. Darling could be found outside the house, and among a crowd of people. Yet, Stella had learned something more. In only a glance at Jill's lines, even on her left hand, Jill's destiny was revealed to the gypsy.

Jill's fortune didn't consist of just a fine home, or her good husband, or the love of her parents. The waltzing and bright lights and songs were not the only affairs the pirate queen enjoyed as she marked time before her escape from Vienna. Those green gypsy eyes had read Jill's palm and, with it, the lady's heart. Stella knew Jill. She knew her to be loyal and true to those on whom she chose to bestow her affections, whether as daughter, as wife, lover, or mother.

The secret Stella had discovered was one she should hold in her own hand, and closely. She must confide in Nibs as her husband. But Stella's father, Jill's husband, would be much more intensely affected. He must not yet learn of the complication Stella's green eyes had seen. While under the dominance of this Doctor Heinrich here in Vienna, Jill's sights were roaming, both near and far, and taking her body along. Once again, Jill— and everyone else who adored her— must deal with the consequences of her own story.

Cautiously, Milady uncovered her ears. The roaring and rolling of cannon on the decks overhead seemed to have ceased. She sat up on the bench in the brig, still wary. The relative silence persisted, accompanied by the sounds of men shouting orders, objects grating over the deck above, and the distinctive speech of Mr. Smee below, dictating repairs to the hull. Not long before, Milady had heard a whack and a crunch that paralyzed her with fear. From the tone of the voices now, she believed all was not lost; the ship had not sunk, nor even listed, nor had swarms of snarling brigands boarded and descended to accost her in her hiding place.

She stood, gingerly, glad to leave the weathered wood of her bench, even with a covering of pillows from the captain's quarters. As she picked straw from the hem of her green gown, the hatchway above was thrown open, and a pair of boots stamped down the steps. She blinked in the new daylight. Expecting to see Tom Tootles, who had escorted her down here, she was startled. Her heart began to thump like the guns as her gaze took in the sight of Captain James Hook.

Any doubts about who was the victor dissipated. His fine-featured face had come alive, more fully, perhaps, than she had witnessed since she'd been exchanged for Red-Handed Jill. His black hair was wind-blown, his blue eyes alight. He breathed heavily, exhilarated with victory, his clothing disheveled, his crimson coat open. In his one hand he held a cloth with which he was wiping his hook. The white of it was stained in places with smears of the same color as his garb. That task done, he pocketed the cloth and grasped a flat iron bar of her cage. His sword dangled at his hip, and a brace of guns were tucked haphazardly in the belt that crossed his chest. The man smelled of blood, gun smoke, and conquest.

With his ears still ringing from cannon fire, he spoke more loudly than was his wont. "I was quite right to confine you, Milady. A rascally lot. The seas are well rid of them."

"What, they are gone?"

"Sunk, or as good as. My men are salvaging what we can."

"And their men?"

"Let us simply say that, should you wish to remain in these quarters, you will not be oppressed by other prisoners."

With a swift intake of breath, she grasped his meaning.

He drew a flask from his coat and pulled the cork with his teeth. As he drank, Milady perceived the strong scent of spirits. She had sampled it, once, when he tendered a taste. He no longer bothered to offer.

She confessed, "I am rather ashamed. I imagine your Jill would disdain to hide behind bars like a coward."

"It is more likely that I would lock her up to restrain her from the fray." He tucked away the flask and thrust his hand through the bars. She laid the key she had been clutching into his hold, the metal still warm from her grip. He unlocked the door to pull it open for her exit, the hinges squeaking and her footsteps rustling the straw. The rising chaff made her sneeze as he pocketed the key. Ever the gentleman, he apologized. "I fear what passes for my handkerchief this afternoon is no longer fit to be of service to a lady."

Queasy at the thought of those bloodstains, she directed her attention to a more pleasant discovery. "Look over here, Master James. You have a new set of crewmates." Leading him by the hand into the cell, she knelt in a corner and, gently, shifted the straw. She sneezed again, then lifted a fluffball from a nest of kittens. Tiny needle-like claws pricked her skin. "The mamma has gone off to find sustenance, I presume. These little kits kept me company. I think they are braver than I."

"Or simply more ignorant." With one ringed finger, he stroked the ruffled black fur. It was so soft it felt almost imaginary. The kitten's head bobbled as it struggled to raise it. The animal was hardly as big as the lady's hand. Now that the cacophony of guns had died down, little mews could be heard from the rest of the litter, crawling over and under one another in blobs of gray, white, and black. "I shall instruct our stockman to watch over them."

Milady smiled her relief. "I was afraid they might end in the sea, like those ruffians." She felt it safe, now, to return the little black ball to its littermates.

"Although only a trifle more disciplined, a litter of kittens proves more useful aboard ship than men of that sort."

She paused, she rose, then with her tone not quite as gentle as was her practice, she dared, "And what sort, may I ask, are we?"

Hook narrowed his eyes, and his voice fell smooth. "The kind who do not stoop to accost women, such as yourself, and sell them into slavery."

"Oh," she whispered, and he seized her as her knees buckled. He set her down on the bench to recover, but she did not. "I came away hoping you would remove me from the life that you left to me. Instead, I am submerged, more deeply, more direly, into life's flow."

"You call yourself a coward compared to Jill. I see you differently."

"I look at you today, Captain James, and I see how you thrive on these clashes. I myself have not the strength to fight for what I so desperately desire."

"May I remind you of those occasions on which I prevented your rash attempts?"

"Not rash enough!" She jumped up from the bench. "*Now*, Sir." In her two hands, she seized the base of his hook. "The gore of your battle already marks this weapon." Finding her courage, she demanded, scathingly, "What's a little more blood— to you?"

As she pulled the point of his claw toward her throat, Hook arrested her effort. He held his barb poised, inches from her skin. "The bloodlust, is it? The Storyteller made you more similar to herself than you know." With a twist of his arm, he freed himself from her grasp, then he gathered her hair at the back of her head, commandeering her long curls to hold her. She snatched at his hand, struggling, but he pulled to force her face upward, exposing her throat. As she stilled, his gaze bored into her violet eyes. He felt his own eyes burn as they changed. "Shall I make you more similar still?"

He held her firm. He bared his teeth. In a low, threatening sentence, he uttered, "I'll show you the road to dusty death."

"Master James...your eyes. Your eyes are purple." She blinked, then, gasping, she looked away. Seconds passed in terror, and when she looked again, his gaze appeared as she was used to viewing it, the heavenly blue of forget-me-nots. But his hook descended. The lethal tip felt cold as it met her neck.

With a flick— a light, quick curve— he cut a line of scarlet, a mark to match Red-Handed Jill's. He shunted her away, then threw her his cloth. "Indeed, Milady. A little more blood is as nothing to *me*." Pivoting toward the door of her cage, he strode out, then stopped to speak over his shoulder. "Is it nothing, or *something*, to you?" He slammed the door. The metal still reverberated as he turned the key in the lock.

Pressing her hand to the pain, Milady sank backward onto the bench. She was trembling, panting. The cut smarted. The blood beat at her throat, and, soon, she felt her pulse pound throughout her whole being. "Captain," she called. The strength of her own voice amazed her. "It *is* something to me." Sticky, warm fluid painted her fingers. Her lifeblood.

With one black boot on the step, he turned to observe her. Looking more vibrant and alive than she'd witnessed since he'd grown to a man, his sword dangling at his hip, pistols in his belt, and his hair blown about his shoulders, he smiled, half-way.

"All is not lost; the ship has not sunk. If you decline to bleed to death, I shall descend again to your hiding place. To accost you."

On an evening not long after her meeting with Stella, Jill flew on the wings of the freezing evening sky, sensing that the storybook of her romance had reached its *dénouement*. Before ever she pushed off with her toes, she felt wobbly. Her path was erratic even there in the air as she fled over the treetops toward the canal. As she predicted, when she ascended the ladder to board *Le Paradis*, one glance at de Beaumonde's eyes showed the blue pools of his tears. He swept her into his copious hold to carry her below, and his arms let her free only long enough for the couple to draw off one another's garments and recline on his bed. Then it was that the drops fell from their eyes and mingled, to form a stream not as vast, but as vigorous, as the Danube on which they rocked.

They spoke little, but made love a long time, accompanied by the serenade of the river as it slipped by the ship on its way to elope with the sea. Exhausted afterwards by the pain of emotion and the gratification of their physical love, they donned warm robes and dined, and now the two lovers inclined close together, two hands adjoined, massive and petite, flesh-colored and scarlet, a scion of France and a buccaneer beauty, planning a future that, hand in hand, they could no longer share.

Jill spoke of her news with dulled animation. "So you see, although I thank you for arranging it, we need not stage the contest, after all, between your man and Heinrich. Nor need we count on your associate to remove the parchment from Heinrich's pocket upon victory. If my friends can follow through with the course Stella indicated, Father and I will find ourselves among our liberators within the next month, and they may spirit us away.

Should this rescue come to pass, neither of the doctor's documents can harm me."

"At this occurrence, you must feel relief." The baron's touches tonight felt even heavier than usual. He pressed his lips to the scar at her throat, paying homage again to her courage. "Like you, your gypsy daughter-in-law is a brave one. A good omen for your son! To risk such a venture for your sake, she must, I think, care a great deal for you." The lines upon the face that always showed his emotion deepened so that he appeared more serious than Jill had seen him before. "*Mais*, I am not surprised. I, too, risk very much for you, *ma Sirène.*"

She ran her fingers through his thick silver hair. She would miss this treasure. "Your affection sustained me through this darkest of wintertimes. I am not unacquainted with magic, but the enchantment you practice upon me is unique. I will never forget *mon bon Baron*. My dear, gentle giant, I shall remember you, and recall with fondness your abundant loving on the waters of the magical Danube."

He, in turn, fondled her copper locks. "Would that I could sail the Seine with you, Lorelei."

With a start, Jill realized, "I never told you my name."

"You have told me enough that I am knowing I do not want to know it. As I have indicated, in our association lies a risk to the house de Beaumonde. Therefore, I have rechristened you for my own security, and, of course, in my fond affection."

"Our two kingdoms may not acknowledge one another. *Tant pis.* It is too bad."

"*Oui, et quel dommage!* But now, instead of bewailing our fate, let us celebrate something new." His translucent eyes dried, and his mercurial temperament altered, again. "Congratulate me! One last time, I am made to be a proud papa."

Jill said, astounded, "But Victor, how is this? You have not seen your Margarette these many months."

"Do not remind me! I can delay no longer to claim her. The timing, it is everything in these matters. I must fly to her side before she tires of her Count. For our fullest experience *après la réunion, la baronne* must believe she has made a great sacrifice, and all for her love of me."

"You, Sir, are a storyteller *extraordinaire*. No wonder I am madly in love with you."

"*Alors*, you are shrewd, you see that my strategy is successful. Are we not doing the same? We two part now, this very night, before our love cools. Are we not reeling with the exquisite pain of our sacrifice? Our respective mates will reap the benefits of such passion, is it not so?"

"It is so. And I adore you, you clever, calculating man. Now reveal this other secret to me. How have you produced another blessed event?"

"Ah! But this child did not come to me in the traditional manner. The little one is a veritable Minerve— like yourself, a goddess worshiped here in this city— sprung from the thigh of her father, the almighty Jupiter." With a wily smile, de Beaumonde slid open a drawer and fished out some parchment. "No, *ce bébé* was not delivered to me by the toils of my darlingest wife, but bloomed instead, within my very own arms." He unrolled the documents. "You see? She is born, like your stories, with ink for blood and her flesh made from paper."

Skeptical, Jill remarked, "A miracle."

"*Et voilà! Une citoyenne de la République*, and my dear, adopted daughter." Like all expert raconteurs, he paused for dramatic effect. "I introduce to you…Lady Lorelei de Beaumonde."

"Victor…the only papers I looked to find were in regard to your offer. You were to have documents drawn up for me, so that I and my father may travel out of Austria under false names. What further scheme is this?"

He placed the parchments in her hands and, disbelieving, she read them over. "But…but this is a favor far more generous than I requested." She took a few moments to consider the ramifications. "And this gift is far more protective. If I accompany my father all the way back to London— as a de Beaumonde— I need not be concerned about the official inquiry of which my mother gave warning. I am no longer the woman the Admiralty seek to interrogate. As the daughter of *le baron*— as Lady Lorelei— I can move freely." She exulted, her sapphire eyes wide as the wider worlds she envisioned. "I may go anywhere on Earth!"

"My, my," the baron commented, dryly, "I had not thought of that." A silver fox, he smiled sideways. "But the drawback, *naturellement*, is that as your father, I may no longer make love to you." He tutted, "Such a shame, and yet, we were destined all along, by our love for our spouses, to relinquish these delightful nights. And, with this alteration of our circumstance, you may write to me, to tell to me how you fare. For I *will* be wondering, *ma Sirène*, and caring, if you are safe, if you are content. Should you have need of your Papa, you must not hesitate to request my assistance."

"Victor, will I ever repay the kindness you have shown to me?"

"A thousand times, *ma bien-aimée*, you have done so."

Emotion thickened her throat, and Jill threw her arms about him, his shoulders so broad that her hands didn't meet. For the last time, she reveled in his strength, inhaling his familiar, masculine smell.

He sheltered her in his arms. "It seems that I have lost one of my sons to a desert, yet, upon the seas, I have gained a new *fille*."

"And now, I enjoy the care of two fathers."

He kissed both her hands, and held them. "One caution, *s'il te plaît*. As I pointed out, I am trusting you, my Queen. You will not stoop to involve my good name in any, shall we say…nefarious?… doings. But, by all means, if apprehended by sea rogues, you must see that they sue me for ransom. Or, should you run afoul of any authority, you will claim you were captured, and use my name to save yourself."

Jill tarried for a while, appreciating her *baron* with adoration and gratitude, then she assumed her most regal bearing. "And now, *mon Chevalier*, one final time, you will do as your Queen commands." She drew him closer, if it were possible. "You will tend to yourself, and you will shelter your Margarette from all harm. If I cannot keep you, I cannot not bear to think of either of you languishing without the other." Her breath caught. The tears stung. "All the misadventure I can tolerate, now, is to part with you."

His low voice comforted even while it carped against Fate, *"Ma Sirène."* Softly, and sweetly, he kissed her, then he set her apart from his larger-than-life self. "From tonight, from afar…I am your lover." With his island-blue eyes gazing into her own, he read her, again, like a storybook. "It has been written: in certain great men lies a touch of the feminine, and this gives to me the intuition. As I look upon you now, it is my feeling that, one day, some teller of fairy tales will join our paths together again, in some other kingdom, in another enchanted forest."

27
Sugared Shards and Sweet Deceit

As the horizon purpled with sunset, Jill and her father sat together at the painted table in her sitting room. Settled in for the evening, she wore her plum-colored robe, and he his slippers and smoking jacket. As pledged to her mother he would do, Mr. Darling monitored Jill's health, and he remarked upon Jill's doldrums today. Jill didn't explain the cause, but she well understood it. After last night's heartbreak at parting from *le baron*, Jill was listless from a lack of sleep, and low in her spirits. Her father's company did cheer her, and she readily agreed to host this tea in her sitting room, to enjoy the treat he ordered for her— Jill's favorite of *Frau* Lieber's *Torten*, and a delicious liqueur from the Black Forest. The sweet cherry cordial made her smile once again.

"Thank you for watching over me, Father, but you needn't worry. My mind is preoccupied, dealing with the events set in motion by our meeting with Stella."

It was unlikely that anyone might overhear them, yet both spoke quietly. Their designs for escape from Heinrichhaus must be carefully guarded. Mr. Darling was eager to learn more of the details. "This Stella, she's that gypsy girl at the park, with dark ginger hair?"

"Yes, and I trust her implicitly. She is my husband's daughter, and remarkably poised. Despite the cold, she waited patiently outside Heinrichhaus while she attracted my attention, and then she conveyed what I needed to learn by employing just the basics of English."

Mr. Darling's forehead wrinkled in confusion. "But you are fluent in Italian. Why didn't you speak her own lingo?"

"I hesitate to behave in any way that might alert Heinrich. Were I to talk with a stranger in a language he cannot follow, he might grow suspicious."

"Quite wise of you, my angel, quite wise. As for learning languages, that Miss Liza is a sharp little thing. Picked up Austrian as quick as you please. She won't speak, mind you, but she understands."

"Indeed, and I feel much better leaving her here, knowing she can fit into her surroundings, and that *Frau* Lieber will undertake her care." Feeling optimistic that the possibility of returning home had increased, Jill's appetite returned, and she helped herself and her father to more cake. "Thanks to Stella, we now know where and when to look for our rescuers, and they'll know the right moment to approach us."

"After these seasons away from London, it seems too good to be true."

"I'm also happy to see by Stella's ring that Nibs and she are now husband and wife."

"And he is the young fellow who wrote to warn Mary."

"Yes, one of my Lost Boys, you remember. I do hope you will meet him. I haven't a clue how our next adventure will be managed, or who will manage it. We shall have to trust in whatever plan they've concocted."

"I should like to write to your mother with the good tidings, but I suppose it would be imprudent."

At this idea, Jill set down her glass with a clack, and waxed strict. "You mustn't do so, Father. No warning can be given to anyone, not even *Frau* Lieber or Liza. Tomorrow I'll think it through. Before the event, I will advise you how to prepare." She stroked her throat, uncluttered at the moment with any ornaments. "One thing I know. I'll sew my best baubles into my gown, and give you the rest to conceal in your money belt. Do wear it when we attend the opera."

Mr. Darling grinned, and hiked up his waistcoat. "It is upon my person at all times!" He patted the belt, then concealed it again to pick up the bottle and smell the aroma of fermented cherry. "Excellent stuff, this!" He filled the little stemmed goblets again and clinked his glass against Jill's. "You'll need your rest if you'll be scheming tomorrow. Humor your old man, and allow me to tuck you in tonight, as I did when you were just a wee girl."

"All right, Father. But you needn't read me a story. My head is full of plots as it is!"

They laughed together, their hearts lifted by their secret, and by their affection for one another. They finished their repast, then Jill rose to prepare for her nap. Tonight she expected Heinrich to visit her boudoir, so, after brushing her hair at the vanity, she removed her wedding ring and laid it in an alabaster box beside her *brisé* fan and the cut glass container of scent. When *Frau* Lieber came to wake Jill and take her place, the housekeeper would slide the ring on her own finger, and dab rose cologne on whatever parts of her body Heinrich expected to enjoy it. With a sly smile in her mirror, Jill felt her spirits recovering from this ordeal. The sky outside her window was indigo now, past twilight. The house stood still and quiet with the snow outside dampening the street sounds, and she expected a comfortable snooze before she must remove to the cot in the dressing room.

Jill closed the drapes. *Frau* Lieber had advised Jill when she and Heinrich dispensed with the blindfolds in favor of the dark arts of the curtains. In the blackness of the boudoir, the two lovers felt free to release themselves from the world, from convention, and from inhibition. As she spoke of her trysts, the housekeeper's sweet face always colored, but she smiled. In a roomful of darkness, she had found inner light.

"I'm ready, Father." Jill laid her robe at the foot of the bed, sat down in her nightie, and kicked her slippers to the floor.

"You haven't finished your pickled cherries. Drink up, like a good girl, and you will sleep like a baby."

"I will, and thank you for arranging our treat." She drank the last drops of cordial, then set the little glass on the bedside table. She laid down, and her father drew up the covers. Instinctively, Mr. Darling reached for a lamp there, to put out the light. There was none.

"No lamp or candle, Jill?"

She and *Frau* Lieber had removed all sources of illumination around the bed, in order to prevent Heinrich from following any impulse to light one. "No, just leave the lamp burning over there on the vanity. Good night, Father, dear. Sleep well yourself, and we'll talk tomorrow."

He kissed her forehead, and Jill smelled the scent of his pipe tobacco. "Sweet dreams, my angel." He watched as she closed her eyes and nestled down, then he padded to the sitting room. From the painted table, he picked up a tiny vial, and corked it. He poked it back into his pocket, popping a last bite of chocolate cake into his mouth. Enjoying the moist, fulsome texture, he tugged his waistcoat into place, rubbed his slimmer stomach in satisfaction, then returned to the bedroom.

Already, Jill lay in a deep, complete sleep, her breathing even. He nodded to himself. That Doctor Heinrich might be a scoundrel, but he was a man who knew his medicines. Ever since that blighted storm at sea, Mr. Darling swore by Heinrich's sleeping potion. Believing Jill would now enjoy a restorative rest, to wake fresh and chipper the next morning, he gazed upon the Storyteller, thinking how the pretty vision of her conjured her old romantic tales of the Sleeping Beauty. He sighed. Although their Wendy had chosen a more dramatic type of life than they'd planned for her, he and Mary were proud of their only daughter. His time with her aboard ship and in Austria increased his esteem. One drawback to leaving Vienna would be her return to her life of adventure, leaving her parents bereft again, missing their little girl even more sharply. In bittersweet spirits, he tiptoed from her suite.

An hour later, Jill didn't hear the tap at her outer door. *Frau* Lieber opened it, closed it, and clicked the lock. In her reliable shoes, she walked soundlessly across the carpets of the sitting room, lowering the lights. As she stepped into the boudoir and closed the sitting room doors, she found Jill asleep. The mistress had appeared weary today, so *Frau* Lieber allowed her a few more minutes of rest as she removed her spectacles and changed into her peignoir. She let down her pale, shining hair, brushed it out, and slipped the diamond and ruby ring on her finger. After a few dabs of perfume, the room smelled of roses again, a scent that, forever after, would bring bliss to Katje. She glanced at the clock, then moved to the bedside to rouse the mistress from slumber.

"Madam," she crooned, serenely, so as not to startle the lady from what appeared by her face to be a pleasant dream. "Madam, it is time now." *Frau* Lieber laid her hand on Jill's arm. "You must wake now, Madam." She gripped her mistress' shoulder and shook her. "Madam…*Herr Doktor* is expecting to enter." Her soft voice grew louder. "The time is come to awaken." But Jill did not stir. Like a fairy tale princess, she dreamt on, her red-gold hair spread over her pillow, her blue eyes closed, and her cherry-stained lips shaped in a smile.

Minutes passed as the clock ticked closer to the hour of the doctor's arrival. *Frau* Lieber tried to rouse Jill again, this time by seizing her fan off the vanity and vigorously waving it over Jill's face and neck. When this effort failed, she resorted to slapping it across her cheeks, which also produced no effect. As panic suffused her body, the housekeeper tried to discipline her thinking. With her lips pressed together, she surveyed the room, ensuring nothing was out of place. The curtains were closed, Jill was dressed in her nightgown. *Frau* Lieber slid the bed curtains closed on three sides, then, checking the clock again, dashed to the vanity to snatch up the bottle of perfume. She placed a few drops on Jill's throat, then hurried back to the dressing table, where she pinned up her hair. As the clock clicked— more loudly and insistently than it should— she yanked off the peignoir and slipped on her stark black wool gown. Her fingers worked to secure her buttons, then she threw the night attire into the dressing room and shoved her sensible shoes on her feet.

The doctor's tap sounded upon the adjoining door. Patting her hair, *Frau* Lieber answered before she remembered her spectacles, "Enter, if you please, Sir," and she flew to the vanity to retrieve them. As she pushed the glasses onto her face, Heinrich walked in, wearing his slippers and a long brown robe with satin lapels.

Frau Lieber drew a breath, and with it her courage. "*Herr Doktor*, I am sorry. I came to prepare *Frau* Heinrich for retiring, but…as you see," she gestured with a quivering hand, "the lady is already asleep. In fact, I cannot rouse her." Behind her tinted spectacles, her hazel eyes blinked. "I am afraid the mistress must be ill."

Adopting his professional demeanor, Heinrich tendered the usual physician's phrases. "Do not fret yourself, *Frau* Lieber. I will attend to *Frau* Heinrich." He had moved to the bedside. "Bring the lamp to this table." As the housekeeper obeyed, he took Jill's wrist between his finger and thumb. "Her pulse is regular….No sign of fever." He moved his hand from Jill's forehead to pick up the glass from the tabletop. Inspecting the dregs of the drink, he sniffed it. He smiled.

Turning to his housekeeper, he said with good humor, "I believe Mr. Darling supped with *Frau* Heinrich this evening?"

"Yes, *Herr Doktor*. At Mr. Darling's request, I served *Torten* and cherry liqueur."

"I understand. Be assured that my wife will awaken refreshed in the morning. My sleeping potion is harmless, as Mr. Darling has cause to know. You may leave us, and good night to you."

Unwilling to abandon her mistress to the mercy of the one man she dreaded, *Frau* Lieber delayed. She fingered the copper watch pinned to her bodice. "But, Sir…you are certain the lady is well?"

With just a hint of impatience, Heinrich eyed her. The scars on his face— which she had traced so often with her fingertips as she lay entangled with him, right here, upon her lady's bed— tightened with his jaw. "Unless you know more of medicine than I, yes. I am certain."

At a loss, she bowed her head.

"You are dismissed, *Frau* Lieber."

The housekeeper curtseyed, and tried to resume her duties. "Then…I will just clear up the dishware." She held out her hand to remove the glass he was holding. She saw the doctor's eyes fill with amazement, and, too late, she realized her mistake. In the light from the lamp, the diamonds and rubies on her finger glinted like shards of ice. He stiffened and slammed the glass down on the tabletop. Despite his dressing gown, he was every inch the outraged employer. His cutting tone pierced her.

"*Frau* Lieber. Kindly explain why you wear my wife's ring."

While her heart palpitated as rapidly as on those nights she shared with her master, *Frau* Lieber swallowed. She answered, "I am sorry, *Herr Doktor*. I have acted foolishly. The mistake is entirely my own." She pushed her spectacles higher up on her nose, thinking quickly. "Madam asked me to take her most precious piece to the jeweler. She fears that perhaps one of the rubies is loose." Removing the offending article from her person, *Frau* Lieber offered it to Doctor Heinrich. "I…I found it upon the vanity this evening. I only wished to keep it safe. *Bitte, Herr Doktor*…accept my apologies."

Unwilling to touch his flesh to the servant's, Heinrich cupped his hand beneath hers and accepted the ring as she dropped it in his palm. "I see." With his head on one side, he examined the stones, his expression not quite suspicious, and not quite satisfied. "I myself shall manage the repair, if it be necessary. I trust it will *not* be necessary for me to instruct you in the proper handling of your mistress' treasures."

"No. No, not at all, Sir."

"Very well. You will leave us."

Mortified, *Frau* Lieber curtseyed again and turned away. Wishing to recede altogether from his every sense, she lowered her head and pressed her hands to her thighs to suppress even the rustling of her skirts. She left by way of the sitting room, shutting the double doors behind her without a sound. Before leaving the suite, she stood on the silencing carpets, attempting to restore her jangled nerves. The clamminess of perspiration had broken out on her body. Unthinking, she rubbed the empty finger where Jill's ring had lodged on so many other occasions. Once she felt calm enough, she leaned her ear on the door of the boudoir, to listen. She soon realized how foolishly she was behaving. From her own nights in that room, with that man, she already knew.

No sound of his voice would emerge from there. *Herr Doktor* would make love to his wife, silently and sensually, and, consensual or no, tonight would be no different from any other. He would have his way with her, and with her body. Of all women, *Frau* Lieber knew the increasing intensity of the physician's desires— not simply for his physical gratification, but for asserting his dominance. Authority, now, not his philter, was the drug that drove him. Wishing to benefit from her mistress' advice, she had confided in Madam a knowledge of his growing proclivities. But in bearing the lady's ring, the housekeeper had, tonight, openly broken the bounds of propriety. By no means could she interfere with the intimacies of her employer. Not, at least, in any way of which he would be aware and, with certainty, not this evening. She, too, must remain voiceless.

Shaken and concerned for her mistress, *Frau* Lieber left the suite. She turned around and entered again, to fetch out the remains of the meal. With a last, hopeless glance at the white and gold doors to the boudoir, she retreated.

On the other side of those doors, Heinrich dropped his robe and stretched out on the bed, beside his wife. Like the prince in one of her tales, he took his time before rendering the magic kiss, admiring her in the soft light of her room. He had not enjoyed a view of his Sleeping Beauty for a very long time. The first occasion was that night on the *Roger*, when, as tonight, she imbibed his potion. She trusted him then to behave like a gentleman. As a gentleman in love, and as a man disappointed, he had been angered by her absence of awareness. With both love and hostility, he left his impression on her, only discovered when she awoke. But, tonight, behind the doors of the suite in which he kept her, he welcomed Jill's passivity.

Always, when he beheld her in the daylight, she was animated and clever, her blue eyes alive and her quick mind at work. This evening, within his two skilled hands, he held control over her, completely. This regal woman, this wielder of power, was now his doll. He played with her, arranging her hair upon the pillow, draping her copper curls over her bosom. Placing her stained hand upon his cheek, he bent to her lips, which looked and tasted of sweet, liquid cherry. He was not expecting her to magically awaken at his kiss, yet he indulged in the fantasy that she did, and that she lay beneath her master, a woman of spirit— whom he'd made obedient, submissive, and still.

He pulled open her nightdress, to feast his eyes upon the curves of her breasts, the low mound of her stomach, her hips, and the fulcrum of her femininity. In spite of the unpleasantness with the housekeeper, he felt aroused. With Jill's diamonds and rubies crowning his little finger, he applied his two hands to stroke her all over, slowly and methodically, as if examining her, not for illness, this time, but for imperfection. Although this woman had matured since that first night he indulged his desires with her, the only marring he found was the scar at her throat, which he insisted she hide from him. After a thorough assessment, he toyed with her most intimate areas, to stimulate her arousal in sympathy with his.

Subservient, she responded to his touch. He wasn't certain of her love for him, nor did her emotions much matter now that he commanded the pirate queen, but he could count on her physical avidity. A more sybaritic woman he could never find. He watched as he prompted the manifestations of her pleasure. Her body knew what his fingers did with her, even if her mind only dreamt of him. She twisted a little, as certain parts tightened, and other regions relaxed. Her respiration became deeper; her eyes rolled beneath the lids. Incited by both her reactions and his own, Heinrich straddled his creature. He kissed her again, on the lips first, then her hair, then everywhere, tasting with his tongue, too, in and out, over and above, down to her toes until, allowing himself an audible sigh, he mounted her, his rigidity invading his way between her yielding, intimate tissues.

Strangely, he felt this passive reception to be just as erotic as her wildest passions. He moved as his urges bid him, uninhibited by demands from his subject. The seam on her neck, though, offended him as a mark made by some other male. He circled her throat with one hand, to obscure it. His thumb rubbed the blemish as if to eradicate it, then he followed his impulse to press down on the scar. She coughed, and a rush of ascendency infused him.

The woman lay at his mercy, his fingers tightening as he experimented upon her, exploring his professional control over her life or her death. As a physician, he knew the tube of her trachea that enabled her bronchi to breathe, the tongue and the larynx that allowed her to tell revelatory tales. Under his thumb lay the soft, supple mechanisms that enabled ingestion, imbibition, those workings that kept life alive. All this precious flesh lay in his grasp in this moment, membranes susceptible to his motions. Allowing her airway just enough scope to survive, he watched her suffer.

With an increasing sense of supremacy, he administered his phallus to her vulva. Slow at first, his thrusts grew in vigor as, with gags and gasps, she struggled for oxygen. His effort graduated from manly, to masterly, to monstrous, and, in the fullness of time, he threw back his head with his exhalations spitting through his teeth, releasing his stream to her unknowing receipt. Passive himself now, he let go her throat, and as her lungs battled to refill her, he lay still, savoring the fading of this feeling. Almost on top of her, he inhaled the scent of rose on her skin, and he rested. And then he reared up again and rolled her onto her belly. With her scar now concealed, he affirmed his command of the slopes and the valleys of her delightful, inviting backside, enjoying the indulgence of his dolly's docility, all over again. And again, his masculine passion burst forth, a fount virile and robust, in celebration of his sovereignty.

The clock ticked on. When eventually he left her tucked up snugly in the bedclothes, he turned down the lamp. He retired to his room with the scent of roses and cordial all over his flesh. Briefly, his drive roused again when the thought crossed his mind that next time he came to her, he might apply the sting of his walking stick to her delicate flesh. He fell into his bed with her ring on his finger. He believed that, like the prince in children's stories, he had rescued his princess, and carried her home to his castle. However fragile his lady might be, with his physician's skills he could keep her thriving. Whatever his designs for her— whether in the tower of consciousness or confined in the dark dungeon of the drug— she lay in the domain of a master more adept than her last. When he slept, it was only to dream of unchildlike adventures in amorousness, an overlord enshrined with his fairy tale bride. In time, if she was not already, she would be bound to him by unshakable chains.

This time, as *Frau* Lieber shook Jill's shoulder, the lady came groggily aware. She blinked, then rose to her elbows. A stale, sweet taste lined her tongue. Her copper hair flowed over her shoulders, and beneath the covers, her nightgown gaped open. She drew it together again and sat up.

"Madam, I hope you are feeling well?"

Jill stared at the woman before she registered that the housekeeper's face was creased in anxiety. The tinted glasses reflected the morning light as *Frau* Lieber spoke.

"I have to inform you that, last night, our plans went amiss."

Jill looked around the room, realizing that she was missing hours from her memory. Her voice croaked. "*Frau* Lieber, what has happened? I don't recall anything after my father bid me good night." Sleepy still, she tried to shake off her drowsiness.

"I apologize, Madam. I simply could not wake you! I dressed for our tryst, but when *Herr Doktor* arrived, he found you deeply asleep." As Jill came alert in alarm, *Frau* Lieber assured her, "He did not discover our secret. I resumed my proper role and clothing just before he entered, but, I am afraid…"

"You don't have to say it." Jill's heart felt heavy in her chest. "I already know." Her body knew; Heinrich had used her. Her innermost precinct was damp, and parts of her ached. She swallowed, feeling a sharp kind of dryness in her throat, and when she fingered it, her skin there was tender. As she threw off the covers, the bedding smelled of him. Jill's lip curled. "I know this feeling. I know it too well. I was drugged. And I was—"

"Oh, Madam! I tried to prevent him from remaining with you, but there was nothing I could do! The master looked so determined, and he became angry at me."

"Angry? Whatever did you do?" But Jill guessed that answer, too. With her instinct for the presence or absence of jewelry, she felt the nakedness of her hand. "You had no time to take his ring from your finger."

"Just so." Near to tears, *Frau* Lieber fiddled with her watch. "I said the first thing I could think up, that you asked me to take your ring to the jeweler to have the rubies secured. I cannot know if he believed my tale, but he took your wedding band from me."

"And did he expect to find me unconscious, or was he alarmed?"

"He guessed that your father had administered a potion. But he was not displeased."

Jill's tone was flat. "Father." Again, Mr. Darling's good intentions led to disaster. Jill decided then and there to keep every new detail of her plans for escape unknown to him. Most likely, he and she would be granted only one chance to break away. However well-meaning, her father must not be allowed a chance to bungle it. And…"Had I known he had some doses…"

Frau Lieber helped her to don her robe. The housekeeper intended, a little later, to advise her mistress to dress in a high-necked blouse, to conceal the bruising. On second thought, the lady might do best to choose to reproach the doctor with the sight of those marks. And soon, *Frau* Lieber must consult the mistress on how best to safeguard herself when next in the physician's hands. "I have prepared our tea, Madam. Do you feel well enough to take a cup now?"

"Yes, now. Especially now." The familiar scent of the brew wafted Jill's way, and she felt comforted. This tea protected Jill. She thanked the Powers that she had imbibed it unfailingly, every morning of her months in Vienna. Although flaming with anger at her abuser, Jill triumphed in the knowledge that, on this level, she thwarted his wishes. Lelaneh's infusion never failed to prevent conception. *Frau* Lieber also drank it, daily, to avoid the too-likely consequences of her couplings with Heinrich. Like the women of Cecco's gypsy tribe, Jill and her sister in deception kept their mysteries. Heinrich wasn't the only party to use potions to his benefit.

Sitting across from Jill, *Frau* Lieber served the tea from a tray at the bedside, and dished up one of the cook's fragrant cinnamon buns for Jill, to restore her energy and fill her empty stomach. "I am sorry you underwent the experience you expected to avoid, Madam. *Herr Doktor*, of course, believed you to be the same woman who always lies here with him, of her own choice." Vowing to herself to prevent any such mishap again, she declined to disturb her lady further with her own darker encounters with the master. "Still," with years of service behind her, this woman of discretion hesitated to denounce an employer, "to act thus, while you lay helpless…it is unchivalrous."

"The consequence, in small part, of my own decision, but one of which no worthy man would take advantage." Jill bit into the bun in time to stop herself from swearing to *Frau* Lieber that she would not long tolerate this life in this household. Again, no hint of the anticipated departure must be communicated to anyone. "*Herr Doktor* is no knight in shining armor. Last evening was not the first time he violated my body with the administration of his medicine. He did no damage that will not heal, but he wounded my dignity." Jill jutted her jaw. "I will survive."

If she could, Jill would challenge him to a duel, as she'd threatened when confiding in one of her champions, the genuinely chivalrous Mr. Davies. What stopped her from this impulse today was the need to keep up her pretense until her rescuers could enact their plans. Heinrich must remain unforewarned of her departure, under the delusion that she was content in her role as *Frau* Heinrich. No ripple must stir the waters of his peaceful pond until she could sail well away. Although her bloody hand craved to kill him, when the hour came to run, she must be satisfied merely to rob him of his wife, his jewels, and his domination. Jill's desertion would pierce him in a stroke as painful as that of a sword point, right through one of his weak spots. Like her dignity, the status he prized would suffer damage— not mortal, but enough to cause torment. And, Jill reflected, he held one other belonging that should be stolen away from him...

She brightened. Thoughtfully, she said, "*Frau* Lieber." She set aside the remains of the pastry. "I've had an idea."

The good woman didn't know whether to be glad or afraid. The mistress' ideas were daring, always. Dangerous, sometimes. "Yes, Madam?" She set down her teacup, and waited.

"You mentioned that a man in Doctor Heinrich's position usually prefers a son to a daughter. But what if his daughter should be the one to follow in his footsteps?"

"We have discussed, Madam, *Mademoiselle*'s wish to practice medicine."

"Yes. I believe it is time to turn his ambitions toward this end. We must use his influence to enroll Liza at Heidelberg."

"But...from what we know of *Herr Doktor*, he will not approve such a plan, much less facilitate it."

"Won't he?" Jill sat back, considering. "Just think how his precious reputation might be enhanced by a brilliant daughter who takes after him. And more, under the inspiration of her venerable sire, she will blaze a trail for female physicians."

"While this idea is noble, it seems to me impossible to execute."

"Stranger things have come about, *Frau* Lieber." Jill sat up, now energized to meet the new day. "First draw a bath for me. Let us finish my toilette, and I will settle into my desk. I have a new story to plot." Craftily, Jill smiled. "Give me an hour, then send Liza to me. I will discuss the proposal with her, and if she is inclined, we shall write up a letter of application. And at your convenience, *Frau* Lieber, please visit the doctor's surgery and bring us a few sheets of his personalized stationery."

Frau Lieber's lips parted, but she remained silent. From her reaction, Jill knew she'd hit upon the right scheme.

"After all, Johann is honored and respected among Viennese medical professionals. If he himself appears to approve a petition to his alma mater to admit his daughter, once she is accepted he cannot easily retract his support for her education. Can he?"

Frau Lieber meditated for some moments, but could not disagree. "Indeed, Madam. Our doctor is known for his innovative thinking. His reputation is founded, in fact, on progressive advances. He might find it awkward to deny her."

"And he regards his reputation as his lifeblood. Liza has all the qualities she needs to thrive at university. For once, her similarity to her father may do her some good." Jill rose to begin her bath. "By now the girl is familiar enough with his library to locate any reference materials on Heidelberg University. Having spent some years there, *Frau* Lieber, by the side of your uncle the professor, you yourself might advise us as to the faculty and customs. And you will be her best tutor in how to behave there. With her background among ruffians, she'll require your guidance in the basics of deportment."

The housekeeper stood too, still willing and ready to wait upon the lady. On her amiable face shone admiration. "Such a bold gesture— enrolling his daughter in medical training— can only be made by a practitioner of new ideas, a man brave and forward-thinking enough to challenge tradition. Of course, it is you, as the good wife behind the husband, who enhances his standing." She blushed. "You may think me foolish to devote myself to a man with such flaws, now that I am better acquainted with his character. When I had to give him up, I held no prospect of marriage or children of my own. I determined that the next best thing to making a home for a husband is to keep the house of a great man.

I will help you gladly, Madam, for the sake of young *Mademoiselle* no less than to foster the advancement of my employer's vocation… and my own."

"*Frau* Lieber, you have the soul of a philosopher. As ever, I welcome your assistance." Jill had enjoyed her breakfast of cinnamon buns, but a sweeter treat now lingered on her palate to replace the cloying aftertaste of the drugged cherry cordial. If she conducted this intrigue adroitly, the good doctor might be compelled to grant his daughter the freedom his wife so badly required. Last night, Heinrich toyed with Jill's body. Now Jill might toy with his mind.

"I am breaking my rule, you know, allowing a subject to speak while he sits for a portrait."

Mr. Smee's eyes twinkled. "Show me an Irishman who can sit without gabbing, and I'll gladly be giving him my place."

Milady captured that twinkling eye in her miniature, and gave Mr. Smee her shy smile in return. "I am afraid we are both bound to this task. The captain insists." Her dark hair curled over her shoulder where she perched beside the captain's desk, her paintbox at hand and Smee on the plush stool of the harpsichord before her, his red beard trimmed neat and his sturdy frame dressed in his best shore-going blouse and breeches. These days the room smelled of Milady's lily of the valley mixed with the odor of linseed rising from her paints, a blend that obscured the lavender scent of the days of Jill's habitation. Smee wrinkled his nose, regretting the loss, only to see Milady's smile turning stern.

"Ahem."

As lovely as this lady appeared in her mellow middle age, she was too often desolate, without the vivacity Smee believed could keep a woman of any age youthful. He tried to restore her good cheer. "You'll not be making my likeness come alive, then? I'd fair be spooked, to see myself winking back at me."

"No, Mr. Smee, I used my allotment of Jewel's magic dust on the portrait of the *Roger*." In the clear white light of an early afternoon at sea, Milady looked up to appraise that painting again, her masterwork. It hung in a position of honor in what had become a gallery, on the starboard wall of Hook's quarters. The figurehead in Jill's likeness smiled at her, supreme in her serenity. With all she'd learned of Red-

Handed Jill, still, Milady could not comprehend her. "After his exile, he chose a veritable queen after all. I wonder…how is she bearing being torn from her king and her court?"

Smee's gaze had followed the woman's. "Aye, I'm wondering, too. I've every faith in our lady's skill in managing desperate turns of fortune, but herself has been trapped in Vienna with that villain these many long months." He dropped his pose, and his rough features darkened with concern. "Even if he treats her like the queen she is, I hate to think what she's enduring at his hands to pay for her position."

"I've observed that all the crew are anxious about Jill Red-Hand's well-being, but you yourself have, I believe, a unique relationship to her?"

"I was thinking it unique, until you were deposited on deck."

"I?"

"Cap'n will have been telling you about it, by now. How the Storyteller conjured the *Jolly Roger* for him, and how, in her yarns, she dreamed up me and all of our mates to serve him here. It started as a children's story, back in the nursery. She didn't realize the cost of her tale-telling herself, until she entered the scene she had crafted." Smee chuckled as he recalled that young girl and her courage, who, smart as she was, was outwitted by her own creation. "She wasn't long about matching him in mind and mettle, once she learned what she'd done."

"No doubt the girl experienced quite a shock. Having stepped into the captain's world, I, too, felt its impossibility, right along with its reality. A most confusing paradox."

"Aye, she conjured you, too. You and I, his closest confidants, were made to suit her purposes— or should we say, the captain's?" Loyal to Jill, Smee had to add, "And once again, she'll be reaping the consequences, when she comes aboard to see the pretty picture of yourself tucked in all cozy and at home in her very own quarters." But Smee's outburst was brief. His hearty chest rose and fell as he heaved a sigh. "That Jill, or Wendy as she was then…she's a deep one. 'Tis uncanny how she knew what she knew, and at such a tender age."

Avoiding the thought of the looming consequences of the master's mistress' return, the lady seized on Smee's empathy for Jill. Her violet eyes lit up. "Mr. Smee. My suspicions stand confirmed. You are in love with her."

The bo'sun had long passed the stage of discomfiture where his emotions were concerned. "She and he, they're one and the same. You can't be feeling for one and not for the other."

"*You* cannot. I cannot yet know your pirate queen." With a shiver, Milady envisaged the coming encounter. She hadn't required Smee's reminder to reawaken the dread. Not only the long arc of her existence, but her demise as well, lay within the power of the pen in the Storyteller's blood-red hand.

Smee rejoined, "All the same, you lived for him. You're living *only* for him now, and, if what you've been claiming all this time is true, you'll be dying for him. Mark my words, lady. You may have never met Hook's mate face to face, but you're as tangled up in the pair of them as any of us sailing upon his ship."

Milady had ceased her brushstrokes long minutes ago. Now she sat trembling as if with trepidation. Seeing her distress, Smee, the ship's ladies' man, rose from his stool and hunkered down at her knee. He took her delicate, artist's hand in his own, and soothed her with his Irish lilt.

"Don't you be fretting, now. Facing the truth is hard, but not unbearable. And I can tell you, a life spent serving James Hook is a life well lived. Not an easy life, mind, but I've no regrets." He shook his red head. "Not a one." With his keen blue eyes, he peered over his spectacles at her frightened expression. "Have you?"

Milady turned her own eyes to gaze upon her recent, full-length portrait of Captain Hook. She experienced again the aura of authority that had possessed her paintbrush as she translated his form into art— the jewel-blue eyes set in his magnificent head full of black curls, a neat beard like a medieval king's, the sculpture of his shoulders enhancing a bright crimson coat and a gold-colored silk shirt. He held his hook poised at an angle that left no doubt of his readiness to strike, and a look of command enhanced his aristocratic face— all edged with a gilded frame mounted next to the image of his beloved *Roger*. For this painting, no magic dust had proven necessary. Every stroke of pigment Milady laid on the canvas contained the enchantment of her own emotion. He in his portrait, too, came to life whenever she gazed upon his semblance. The woman's brow creased as Smee's question echoed the conundrum at her core.

"It's no shame to admit that you love him."

She regained her ladylike posture, sitting up straight. "Love was never the basis of our association. He was barely past boyhood when he sought me out. To form an attachment would have been unseemly."

"Unseemly, maybe, but nigh irresistible. Well, and now that you've met him in his manhood, and you've slipped into his lady's place everywhere but in his heart and in his soul?"

Her gentle voice took on a touch of defensiveness. "Are you saying, Sir, that you know James Hook's heart and soul?"

"Aye. I know her."

She gasped, pulling her hand from his grasp.

Although the baroness was persuaded to set her pride aside for Master James in their past and in the present, she retained enough refinement of feeling to resent such presumption. Besides, she herself did not know the answer to the bo'sun's very personal question. Did she love the man Hook, or, as the woman he'd elected to apply a final finish to his youth, had she been so invested in his formation that he seemed part of her own heart and soul? Milady's guidance helped to shape that young man into the master of today— yet another masterpiece created by the strokes of her talented hands. Perhaps this surge of proprietorship was the very same feeling that engaged the heart of Red-Handed Jill as she gazed upon the character she first formed in her deceptively innocent youth. The queen of the *Roger* was another female who set pride aside for that demanding man. Abruptly, Milady turned on Smee.

"In breaking my rules, I have received what I deserve. Kindly sit down, Mr. Smee, and let us comply with the captain's order."

Smee complied, but he kept on breaking the rules. "So you do hold regrets. But not to worry. I spilled my own sweet secret to you. I won't be breaking your brittle trust by gabbling to anybody else about yours."

He sat back, shut his mouth, and, to humor her and to obey the commands of his captain, crossed his arms and expanded his chest in his best bo'sun's pose.

◢

Like Jill said I might do, I am changing my story. It is a thrilling mystery, because I do not know how it might end.

She said my writing is improved, and she helped me compose a letter to the University asking to let me study there like my famous father.

I copied it over onto his letterhead, so they would know I am who I claim.
I described my interest and experience, and named the books I have read,
and how I have been learning Latin. Jill judged the letter worthy, but I
did not expect an answer.

It came today.

The family sat together at breakfast, as usual, and when Father
examined the tray of mail at his elbow he looked gratified to see the crest of
Heidelberg University. He slit the envelope, unfolded a thick, whispering
paper, and read. I watched his eyelids shoot up, then his wide lips turn
down.

Jill and I did not look at one another. We waited, and my spine
rippled in that feeling I get whenever I earn his attention. He read the
letter again. Mr. Darling, not knowing our scheme, helped himself to
more eggs. Father, Jill, and I had forgotten about breakfast, and the clink
of Mr. D.'s fork on his plate jarred my nerves.

Father kept us in suspense after reading, looking around at Jill and
me with a cold expression. When he questioned me, I looked right back at
him. He asked if I truly want to study where he studied, and if I believe I
resemble him enough to apply myself to the rigors of becoming a physician.
I kept silence. I nodded.

He told me, "Whatever you wrote to Heidelberg, you seem to have
made a favorable impression." Even saying this good thing, his voice
sounded crisp, and he did not appear to be pleased.

Jill asked the question I couldn't: had my appeal been amenably
received? I could hardly breathe as I waited to hear, teetering on the edge
of my chair like it was the rim of a glass. He said, "Provisionally." He
read out the line. "Given that you yourself as a revered alumnus encourage
Fräulein Heinrich, if she continues in her dedication to independent study
and makes good marks on our entrance exams, she will be invited to attend
the University as a legacy aspirant in the autumn term of next year."

I sat stunned. Jill smiled and shook my hand, congratulating me.
Mr. D. looked up from his breakfast and beamed on me. He declared
how proud Father must be with his daughter so clever as to be considered
for enrollment in such a venerable institution. Father's tone was scolding
when he told Jill he believed she'd had a hand in this plan to pursue my
hobby. She told him yes, as my stepmother, her duty is to help him prepare
me to be of use to humankind. She claimed that my concentration on
medicine is more than a pastime. It is my vocation, just as it is his. He
said if I were his son instead of his daughter…stated in a bitter way that

meant that his son is dead. I had to look away when I felt the tears burn. But Jill carried on. "Liza's success will be your legacy, Johann. A living legacy."

In the end, Father answered that he must act in my best interests. There is plenty of time, he said. He tossed the letter aside. With his professional air, he shot his cuffs and pronounced that I suffer from delicate health, and my physical condition too must be taken into consideration along with his concerns for my social prospects. He will give the matter serious thought before deciding whether it is acceptable to allow a young lady— his young lady— to study medicine.

He gave it thought. He came to my room tonight in his long brown velvet dressing gown. He stepped in on the parquet floor and clicked the door closed. I smelled that masculine, musky smell that hung in the air of the quarters we shared on the Roger. Just like when he makes love to Jill, his mouth remained sealed, but he made it clear that he did not want me to speak to him on the subject of Heidelberg, or anything else. Nor did he want to talk, himself, about my formal education. He had a lesson for me, but he had not come, tonight, to talk at all.

Instead of displaying rage or ridicule, he acted as he used to do aboard ship. He wooed me. As he set his practiced hands upon my face, my thoughts emptied of my plans for schooling. He teased my lips with his fingertips, the way he does that makes my mouth water. He leaned down and kissed me, giving me that warm, liquid feeling again, and then with his body he urged me backward. With the strength of his arms around me, he eased me down on my feather comforter. My nightgown gave way to his fingers. Under his caresses, I felt what I had not felt since my sailor lay with me, the throb and heat that a man's touch kindles. I had only moments to think whether I wanted it with him tonight, or whether I wanted something else, something maybe more, maybe better. Into my head flashed an idea— the notion that Frau Lieber had tempted me with an enticement my father never plied.

She offered me choice.

Some time ago, Frau Lieber brought up a pewter tray laden with heavy dishes and silverware, and she left it sitting partly over the edge of my night stand. Levering my hands, I gestured to show her how it might overbalance, but she told me to just leave it there, exactly that way, in case I ever needed it. She promised that if she heard the platter clatter to the floor, she would come to my room as quickly as she could, and ask me no questions.

I have been watching our housekeeper, as I watch everyone. I notice how her proper stance softens when Father talks to her. I hear how her voice becomes milder. I see how he overlooks her. To him, she is an efficient servant. With his gray eyes, he does not perceive her admiration for him, but I and my own gray eyes do. Yet when she set up that tray for me, I heard her say without words that she understands my father better than I suspected. I think she made it her job to watch everyone, too.

As Father pressed his weight down on my pelvis, I felt the clash of feelings inside me. I hankered for his strong, hard physique, and for those movements that please me. I thought of my mother's body, frail in comparison, and remembered the sight of her hand dangling limp over the edge of their bed. I felt the firmness of my breast between my fingers while our baby mewled and struggled with his tiny, weak mouth to suck milk from me. I saw Pierre-Jean's blood on my father's hand as Father reached for me, and the long blond braid tumbling after his body down the burbling stream, to sink in the sea. I heard the deep resonance of Yulunga's laugh, as he challenged me. I remembered the whisper of the letter from Heidelberg between my father's fingers, those expert fingers that held me in thrall where I lay pulsing with passion, right at this moment.

I understood my story right then. It is being not safe that excites me. I choose danger.

I pressed on the tray, upending it onto the floor. The metal clanged, the glassware shattered. Father sat up, his bare chest heaving, and in the yellow light of my lamp I saw a look of shock on his face, his twin dueling scars sharp against the paleness of his skin. Then he stood to fling on his robe and tie it closed.

"You expect to enter Heidelberg. Now you know what I expect."

He stalked out the door. His slippers made no noise, but I heard Frau Lieber hurrying up the steps, calling, to learn what the crash was about. In his most civilized tone, as if he hadn't just raised his thick lips from my naked nipples, he told her I'd had an accident and he directed her to attend to me and to the other broken things. Then he strode away down the hall to his suite and I heard him shut the door.

I couldn't read her eyes because of her spectacles. She maybe admires him a little less now.

Oftentimes, Jill says, people communicate without language. That is what I have been doing ever since she first met me. When she confirmed my hopes for Heidelberg and began to prepare me for schooling, she told me that if I attend university, I will have to converse in words. She said I should speak for myself, the way I spoke for my baby. She explained that I will not be required to discuss my past, but that I will be expected to discourse in regard to my future.

I know now that the metal tray with the dishware was another way of speaking without saying. I made a statement with it. Instead of yielding to my father's temptation, I surrendered to the risk of saying no to him. As I thought about doing with the glass wall of his medicine cabinet, I made a sharp sound. I made a breaking.

When I unstopped my mouth, Frau Lieber looked shocked, too.

In my rusty, low voice, I told her, "I will help clean this mess."

The housekeeper keeps not only the house. She keeps our secrets. When she heard me talk out loud in good, solid Austrian, she smiled.

I know I resemble my father. With help from the women around me, I can be strong, like him.

I cannot know how it will end, but I am retelling my story.

Grand Performances

At the tap on the white and gold door of her suite, Jill called, "Enter!" and *Frau* Lieber stepped in with her dependable shoes and a curtsey. The evening was young, the hours of sunshine growing longer each day as spring crept closer and, with only a small fire for warmth, Jill had lit the one lamp at her escritoire to brighten the page for her writing. Just as the housekeeper designed it, the room lent its service along with its comfort. Jill soaked up the atmosphere this afternoon for remembrance, hoping today would be one of the last she might spend here in this elegant cage. With her thoughts and her longings returning to her role upon the *Roger*, she greeted *Frau* Lieber, smiling in friendship, memorizing, as she did for the room, the serviceable and comforting sight of her for recollection in future, freer days.

"It is time to dress for dinner, Madam."

"So soon?" Jill glanced at the enameled clock. "I didn't expect you for another hour."

"*Herr Doktor* has ordered an early supper this evening."

"Did he say why?" Jill began putting away her writing utensils for the day, and, maybe, forever.

"No, Madam. But he instructed me to hold back the roast you ordered and serve a light repast instead."

"Perhaps he is planning some entertainment for us after dinner. Father wanted to teach him a favorite old card game. Well, I've finished my work, and supper is welcome." Jill rose, and the two women prepared her to appear as mistress at the head of her dinner table. They had recently refreshed the tint of Jill's hair, and, as always, Jill donned the netted gloves she wore on Heinrich's orders when in the presence of their servants. Although the shade of her hair had changed, the hue of her scarlet hand remained as vibrant as on the night she and Hook mingled their blood to mark it. Like his passion for her and hers for him, Jill understood that this ruddy color could never fade. She picked up her fan with its similar tint, to hang it at her waist. Whatever Heinrich had planned, Hook's consort, Red-Handed Jill, would cope with it.

When she entered the dining room, she sniffed the steam of fresh bread rising from a linen-lined basket. The cool pats of butter, shaped into shells, looked too pretty to eat, until Jill's stomach registered its hollow state with a pang. Her father and Liza sat at their places, with the gleam of china and the sparkle of crystal cups before them. Heinrich stood behind her chair, waiting to seat her. He looked genial, eager to partake of the meal as well as the company, as if pleased with his wife, his family, himself, and his world.

"Johann, you appear in good spirits this evening. Have you something special planned for us?"

"I have something special for *you*, Jill." From his coat pocket, Heinrich produced a small black velvet box, to hold out before her. Slowly, as he watched her face, he opened it with his impeccable hands.

Any such prize stimulated the pirate queen's senses. She felt hungry for supper, but now she craved this feast of treasure. As the brooch in the box came into focus under the rays of the chandelier, she was dazzled by a golden figure of a cherub, surrounded by a heart made of garnets. In the figure's little hands lay an arrow shaped by a line of tiny pink topazes, the point a chevron of silver. The pin wasn't large enough to seem garish, but it wasn't small enough to seem ungenerous. Jill's pirate heart leapt as she viewed it, and she exhaled, "Oh. Oh, Johann, how beautiful."

She made plans for this brooch immediately. Unlike her other jewels, which she was preparing to smuggle out of the house within her garments as she departed for the opera tomorrow night, she would fasten it to the bosom of her gown. Even now she was attached to it, and she would not leave such plunder behind.

"This piece caught my eye the day I retrieved your wedding band from the jeweler. I saved it for a particular occasion."

Taking the brooch in her hands, Jill continued to appraise this new prize. "I thank you, Johann. But," she looked up to her *faux* husband's eyes, "today is no birthday or anniversary. What occasion are we celebrating?"

Gently, he touched her cheek, observing her features. "I shall inform you later tonight. Now we will dine, for I have ordered the carriage to be ready at seven o'clock." Heinrich took his place at the other end of the table, flicked his napkin open, and laid it on his lap. He served himself with thin, savory slices of veal smothered in cream sauce, then passed the platter to Mr. Darling on his left.

"Ready for what?"

Heinrich cocked his head, as if astonished. "Do you not remember, my darling? We are attending the opera."

All the satisfaction Jill gained by the feel of the sharp, precious jewels in her fingers gave way to panic. It broke out in twinges under her skin. She set down the brooch. "But..." With every nerve strained to hold her voice in control, she enunciated, "But you told me our reservation was set for tomorrow."

"I told you I wished our outing to the opera to be a surprise." Heinrich's scars bent outward with the spread of his smile. "Have I succeeded?"

She choked out, "Yes!" Barely able to contain her shock, Jill paused as she tried to collect her thoughts. "But my gown..." Her gown lay on her divan by her sewing box, awaiting the last of the jewels she'd chosen to stitch into its recesses. "My ensemble isn't quite ready. And Father—" Cautiously, lest Mr. Darling allow his anxiety to give away their hoped-for escape, Jill placed her hand on his arm, willing her gesture and expression to convey a calm she did not feel. "Father, I must have your best tail coat laid out, and your hat and cape brushed."

As he goggled at Jill, speechless, she patted his arm. "Never mind. *Frau* Lieber will see to all our needs, and speedily." Finding a smile for Liza, who looked bewildered, she assured the girl, "And the maid will help you with your attire, Liza. As we planned, you may wear your finest frock, the new yellow satin." She returned her gaze to Heinrich, feeling able now to present a demeanor of composure. "Although I had not prepared any of us for an outing tonight, I am sure we will all be pressed and primped on time to enjoy the presentation."

Luckily, Jill's appetite had not evaporated with her ploy, and she seized the bread from her plate. While she filled her mouth with the warm, buttered taste, she used the time of dining to consider this catastrophe. The supper progressed, with talk led by Heinrich, of the performance they were about to attend, the composer and his other works, and which piece might be their favorite. Jill felt that her own performance at the stage of this table, holding her poise while digesting disaster, might merit applause from even a professional troupe.

Employing the excuse of coordinating her costume, Jill rose from the board at the earliest chance. She dashed upstairs, intent on secreting the remainder of her treasures within her raiment. But first, she hurried to the window overlooking the park. She opened one of the double panels, feeling the rush of late winter air against the flush of her face. In an agony of hope, she searched through the park— the grounds, the trees, the benches resting in the fading rays of sunset— for the figure of a petite, auburn-haired gypsy. Although a flock of eager birds had returned with milder weather to chirp their good-nights against the waning sky, Jill perceived no trace of the visitor she needed to see.

Of course Stella wasn't there. During her fortune-telling, she had been informed that Jill's excursion to the opera house was arranged for tomorrow night. Frustration filled Jill's soul as, now in the privacy of her rooms, she experienced the full effect of her disappointment. Her body felt as leaden as her heart. She pushed the window closed to drop onto the divan, despairing.

Even if by some miracle she were able to contact Stella, time had run out. The groom was hitching up the carriage. The men were donning their suits. At the pull of her bell, *Frau* Lieber would enter to stand by the vanity in her tinted spectacles, brush in hand, to dress Jill's copper locks in a style appropriate for the occasion. Whoever was meant to help Jill and her father escape, whatever their means and their strategy, they would miss the opportunity.

Jill's spirits drooped further as the probability solidified that Heinrich had developed a suspicion at the first, on that white, snowy day at the park. With no indication of his distrust, he named the wrong date for the excursion. Perhaps he mistrusted Jill, too, along with the fortune-teller. On reflection, Jill interpreted his mood at the dinner table as a pinnacle of self-satisfaction. The more she pondered, the more convinced she grew that he had deliberately seized control, again, to direct Jill's destiny. Like Jill, he staged a grand performance.

He may not know for certain that the gypsy girl was an agent of escape, but he had acted to thwart any chance to find out.

Escape was so close, and disillusionment so deep. Jill felt nearly crushed enough to plead illness and stay home altogether. Venturing out only to pretend to be cheerful the whole evening long seemed like torture. In the brief time at hand, Jill considered her options. To abandon her father in this distress would be unfair to him. To display any kind of upset to Heinrich might increase his conviction that he had scuttled a scheme, thus increasing his vigilance and diminishing her odds of success in some future attempt. No, as always, Jill must summon her strength and rise from the ash of despair. She knew from experience that she would endure. Tonight's disappointment was not her first.

She straightened her spine, opened her sewing box, and set to work again. All might not be lost this evening. If she found a moment to grasp her father's elbow and run, Jill would be ready. Setting her jaw, Red-Handed Jill plucked off her gloves and caressed the bright, hard jewels of the new brooch on her breast. This treasure alone would buy passage out of Austria. Her red *brisé* fan hung at her side, a feminine weapon to deploy at her need. The brass knife from Cecco could be easily concealed in her garter. And the papers that her dear champion, *le baron*, had drawn up for her rested secure within the folds of her gown. The time had come— one day early and with outside assistance or no— to break free from this dungeon of Heinrichhaus.

As the carriage bowled through the gates of the courtyard to turn east on the boulevard, Jill returned *Frau* Lieber's cheerful wave. After that gesture, she did not look back. The good woman had followed her mistress' directive weeks ago, visiting the city's hall of records to obtain an architectural layout of the opera house. Jill had studied these blueprints thoroughly, and this evening she found a few moments to look over the drawings again before thrusting them into the fire, where they burned with a chemical stench. No evidence of *Frau* Lieber's involvement in Jill's hoped-for escape must remain for Heinrich to find.

While the party of theatregoers set off for their destination, in her mind Jill traced the quickest passageway from the lounge to a back stairway, and thence to the delivery doors in the rear of the building. She was as equipped as possible for flight with her father in tow. Even after insisting that he exchange a few English pounds for Austrian coins, Jill had kept the finer points of her design a secret from Mr. Darling, but she knew he too was ready to wave goodbye to Heinrichhaus and head for home.

Jill wore her green velvet cape, trimmed and lined with fur. She had covered the scar at her throat with the adornment of her pearl and diamond choker, which was too heavy to hide. Since she knew Heinrich would be handling her wrap for her, she chose not to weigh it down with her riches. Her gown, though, black taffeta with a low, scalloped neckline, elevated waist and sash, sleeves that tapered into bells, and a train behind a loose, flowing skirt, was overlaid with a sapphire-blue network of lace to match her eyes. The latticework veiled any irregularities her hidden jewels might cause, and if the dress hung more heavily on her shoulders than it should, Heinrich would never know. Black gloves obscured her many rings. As always, Mr. Darling wore his money belt under his formalwear, to which Jill had added a few more trinkets. She secreted his new identity papers within the lining of his waistcoat, and tucked her diamonds in his hatband. As a result of the latter cache, tonight he was monitoring closely both his daughter and the drafts.

Mr. Darling, too, declined a last gaze at Heinrichhaus, patting Liza's knee for encouragement instead. He knew only that the little gypsy's fortune-telling had opened an avenue of absconding that connected with this trip to the theatre, and he kept his topper wedged securely on his brow and hoped for the best. By now he knew to trust Jill, and to obey her commands directly, without question. Just then he remembered to cough, as she had instructed. For good measure, he shook his shoulders a bit.

Of all the wonders he had witnessed in Vienna, the one thing he might miss when at home at last in London was this girl, little Liza, in whom he had vested his fatherly affection. Never once had he seen her real parent unbend toward her, and a pinch of regret afflicted Mr. Darling to think of leaving Liza here, under Heinrich's uncaring control. He did, however, hold faith that Jill made some arrangement for the girl's future. In Jill's girlhood as Wendy and even more in her maturity, Jill was too motherly to abandon any child who required her care. He managed to produce another cough.

Liza felt the excitement that rode along with the company in the carriage, although no one spoke of it. With his satin-lined opera cloak, Heinrich wore a confident smile above his cravat. The knot was adorned with the emerald stick pin with which Jill had gifted him. His silver-topped cane lay against his seat, and while he watched the city roll by he rubbed his watch with his thumb. Jill fluttered her slatted fan at her cheeks, even in the cool but newly humid air of winter's end, and Mr. Darling hummed a tune between coughs as he twiddled his fingers on his knees. Wearing her best gown, Liza sat immobile within her warm woolen wrap in order to avoid wrinkling her frock of pale yellow. *Frau* Lieber had crocheted a snood in gold-colored ribbon for her, and helped arrange Liza's locks in it. Fidgeting like her companions, Liza kept her hands busy by toying with the brass opera glasses her father had bestowed upon her for the occasion.

Jill, of course, had caused both the gown and the glasses to be presented to her, but Liza's pleasure in them did not diminish due to her father's thoughtlessness. Even if he did not deign to say so, Liza knew she deserved this treat. She labored every day at her studies, and when she felt brave enough to speak aloud, she was able to query her father about the subjects in his medical books, and even discuss them in Austrian. By now, the language of the culture she inherited on his side came to her as naturally as the color of her eyes. She only hoped that, this time, the dream to which she aspired was not too good to come true. As Mr. Yulunga in his canniness had predicted, she found a happy change in striving for something she could accomplish through her own effort, rather than something she must depend upon a man to do...or to feel. On the whole, she preferred her father not to think about her.

Heinrich leaned closer to Jill, caressing her shoulder with his. "A theatrical evening to which we have looked forward, and one to remember, is it not, my darling?"

His lady smiled and nodded, but she returned her gaze to the window. The carriage rattled over the little bridge above the canal. As they passed between the tall stone markers that guarded the span, Jill peered down to the green waters running off with the river. A few small craft drifted with the flow, where, wistful, Jill remembered the baron's boatman rowing, and with some pain of poignancy she recalled the sweet release of the hours the French nobleman devoted to her in the darkest part of her winter in Vienna. She couldn't see, but she intuited that the coming spring had stirred the current of the canal to life again. The same pull stirred Jill; soon, she herself might be released to rejoin the sea.

But as she followed the carriage's progress, alarm made her feel the cold again, on her insides. She stilled her fan. The rig turned too soon.

She ventured, "Have you some further surprise for us tonight, Johann? Should we not continue on at this crossing?"

"No, Jill. This is the correct way to the State Opera House."

"The State—" She drew a slow breath. "I see." Jill's fears were confirmed. Heinrich had misled Stella about not only the date, but the destination. It hardly mattered. Either piece of information was valueless without the other. Jill made her words obey her will, expressing only a mild interest. "I have yet to have the pleasure of visiting the State Opera House. I was under the impression that you had named the *Theatre an der Wien.*"

"I may have said so, in my astonishment at the gypsy's prediction. Nevertheless…ah, here we are! I must say, the State is my preference after all. Tastefully appointed, elegant…and the orchestra excellent." As his groom jumped down from the box and held the door open for him, Heinrich disembarked and tucked his cane under his elbow, offering his support to Jill. "Once again, I am guilty of the sin of pride in showing off my wife and my family. Do take care, my darling, I shouldn't want you to slip in those pretty slippers, and twist an ankle. Father, wrap your throat, the air is still chilly and I notice you are subject to phlegm this evening." Having assisted his father-in-law, Heinrich reached for his daughter.

She was gazing at the bright façade of the theatre. Its arching porticoes, stretching for a city block and more, were lit within and without, casting a soft, becoming glow upon her face. Due to her intervals of voicelessness, whether enforced by her father or by herself, Liza had developed a special affinity for sound that became more sophisticated as she attended concerts and operas in Vienna. She was eager to fill her ears with music tonight. "Liza." Heinrich interrupted her reverie, pressing his scarred cheek to hers. She pulled away, but he pursued her, murmuring in her ear as his grip bore painfully into her forearm, "You look enticing this evening. I hope that, in public, you will continue to behave like the chaste young lady you now pretend to be when we are alone." In a gesture he believed only Liza would understand, he raised his cane to the level of her eyes.

Struck dumb again, Liza dipped her head and hurried to Mr. Darling, who linked her arm through his own to guide her through the throng. He kept one hand on his hat.

With a foreboding that her opportunity had closed, Jill heard the groom slam the carriage door, then Heinrich instructing him to stable the carriage and return to the theatre to wait for the family in the front lobby. Their equipage trotted off, and other horses with brushed, shining coats clopped up to chew at their bits and paw the pavement as more patrons arrived to spill out at the opera in glossy silks, twinkling jewels, gold or gemmed tie pins, and top hats. As the Heinrich party entered the spacious, vaulted foyer, the scents of potted flowers mixed with cologne. Cloaks and canes were checked, coiffures patted back into place, and skirts shaken free. Jill's fortitude wavered as she gazed around the vaulted hall, listening to the voices of a multitude of celebrants. The place was palatial. Clearly, the front door would be watched by the groom, and without the guidance of a floor plan, she and her father, in their quest to break away, might become hopelessly lost within its labyrinth…only to be found again, and dragged back to be even more heavily guarded for ever-after, within the fortress of Heinrichhaus.

Heinrich escorted his wife up the wide, lavish carpet over the marble stairway, turning to the left when, at length, the steps diverged with options into two opposite flights. Ushers in emerald green coats with gold braid milled about, guiding the patrons under the paintings in the pediments and through the towering doorways to their seats. One young man with a slender build and sloping shoulders seemed to be watching for them. He came forward, touching the shiny bill of his cap.

"*Herr Doktor, guten Abend.*" Changing to English, he greeted Jill, "Good evening, Mrs. Heinrich. Allow me please to show you to your box."

They strolled after him down a quieter hallway. Looking up, Jill saw white molded ceilings, encrusted with gilded wreaths encircling gold-leafed laurels. Every inch of this edifice, above and below, bespoke luxury. The young usher pulled the polished handle of a baize-covered door and held it open for them. Helping the ladies with their cloaks, he hung their garments on a coat tree at the back of the box, then did the same for the gentlemen's hats and capes. Jill saw Heinrich slip a tip to the usher. Glancing at the bill in his hand, the youth thanked him with a tremor of gratitude in his voice, then exited the booth and soundlessly shut the baize door.

After noting where each of their wraps hung, Jill turned to approach the red velvet edge and looked over the theatre. She and Heinrich took seats closest to the stage, with Liza at her father's side and Mr. Darling perching at the end of the row. From here, Jill could look left and right to see other boxes' occupants, and across the oval of the theatre she saw rows and rows of similar alcoves. In the center below, seats were arranged over a decorative flooring, filling quickly as the hour for the performance advanced.

This auditorium was as grand as the hallways, appointed with more gilt embellishments and an elaborate chandelier, but the feeling it exuded was one of intimacy. The stage, too, appeared more graceful than grandiose. It lay close enough to view without glasses, yet it was deep enough to hold a complex theatrical set in front of a full orchestra. The black-suited musicians tootled and blew, and drew bows over strings in a chaos of tuning. Even this cacophony was glorious. Then, in a multitude of sconces, the light dimmed.

When the conductor tapped his baton, the drone of dissonant tones died away. Beats of silence filled the hall with anticipation. His arms poised, the maestro held the audience in this thrall of suspense until he flung up his hands, and the instruments erupted in an overture. Jill found the acoustics to be exquisite. If only she could sit back and enjoy the splendor of this music! But she could not. She felt her tension stretch instead as she awaited her excuse to exit the booth— in the form of a much more humble sound: a prearranged fit of coughing from her father.

Halfway through the first act, Mr. Darling managed it. He leaned forward, covering his mouth with his fist. Persisting, he tried to cough quietly but annoyingly enough to disrupt his box-mates' pleasure in the measures of a full-throated chorus. Liza bestowed a look of concern upon her companion. Heinrich turned to him, too. "Father," he whispered, "let me escort you to the hallway."

Jill rose and laid her gloved hand on Heinrich's shoulder. "No, Johann. You enjoy the program and watch over Liza. I'll attend to Father." Before he could object, Jill acted fast, sweeping up her taffeta train and pushing her sire ahead until they exited the booth. She looked back to see Heinrich settle in again, his face turned toward the stage, his head swaying to the beat of the measure. She snatched her cloak and her father's hat and cape, and shut the door behind her. She lost no time in stepping away from it.

She was brought up short by the young usher standing in her way. "Madam? May I be of assistance?"

Taken aback, Jill fumbled to find a smile for the young man. His manner was respectful, and when Mr. Darling made another foray into his coughing fit, the boy's slender face turned solicitous.

Jill seized the moment. This youth could be of use. "Yes, please do show us to the lounge. My father is fighting a cold." She made a show of wrapping Mr. Darling's cape around his shoulders, then offered him his hat. "Here, Father, we must protect you from the draft." She flung her own cloak around herself, and followed their guide down the lush, padded hall and past many more baize doors of other boxes, toward the Gents and the Ladies.

"I shall moisten a towel with warm water, Father, and I'll wrap your throat. This remedy is one the doctor taught me this winter, if you recall. I will be only a moment."

"Er…yes," her father rasped out, "yes, thank you, my angel."

She slipped into the powder room. She sighed but did not hesitate, and a wave of relief washed over her as, at the back of each stall, she found a window opening onto a piazza. She twisted the lock of one casement and lifted the pane. Looking down to the ground she saw a thin coating of snow with soft earth beneath.

But it was too far beneath. Assessing the distance, Jill couldn't be certain that, even after his walks and activities had reduced his weight and enlivened his physique, Mr. Darling could land under his own power with safety. Gazing down, Jill herself felt a bit dizzy. For the first time since gaining the power of flight, she thought twice about employing it. With this gown and its train and the weight of her treasure, would she manage to float down, supporting her father to boot? Begrudging her own caution, she discarded the idea, then, removing only her left glove, proceeded to dampen the promised towel for Mr. Darling.

Hoping the usher had vanished, Jill was disappointed again. She continued the charade, loosening her father's cravat and applying the remedy. She donned her glove again as she turned to the younger man. "Would you be so kind as to find a hot cup of tea, please? We are English, you know. Tea is our remedy for everything."

"Yes, Madam."

"And do add a drop of honey, if you can find some."

The boy bowed and, as he collected the coins Mr. Darling offered, the slope of his shoulders perked up a little. He left the wanderers there in the lounge. Once his green coat disappeared around a corner, Jill spun to grasp her father's hand.

"Quickly!" Leading the way, she sprinted out of the lounge and down the hallway, the opposite direction from which they had come, and, she hoped, toward the back of the theatre. At the end of the passage, a sign over a door reading '*Ausgang*' made her hopes surge. Mr. Darling pushed the portal open. The two fugitives swept their capes to the side and, grasping the bannisters, ran down their length. This passage was meant for service and emergencies only; its iron bars were plain, the wood of the handrail worn smooth, and the light dull. But Jill could smell the outdoors in the air; an exit must connect to it. With her heart pounding, she fled down the bare, echoing enclosure to the base of the stair.

Jill's breath came in hope-filled gasps. Mr. Darling puffed, but he wore a giddy smile. Before them stood a broad metal door. Mr. Darling took the knob in his hand. As he rotated it, Jill heard the sweet sound of a click, and the creak of the door opening. She anticipated the gust of fresh, cold air on her face. Yet the atmosphere of the lower level of the opera remained dank and still. Nonplussed, Jill discovered that the knob had not turned, and the portal remained sealed. Her father's smile metamorphosed to a look of confusion.

The exit was locked. Behind the runaways, footsteps trod down the stairs. The sounds they had hungered to hear had come not from this door, but from the one up above. Searching for a corner in which to conceal themselves, Jill cursed under her breath. To the left of the door stood a wall. To the right, a vast, open space. Clearly, this area was the loading dock for the theatre's sets and equipment. Large barn doors, padlocked, dominated the wall, and this side of the bay was bare. No packing crates, no scenery, no carts stood near enough or at convenient angles to offer a hiding place. The amber illumination of gas lamps showed that the only path was to run deeper into the basement of the theatre, rather than out of it. The timid voice of the usher arrested them.

"Madam, Sir, I fear you have lost your way." Offering a steaming cup to Mr. Darling, he remained diplomatic, disguising any surprise these foreigners might have prompted in him. He tendered his salute, touching the bill of his cap. "When you are ready, I will show you back to Doctor Heinrich's box."

"Why, thank you," Jill answered, employing all her skill to act grateful. "Father, drink up, sweet hot tea is just the thing for your ailment. There, I am sure you will be quite recovered...after a breath of fresh air from outdoors." Jill turned her blue gaze upon their guide, feeling for her fan, then tapping it cajolingly on the gold braid of his sleeve. "Would you be so kind as to open this door for us? Another quirk of the English. We believe in the restorative powers of cold, crisp winter air."

As her eyes engaged his, the usher blushed, but if he fell under her spell he withstood her. His bony shoulder blades drooped again. "I apologize, but *Herr Doktor* asked me most especially to watch over the needs and the whereabouts of his family this evening."

"Oh?" Jill's face flushed, too, but in anger. She drew herself up, straight and queenly. "If this is so, you should follow your benefactor's wishes and grant his lady wife's request."

"*Entschuldigen Sie, meine Frau,* but if I wish to keep my position here at the opera, I cannot cross the doctor's will."

Jill paused only a moment, for effect. A pregnant silence reigned, as when the maestro raised his baton before the overture. Instead of a burst of music, the shriek of rending lace filled the empty bay as Jill yanked the heart-shaped garnet brooch from her gown. She thrust it toward the boy. "I am English, but *I* can speak your language just as fluently as Doctor Heinrich."

The young man stared at the precious pin, his eyes wide. He made no move.

"If you are too shy to accept a bribe, I will drop it in your pocket. Now...get us out of this theatre!"

Tears sprang to the usher's eyes. He blinked to banish them. "I would...I would, Madam, but...it is because of my mother. She is due to deliver soon. She is too old and...we cannot afford a good doctor." He wrung his hands. "She needs the help of your husband!"

Mr. Darling coughed again, not feigning his affliction this time. Pushed to the extreme of vexation, Jill bared her teeth. She felt her eyes burn, and she seethed. Bringing all her wits to bear, Jill declined to seize the knife from her garter, seeking instead to curb her urge to murder. She commandeered what little control she could exert over the remainder of this misadventure.

"I understand you, boy. I trust you will not cross the doctor's will when you return us to the lounge— *without* mentioning to him where you found us."

In sheer relief, the boy smiled a wide smile. His shoulders climbed toward his jaw. "*Ja, ja, this* I can do for you. But we must hurry. The entr'acte is about to begin."

Later, with her brooch pinned over the rent in her gown, Jill listened to a grand performance, her crimson hand trapped within Johann Heinrich's. Employing her fan as a stage property, she kept up the appearance of pleasure. Every so often, Mr. Darling remembered to clear his throat, for the sake of consistency in his act, too. Fittingly, this opera echoed Jill's experience, portraying a tragedy in which the villain prevailed over the lovers, with Fate weighted to his side, and Jill, staring blankly into the darkness, felt the cleft that tonight's drama left in her heart. She could be pardoned for chasing from her cheek, with one gloved finger, one single tear drawn from the evening's emotions.

Weary, Jill gazed out the window of the carriage all the way home, aching for the solace of her boudoir. With the orchestra's final strains still ringing in her ears, she steeled herself, expecting the finale of this night's performance. How very in character Heinrich behaved when, as the curtain fell, he asserted his dominance again. In a quiet aside to Jill, he insinuated his intention to join her in the setting of her bedroom. Like a virtuoso, he had arranged this evening's program. Next he would stage a command performance from Jill, rousing her for the climax, then, as arrogant as any actor, he would take his final bow.

Jill's only chance to avoid this scene was an appearance by *Frau* Lieber— if the two women could contrive to prepare it in time. At this late hour, such a feat was uncertain. Jill very much doubted today's farce could end so happily. The coach lurched in tune with the lady's anxiety, her insides roiling as the wheels beat in percussion over the cobblestones, through the gate, and into the courtyard of Heinrichhaus.

The horses, too, seemed nettled, whickering so that the groom remained on the box to hold them in check while the stolid form of the houseman Karl arrived, to open the door for the passengers. The fresh air Jill had longed to inhale at the back door of the theatre poured into the carriage, cool and plentiful now. Heinrich climbed down from the rig. Liza, eager to share with *Frau* Lieber the wonders her ears had taken in at the theatre, accepted with a brief hesitation the hand her father offered to help her jump down. Mr. Darling, in keeping with his role as he waited his turn, shivered and expelled a few dispirited coughs...for good measure. Averse to observing the scenery of her imprisonment, Jill continued to look away from it, staring out the window on its opposite side, wishing she might miss her cue and wait in the wings, forever.

The coachman appeared to her view, ambling over. Boldly, he paused at her window and peered in at her. As, in confusion, the mistress' eyes met the servant's, his audacity caused her to gasp. The groom's form was altered, no longer familiar to her. The man wore a grim grin on his face. Seeing Jill's shock, he raised his topper to display a full head of dark hair, bound with a bright orange kerchief.

He was nodding.

He was Nibs!

Father's Loss, Mother's Love

In a flash of fresh energy, Jill grabbed her father's knee and shook him back to life. She gestured vigorously, urging him to embark upon another bout of coughing.

As he hacked, Jill exclaimed, "Father! We were wrong to keep you out so late in wintertime. Johann…" Turning an imploring gaze upon Heinrich, Jill said, "Johann, please tell *Frau* Lieber to run and fetch Father's greatcoat. This opera cloak is no shield against the cold. I won't allow him to set foot outside this coach without his good English wool. And have the maid draw a warm bath."

Heinrich sent a skeptical look her way, then examined Mr. Darling, whose face had turned cherry red with his efforts. "Very well, my darling. Perhaps you are right."

"And do shut the door. The draft is aggravating this attack, I am sure of it."

Before acting, the doctor lifted his gaze and looked to the gate, where Karl was turning the key in the lock. Judging it safe to relax his vigilance for a moment, he closed up the coach and stepped away from his wife. As he strode to the house, he raised his silver-topped walking stick, hailing the housekeeper, his breath puffing like a cloud in the wintry weather. He stepped over the threshold.

Jill shot to the window for another glance of Nibs. He had vanished. She heard a whistle pierce the air and Nibs' voice hollering, "Yah!" He snapped the reins to whip up the team. With a jerk, the carriage jolted forward. Nibs guided the horses to turn in a tight curve, then drove them headlong for the gates. Where the coach had stopped to drop its passengers, the groom lay on the drive, as if sleeping.

Looking ahead, Jill exclaimed in surprise. Karl was pulling the gate open for them. As the rig passed through its gap, Jill recognized the burly figure of the houseman to be the barrel-chested body of Tom. As soon as they sped through the gate, he banged it closed. Tom ran alongside the coach, grasped its lamp and, in a flying leap, he landed on the box. The vehicle listed again, as it had rocked just before entering the courtyard— when Nibs and Tom must have commandeered it. Free of the confines of Heinrichhaus, the coach raced away. At last, Jill's soul soared with the long-sought feeling of freedom. Wondering how it came about, and wary that this liberation might yet prove illusory, she clung to her hope like she held to the carriage, for dear life.

A great many thoughts crashed through her mind, striking like the clash of the hooves hitting the paving stones. Nibs cracked a whip, and so wildly did he drive the team that Jill felt sure the coach would overturn, that— in a wreck of splintering wood and spinning wheels— this last chance of escape must elude her.

Her notions churned with the spokes. The limits of the city lay miles from this district, the side streets were narrow and, even at this time of night, the avenues were sure to be crowded. She had seen enough of the town under Heinrich's escort to know no road allowed easy egress from Vienna. With the clatter the carriage made, their passage must be noted. Heinrich was certain to follow the runaways, and easily. She saw her father brace his arms against the rig's sides, she heard him wheezing, "By gad!" Whenever possible, he clutched at his hat, as if to secure the valuables she had secreted there. Jill feared that, under the exhaustion of this night's turmoil, once the carriage stopped he would be unable to move quickly enough to reach whatever refuge the boys had in mind. What were her sons thinking? she wondered.

But soon Jill recognized the guardian stones that marked the bridge over the canal, mere blocks from Heinrichhaus, and understanding dawned. Nibs turned the rig just short of the span and hauled on the reins, hollering, "Ho, there, ho, there, girls!" and next thing Tom was tearing the door open with such violence that it twisted on its hinges. He urged, "Down the steps. Hurry! We'll take the old man in hand, Jill, you just follow us. Take what you need from the coach and follow!"

As the horses snorted and the carriage teetered and creaked, Jill bundled her skirts and jumped down to the lane. Nibs and Tom hauled Mr. Darling out. With one man at each arm, he protested, "A little more gently, there!" but they hustled him from the street to the slippery stone steps toward the waters that led to the Danube.

Having rushed down this flight toward her trysts with the baron, Jill thought to caution her sons, then she realized that none of the men's feet touched the pavement. Nibs and Tom were lifting her father up, skimming just over the stairway. Of course they skimmed, they were flying! She raised the heavy hem of her black taffeta to follow. Her pulse beat painfully in her anxiety to get away from this coach, from this street, from this city…from this man, whom, with horror refilling her soul, she now heard calling her name from horseback. The iron shoes of his mount rang only paces behind her. Even so, Jill's instinct betrayed her intentions. She must buy the boys time. She froze at the head of the steps, and felt the nip of dread freeze her blood, too.

"Jill! Jill, do not fear, my darling." Heinrich leapt from the horse and abandoned his steed as the animal danced away. He still clutched his cane, and this time he gripped it like a club. Quickly, his gaze rummaged the vacant carriage. "So, they have taken your father." From his position by the coach, some strides away, he looked Jill over where she waited in the light of a lamp post, and he assessed her well-being. "Strange that they did not first seize your jewels."

Her hand hovered over the choker at her throat. The emerald on her captor's throat, she noted, on his necktie, gleamed, as if reminding her why she had pinned it there.

Cautious not to startle her into bolting, Heinrich took a single, tentative step forward. "But I know how valiant you are. I presume you fought bravely, and now you intend to overtake these ruffians." A wry smile on his generous lips gave the lie. He, too, had expected her sons to come calling someday, and they were still close enough for him to recognize them. With his sand-colored hair agitated by the breeze, he stole another step. "Of course I forbid you to attempt to apprehend them. I myself will see that your father is rescued from these…kidnappers."

His meaning was clear. He was offering Jill a chance to surrender to him, to return to her role as his wife, free of consequences for this evening's rebellion— if she submitted. Holding fast against her reflex to fly, Jill stood half turned from him, poised on tiptoe at the top step of the stairway. She perceived that her presence there, threatening to run, prevented Heinrich from marching down the steep flight of stairs after her father. Clenching her fan in her hand, she found that its slats were cutting into her glove. The horses behind Heinrich puffed and pawed in their fretfulness. She stalled, as if undecided.

With her eyes only, she followed the threesome's progress. The inky billow of her father's opera cape streamed behind them. Jill's spirit sank under the certainty that, encumbered by his weight, the fugitives would be unable to get far enough, fast enough. Mr. Darling sagged in the two men's grips as they completed their deep descent, less quickly than she willed, to cross the landing, aiming to leave it behind and take to the canal. The channel suddenly looked wider than Jill remembered. Once again, she smelled the scent of fresh water and heard it lapping, a gentle sound in contrast to the rocks that edged its trench and the dangers faced by her family. The waters called her to follow the men, to hurry homeward. To happiness. To Hook.

As the scope of Jill's gaze broadened, she realized that the waterway was cluttered with boats. Where at the outset of the evening only one or two craft drifted down the stream, vessels of all shapes and sizes now lined the canal, two and three abreast between its walls, all sailing past her, toward the fuller straits of the river. From the street level above, gaslight reflected here and there on the surface as it undulated. Lanterns on the boats bobbed downstream like so many out-of-season fireflies, beckoning to Jill to join their procession, toward liberty. Still, Jill fought the impulse to rush away with them.

Instead, she allowed Heinrich to catch her. His soft-leather shoes offered him a firm foothold on the cobblestones. He reached for her. She felt his grip on her shoulder, restraining her in his firm, practiced hand.

"I instructed *Frau* Lieber to send for the constabulary." Again, he offered her choice that was no choice at all. Voluntary captivity, or forced.

Jill stood her ground. She surmised that he had no preference as to how he exercised his power. As with his lovemaking, his domination had become all to him. Her option was to choose how harshly he would enforce his control— and she could make that choice before, or after, the law arrived. She eyed his cane, which once upon a time menaced Liza. His hand lay heavy upon her.

She spoke then, and, as always, she told him the truth. "I can trust you to act as you believe for the best."

He studied her face for sincerity. Seeming assured by her stillness, he descended the stairs, the cane poised against need. Shuddering from the repulsion of his touch, Jill backed toward the carriage.

The horses stamped, agitated and wild-eyed, but even with no apples to treat the beasts as she'd done for gypsy ponies, she braved them. She tucked her fan away in a secret pocket in the bell of her sleeve, where the papers that named her a daughter of de Beaumonde resided. She had no need to hide behind her fan now. No matter what the physician believed, Nibs and Tom had released her from her captivity. Grateful as she was for *la matriarca*'s gift of protection, it could do no more for that lady's favorite son's wife. Nor, now that the boys had flown, could her sons defend her. Tonight, Jill must safeguard herself. Another beast needed to be treated.

Stripping off her right glove, Jill felt the damp of river air on her palm. For the first time since her arrival here, her blood-red stain became visible to Vienna. She hiked herself up to the driver's box, where she confirmed her guess. Her sons had furnished her needs. She wrapped her red fingers around the grip of the horsewhip. This tool was no buggy switch. It was long and supple, her own leather lash, transported from the single hand of her lover on the *Roger* itself to extricate her from her enemies. Red-Handed Jill held the familiar grip of the handle, supple but brutal, more powerful than the feminine weapons that guarded her thus far in her perils. She smiled.

She pulled the brass knife Cecco had given her from her garter. Securing it in her sash first, she climbed down from the box, and, leisurely now, she sauntered toward the man who called himself a husband. Splendid in his concert finery, top hat and tails, his cape thrown back over one shoulder with the gray satin lining exposed, Heinrich paused at the brink of the water. With one ear cocked for Jill's movements, he was searching through the darkness for his father-in-law.

Jill unclasped her cloak and shrugged it from her shoulders, to discard it in a green velvet heap on the ground. She scanned the canal but, between the parade of boats and the midnight shadows of the arches under the bridge, the three men had vanished. She felt another knot of worry unravel. Where would she find them when, in good time, her own moment to flee arrived? As she stared down at Heinrich, the anxieties of the past months dissolved. All concern for her own freedom dissipated. Her sons, her father, were stowed safely away. At last, after her long term of bondage, Doctor Johann Hanover Heinrich had no hold upon Red-Handed Jill.

But Jill had a hold upon him, in her red-as-ruby hand. She glided down the steps, to stand level with him, yet keeping her distance.

He gave up his search and turned in full to her. Instead of the look of loss she expected, he wore his accustomed expression of victory. "I will miss your father's company, but we no longer have need of him. Our little family will be just as complete."

"You are correct. We will do very well without you."

His eyes narrowed. "There is no going back for you, Jill. As I attempted to reveal to you on the day you left him, Commodore Hook took a beautiful mistress. And not a new lady. One he has loved for a lifetime."

Jill now allowed the knowledge she hid from herself to flow free. She did not miss a beat. "No secrets can survive between Hook and me. I dictated his story." She raised one eyebrow. "Shall I tell you the ending of ours?"

"I can tell you how we shall continue. Thanks to your sons, I need not fall out with Mr. Darling when I write to Heidelberg. Because of Liza's 'delicate health,' she will remain safe with her family. No doubt Mrs. Mary Darling will be happy to welcome her husband home. If, that is, your pirates feel he is worth bothering to return to her. Or, perhaps, we might have him restored to us…with an offer of ransom?" He gave his gust of a guffaw, the irony of his speech entertaining him. "You, at least, have eluded recapture."

"No, Johann, I did not escape capture. But I'll be a free woman soon." She stepped closer, mocking as she delivered her own line of humor. "As you like to say, maybe even…'Today.' " She lifted her whip.

"Is that weapon how you fended off your brigands? Our social circle will applaud you." Amused, self-confident, he smiled more broadly, and his scars puckered the flesh of his handsome face. "My clever wife. Ever the pirate."

"Your pirate wife will steal that document from you, Doctor. Please to hand it over."

As if relaxed in a stance by his fireside, Heinrich pulled the watch from its pocket and massaged the gold case. "What I wrote was too harsh. I cannot let you upset yourself over it. Not in good conscience, not knowing what I now know. Jill, my darling, I shall tell you why I chose 'Today' to give you that garnet heart brooch."

Jill strode one step nearer. She dropped the coils of the whip. She shook them loose. "Never mind, Johann. I shan't trouble to ask for your paper again." In the light of the gas lamps, she felt the blue of her eyes flicker to green. They began to burn, and she welcomed the feeling. Her Island tigress surged into life.

The flotilla of boats streamed silently by, fewer now, and seeming to Jill to flow more slowly. Which vessel sheltered her sons? From which porthole did her father watch her, and worry? She could not ponder these questions now. She and her false husband were sheltered to some degree by the lofty drop from the bridge. An occasional carriage could be heard rumbling above, but not seen completely. This scene proved a favorable place and time for her, in Vienna. She snapped the whip, and the sharp sound bounced off the old stone walls here by the waterside. Here, below the city of her servitude. Jill lifted the whip again.

Alerted at last, Heinrich dropped his watch to dangle on the fob, jolting up to regain his perfect posture. As comprehension grew, his smugness changed to alarm. Jill flicked the lash. He cried out, raising his cane to fend off the blow. Her whip entangled it, and Jill ripped the stick from his grasp. It clattered to the landing. With metallic tinkles, the silver handle broke into shards.

"Jill, you know of the duplicate letter in my strong box. A dire fate awaits you if I come to harm. The authorities—"

"*I* am the authority."

Heinrich backed toward the water, shaking his head. Refusing the death of his illusions, he uttered, "No….No— Jill!"

Her leather snapped, his gasp was strangled. With his manicured hands, the doctor clutched at the layers of straps that wrapped his throat round. The silk hat tumbled from his brow to plunk in the canal. It bobbed down the current, tagging after the last of the boats. His dueling scars turned to red gashes against the shock on his face, symmetrical from cheekbone to jaw.

Jill said, "My crimson hand bears something more potent than a lady's fan, now."

"Yes...yes," he choked out, "and you will bear more than this." Applying his physician's skill, Doctor Heinrich tried to weave his fingers under the lashings. His clipped accent grew desperate. "I see it in your face, Jill, the radiance— the veil. To a physician, these are unmistakable signs."

"A physician who kills."

"You don't yet know—"

"I know that you are a dead man."

"...I fathered the child in your womb!" He stopped struggling. Offering one hand to her, the hand wearing his wedding band, Heinrich recaptured his poise. He stood erect, his neck trussed in her trap, relying on moral certainty, his lifelong conviction that his sense of right must prevail. "My darling. In a matter of months, you will become a mother." He waited, gambling his life, sure that his magnificent woman, his pirate queen— like any lesser woman— would be stopped by the shock of his revelation.

Jill did stop, and she remembered. She recalled the taste of her tea.

When had it changed? "You altered the formula."

"I did. When you did not conceive, I grew curious. I found your tea leaves, and I analyzed them in my laboratory." He seized another means of persuasion. "You are well past your youthful bloom, Jill. And under this burden of maternity, your buccaneer lovers cannot cherish you now."

With a lurch of her insides, Jill knew that her morning draught no longer shielded her, and had not done so for months.

In a flash of intuition, in the break of one breath, she thought of her bargain with *Frau* Lieber. Their pact carried consequences for the housekeeper, too. She would suffer for relieving Jill of this monster's attentions. The elements of Jill's life in Vienna— her sacrifice for her father, her schemes to break free, her fantastical affair with de Beaumonde, that single night Jill fell helpless into Heinrich's hands...her care of his daughter, her compulsions as a mother— all combined like an alchemist's distillation, in a fiery furnace of insight, to make her a mother in truth.

Staring into the gray light of his eyes, she retorted, her voice ringing clear, "Yes. I am a mother. And a mother protects her children."

With all the strength she possessed, Jill yanked the lash taut.

She heard the crack of bone. Disbelieving to the last, Heinrich jerked sideways. He wilted, then collapsed. His athletic frame lay depleted, sprawling on the bricks of the landing. Jill's green eyes felt like coals. The blood-rage burned, and this time she controlled its flames so that they did not consume her. The tigress inside her raged at his treachery. She triumphed at his demise.

Many thoughts crashed through her mind...and she had all the time of a journey home in which to master them.

She knelt down to the body of her *faux* husband. Rifling his pockets, Jill searched for his papers first, and as her fingers closed upon the dry feel of parchment, she stuffed the document in her sleeve by her fan. She robbed him of his keys, his pocketbook, his wedding band, his cufflinks, his tie pin— the emerald tie pin she had bestowed upon him, to mirror her tigress eyes. And, last, as she'd done that fatal day aboard *L'Ormonde* when she foretold that she'd come away with him, she stole his watch and its fob, and dropped them into her bodice.

Withdrawing her dagger, she threw his cape aside. She slashed the collar of his tailcoat. She thrust her knife between her teeth, tasting brass at her tongue, then ripped the coat in half. With pleasure akin to that inspired at the opera, she listened as the cloth screamed, echoing off the walls of the canal. She did the same for his shirt, to view the carving that Cecco cut there.

"'Tonight,' Johann," she murmured, and her voice in her throat felt like purring. "We will each of us find our homes in the water." On her knees on the stone, Jill rolled his body to the edge of the embankment. Slowly, with the Fates weighted in her favor, she slid her villain of a husband into the river and left him floating, face down, in the Danube.

On his back, in big, bold letters of flesh, seamed over with scar and exposed to the eyes of any in Vienna who wished to witness his infamy, lay the name of his darling, and his destroyer.

JILL.

Fleet Afoot

A s she wondered which way to fly, Jill heard a flurry of footsteps behind her. Her first thought was of the police, but no boots approached, and no whistles waylaid her. She descended from her toes, whirling to see two slim figures hesitating, one in black, one in yellow, in the lamplight at the top of the steps.

Wrapped in a thick knitted shawl and with her arms around Liza's shoulders, *Frau* Lieber stood as if taking in the scene. The three horses edged nose to nose now. The boats had deserted the canal. No longer visible, the body of the head of their household slipped silently, silkily, away down the stream. All that remained of the man was the litter of his cane, and his cape.

"Madam!" A good housekeeper, *Frau* Lieber picked up after her mistress. She plucked up Jill's cloak and shook it free of debris. *"Mademoiselle,"* she said to Liza, in her soft, calming way, "perhaps you should take the horses in hand?"

With her eyes wide as the Danube, Liza nodded. She was not unwilling to speak now, she simply did not know what she should say. Confused, relieved, and in shock, she saw her father's wife much as in the first glimpse she'd had of her, leaning back against the mast of the *Roger*, her skirts wrapped round her, lovingly, by the wind, and her jewel-blue eyes glorying at the plunder of the *Julianne*. Liza turned away from the wild, unfettered vision of Red-Handed Jill, to soothe the tamer members of her family, the animals she had come to love.

As *Frau* Lieber scurried to descend and drape her cloak on her shoulders, Jill asked, urgently, "Are we expecting the constabulary?"

"I am afraid I neglected *Herr Doktor*'s last command." Scanning the landing, *Frau* Lieber drew instant conclusions. The lady before her induced no indecision. Whatever transpired here a moment ago, Jill was the mistress of victory. "My intuition told me you had the situation in hand." As she observed that hand, she realized that Jill's bloodstain lay revealed. *Frau* Lieber's face turned as white as her celebrated throat. This sign was definitive. "You have—" She trembled. "Johann is gone, then?"

Jill held the housekeeper's hand in her garish one. *Frau* Lieber did not flinch, and Jill appreciated the woman's resilience. "Know that I regret that I caused you grief. I believe, however, that soon you will also feel joy."

A rush of blood now suffused *Frau* Lieber's complexion. "I was about to confide to you...but how did you know?"

"I seem to be in a similar state. With his last words, the doctor enlightened me." Her bitterness made her words brittle. "Believing I protected myself, I never looked for the signs." She shook her head. "You must throw away the rest of our tea. Our overlord was a canny adversary, but..." with grim satisfaction, Jill cast her gaze over the damage, "not cunning enough. Now we must hurry. Let us toss these remains in the water." The two women set to work to sink the cane and its shards. Jill hung the doctor's cape on the housekeeper's arm, to return to the carriage. "When you are asked, *Herr* and *Frau* Heinrich were accosted by robbers, and vanished together into the night. You know what to do with my papers." Jill awarded to *Frau* Lieber the master's keys. "The very moment you return home, you will kindly destroy the affidavit in the doctor's strong box. I entrust *Mademoiselle* to your care. She is an heiress now. *Herr Doktor* leaves you and his children well provided for." Not stopping to unclasp the brooch on her bosom, Jill tore it off again and thrust it into the housekeeper's hold. She wrapped the woman's fingers around the prickly, gem-studded surface. "Bring Liza to the State Opera House tomorrow, and enquire after the usher who attended us. His mother needs this piece much more than I."

"I will do so, Madam."

"And Katje," gently, Jill removed the tinted spectacles from the lady's face. "Your eyes are a lovely shade of hazel. You have no need to hide them. Not ever again." She smiled. "I hope your little one will favor your side of his heritage, and take after the professor, your uncle."

"'His,' Madam? You know this?"

Jill's mirth turned mysterious. "Remember. I am the Storyteller." Serious now and anxious to fly, Jill quickly finished her business. Coiling her whip, she instructed, "You will write to me at my mother's, and expect a French noblewoman to reply. I see Liza is waiting for you. Hurry now!"

Katje pressed her fingers to the copper watch over her heart, "From this day on, my lady, may love be kinder to you."

"To the both of us."

Katje picked up her skirts, and, in her sensible shoes, dashed back up the steps.

Raising her scarlet hand, Jill saluted the girl. Gravely, Liza waved a goodbye. Jill held a bold pose where the water met the shore: the Pirate Queen, garbed in a gown stuffed with plunder, her red hair tumbling down around her shoulders, her weapons in her grasp, and her voice commanding. "*Fräulein* Liza Heinrich. I grant you your freedom. You may go wherever you wish." Red-Handed Jill hoisted her whip, warning the girl, one last time, "With the exception of the sea."

The footsteps she had expected to hear advanced, becoming audible. The two other women spun from Jill in alarm, and she stole away into the shadow of the bridge. With limping tread, Karl and the groom huffed to the carriage, voices raised in relief to see the ladies safe there, and then lowering in moans after hearing the tidings. Drawing farther under the span, toward the other side of the bridge, Jill listened to the men tramping closer, to the edge of the canal, to search for hints of their missing master and mistress. She had lingered too long. Time to fly.

She closed her eyes and lifted her face, allowing herself to believe in this feeling of freedom. The longed-for dream was real this time, not a promise to be stolen away. Jill's spirit housed so many happy thoughts, taking to the air again was simple. The gift of an instant. Heinrich and his schemes lived no more. Her father was safe, on his road home to her mother. Nibs was beloved of Stella, and Stella was restored to her father. Those Jill left in Austria were free at last, too. The waters beneath her feet poured, in a long, winding flow, into the ocean, on which, after riding the wind, she would hold her lover again. For ever and for always, Hook was hers and she his. There with the fleet, her true husband's love, too, would enfold her. What more could a woman, touched by the fairies, require to rise into the sky, to swoop with joy, and rejoin the adventure of a life begotten by the magical Neverland?

The wind fingered her hair. Fresh, cool air filled her lungs. Beyond the lights of the city, the stars sang with their salutations. Jill's heart soared upward, toward the firmament.

But her feet remained motionless, firm as the earth on which she stood.

Magic had not deserted her. Jill felt it tingling, still. It uplifted her even now...but differently. With a heart full of love, yet she weighed very little. But even further inside her, something else weighed like gold. Life, both separate and dependent, gathered every grain of enchantment to which its mother laid claim. As the reality of her condition entered into Jill's thinking, the miracle of flight was waylaid by her new little passenger. Her eyes, returned to their usual hue of blue, moistened with emotion. And, although this story was one Jill had not foretold, she was, again, presented with the consequence of her own actions.

But this woman had grown up long ago. She straightened. She drew her cloak more warmly about herself. She was a mother, and a mother looks after her children. Her mind went to work on how to bring herself and her new burden home.

And none too soon. Heinrich's men were not satisfied just to crane their necks gazing down the canal. They began hunting all around, and would soon seek beneath the bridge. Several wagons rolled onto the street up above, to stop there. Men in helmets and uniforms poured out of the drays, some leaning over the guardrails, others tumbling down the steps to join the servants, with lanterns in hand to shine into the gloom. Clearly, the police were alerted after all, by Karl, perhaps, after Katje left home.

Jill pressed herself against the cold stone of the understructure. If she could climb around the far side of this arch, and if she could reach the carriage unseen...but she heard the horses' hooves, placid now under Liza's guidance, clumping down the lane, carrying the innocents away from the scene to a new life in their old home. Reassured for their sakes, Jill searched for another way to exit the area. To be found with her knife and her whip, the jewels, and her very red hand, whether she was recognized as *Frau* Heinrich or not, could only lead to imprisonment. After this taste of liberty, her spirit was strong, but recapture might break her heart.

Even with proof of her new identity, Jill could not choose to spend the time it would take to enlist the help of the baron. Without doubt he was in Paris by now. Jill had no wish to involve him in scandal, however willingly he had lent himself to it. And unless she was certain that he was a papa— again— she desired to take nothing more from him. She owed her rescuers, too, who would even now be wondering where she was, why she had not yet flown over the Danube to find them. She knew lights were burning on their regatta, and calls tossed from boat to boat, asking which of them held her. But how, now, to reach them on the broad expanse of the river? Lorelei de Beaumonde was no water bird.

Jill's breath stopped. While she considered these points, the forces of the constabulary had strung themselves out and a harsh shout rose downstream. The murdered man was found. At first Jill believed her troubles over, for a surge of men headed that direction. She could slip up the hill, head the other way down the side lane, eventually to enter the highstreets of the city. But no, another group took the duty of searching beneath the bridge. Soon they would leave the banks of the canal and examine the shadows. She ventured to poke her nose out of the underpass, and peered up to see the helmeted heads of two officers looking down from the span. Until those men were distracted, Jill was pinned, within the darkness.

She could swim! Welcome as it was, the water would be frigid, and the time she could safely dip in it limited. The jewels stitched into her gown, too, might drag her down. But she need only get as far as— as that boat. Jill blinked, and the boat became two. Three…the armada had returned. Once again, vessels large and small navigated down the canal. This time she paid attention to the men attending them. Sparkles of silver and gold caught the streetlights. Snatches of Italian played like music in the air. She deserted her hiding place, creeping carefully under the arch and then down the bank, shifting away from the policemen.

Her stealth was in vain. Once out of the dimness, she was spotted. An authoritarian voice hollered, *"Anhalten Sie!"* Discordant whistles hooted, and the sound of boots began to thump her direction. Jill broke into a run, her pulse throbbing, her whip held tight in her grip. The weapon she wielded so successfully against her rogue of a husband was useless against a force of so many. She had no other course but to shout out herself. She waved her arms, she hailed the men who poled their crafts, "Ahoy, there, the boat, ahoy!" At the brink of the stream, she threw off her cloak, she wrapped her whip round her waist and tied it. Ready to plunge in the current, she hoisted her skirts…and jumped instead onto the dory that nosed just close enough. The flat of its bottom rocked beneath her feet. She swayed for balance. The sailor who handled it pushed off from shore, and another boat approached. A man reached for her with an arm bedecked with bracelets in a wide, bright-colored sleeve. He pulled her into his dinghy, and while he steadied her he fitted his fingers to his lips and whistled, in three sharp blasts, for the next craft, and the prow of that boat swam up to them. Brother Trinio handed Jill to another gypsy gentleman, and she found herself leaping from boat to boat, the dark arch of the bridge looming overhead, and then its land-based structure fading in her wake. She vaulted her way across the canal, vessel by vessel, the planks underfoot swaying with her movements as she readapted her body to the shifting of the waters, always supported by hands strong and true, until the shouts of the constabulary dwindled with distance. As she plunked down on her feet to land on the boards of the last and the largest boat, Jill felt two arms surround her, and she was pulled through a hatchway and hidden within a lower deck. Unable to satisfy her laboring lungs, she panted instead, her panic abating as she felt, rather than saw, that she had won a place of safety. A familiar tinkle of chimes struck her ear, she smelled the pleasant scent of skin tinted by the Mediterranean sun, and Jill knew that she was caught and captured, once more.

This time, she greeted her captivity with contentment. Cecco secured her, limp but willing, in his muscular embrace. No words could escape through her lips, but none were expected. Her husband picked her up in his arms, imprisoned her close to his chest, and kissed her for a very long time, vowing, without language, that he would never let her go, ever again.

The wave of Jill's joy was so forceful that, away over seas and continents, Hook felt it surge throughout his being.

He stabbed his hook in the surface of the table, cutting his crude kind of signature in the woodwork, and hauled himself up to his feet. His nostrils flared as he inhaled, a deep-as-the-sea breath. Bound by the leather lashes of his bracing, his chest swelled against it.

He closed his eyes to the scenery of the galley: casks and kegs against the bulkheads, provisions swinging from the beams as the ship shifted beneath his feet. He escaped the mundanity of his backdrop to listen to the opus of the song in his soul. Unwilling to exhibit his own feeling, Hook accrued Jill's like a miser, locking it away. Then he darkened his heart to her, to shield her as she indulged in the final acts of her performance ashore.

Smee had caught the goblet of fine, old wine before it overturned. Bracing for action, he sat up straight. The planks of the *Roger* creaked beneath his bulk. "Is the news good or ill, Sir?"

"Fine tidings for us, Smee. Jill has broken free."

Smee shouted his gladness with an Irish oath, but Hook remained where he stood, indulging in the revels of his relief. Jill's freedom meant his own release, too. Yet he knew, better than anyone else, what a trickster was Time. As for Milady's liberty…"Even so, 'tis but the beginning of our story's end."

He quaffed the blood-red wine to the dregs, even more able now to appreciate the taste that came with its aging. "They've a long journey ahead. I will allot Commodore Cecco six days." He turned on his heel to doff his garb and lie down with the lifelong lover who slumbered in his bed, hemmed in by Time, by Fate, and luxurious curtains.

For good or for ill, Hook felt older already.

Dearest daughter,

You must forgive my scratches here, as I am scribbling quickly before my escorts must turn back homeward.

Our gypsy acquaintance, Miss Stella, is as enchanting a vision as I remembered with her ginger curls, and now I see the lovelight for our Nibs shining from her eyes of garden green. She did not let us down, my angel! As it turns out, she and your sons were keeping watch from the rafters of Heinrichhaus for days and days, ready to jump whenever opportunity arose. Seems they didn't take Heinrich at his word, as you and I committed the error of doing.

After a brief float down the canal, your gentlemanly sons Nibs the Knife and Tom Tootles pried me from the boat and bundled me into Stella's wagon. On the instant, she crooned to the ponies, who took to their hooves as if charmed. She and Nibs and I are now trundling down rough country roads to Salzburg, where I am to embark upon the long rail ride to Calais. Tom will take to the air with this note to you, as soon as I sign it.

I have been provided by my rescuers with somewhat less elegant clothing so that if the Austrian law is looking for the runaways, I shan't draw attention to myself. My formalwear is rolled up and preserved in a rucksack, and I have cut the papers proving my identity from the interior of my waistcoat, and pocketed them. I am uncertain as to the benefit of this change of costume, for whoever heard of a French employé de banque *traveling to England done up like a Tyrolian climber? But beggars cannot be choosers, and I am most thoroughly grateful to your numerous accomplices for their assistance.* Vive la France, *hail the gypsy King, and ho! for the Matterhorn!*

I must say, this adventure thing about which you are always spouting is hair-raising, but invigorating. Upon my return to Number 14, your dear mother will not know what to do with me. I expect that henceforth I shall spend a good many afternoons in the park. After all, I have had commerce with gypsies, murderers, pirates, and privateers! My tales cannot be as enthralling as yours, but they may do to prevent some of those boys being Lost. This thought alone affords me a kind of ever-after happiness.

I shall miss the little ones I befriended in Vienna. And I will, of course, quite deeply, miss you.

Farewell, my angel. May you descend safely on your destination. I shall deliver your kisses to your mother, with many more of my own.

Your affectionate father,
"Georges de Chéri"

Wider Waters

Commodore Cecco's regatta sailed quickly and calmly down the canal, their lanterns like brothers to the lights on the shore. Upon gliding into the wider waters of the Danube, the boats spread out in order to appear innocent, coasting the current to a rendezvous point marked by a fire, on the far bank a few leagues to southeast. True to his vow, Cecco never released his wife from his loving hold until his boat nudged the shore.

The new-made sailors abandoned their craft there, and with the rattle of bridles and creaking of saddles readied their horses. Hurriedly, Jill exchanged her gown for a blouse, a warm coat, wide gypsy riding breeches, well-worn boots two sizes too big, and a felt cap in which to tuck up her hair. While her husband packed her dress and its treasures and her pearl necklace into his saddlebags, Jill threw Heinrich's affidavit onto the fire. She waited only long enough to be sure it shrank in the flame, watching it curl and blacken to ash. Looking up, she recognized the men from the tribe, and she greeted them appropriately, offering hasty thanks and sending her affection to their families.

Materializing among the trees, Tom squeezed his mother in a hug worthy of a Bavarian bear, and showed her Mr. Darling's quick missive. He stuffed it into the saddlebag. "From your honorable pa. Get moving now, and read it when you're far enough to stop for a rest in safety." He touched his forehead to Cecco, nodded to the Romani troupe, then headed into the woods again to take flight toward, Jill deduced, the *Roger*. He had not invited her to fly with him.

With a pang, Jill remembered Heinrich's allegations of Hook's intrigue with another mistress. Her own intuition supplied vivid inklings of the explanation. Before she opened her eyes on the flagship of the regatta, part of her had hoped, against reason, that the man whose arms recaptured her was Hook. To resurface anywhere in Europe, however, was far too risky for a most-wanted man. The danger he'd dared in his flight to warn her in Italy last summer had turned one or two of her hairs white. In any case, another female aboard the *Roger* meant that Hook's single hand was filled, and Tom's rare reticence confirmed it. Even if Jill were able to wing her way to the *Roger*, she must wait. Not for the first time, Hook and his storyteller must come to terms.

Before mounting up, Cecco introduced Jill to the brothers she had yet to meet. She seized the moment now to express her gratitude to Giorgio and Jacqui, who, years ago with Nico, had so daringly saved Cecco from his imprisonment in a brutal cell ruled by a cruel overseer at Gao. Nico was not among tonight's band of rescuers. He remained watching over Mamma and Papa and the *Padre* in Italy, counting the days until his firstborn would enter the world. Trinio laughed, and with his flashy garb flaring, picked Jill up to twirl her round, then set her before his brothers Pietro and Mischa, who had married sisters in another troupe. Always watchful of the law even now that the bounty was paid and the outlaw presumed dead, Cecco's *compagni* pledged to swear he was Nico, should any trouble arise. While none of these five brothers were as similar in appearance to Jill's Giovanni as Nico, the family resemblance was marked. Strong chins and wide shoulders, dark eyes and white, shining smiles. Mamma and Papa Cecco raised seven fine men.

Cecco held his hand to his heart, bowing his head to his brothers. He had left off his conspicuous headdress, and bound his brow with a brown scarf. His jewelry shimmered in the light of the signal fire. "*Grazie mille, i miei fratelli.* The debt I owe you has more than doubled. You once saved my body. Now, you have rescued my heart."

Ever ebullient, Trinio said gaily, "It is Mamma you should thank, Brother. The *Padre* had no choice but to bless our venture when she invoked her mysterious charm and went to work upon him." He kissed the air at his sister-in-law's cheeks. "Ever since her 'brilliant Jill' sent her Giovanni home to us, *la matriarca* has sung and danced in her new daughter's praises."

But the law was hunting their Jill, and the brothers and tribesmen faced a long journey. Those who had waited with the horses sloshed pails of river water to smother the fire, and in the cloud of its smoldering smoke, every man leapt in his saddle and put his heels to his mount.

Cecco lifted his precious wife to the back of his glossy black stallion, then swung up behind her. With his arms safely round her, he clicked his tongue, and Jill felt the flow of the animal's muscles as it picked up its heels and cantered, smooth as glass under its master's guidance, toward Italian lands. She and her husband would soon speak of their many adventures, name their regrets, and reclaim their love. But for now, Jill felt her eyes droop closed. Her limbs relaxed to release the night's tensions. She leaned back on Giovanni, grateful to give over her cares. Inhaling the fresh scent of the woodlands and with the air of a soft Austrian spring on her face, she drifted into sleep.

Cecco kissed the back of her neck, then set his gaze on the path. In their rush and the hurry, Jill had time to tell him only the two things he most wanted to learn. Far from innocent, her eye held a spark of green as she informed him: her love for him lived, and the doctor died, by her hand.

When she roused, Jill recalled her initial visit to Italy. She cherished the gift of that experience. She rejoiced that she and Cecco rode together, now, tonight, under the spiced, celestial skies of his homeland. Within her husband's embrace, the atmosphere was as romantic as she imagined while she dwelt here in the care of his kin. The journey was a long one, yet the days and nights were filled with song and camaraderie. Halfway south between the long country's borders, the riders parted ways. The gypsies whooped and waved, performing tricks on their ponies, and Cecco watched their antics with a sorrowful smile until the many colors of their jackets dwindled away with the drumming of hooves, heading eastward in the tall, swaying grass of the countryside. A trio now, Trinio, Jill, and Giovanni rode southwest to the shore. Jill had made friends with the stallion, and she was cheered to learn that instead of selling him at the seaside, Cecco intended to toss his reins to his brother. Trinio would gallop the handsome horse homeward. The steed was a present to Papa, who loved him at the first glimpse and would work him and care for him until Cecco's next return to his tribe. Jill understood that Cecco, too, cherished a gift. No matter what troubles had arisen for himself and for Jill, these trials had mapped his path home.

Farewells were exchanged with his youngest brother at the coastline. After Cecco's inspection for seaworthiness, passage was paid on an island hopper. Glorious sights passed by Cecco and Jill between two shores— steep, stark rocks, exuberant vegetation, and fearsome fortresses. The tang of salt air reawakened Jill's yearning for her life on the sea. The pirate pair examined with professional interest the tall ships of war where they moored, menacing, but the couple kept their heads low. At a far western point on a sun-saturated beach, the *Red Lady*'s dinghy lay waiting. Guillaume, dressed in his dapper blue and red uniform, was all smiles and salutation as he handed Jill aboard. A bright fairy light rose from the French first mate's shoulder. With a musical strain of welcome, Jewel swirled around the lady's head. Filled with nostalgia, Jill flicked a kiss to go with her before the fairy shot off over the brine. Jewel jingled out her affirmation that she would, with delight, deliver that kiss to her master. Even as poignantly as her heart ached, Jill had to laugh, comparing the iridescence of the creature's peacock blue wings to brother Trinio's bright garb.

Commodore Hook arrived upon the *Red Lady*, descending from the sky in a crimson blouse, black breeches, and boots, to board her long before the voyagers. He left the *Roger* waiting many leagues afar, rocking in safer waters. When the dinghy hooked on, Mr. Yulunga saluted Captain Cecco and the queen of the fleet, and, having warned them of the pirate king's presence, he ushered Jill up the companion-way to the quarters of the *Lady*'s commander. Cecco opted for discretion. He had enjoyed days and nights in Jill's company. The time had come to award the same privilege to the commodore.

He intended to use the time of the couple's reunion to break the tidings to Mr. Yulunga that Red-Handed Jill granted Mrs. Hanover her freedom…but banished her from the sea. Knowing his first mate's disposition, Captain Cecco would also advise his sailors to keep at a distance from Mr. Yulunga for the near future. He understood though that, in the long view, the African prince would take pride in his little woman's efforts to better herself. After all, she followed his own advice. He, too, had allowed her a choice by releasing her for her sojourn. Now that her father was dead— and by the lash he deserved— *Fräulein* Liza Heinrich should be no man's slave, forever after.

Having warned poor Pierre-Jean of the risks of championing the girl, Cecco agreed with Jill's conclusion that Heinrich murdered the faithful young sailor. The tragic news that Pierre-Jean died for his sweetheart would occasion mourning among the company, and, soon, their captain would lead a vigil. The young man's Gallic smile and his china blue eyes would be missed by friends and females alike, and Pierre-Jean's fate would confirm yet again the bad luck the girl brought to the fleet. On the whole, everyone was better off for her shift of residence to Vienna.

As Yulunga escorted Jill toward the commodore, his throaty tone held the respect she had earned from him. "Congratulations upon your escape, Lady." His wide grin grew across his dark face. "Welcome home." Arrived at the door, Yulunga raised a fist to knock.

After her rush up the steps, Jill hung back, feeling a compulsion to pause, to master her emotions. She smoothed the blue-lace-bedecked gown she had worn to the opera, donned for this occasion and still heavy with treasure. In spite of the months of craving to fly back to Hook's arms and regardless of the anticipation she savored all along the journey homeward toward this collision, his consort now found herself drawing up to stand proud, rallying her forces to take on the reality of Commodore Hook, once again. The air felt charged, raising the hair upon her arms as the power between the pirate king and queen crackled.

Yulunga's knock thundered.

"Come!" Hook commanded, and the deep, velvet tenor of his voice stopped her heart— just as it had done the very first time she overheard him speaking to Smee.

Yulunga swung open the door. Jill got one look at her lover.

He seemed larger than life. Like Jill his counterpart, he was wild, he was tamed, he was magnificent. He was Hook, and he was sweeping her into his embrace and kicking the door to slam shut, and no past or no future created any barrier between them. Hook and Jill stood as one, yesterday, now, and tomorrow. She had never left him and he never let go. His grasp was heated, his body solid as he pressed against her. His tempestuous kisses endured until her embraces relented. He sensed where she'd gone and intuited what she had borne.

And now that they touched, he knew of the jewel in her womb.

He pulled back to study her. With his iron claw, he brushed a stray lock of copper from her forehead. He said, "I have been expecting you. And I find, my love, that you, too…are expecting."

The single streak of silver running through his black hair told Jill a story.

With her passion pressed into a whisper, she rejoined, "You wrote to remind me: 'I am wherever you go.' Whatever world I enter, its episodes bleed through to yours."

"From our beginning, it has always been so." His sapphire eyes fired as he fixed his gaze upon the woman who coined him, and whom he transformed to woman from girl. "The Storyteller decreed it."

She steadied her breath, and she sighed with it. Hungrily, she caressed his altered strands, silky and rich, just as she remembered the silver of the baron's to be. "Our experiences, here and there, leave our marks upon each of us."

"Our experiences affect the *four* of us." With a light, brushing touch, he stroked the scar at her throat, reproduced upon Milady's neck by a more severe stroke of his hook. "By now you've some sense of the paramour whom Heinrich, in his conniving, so artfully reintroduced to me."

"One you have loved for a lifetime, is how he described her."

"As I would describe you."

"He also warned that you will no longer cherish me. With one thing and another," she guided his single hand to lie lightly on her abdomen, "I am past desirability."

"And how did you leave him? Desirous? Or dying?"

"He is dancing in the Danube."

"Why, Jill, have you no thought for your child?" As her sly tigress' smile slipped onto her face he, too, became guileful. "Ah. So you hold hopes of another source of paternity. I shall endeavor to be shocked. But I am familiar with such hopes. These Heinrichs…." He tutted. "They will insist upon being irksome."

"Time will tell."

"Our old friend, and our foe." Above his kingly black beard, Hook's expression held a balance of bitter and bountiful. "I cannot pretend to be less than outraged. I crave to have his kill on my hook. But we will use Time to our advantage, and manage this new proposition. Perhaps the hour is come to bid your husband—" Jill flinched. "Your *true* husband, to join us as we relearn our collective adventures."

"But Hook. This time the consequences of my blunder bring a longer-lived challenge! I cannot expect you to welcome it."

Angered and energized, he tossed his head, setting the golden filigree of the earring she so well remembered to swing in the afternoon light, "What has changed? Everything, and nothing. As when we first found one another, I am a pirate. You are a mother. I predicted before your departure that we should become more ourselves with each day."

"And we are the richer for our difficulties. I recall your counsel." That bold flash of green lit her eyes again. Her gaze sharpened as, with proximity, she more fully pictured the mistress she made for him. She had never articulated that story, yet it was as intrinsic to his history as his hook. And although Commodore Hook had suffered much time alone in his years, he was not alone in his tempers. She retorted, "You and I both seized the prizes our trials presented."

"In my case, the prize was a pleasant memory of the past. In yours, *one* of your lovers— pleasantly— engendered a duty toward the future."

"We both plundered the comforts that we required to return us to…" Jill's jagged timbre transitioned, from seething to smooth. "To our unity."

Hook reclaimed her in his arms, and tightly. He would brook no divide. "Indeed, and now, thank the Powers, here we stand." Nonetheless, the long-parted lovers felt a step of separation, a small, stark breach between them. Never one to prevaricate, Hook demanded that she gauge it. "Is our tale a tragedy, after all, in which the villain prevails over the lovers?"

Red-Handed Jill jutted her chin. "The villain is slain, by my scarlet hand."

"And are our designs intact, or do you intend a return to the nursery?"

"A pirate fleet is no place to raise a daughter."

"No more sons, Jill?"

"No, no more sons. Giovanni read my palm long ago, and his mother confirmed his prediction. While immersed in his Romani tribe, I gained every faith in their prophecies."

"Which brings us to our very next adventure. It will consist of informing your husband of our respective *amoureux* in such a manner that he will not set fire to the fleet."

"You've reminded me." Difficult as she found it to undertake, Jill disengaged from Hook's hold to turn to Cecco's desk. "Giovanni advised me he left something for me." Following his instructions, she located a niche and found the letter. As she read, her eyes stung, matching her heart.

You love me; I love you. It is enough. His words caused her voice to vibrate as she read again, aloud, to reassure herself before putting the love he professed to the test. " 'No other lover can pull you from my heart.' "

No matter what troubles arose for Giovanni and for Jill— and for Hook and his paramour— these trials had mapped their paths home. And the Storyteller herself must strive to set their world right, by unfolding, like her fan, an ever-after end…for Milady.

Pulling his fine linen handkerchief from his sleeve, Hook dabbed the drops from Jill's eyes. Like beads of rain, the lifelong lovers drew together. Time drenched them in its blessing. Acting this time as a friend, it held as still as a mirror for them, and they basked in one another's reflection. The sea cradled the ship, and the ship played host to their bonding. Gradually, reverently, they laid aside gown, garb, and claw, to recline at last upon the captain's bedstead. Below them, they sensed the creatures of the deep, insensible to any dilemma and living by impulse alone. So, too, did Hook and Jill reunite, body and soul, forever and again wrapped and rapt in each other's embraces, on this vessel— a bastion of security on the bosom of the sea, a substantial plan of planks, ropes, and canvas. A home and a haven for Hook and his Jill, upon ever-widening waters.

The Ever-After End

Long absent from one another, the fleet's leaders reconvened. Yesterday, and not without turbulence, the threesome exchanged tales of their trials. They considered the implications, and came to grips with the consequences. On this first day of their future, Red-Handed Jill felt prepared.

She had gathered all the straws of her story. Acclimated and at ease in Cecco's cabin on the ship he had named for her, with her back warmed with sunlight and her beloved sea peaking in sparkles behind her, she faced Commodore Hook and Captain Cecco. She spread her skirts and took her place on the bench before her imaginary wheel, one foot on the treadle, ready to spin chaff into gold. Jill, the Storyteller, owed a certain lady a lifetime. As always with tales of enchantment, a price must be paid.

Her firstborn.

Jill spoke the words, beginning the end, and ending at a beginning.

How to begin this commission? Despite her beauty, she is modest. This portrait will be smaller than the others. She pauses to select a favorite gown from her memory and recall its details. She had dressed in so many frocks, over so many years, becoming less splendid as, of necessity, she withdrew from society. She decides on a silk of pink, so pale it made the dark spirals of her hair glisten against it. Wide layers of skirts, half-length pleated sleeves as was the fashion, and a narrow waist cinched in with lacing. After she shed the final grays of her mourning, she wore ribbons of violet on the decolletage that made her matching eyes appear vivid. Most of the gown will not show in this portrait, for she will turn her profile to the viewer, bent elbow leading to shoulder, to draw the eye toward only one half of a delicate face. Hers is not the visage of an eager, carefree girl. The countenance is one of a woman twice widowed, left on her own without love. Is it mere chance that this ensemble is the one she wore to the opera one fateful eve, which, in the interval, brought his introduction? On that night a young man initiated another kind of commission. Not an affair of the heart, but a lifelong liaison.

She inhales the smell of her paints, comforting in familiarity, and studies the canvas, imagining the life she will bring to its surface. She must imagine, because the mirror cannot reproduce the face. She has aged. Kindly, it is true, but even a kind ripeness cannot compare with the rose-tinted skin of a much younger woman. She learned, however, that what is lost in unworldliness and in suppleness may be balanced by knowledge, and grace. With no bitterness, she imagines the Storyteller transitioning too, in time. That lady, though, may hold the consolation of not just her calling, but the comfort of his love.

Her gaze slides past the canvas to another who personifies the lesson she learned. Robbed of a legacy in which he should have dwelt in luxury with position and power as his portion, yet he endured degradation and exile to forge his own kingdom. Like her lost-in-time face, she remembers his other hand, lost in a land in which Time roams unconfined. His eyes, the color of the cobalt in her paint box, remain fixed upon her. His eyes never falter, and they do not inquire. They command.

Leaving her paints and her brushes, she rises to obey.

The sea is calm this afternoon, rocking his bed with mellow swells. The beams above croon, and the sun splashes its watery reflection there. As he pulls her down to his side to recline with him, the brocading of the curtain sways, making a hushing sound. On his few, ringed fingers she sees glints of gold. He caresses her shoulder, leaving a bright, fine-grained trail on her flesh.

He is gentle, this time. As they roll together, her back and her arms and her thighs and her breasts pick up a littering of glitter. It lies in the newly-limned lines on his face, too, and collects along the muscles of his arms, and his chest. Some golden flecks mingle with the black of his hair, and, mixing the elements, cleave to the silver swath flowing through it.

He kisses her, and his lips, flaked with gilding, taste like those roses her cheeks used to rival. A sprinkle of this substance brought to her portrayal of his ship a depth of dimension far deeper than her skill to render it. This stuff of the fairies can make a man fly, if he believes enough in his passions. She wonders what it might do with a woman whose dreams are already spent, whose highest ideal distilled over decades into a wish for— rather than roses— the lilies of peace.

As if gifting her in return for her giving, he grants acts of love. Weak but not beaten, her heart throbs in response. Accustomed to one another's desires, they linger in pleasure, then arrive at their height to descend into *la petite mort*. Pleased and pleasing, she opens her lips to speak. With one gilded finger, he silences her.

"You wonder why I request your self-portrait, then prevent its conception." He raises up on one elbow, to gaze over her shoulder, at her easel. "But see. You are begun."

She turns. She blinks to clear the film of lovemaking from her eyes.

The canvas is blank, but dusted over in gold.

After long years, he pronounces in his rich, textured voice, "Our contract is fulfilled. All promises kept, all duty done."

Milady feels the bed tilt, just a little. She is dizzy. Raising her arm to seek her lover's support, she finds her limbs feel light. Insubstantial.

He sets his one hand on her cheek. She feels its weight, and then she doesn't. Her bones no longer support it. A breeze enters through the bedside window. With fresh scents, it shifts her hair, whirls the golden granules. As if stirring petals and leaves on spring trees, it raises pieces of pink. They float toward the canvas. They settle there.

"I release you, Milady."

Is this what it feels like to fly? Flimsy and feathery? Afraid, she asks, "But where do you send me? How will I go?"

Now the floating leaves are peach, and violet, and brunette. They waft away to adhere to the portrait, arranging themselves. An image begins to take shape.

"Commodore?" The lady's voice loses strength.

No longer able to enfold her, he lets his hand fall to the bed. His eyes hold her now. Cobalt blue, gazing deep into her eyes of violet.

He shakes his head, once. "Ours was never an affair of the heart." Like a cool puff of air, tenderly, he kisses her thinning lips. "Never... until today."

As if reality has dissolved with her body, Milady whispers, in disbelief, "Sir...Master James..."

His irises become tinged with purple, then crimson. "I am no longer your patron. You may call me by my name."

Her flesh burns. No, it tingles. Her eyes and her fingertips flare. "James."

He answers her, with love letters...

"...Jane."

Little by little, the lady learns to fly. With enchanted grains from the bed, in the paint, piece by piece, she flutters toward her canvas. Bit by bit, she shimmers inside it.

Like a band of butterflies, what remains of Lady Jane rises up above the bed, swirls in the sunlight, then descends to her easel, assembling into a portrait. Whole at last, at peace, and at an end, she appears as she did that fateful evening, her dark curls flowing, her face turned away from the viewer, beautiful but unassuming, a woman wounded, and now restored.

Enchantment is broken, its price is paid. And still, just begun.

With a cobalt blue gaze, Hook looks upon his mistress. He may be pardoned for flicking from his cheek, with one gilded finger, one single tear drawn from a lifetime's emotion.

New Duty

The stranger didn't stop to ring the bell at Number 14. He followed the stars, and flew through the nursery window.

With infinite care, he set his burden down. The fairy who guided him chimed a gentle melody and settled in a vase. Ensconced there, her aura cast a glow as soft and as warm as the watchful eye of the nightlight. The room smelled of down, of books, and of blankets. A fireplace warmed the corner, its embers dozing, but cozy. The old nursery clock on the mantel ticked and it tocked, the pendulum swinging forever.

Leaning upon his shoulder, Jill regained her balance after the long, wearying flight. Bundled up as she was against the chill of night air, still her cheeks felt nearly as ruddy as her right hand. She looked around the restful room, absorbing its changes and familiarities. The many stories Wendy told here echoed through her grown-up mind. The sounds of childhood, of music boxes, toy weapons clattering and shouts from her brothers, lullabies sung in her mother's sweet intonation— those songs soon to fall from Jill's own lips— and the barking of a dear dog. All these memories faded to the silence of her sadness as she returned her gaze to her escort.

She said, "The years have been kind to this nursery. Mother kept it ready."

His voice was velvet. "Are *you* ready, my love?"

"Oh, no. It is a pretty story to tell, but it is a lie. No one is ready for motherhood." She smiled, half-way. "When I was Wendy, I believed I was suited to it. Now, nothing can prepare me...to lose you."

"Nor can I countenance it. With one thing and another," he laid his remaining hand, lightly, under the curve of her abdomen. She was swollen with child. "You are not past desirability." Then he pulled her blood-marked palm to his lips, and gifted her with his kiss.

She closed her eyes to bask in the balm of his love one last time, and feel the fire of his touch. But only for a moment. Tonight, as ever, Time was capricious. To her most-wanted man, she urged, "You must fly away now, and quickly, before the light rises. You chose to take this terrible risk, Hook, as my champion, but your queen will suffer, too, should you be apprehended."

Before she took wing from the *Roger*, sustained in flight only by love and her lover's arms, she had looked about her at the comfort of the commodore's quarters. She breathed in the scents of lavender and tobacco. She fingered the brocade of the bed curtains, the silky grain of her escritoire, where she inked her stories into life. Those tales had caught up to curse her, but, still, that room was her refuge, enhanced now with renderings in oil paint, of Hook, and Mr. Smee, the Lady Jane, and even herself as the commodore's mermaid at the prow of the *Roger*. After Hook gathered her into his embrace to be encumbered by the weight of her flightless flesh, she looked over his shoulder to witness the white wings of their vessel spreading behind, diminishing with distance. As she stood in the nursery, the surge of the sea still threatened her equilibrium. Assigned her new duties, she might not miss their quarters, nor the ship, nor the sea. Not unbearably. But she expected that, without limit, she must miss the commodore.

"I kept this token from you, Jill. I believe you will absolve me." From a pocket of his waistcoat he pulled a violet ribbon. At its end, in an elaborate frame, dangled a portrait in miniature.

She seized it. "Oh!" Tilting the image to the light, she traced the face with her finger. "She captured you. A perfect image of our perfect pirate." She sighed in appreciation. "I will remember her, with gratitude."

Roused not by sound, but by a feeling, Mrs. Darling could be heard, her bedroom door clicking closed, then her dressing gown sweeping down the hall. Candlelight wavered as it spread toward the door.

Hook raised his face, one eyebrow lifted. "Her Grace is upon us. I must fly."

Attended by his fairy, her radiance casting sharp shadows across his features, he strode to the window. Always open, the casement invited adventure on one side, and offered the contentment of home on the other. With a last look behind him, he flourished his single hand in salute to his Jill, the jewels of his rings glittering, and, with his coattails flying behind him, he leapt to the feathery sky on a pathway illuminated by stardust.

Jill ran to the window. She toed the final edge of the sill. As she clutched his miniature image to her heart, Hook dwindled from her sight. A flash of fairy light bounced off his claw— the last inkling she had of him. Joy and pain clashed inside her soul, the pathos of homecoming, the stabbing jab of her loss.

Looking down at the ground, she viewed a lovely little neighborhood, with the small, familiar park across the cobblestones. In the silver of moonbeams, fading flowers speckled their boxes with late autumn color. The square was quiet, and kind. As Mr. and Mrs. Darling understood, this homely place was an ideal spot to raise a family.

But it was no place for Red-Handed Jill.

Her mother called to her, "My dearest! Our Lorelei…" She hurried to meet her wanderer, whatever name she must use, her secret kiss apparent at the corner of her mouth to the daughter who shared the same feature. She enfolded her lost girl in her loving embrace. In the bliss of reunion, the two women wept.

But even Mrs. Darling could not hold her daughter for long. The ticking clicked on, and, soon, the child's birthing time would come. Of all people, Jill understood how quickly the two hands of the hours could circumnavigate the old nursery clock. Anticipating, she felt lighter already.

A happy thought sustained her. She raised up on her toes.

Only Time stood between Hook and Jill. With her world of experience, she expected its tricks.

She would stay close to the window, keeping watch with the nightlight. Because from here, he could reach her.

From here, he was hers.

Postscripts

Dear Madame, *my Lady de Beaumonde,*
So much good fortune visits us that it is my great happiness to report it to you.

The Fräulein *is accepted to University, but received the consent of the governors to delay her entrance for one year. She wishes to remain at home to help me care for my little son. She is very good with him, seeming to know just how to handle a baby boy. She has not confided in me, but, due to your discreet hints and my own observations, I can guess the extent of the misfortunes she has borne. Given the situation, I have named my son not after his father in first or in surname, but for my uncle, so that, as I know you hope, too, he might grow in that dear old man's pattern.*

Fräulein Heinrich *persuaded me to adopt a less severe uniform, and as I no longer need to guard my identity, I now enjoy to wear pretty shoes, and to dress my hair in a looser coiffure. I in turn have persuaded her to accept invitations to the salons of her father's associates. Small steps for each of us, but substantial in value.*

Our newest member of the household is proving his worth. In taking over the practice, Herr Doktor *has succeeded in retaining a good many of Doctor Heinrich's patients. We granted him this position upon his agreement to mentor the* Fräulein *as she works to earn her Dr. med.*

You will imagine my white neck blushing again when I tell you that he is a nice-looking fellow, and appears to appreciate my companionship. He is a widower, decent and respectful, and in regard to my child he reserves judgment, accepting us with no questions. I find it a refreshing change to run the household for a gentleman who...well, let us simply say...for a gentleman.

Herr Doktor *has a grown son who has seen quite a bit of the world. By the standards of Viennese society, he is considered a little wild. His prominent feature is a most resonant voice. The* Fräulein*'s gray eyes brightened when he and she were introduced. She still holds her own counsel, but one who knows her, as I now do, understands her by looking. In time, perhaps, when both these young people are more settled in life, might we see this liaison lead to a fairy tale finish?*

As you might imagine, we have scaled down the opulence of Heinrichhaus. Although the family hold the surety of our former master's investments, we are frugal, and thus, secure. I believe you are also secure, for only I know who Lady de Beaumonde really is.

No trace of Frau *Heinrich was found once she sailed down the canal, and although she is suspected of having a hand in her husband's death, the English ambassador recommended that the constabulary close the investigation. I need not say that she must never again set foot in Austria.*

One of the ladies upon whom she made an impression at a salon came calling. She inquired how she might help the family after the tragedy. The Frau *is chagrinned that she had not understood the lady's plea for assistance. It is she who has taken* Fräulein *Heinrich under her wing and introduced her in the company of the Heinrichs' acquaintances. Several weeks later, a letter arrived addressed to 'The Housekeeper' from an Englishman, a Mr. Davies. He asked very frankly where he might find 'Mrs. Jill.' If he is who I believe him to be, I quite admire him. In any case, I shall strictly follow your wishes in my reply.*

Your correspondence takes rather a long time to arrive, so in order to ensure that you received my own message I will repeat what I conveyed in my first letter: I trust you are in receipt of all the papers I forwarded to your mother. You may trust that the particular paper you found so offensive perished in a grateful blaze.

The Fräulein *and I were disturbed by a missive written in a hasty French hand, which, as far as I am able to translate, rather rudely demands that my deceased master initiate contact with him. He writes with no name and no address. I have locked this letter in the strongbox.*

One question remains, on which the doctor's daughter and I most earnestly require your guidance. In the strongbox, we discovered the formula for his famous— or infamous— elixir of love. You and I both know its potency, and its potential. I cannot presume to advise my young mistress whether to preserve or destroy it.

Fräulein *Heinrich and I send our congratulations on the birth of your daughter. With a mother as loving and dedicated as yourself, she has every benefit that life can require. I can picture our dear Mr. Darling puffed up with pride! I cannot help but wonder, and please forgive me if you find my inquiry impertinent. Do the* Fräulein *and my child now share a sister?*

I look forward to hearing more news from you, as I will write ours to you, also. We think of you. For our own sakes only, we regret your absence.

Ever your faithful friend,

Katje

Mon cher *Victor,*

Although I think of you fondly and fervently each day since we parted, I waited to write to you until the story we created reached completion. While it is unexpected, the two of us within our fairy tale achieved a most happy ending.

The assurances I gave to you were sincere. It was the will of another that, unbeknownst to me, caused me to conceive of this issue. Given time to adjust, I hope you will greet my news with all the delight you experienced on six previous occasions.

Any doubts I held dissolved when I looked down into her island-blue eyes. My own eyes fill with tears of tenderness when I gaze upon the richest treasure this pirate ever beheld: our little Lady, our lily of France— Victoria Jane de Beaumonde. When she comes of age, I will follow the gypsy tradition of my mother-in-law, and present to her my Oriental fan. I shall tell her the story of how a lovely little ladies' accessory shielded me, defended me, beckoned to you…and folded us together.

S'il te plaît, Monsieur, lay your concerns to rest. She is safe ashore, thriving in the loving care of her grandparents, Mr. and Mrs. George Darling of London. Ever since I flew the nest as a very young lass, they grieved for me. Opening their arms to a new baby girl repairs the rents in their hearts. For your many acts of kindness, we all owe you a great debt of gratitude.

If you wish to follow her progress, you are welcome to call upon your namesake at any time, as will her lady mother in the rare occasions when opportunity allows. Thanks to your generosity, I am free to travel earth and seas without fear of consequences. I find, though, that while my daughter resides there, the noblest destination in the whole, wider world is my very own childhood home, the nursery at Number 14.

We Peers of the Realms of Water and Wine produced a perfect vintage. Of the ships I have sailed, the vessel that transported this Queen to the farthest and most unknown shore is your very own Paradis. *Although only from afar, let us now revel in our happily-ever-after.*

Your loving

Lorelei

To: Mr. George Darling
From: City of London, Registration Bureau Westminster
In re: Recent Inquiry

Received your query re marriage Wendy Moira Angela Darling, Spinster, London.

Confirmed in office: spouse Giovanni G. Cecco, citizen Italian States.
Registered: aboard Merchant Ship Unity, London & Lisbon.
Officiating officer: Capt. Edmund Greer.
Witness: Dr. Thos. Hastings, Ship's Surgeon.

Inquiry closed this date. Official apology for delay. Trusting no inconvenience caused in consequence.

Author's Note

Upon this time of *The Wider World's* publication, the Neverland turns 120 years of age. J.M. Barrie's brilliance shines as a constant light, and I honor him. I recommend that our readers indulge in his numerous other works in addition to his modern mythology of Peter Pan. Three of Barrie's plays involve islands with magical effect, and I wish you the wonder of reading them or seeing them staged: *Peter Pan*, of course, but also the comedic social commentary *The Admirable Crichton*, and the hauntingly beautiful ghost story, *Mary Rose*. Timeless genius dwells within their scripts, and may the enchantment under which Barrie enthralls us never fade.

I also honor the readers who kindly responded to my own literary efforts by writing tributes to my Saga. It is these readers whom this pirate author celebrates in this volume by breaking the "rules" of publishing. The Reginetta Press printed a sampling of these bibliophiles' "nonprofessional" but so lovely blurbs on the back cover of *The Wider World's* dust jacket. With a flourish of salute, I express a world of appreciation. I thank all my readers who offer such accolades, whether printed here or expressed on other platforms.

The author photo on the dust jacket reveals the daybed on which I experienced a dream that turned into *Hook & Jill*. It is the elegant divan where I composed the first chapters of the Saga, and this distinctive piece is the couch with which I furnished Captain Hook's quarters— with satiny medallions on the fabric, and a flightless swan carved into the back. It is my favorite reading seat, and now Captain Hook's as well.

A note about the Saga's timeline. I caution my readers not to trust to Time as if its bounds can be set within the fantasy. As we discover in this volume, Hook has existed for generations, with unmeasured Time behind him to become who he is. If we take Barrie at his word, Hook was once Blackbeard's bo'sun. Blackbeard himself was beheaded by a Highlander's broadsword in 1718. In this book we visit Vienna in 1908. And who came first— the Story, or his Storyteller? Like magician's tricks, some mysteries ought not be solved. Instead, let us release reality and revel in the resulting mix of fiction and history, in what I now dub "factory."

Having sailed the wider world myself, I expect the unexpected. As I endeavor to pen *The Ever-After End: Book Five of the Hook & Jill Saga* before meeting my timely— or untimely— demise, my highest aspiration is that, another 120 years from today, my stories may be read hand-in-hook with those masterpieces of the Time-honored sage, Mr. Barrie.

Acknowledgements

No ship sails without her officers, her rudder, and her lucky stars.
For your friendship, guidance, and patience, I owe a
wide world of gratitude...

Jolene Barjasteh, Scott Baseler, Catherine Leah Condon-Guillemette,
Stacy DeCoster-Wisneski, Erik Hollander, Celia Jones,
Jonathan Jones, Beth Kirkpatrick, Mary Lawrence,
Cynthia Ripley Miller, LuAnn Morse, Admiral Morgan Ramirez,
Ginny Thompson, Peter Von Brown.

And to the master, the magician, the mage, the man of the play,
whether in park or performance...

J.M. Barrie.

About The Author

Tended by the green thumb of Andrea Jones, the Neverland grows ever more gripping. Like Mr. and Mrs. Darling, Mrs. Jones raised three children. Author of the *Hook & Jill* Saga, Jones is also the editor of a classics restoration program. In tribute to J.M. Barrie, she returned the story that will never grow old to its 1911 origins in *Peter and Wendy: The Restored Text* (Reginetta Press).

Jones' Saga appeals to a variety of readers, not only those who love literary fiction and a poetical turn of phrase, but also fantasy fiction readers, J.M. Barrie scholars, Peter Pan (and Captain Hook) enthusiasts, pirate reenactors, and mavens of women's studies. Jones finds followers at her appearances at— to name only a few— Renaissance faires, pirate festivals, Highland games, and Tall Ships celebrations.

Rooted in Barrie's lore, Jones seeds new and memorable, even powerful, characters of her own. Five books are plotted for the Saga, beginning with *Hook & Jill* and, coming as close to an end as is possible with such perennial content, finishing with *The Ever-After End*. Like her luminary, Mr. Barrie, Jones allows plentiful space for more stories to thrive between the furrows.

Jones studied Literature at the University of Illinois. She enjoyed a career in television production and received theatrical training, and these experiences form the essential environment to nurture her writing. Jones garners a rich harvest as a storyteller extraordinaire.

Visit Facebook.com/HookJill and www.HookandJill.com.